D1603738

Dulcinea

BOOKS BY ANA VECIANA-SUAREZ

NOVELS
The Chin Kiss King
Flight to Freedom
Dulcinea

NONFICTION
Birthday Parties in Heaven

a novel

Dulcinea

Ana Veciana-Suarez

**BLACK
STONE**
PUBLISHING

First edition: 2023
ISBN 979-8-200-81341-4
Fiction / Romance / Historical / Renaissance

Version 1

Blackstone Publishing
31 Mistletoe Rd.
Ashland, OR 97520

www.BlackstonePublishing.com

For David,
mensch

Prologue

29TH OF APRIL, 1616, MADRID

In Which I Am Where I Should Be, at Last

Much has been said about me, much written, and most of it such slanderous tripe. Lies, deceits, falsehoods—a deflowering of the truth. Of all the woes visited upon me by God and, perhaps, the Devil himself, having my reputation besmirched has been, if not the most painful or long-lasting, certainly one of the most confounding. I've done nothing to deserve this calumny except love a man who isn't my husband and never can be, a man who belongs to another. I loved him before the bittersweet elixir of fame, before I danced my first sardana or prepared my first palette with paint, and I've loved him as steadily as the Llobregat flows to the Mediterranean and as predictably as the budding of the quince trees in spring.

This is why my carriage has stopped in front of an unfamiliar building on a strange street in a city foreign to me. I cannot move my feet, and my arms hang limply at my sides. Only my hammering heart is awake. However, I must rouse myself if I am to accomplish my mission. A secret released will lighten the heaviness of heart that has beset me so.

"Calle de León," the driver announces.

Though small, the house possesses a respectable air, and this surprises me. Miquel has always lamented his financial situation. Yet the green shutters appear freshly painted and red geraniums fill the window boxes. Rose bushes bloom in a side garden.

Suddenly I'm startled by the neighing of a horse at the carriage window. Jaume has dismounted and appears eager to get on with the task at hand. He is accustomed to assuming control, and proof of this is how well he has overseen my late husband's affairs.

"Is this the address?" he asks.

"I've never been here, but if it matches what I gave you . . ."

"It doesn't look like anyone's home." He eyes the property as if sizing up an unwanted purchase.

"A dying man wouldn't be left alone."

"Very well. Who should I ask for?"

I hesitate, dread squeezing my throat, but manage to reply, "I don't know anyone in the household except Miquel."

"And who shall I say has come calling?"

"Me. Who else?"

"Are you sure?" he asks, doubt creasing his brow.

"Yes, most definitely." Is Jaume dallying? After all, he has escorted me here only after a considerable number of threats and simpering on my part. Though I originally intended to keep my journey from him, as he would have forbidden it in his high-handed way, I will concede that his presence has afforded me comfort these past few days.

"But there may be some—"

"Objection?" I finish for him. "I understand, but there's not much I can do about that now. Just go ahead and tell the maid."

We exchange a few more words, and I motion for him to move along. He turns on his heel and strides the short distance from cobblestoned street to stoop, taking the steps two at a time. A woman in a white cap answers his knock. A conversation ensues, but it's impossible for me to hear what is said. She closes the door. I'm left to wonder if we will be sent away, if the message delivered by courier last night will serve as an excuse to bar me from seeing Miquel.

Shortly, another woman appears at the entrance. She must be diminutive because neither her shoulders nor her head is visible, only the hem of her black gown. Is it Miquel's wife, Catalina? Or his niece, Constanza? Maybe his daughter, Isabel, who has mended their estranged relationship during his illness? As my thoughts wander through a labyrinth of possibilities, the carriage door is flung open.

"She will see you now," Jaume says.

"She?"

"Miquel's wife."

"Is he well?" I ask, but I'm too intent on the figure in the doorway to properly listen to the reply. Trepidation has unsettled my stomach.

Since my eyesight is failing, I must content myself with a blurred image, though as I draw closer, her features take shape. Like the house, like the neighborhood, this wife is not what I imagined her to be. Her face is angular and plain, neither beautiful nor arresting—details I note with satisfaction. She is several years younger than me, but her hair is already graying.

"You've traveled many leagues," Catalina says, after introducing herself. "All the way from Barcelona."

I acknowledge her comment with a nod. I want to explain that her husband sent a letter requesting my presence, but I don't trust my voice to hold steady. As if from a great distance, I hear the clatter of hooves down the street, smell the perfume of roses on a brisk breeze, feel the warmth of the spring sun on my head. I neither budge nor speak. An eternity passes.

"Come in." She opens the heavy wooden door wider. "Come in."

Though I've spent countless hours imagining all the possible scenarios of my arrival in Madrid, I'm not prepared for this encounter with my lover's wife. I turn to look at the armed guards watching over the carriage. Their sheathed swords and holstered *pedrenyals* provide a measure of reassurance. Even the sour-faced driver, whip in hand, could impersonate Death at a masquerade ball, a warning to those who might do me harm.

As if plunging underwater, I narrow my eyes and hold my breath. I enter. A shaft of light cleaves the dim vestibule in half. I know not what I will say. I know even less of what awaits me.

Chapter 1

In Which I Meet Miquel and Become a Woman,
with All the Temptations of That Title

I can't recall the exact date my life veered from its designated course, but surely it was after the festival of La Mercè and before the close of the seafaring season. Summer's warmth had receded, and nightfall required the comfort of shawl or cape. Mother still mourned my older brother, and Father's step had yet to recover its determination. In our home, a grief held too long lived among us, as comfortable as a mouse in its burrow.

On that morning in question, men's voices—one of them Father's—caught my attention just as Tutor Guillem and I were finishing a lesson. I was intrigued, for we had had few visitors in the past year.

"Dolça!" he brayed. "Your father pays a fine coin for your lessons. The very least you can do is respect his generosity and attend to your studies."

Father was indeed kind in allowing my education, especially at the mature age of almost fifteen. But he also knew that this instruction was in his best interest. With Andreu's death, I was now his one and only, at least until a husband seized the reins of my affairs and I produced an heir for the family business. I wouldn't have chosen to be looked upon as a replacement, but seldom does life follow our wishes. Moreover, unlike some of his associates, Father didn't consider a learned woman unseemly, perhaps because Mother was as quick with her sums and letters as Father, and no one dared to cheat her at the market or in the shops.

"How can I concentrate with visitors?" I asked.

"Everything's a distraction for the young mistress."

Anyone else might have delivered such a declaration with the hint of a smile. Not Tutor Guillem. He was a dour man, gray-bearded and hollow-cheeked, thin as the feather grass found in the mountains. More trying than his tepid personality was the fact that he didn't teach the one subject that interested me but that Father considered superfluous, particularly for the only daughter of a wealthy merchant: painting. Left to my own devices, I would have spent my time in front of an easel, not with the ancient Greeks.

"Who's the visitor, do you think?" I stood. I couldn't bear one more minute at my seat, no matter its comfort.

"It's of no concern to you. You must sit."

Did I do as instructed? Of course not. I bolted from the high-ceilinged chamber where I took my studies and ran down the hall, hair flying behind me like a tournament pennant. The door to the room where Father conducted business was closed. Though I could now clearly hear the words spoken, the purpose of the conversation was lost to me. Father was boasting about the recent decision by the Consell de Cent, of which he was a proud and distinguished member, to clear a road from Riells to the barony of Montbui. He sounded more animated than he had been in a while.

My hand hovered close to the door. *Should I knock or burst in?* Tutor Guillem helped me decide when he hissed in my ear, "Return to the room this minute!"

"Father!" I exclaimed as I surged through the door without first announcing myself.

Father's mouth was open in midspeech, but the corners turned upward as soon as I caught his eye. Always, and more so now, I was at the center of his heart, and I knew it.

"Ah, *la pubilla* has run away from her tutor again." He had started referring to me as the female version of the *hereu*, or male heir, in the past month. Perhaps it was his way of accepting the one grievance he couldn't right. Father was as towering and corpulent as a Montserrat oak, or so it seemed to me back then, and he had the unlined skin and the broad shoulders of a younger man. Only the color of his hair, the white of spring clouds, gave away his age.

I looked over at Father's guest, a young man not unpleasant in looks. Neither tall nor short, on the slight side, he had a prominent hook nose that was impossible to ignore and a beard of burnt gold. He wore his collar-length hair, a rich chestnut, combed away from a wide forehead, and his attire, the doublet and shirt at least, was in a style not familiar to me. But his smile—oh, his smile, it encompassed so much! Humor. Inquisitiveness. Sympathy. An ability, or perhaps it was a desire, to believe and befriend.

"Miguel de Cerbantes de Cortinas," he said, and bowed rakishly.

"Dolça Llull Prat." I curtsied. "So named after Dolça de Provence, who married the illustrious Ramon Berenguer the Third, count of Barcelona."

Father added, "Better known around these parts as 'my sweet.' In your inelegant Castilian, Miguel, it would be Dulce, Dulcie, Dulcinea."

"A name not easily forgotten," he said to me. His eyes were neither brown nor green, but the color of a leaf before it turns. I knew I was staring at him but I didn't stop, and it was he who looked away, to address Father. "Does her name suit her temperament, Don Antoni?"

My father grunted. "It depends."

"On what?"

"The time of day. The day of the week. The month of the year. The weather. The food served—"

"Father!"

"I'm simply being honest."

"No, you're not!"

"Maybe she would like to change her name," this Miguel suggested.

"Maybe." Father allowed himself a self-deprecating chuckle. "In the meantime, we put up with her."

"I'd say you do more than that."

I was mortified that the two men, Father in particular, would speak of me as if I were not present.

"Why are you here?" I asked our visitor. However brash it might have sounded, mine was not a frivolous question, considering our dearth of callers. Father glowered.

"You must pardon my daughter. Her curiosity is matched only by her impetuosity, and both are as long as a sennight of ceaseless rain. I wonder if Impudence would be a better name for her."

"Don Antoni, no question should ever be ignored from such a lovely young lady," Miguel said, and a kind of burning colored my neck and face. Then he spoke directly to me. "I'm here, young Dolça, to visit family. You're a cousin. Our great-grandmothers were sisters."

"On your mother's side, the Servents." Father appeared to make a special point of adding this remark, though such distinction of who was who and where they belonged on the family tree wasn't unusual. For a reason I didn't comprehend then (and only later would I under-stand though not approve), my father harbored a dislike, some would say condescension, of my mother's heritage, though she had brought her own considerable wealth and mercantile holdings into the marriage.

"A cousin of Mother's?"

"Many times removed," Father clarified.

Presently, Mother walked in, most likely alerted by Tutor Guil-lem, who thought me manipulative of my father. Though she had aged precipitously since my brother's death, Mother remained a handsome woman, with the type of noble carriage I was expected to mimic. Her hair, now threaded through with white, had once been so black it shone blue in sunlight, and her large expressive eyes, the color of rusting iron, overwhelmed her face, as my own did.

"Dolça, enough," Mother said. "Interruptions are rude."

She shot me a look that admitted no debate, and called for Aldonça, who came in so quickly that I knew she had been lurking on the other side of the door, as she was wont to do. My nursemaid grabbed my elbow and escorted me out, admonishing under her breath: "If you act like a child, you will be treated like a child. If you behave as a young woman has learned to behave, you will then be treated as such."

I disregarded the advice and turned around in time to hear Mother issue an invitation that was an undisguised command. "Miguel, you'll join us for dinner of course."

Father frowned, but I paid his reaction no mind, intrigued as I was by the smile our visitor proffered when our eyes met, a smile I returned with all the flirtatious coyness I had learned from my older cousins.

We weren't separated for long. When I overheard one of the house-maids say our guest was browsing the bookshelves, I sought him out in Father's library. By then Aldonça was preoccupied with who knows what and Tutor Guillem had departed with his litany of reproaches.

As I entered, Miguel was seated on a hard bench, which had neither backrest nor pillow, and was so engrossed in a book that he didn't hear my footsteps. I studied him from a short distance, mindful not to move or make a sound, which was quite a challenge for me. His shoulders were slumped, and his lips moved as he made out the words. He licked his right index finger to turn the page. For all his intense concentration, however, he looked out of place. His faded breeches and mended forest-green hose—for sure, he wasn't a rich relative, which might have explained Father's earlier reaction—were no match for the treasures in this chamber. Father was a collector of all things beautiful, as well as a shrewd *mercader*, and his books, some bound in gold-tooled leather, others with metal stamps of animal and plants, were often considered unparalleled. Organized by subject and alphabetized by author, they populated much of his library, overwhelming the exquisitely gloomy paintings of religious apparitions and biblical interpretations. (There was one painting by the Valencian Juan de Juanes that I happened to like, though.)

"Miquel."

He didn't hear me at first, but when I called out his name again, he looked up, appearing bewildered, disoriented.

"Dolça, what a pleasant surprise. But my name is Miguel with a *g*."

"Well, then I will call you Miquel with a *q*, for that's what it is in my tongue."

He chuckled.

I took one step closer, then another, and he closed his book, leaving a finger between pages to mark his place. From where I stood, I couldn't make out the title. "What are you reading?" I asked.

"*Amadís de Gaula.*"

Of course. I should have recognized its scarlet leather cover and the gold lettering along its spine.

"By Garci Rodríguez de Montalvo."

He didn't appear particularly impressed by my quick retrieval of the author's name. I changed course and pointed at the red-and-yellow Catalan banner that Father so proudly displayed.

"Do you know the story behind our Catalan colors?"

"Should I?"

"I'll tell you," I replied, ignoring his mocking tone. "King Charles drew the four red bars on Count Wilfred I's golden shield with his fingers drenched in blood."

"Is that so?"

"That's so. It happened during the siege of Barcelona by the Moorish governor of Lleida."

"And you believe that tale?"

"Certainly."

"You don't think it was made up? Like the stories in all these books?"

"It wasn't made up." I stamped my foot. "It's absolutely the truth."

"And what happened to this Count Wilfred? Did he survive his injuries?"

"Count Guifré el Pilós, which is his rightful Catalan name, died on the eleventh of August of 897 while fighting the Saracens."

"Interesting." Miquel stroked his beard, but I wasn't convinced he understood the bravery of our principality's father or the importance of this story.

"You do know who the Saracens were?" I asked.

"I'm not ignorant, Dolça, regardless of what you Catalans think of the rest of us."

We had arrived at an impasse, which is probably what prompted him to smile that right-crooked smile of his. Our gazes locked, and I like to think that's when our fates were sealed, when our hearts accepted the inevitable. Leaving the *Amadís* open on the bench, he stood and gestured at the book-lined walls. "This is a paradise."

"It is. Father considers himself a bibliophile." He kept hundreds of shelved volumes and manuscripts, Latin poets of course, but also translations of the Greek masterpieces and such local favorites as *La Celestina*, *Diana*, and the more recent *Brevísima relación de la destrucción de las Indias* by Fray Bartolomé.

"So which book is your favorite?"

No one except my brother had ever so bluntly asked what I liked, so I was quite happy to respond. "Any by a Catalan writer."

"Would I know one?"

"*Tirant lo Blanch.*"

"Wasn't that written by a Valencian?"

"Yes, but Valencian is a lot like Catalan. Have you read it? In Castilian, I mean."

"No, though I now plan to. But why do you like Catalan writers above all others?"

"It's easier for me to read in my own language. And it happens to be the most beautiful language."

His laughter echoed in the room. "I write poetry," he said, "and I hate to think that a reader would base her preference on native language instead of the words I've so carefully chosen and arranged."

I blushed, but he didn't appear to notice.

"What else do you like?"

"Painting." If I hadn't been so tongue-tied, I might have explained how others mistook my frequent church attendance for piousness when, in truth, I visited our houses of worship to study the masterpieces above and around the altars.

"I've come from seeing the world's most beautiful paintings. Masterpieces, really." He then told me he had lived in Rome, where he had become acquainted with its churches' famous diptychs and altarpieces.

"How I envy you!" What I meant was that I found his experience tantalizing. He was a man who had seen the world, a true sophisticate—at least more so than the coddled young men Mother tried to force on me, those parochial *galants* of my social circle.

"I'm sure you'll visit in due time."

"Father won't take me anywhere far from Barcelona. He fears the Barbary pirates on the high seas and the bandits on the mountain passes. So, I'm stuck. Stuck, stuck, stuck."

"He must love you very much to be so protective."

"True love or pointless restrictions?" I glanced over my shoulder, worried somebody might be eavesdropping. "I'm not a child, you know."

"No, that you are not." There was no mistaking his look of appraisal. There was no mistaking my satisfaction at that appraisal either.

"I'll soon be old enough to marry."

"And do you have someone in mind?" His stare felt like the caress of a thousand feathers.

I lowered my eyes and let the silence speak for itself.

As Mother had requested, Miquel stayed for dinner, though it wasn't the grand affair it might have been had we been hosting distinguished visitors. There was no last-minute visit to the Boqueria market, and the long trestle table was dressed with nothing more than a simple linen cloth. Nonetheless, the sweet scent of roasting meat floated upward to the second floor, teasing our senses for hours. (Even on a bad day, Cook was incapable of spoiling an *escudella i carn d'olla* stew or the honey-drizzled cheese dessert of *mel i mató*.)

Fancy measures or not, the lively conversation was a welcome change from the morose silences of the past year when we would gaze down at our plates without appetite or interest. For me, that evening with Miquel was filled with sidelong glances and fleeting looks, a subtle thrust and parry under the very noses of those who would have otherwise forbidden it. I didn't want the meal to end, and I followed his every move—the lifting of a spoon, a sip from the wine goblet, the tilt of his head when listening—as if under a spell. More than once I caught him studying me.

Father also talked a lot more than I would have expected. He complained about the king's ever-increasing debt to finance military forays and the construction of the San Lorenzo de El Escorial Palace, but it was Father's reference to the Inquisition's heavy-handedness in quashing the Morisco uprising in Granada that garnered attention. At the mention of this dreaded institution, Àvia Regina, usually as hard of hearing as a doorstop, sat up in her leather chair. My maternal grandmother was ancient, well over three scores, but she remained impressively lucid and agile for someone her age. Her dark eyes had settled into a bed of wrinkles, as had her mouth, which housed exactly six unevenly spaced teeth. Her nose, I now recognize in retrospect, resembled Miquel's with its high bridge and steep descent. She hadn't said much during the meal until then.

"Ah, the Inquisition," she muttered, sopping her stew with a knob of bread. "Greedy bastards. Those Dominicans will line their coffers any which way they can."

I smiled behind my hand.

"*Mare*, did you say something?" Mother asked.

"No, no, Margarida. Nothing."

Father apparently hadn't heard her comment or had decided to ignore it, but Miquel turned to face my grandmother as if expecting a clarification. When he opened his mouth to speak, Father intervened, "Don't worry about her. Old people talk to themselves all the time."

Àvia refused to be dismissed so easily, however. "*El gos vell quan lladra dona consell.*" An old dog, when barking, gives good advice.

Father rolled his eyes, but Miquel, who couldn't understand Catalan, glanced around the table in confusion.

Later that evening, when Father and Miquel had retired to a game of piquet, Àvia asked me to her chambers.

"I'm not a fool," she said without preamble. "I saw you making eyes at our visitor."

"M-m-me?"

"I don't blame you. He is so . . . so cosmopolitan. *Molt guapo.*"

"Àvia!"

"Well, even a crone can admire."

Àvia also confirmed Miquel's Rome exploits, divulging that he had once been a wanted man. An outlaw! A fugitive! He had wounded a man in a duel, a man by the name of Antonio de Sigura, and a royal decree had been issued for his arrest. Because duels had been outlawed by the king in order to cut back on all that foolishness of honor and revenge, his only alternative had been temporary exile to Rome until the issue was resolved.

"Was the duel over a woman?"

"Most likely. I doubt it was over money."

How romantic! For days I daydreamed of men fighting over me. More precisely, of Miquel dueling and swooning over me. I replayed every word we had exchanged in the library, every look traded across the table. What did that wink mean? Was his smile an acknowledgment of attraction? The mere mention of his name quickened my heart, and I imagined how the power of my beauty and the sway of my charms would bedazzle him. Never did I consider the pain and consequences of a prohibited love, not once, not ever.

During his prolonged stay in our fair city, Miquel rented a room in the Hostal de la Bona Sort on the lane of Carders, a place he described for us in vivid detail. For example, he said his second-floor room smelled as musty as "an ancient Egyptian manuscript." The light streaming through its east window was like "the sun smiling at her reflection in a mirror." And the din that rose from El Born resembled "a band of devils playing sackbuts and viols." His words, his words—even then he was destined to be a man of words, and I, however unworldly, considered this talent the true mark of passion and sensuality.

He also became a frequent guest at family gatherings, usually arriving with some trinket in hand: a plain glass *porró* for wine, a badly tuned shawmsopranino, a pottage bowl of dubious origin. One day he showed up with a small sandstone sculpture of a girl sitting on a bench.

"Does it not remind you of Dolça?" He handed the figurine to Mother but looked at me, his eyes expressing what his mouth could not say.

I gritted my teeth to keep from exclaiming with pleasure. He held my stare for longer than it was proper and went on to explain that he received these odd items as payment for hiring himself out as a scribe. My mother thanked him politely, as she had done with previous gifts, but refused my request to keep the sandstone girl in my chamber.

I expected such behavior from Mother and did not mind it much. She was easy enough to skirt. I had the great fortune that, wittingly or not, Àvia provided other forms of connection with Miquel. I suspect she felt a certain responsibility for his welfare as she had kept correspondence with her cousin, Miquel's grandmother in Arganda del Rey, long before I was born. She became his protectress, his guide to the city and to the extended family. To that end, one day we'd set off on an expedition to admire the statue of the archangel Raphael at City Hall, another day to El Call. On sunny afternoons, we promenaded around La Ribera, admiring the splendid mansions with their mullioned windows and Moorish courtyards or the grand *plaças* where industry and trade were conducted with noisy flourish.

I remember one particular excursion to the northernmost section of the city wall to see the Canaletes, the channels that directed freshwater from the Collserola Ridge to Barcelona. Though a long carriage ride from home, this uncivilized city neighborhood was one of Àvia's favorite places to visit—on the sly, of course, and only when Mother and Father were otherwise occupied, for they would have surely banned any such jaunt. Except for the water seeping from the pipes, there was little else to admire in the area.

"It is said that if you quench your thirst here, you will fall in love with our city," Àvia declared with a grand gesture of her silk-and-lace encased arm.

"But I'm already in love with the city," Miquel said. He half-turned to face me and continued: "In fact, everything and everybody in Barcelona deserve admiration."

I bowed my head in mock modesty but glanced at him through the flutter of eyelashes.

Àvia produced a paper cone and bent to catch the gurgling water, offering this to Miquel. "Drink up, cousin, drink up."

He took the cone, smiling, but before he put his mouth to the rim, he motioned for me to be the first to partake in the ceremony. When I proceeded to take the makeshift cup from him, he wrapped his hands over both of mine and carefully tipped the cone to my lips. I sipped. The water was cold, gritty, redolent of something earthy. It made my head hurt. I didn't care. Then still holding firm, he drank, his eyes never straying from my face. Once finished, he didn't loosen his grip. Instead, he kissed the inside of each of my wrists, his lips lingering over the very heartbeat of my soul. A dozen braziers inflamed my limbs.

If Àvia noticed this flirtation—and how could she not?—she didn't acknowledge it and spoke not a word of it then or later. Back in the carriage on our way home, she informed Miquel, "Legend has it that those waters bewitch those who partake in them."

"How so?"

"The spell, it is said, will always call you back to Barcelona."

Those words proved prophetic, for he returned to us many times thereafter, never permanently but always to my delight and downfall.

On another occasion, we found ourselves sitting next to each other at a family *convit*. An array of goblets reflected tiny rainbows from the candlelight, and olives and cheeses filled pewter bowls. Servants paraded around the room with various dishes, each more succulent than the other: stewed ram, dobladura of mutton, a cilantro-and-chicken pottage. (Even now, my mouth waters at the memory.) Fortuitously, Mother and Father sat at the opposite end of the long table, and both appeared to have indulged in more wine than was their custom. Actually, this was true of most everyone at the gathering.

Under the table, Miquel tugged at the silver chain of my pomander. He said something I didn't quite catch at first. When I spun to face him,

he widened his eyes and enunciated more loudly, "Give me your hand."
I didn't think twice about granting his request. We spent the rest of the
meal clutching each other in this fashion. Later that evening, as the long
dinner came to its natural conclusion and the men began to disperse to
their games and tobacco pipes, Miquel took advantage of the chaos to
pull me close and kiss me full on the mouth. This act was so brazen, so
ardent, that I thought I might faint. I did no such thing, of course, and
merely returned the kiss with as much avidity as it was given. To this
day that event—a celebration of a cousin's betrothal—stands out as the
first in a long line of perilous family gatherings, and the exhilaration of
it all was enough to make me think I was wise beyond my years.

Over the next several weeks, there were more public encounters of
this kind, each punctuated by an intoxicating lust. My heart bludgeoned
my chest when he was near, and the very thought of him made my skin
feel as exposed as a peeled orange. That this infatuation was mutual only
served to make it more exciting. A look expressed a thousand words, a
smile added a million more, and none of them yet discordant. As we grew
to know each other better, stolen kisses gave way to forbidden caresses.
We were fortunate that cousins Quirze and Glòria facilitated our trysts,
each for their own complicated, and perhaps selfish, reasons. Quirze had
grown very close to Miquel and, knowing my relative as I do, probably
sought to live vicariously through a more worldly man. And Glòria?
Only heaven knows why she helped. I suspected then, and maintain to
this day, that my indiscretions offered her what she did not have, what
she did not dare: the thrill of risk without serious consequences.

By the eve of Tots Sants, there was no mistaking each other's intent but
also no dismissing the potential recriminations we faced if found out.
Miquel was not considered an appropriate match for me by any measure.
Too poor, too undistinguished, with little promise for a better future.
Though not without talent, Miquel lacked both the temperament and
appropriate skills needed to earn the *lliures* and *sous* essential for a life

of comfort—and Father had no qualms making this known. Consumed with the thought of Miquel, I didn't heed such warnings, however. And so, increasingly daring, increasingly desperate to be together alone, we agreed to meet in Father's library during the All Saints' Day celebration. The night had begun in its usual way. Mother had placed several oil lamps by the outside doors, hoping to guide our dead relatives' spirits home, and Cook had roasted chestnuts, arranging them on a hammered silver platter along with the baked sweet potatoes. To ease the vigil, our earthenware *gerres* brimmed with the finest muscatel, a wine so sweet it could make your tongue curl. Quirze, Ferran, and Glòria had goaded me into swigging a full goblet so that by the time the pine-nut-topped *panellet* buns were served, I possessed an abundance of courage and self-confidence.

Feigning a headache with the aunts, an excuse embellished by the always imaginative Glòria, I tiptoed down the hallway, trembling with delicious anticipation. I stopped near the room where the men had gathered to drink and debate behind closed doors.

"Money, that's the tribunal's motivation," Oncle Robert was saying. "Ducats, *lliures*, gold, land. Don't for a minute believe this is about religion or faith. It's about filling the coffers."

"You're being cynical," someone countered.

Oncle Robert made a sputtering sound. "True, but only because we repeat what we're told without questioning. Is there any restraint on the powers of the Holy Office? Can there not be—"

"Shush. Remember that the walls have ears. Or at least the servants do."

"Those Protestants will be the downfall of Spain, I tell you," Father said. "Divided as we are by language and government, the one true religion of our Lord and Savior must be the identity to bind us."

"At what price? Our dignity? Our compassion? I'd argue that our duty should be to forgive and render the fallen a path for redemption, as Jesus himself preached." This was unquestionably Miquel's voice, and it thundered. How erudite he sounded! I smiled with pride.

"Redemption was offered," Oncle Sebastià retorted.

"But to burn people as if they were pigs on a pike? That's hardly Christian."

"Those taken to the stake refused to renounce their errors. And without repudiation of this blasphemy, there is no contrition."

"Besides," Father added, "there are those who publicly renounce but then return to their ways."

"Isn't that true of all sinners?" Miquel asked. "In fact, I'd say that falls and failures are a fundamental characteristic of the human condition."

"The heretics say one thing in public and do another in private."

"As we all do, don't we?" Miquel insisted. "It's a matter of degrees. We show one face to the world and another to the mirror. Hypocrisy is a pastime that knows no boundary, regardless of religion or class or sex. I'd go as far as saying that it's part of our identity."

The uncles then began to speak all at once, shouting over one another, and I seized the opportunity to sneak into the library. Minutes later I spotted Miquel's silhouette in the doorway. He called out my name and I jumped into the light cast by the lantern I had left on Father's desk. I motioned for him to come closer.

"Darling," he whispered when I eased myself into his open arms.

He held me so close I could smell the lavender water on his shirt. He kissed my forehead, the tip of my nose, each closed eyelid, my lips as they parted to welcome his. I quivered. We remained like this for a time but not long enough, never enough. Then he took a step back.

"I have to get back to the uncles soon," he said. "Before they come looking for me."

"Not yet. Quirze said he would help distract them."

"Quirze." He chuckled. "That devil." The two young men had become fast friends in a matter of weeks.

I pulled Miquel into a dark corner of the chamber, near the bench where I had found him reading weeks earlier. Father's library was by no means the ideal place for a rendezvous. It was as cold as a catacomb, and the stone often smelled of rain-soaked earth. That night I did not notice any of this.

"What were you talking about so heatedly?" I asked.

"The Huguenots."

I covered my ears with my hands. "Oh, I don't want to hear any more about that incident. I heard they were burnt at the stake."

"And you won't, my precious. Not a word from me, I promise."

He pulled my hands away from my face, turned them over, and kissed each palm gently. Then he led me to the bench, where we sat pressed together.

"I wish I could see you better. Your face is what I fall asleep to every night."

"We can't risk more light."

"Correct, querida, and maybe darkness is what we need anyway."

We kissed, and I felt a queasiness between my legs. He slipped a hand into the bodice of my dress and cupped a breast. He moaned. I echoed his desire.

Then we heard footsteps. Heavy, deliberate footsteps coming our way.

"Father," I whispered in his ear. "I know that sound."

Reluctantly, and only because our reputations depended on it, we separated. I motioned for Miquel to grab the lantern and scuttled under my father's large oak desk. Just in time too. A few heartbeats later, I spotted Father's boots from where I had wedged myself.

"What are you doing here?" Father asked. "Lost?"

Miquel laughed nervously but managed a good recovery. "Your books . . ."

"Well, man, you can hardly read in the dark. And that lantern won't help you. Best you return in the daytime."

"I most certainly will."

The two walked out, but I dared not leave my hiding space, even as my skirt wrinkled and my calves spasmed from the pressure of my new chopines. I was fearful that my father would return to investigate Miquel's unusual foray into this room, so I remained uncomfortably scrunched under the desk until Aldonça, ever suspicious and not easily fooled, stepped into the chamber and called for me. My nursemaid had an uncanny ability to find me wherever I was.

"You can come out now," she said. "Everyone is otherwise occupied."

Unfolding myself like a marionette emerging from a box and then smoothing down my gown required concerted effort, but she didn't bother to help. She simply lifted her lamp to see my embarrassment better. Disapproval was stamped all over her face. I conjured a dozen retorts but held my tongue. The last thing I wanted was for her to tell Mother.

Without a word, I followed her to my chambers, where she undressed me and brushed out my hair. She waited while I knelt on the prie-dieu to pray and then tucked me into bed.

"Be careful, child," she said into the dark. "You have but one maidenhood to offer."

"I'm not a child!"

"A child to me you will always be."

She snuffed the candle and closed the double doors behind her. Though we were well into autumn, a glowing heat spread down my limbs and held hard my heart. I knew there was a weight to what I wanted, an inevitability to what I would get. That night, and for many nights thereafter, desire allowed me little rest.

By the spring of '71, every man in our principality had turned his attention to war. The Holy League had been established with the blessing of Pope Pius V, and allies had begun to assemble an armada to fight the Turks. At the Drassanes Reials near the port, the spacious naves buzzed with activity, and it was no small point of national pride that the royal galley of Don Juan of Austria, the king's half brother, was being constructed, oar by oar, plank by plank, in our Catalan shipyard by our Catalan shipwrights. As a result of all this industriousness, it was difficult to get around without running into someone who knew me or my parents. Nevertheless, abetted by my cousins, Miquel and I were able to filch privacy where we could: at Glòria's meriendas, under the guise of an errand, in the shadows of a church, during the many communal festivities that marked our liturgical calendar.

Of course, in public we kept as much to ourselves as possible. Not that we fooled everyone—or anyone. One day in mid-June, a Saturday, Don Juan arrived in Barcelona, where he was expected to stay for several weeks before sailing to Naples to command our war fleet. When the *consellers* received news of his impending appearance, the city's most important men, Father included, gathered at the *ajuntament* in Sant Jaume, whence they departed on their horses to meet him at Creu Coberta. The prince entered the city through the doors of Sant Antoni and was saluted with a round of cannon fire, a deafening display that, according to Father, pleased him greatly. Flanked by our new viceroy and our *conseller en cap*, Don Juan then paraded into the city, making his way to Carrer Ample, where he was to stay at the mansion of the admiral of Naples. The streets were full of people who had come from nearby villages and hamlets to catch a glimpse of the golden-haired prince. His handsome face and impeccable comportment had already garnered much admiration during his last visit in '65.

From a second-floor balcony facing Montcada, Mother, Àvia, and I were aflutter with anticipation. Our silk fans were hardly a match for the heat, but this didn't discourage us in the least. When Don Juan's entourage at last appeared on our street, it was to the thump of atabales and a whirl of colorful plumes. Excited shouts erupted from the crowd, which the prince acknowledged with a wave and a smile. By then, however, my attention had settled elsewhere. I was scanning the rabble below in search of Miquel, who had not been invited to join us upstairs. That he could mix so easily with plebeians and *pagesos*—an undertaking totally out of my realm of experience—only served to intensify his desirability. Finally spotting him, I waved enthusiastically. He threw me a kiss. We did not, could not, stop staring at each other, even as the commotion around us grew louder.

Then suddenly, I felt a hard thwack on my forearm and turned to see Mother threatening me with the wooden handle of her fan.

"Enough!" she hissed. "Have you forgotten yourself?"

Angry, I rubbed the welt so intently that the pain grew more pronounced. At that moment, I hated my mother, hated the imposed restrictions and social conventions that made my life both easy and suffocating.

After the prince's grand entrance that day, we seldom saw Father, but his preoccupation with patronage and politics—the supplying of soldiers billeted in the city and of galleasses floating in our port—proved a blessing, as it afforded me more opportunities to see Miquel when he chaperoned our group of aunts and cousins. During these excursions, usually to take the air by the seawall, he was attentive to everyone, no one woman receiving more courtesy than another, yet his punctilious manners bothered me a great deal. I was overwhelmed with jealousy, consumed by uncertainty and insecurity. A novice, I possessed a limited understanding of the complications of the heart.

But on the eve of Sant Joan, the night we call La Nit de Foc for the many blazes that light the sky, Miquel was mine alone—or, I should say, Father's and mine. (Mother, I don't remember why, chose to remain home.) In Barcelona, we celebrate the feast of Saint John in ways that appear more pagan than Christian, more pageant than worship. Petards explode overhead, and bonfires burn on every street and *plaça*. Such a marvel it is to witness darkness transformed into light! Such a thrill to admire couples jumping over small flames or brave lads walking barefoot on hot ashes! At El Born, where Father took us to watch the open-air dances, we were serenaded by *flabiol*, *tible*, and *tamborí*. In addition to the traditional *coques de pinyons* cakes, peddlers sold candied fruits, cooked snails, and mulled wine. Nobles mingled with vagabonds, and couples in contorted poses hid in shadowed alleyways. A spectator wouldn't have ever guessed that we were a kingdom at the cusp of war with the mighty Ottoman Empire.

At one point, as the crowd pressed in, I was pulled away from Father and in fright turned to embrace Miquel. Though surrounded by others, he didn't push me away, nor did he take a step back. I felt the roughness of his beard, heard the inhale and exhale of his breath, glimpsed his lips as they curved into a small smile. He kissed my cheek, tenderly and with much longing. My breath stopped, my voice faltered. I thought my knees would give way. Yet I remained resolute in my stillness, in no hurry to leave his embrace. The moment lasted a rooster's crow, but it felt both eternal and decisive.

My gimlet-eyed father didn't fail to notice. He elbowed his way through the crowd, lips set in a menacing line.

"Dolça!" he shouted, and yanked me away, tearing my sleeve from its ties at the shoulder. Then, aiming his wrath at Miquel, he shouted, "Get out of my sight!"

Though I knew Father as a man of strict convictions and relentless ambition, I had never felt the lash of his censure. I was accustomed only to his tender ministrations. Shamed, I hung my head but only enough to witness Miquel slink off into the mass of revelers. Father did not address me on the way home, even when a drunk stumbled in front of us. His silence was crushing, yes, but it could not change what I felt.

Within days Miquel had enlisted in the tercio unit led by Miguel de Moncada. This was not entirely unexpected, as he previously had expressed a yearning to experience the honor of battle. Like so many others, he was swept up by a collective, conflicted passion that was both pious and belligerent, righteous and mistaken.

But I . . . I was devastated, and not only because he no longer stopped by our home to visit, but because of the mortal danger he would face. I blamed Father. I blamed the tercio officers who paraded about town with their rapiers and ornate morions. I blamed the very privileges that gave me the time to hold others responsible for my anguish. Then, when my sulking and refusal to eat got me nowhere—Mother thought these behaviors symptoms of a bad grippe—I plotted. I knew what I wanted, and I intended to get my way. By the time Miquel left, we had become lovers in the truest sense of the word, and the unofficial consecration of our love was made possible in part by the brilliant machinations of others.

I'd be lying if I said I wasn't afraid when we met in his hostal room in early July—lying, too, if I didn't admit to second thoughts and wracking guilt. I feared pain. I feared his judgment and my inexperience, the very real possibility of being discovered. And I feared, of course, the many and varied outcomes of our sin. I can easily enumerate these repercussions now, though at that time I pushed them away. Headstrong, brazen, conceited, and overconfident, desperate to seal what I considered a romance for the ages—all these traits I can, and must, claim. Still, that first time . . . that initiating afternoon, when I was introduced to a world for which I had received neither instruction nor practice, I could not have guessed that our love would become a stage for both pleasure and pain.

"You've come!" he said at the door, his incredulity emboldening me. With a nod, he thanked Quirze and Glòria, who fled the scene so quickly I wouldn't have had time to change my mind if I had so desired.

He pulled me inside, and my eyes adjusted to the dimness. The room had a desk and a ladder-back chair, a bed, a chest—nothing more, nothing less. Yet it still felt cramped. My own bedchamber, the smallest in the house, was many times larger and included more essential, if luxurious, fixtures and fittings.

"Wine?" he asked.

I nodded. He poured, his hand shaking. We supped. He remembered to offer a toast: "For us."

"For us," I echoed.

Our goblets clinked. When we finished drinking, an activity I prolonged for longer than necessary, he led me by the hand across the tiny room, and we sat side by side on the bed. It was narrow and lumpy. He cleared his throat. I pressed a hand against my belly to contain the nerves rumbling there. But it wouldn't be still, my stomach. Nor would my heart, my breath. My dread was equally matched by anticipation and curiosity.

"You are nervous?"

I laughed, embarrassed.

"Don't be. I'll be gentle."

I lowered my eyes, not in modesty but apprehension. Was I expected to behave in a particular way now?

He began by kissing me, softly at first and then with more urgency. He undid the stays of my bodice, removed each garment until I was left in a chemise. I was relieved not to have worn any jewelry. He asked me to stand up, and I did, the thin linen clinging to my breasts and hips. He stared.

"You're so beautiful."

I needed no more encouragement. With my help he, too, undressed, tossing to a corner the doublet, the breeches, hose, shirt, collar, and wrist ruffs. The boots he tucked under the bed. He adjusted the pillows, and we lay down. We resumed kissing. He lingered long enough to remove the last of my dress. Not once did he speak, not as his mouth sought my nipples, not as his fingers stroked a place I hadn't known existed. A strange warmth spread from center to limbs. My toes tingled. Only when he placed the full weight of his body on mine did he ask, "Am I hurting you?" I mumbled a denial, though I was frightened by the possibility of suffocation.

I can't say I enjoyed the first time, but it wasn't unpleasant, and the pushing and wriggling and fumbling, the musk of Miquel's body and the sound of his labored breathing, all receded before I had figured out how to react. When it was done, he held me in his arms, and I thought myself mature and wildly in love. The initial doubts (and fears) were gone, replaced by this sense of wonder at both myself and what the two of us had created. And it was only after I returned home, impressed with my bravery, that I wondered how he would explain to his landlord the spot of crimson on his bed linens.

On a windy day, the twentieth of July, Father, Mother, and I were among the hordes bidding our soldiers a noisy farewell at the port. Out on the water, the oars thumped against their oarlocks, and gulls screeched overhead. On land, horns played rousing music. Don Juan looked incredibly handsome in his scarlet brocade suit. But while the mood was festive, delirious even, I was intent on only one thing: trying to spot Miquel and his brother Rodrigo, whom I had met very briefly, on the ship's decks without alerting either of my parents. This proved an impossible task, not because of their vigilance but because all harquebusiers looked the same from a distance. Our fighting men wore uniforms reminiscent of parrots: yellow-and-red slashed-knee breeches, completed by red hose and buckle shoes, then topped by a red shirt and a leather doublet with cap sleeves and ruffs. For good reason they were called papagayos.

After the send-off (and without once catching a glimpse of Miquel), we strolled to the Basilica of Santa María del Mar, where during Mass I pressed hand to heart. There, snug in a small cloth purse, rested a note from Miquel.

> *Dearest Dolça,*
>
> *In the past few weeks, I have come to know you as a young lady of many gifts, blessed of beauty, spirit, and intelligence. In your presence I am mesmerized, captivated. So it is with a heavy heart that I leave you, yet I hope you understand that I must do my duty for both God and king. While the future cannot be forecast with accuracy, be assured that you, my beloved, will remain close to my thoughts wherever I journey, whatever befalls me.*
>
> *Forever and always,*
> *Miquel*

Though I was terrified of what might happen in battle, I never doubted he would return for me.

From Barcelona the Spanish fleet sailed first to Genoa and then south to Naples, and by September it had joined the Venetian and papal galleys in Messina. Within our city walls, we continued with our routines: working, attending family events, participating in numerous religious processions. Extramuros vintners pruned their vines, and *pagesos* prepared their fields for winter wheat. In short, for me and mine, life settled into its usual pattern but with one notable exception: Father finally relented to my entreaties and hired a painting instructor, a concession I accepted as an olive branch, for we had spoken little to each other since La Nit de Foc. Mother disagreed with this decision. She considered artistic vocation an obstacle to a proper and profitable marriage placement, especially since my choice of subject, commoners at work, was "scandalous"—Mother's word, not mine. In the end, her opinion didn't matter. I learned how to mix ground pigments in linseed and nut oils and became proficient in the detailed labor of making brushes from miniver fur. I discovered perspective, composition, and chiaroscuro, and the joy this gave me helped temper the long wait for Miquel.

Chapter 2

Concerning an Encounter on the Road
We Will Not Soon Forget

One afternoon, decades after my initial lessons in the art of painting and the art of love, I receive an unexpected letter from Miquel. Amber light pours through the west window, and my studio has warmed to the promise of spring. When Aldonça shuffles through the door, I don't glance up at first, as I'm readying to mix the hues for my palette, enough of them to layer my underpainting. To be pulled from my work, to be forced out of my trance can only serve as an invitation to loneliness—and why entertain the dark mistress when her exile is such a blessed reprieve?

"*Senyora*," she says, "a letter from Madrid."

"Madrid, Madrid, Madrid," I singsong, wiping my hands on my painter's smock. "Who could it be? The queen calling for me?"

"Dolça," she says, pressing the letter to the imposing mound of her breasts, "I hope you'll behave with decorum."

"When have I not?"

She rolls her eyes. I snatch the letter from her hands and wave her away, but she ignores the gesture in that stubborn way of hers. In spite of her social limitations, Aldonça understands the secrets of my heart, its dark undercurrents and light-filled swells, and so she prays for my lost soul with the ring of every compline bell.

I recognize the handwriting, the intricate loops that never sag no matter the length of sentence or depth of emotion. However, this particular missive bears an unfamiliar address—the corner of Calles de Franco and León. Has he moved from the house on Calle de la Huerta since his last letter? No matter. I slash the wax seal with one of my scrapers:

Dearest,

Time is short and I desire to allow my tired eyes, aided by these Florentine spectacles, to rest on the sweetness of your smile. To see you again would be a blessing I have long been denied. Can you not grant me one last wish?

These past months have been a period of professional success, but I must admit that recognition has arrived too late, even as I do my utmost to savor these triumphs without scruple and, more importantly, without my foremost muse at my side. (You.) In the midst of these celebrations I think of us, of our days together, but also of this separation neither of us deserves.

My life has been reduced to the confines of a spare room with a pallet and writing desk. I can no longer ignore the obvious. Or the inevitable. I have been diagnosed with the dropsy, and the juice of the large leaves of wormwood has been recommended. Still my thirst cannot be slaked. I retain water and my ankles bulge grotesquely. I have grown spent and weak.

Let the past be past. Let us be brave, braver than we ever dared to be in our youth. We must forgive ourselves and each other. I await you, my love, knowing this is a call both godly and selfish.

Miquel

I turn my attention to the date: 5 de marzo de 1616. Thirteen days ago.

But there's more. Under Miquel's signature, a delicate, feminine scribble: *Make haste. His days are numbered.* Who would add such a message?

Though Quirze mentioned at Christmas that Miquel has been ailing, I did not expect this sweet-worded request. Not after our last argument.

Aldonça taps my shoulder. "Wasted minutes can't be rescued," she says, and points to the quill and inkwell on my desk. "You must answer."

I heed her suggestion and prepare the ink to dip the quill, wondering who might read my note, Miquel or the mystery woman who added her own message.

Miquel, I write, *I am coming.*

I dry the ink with cuttlefish powder and then copy out his new address. I don't, however, sign my name, and too late, after Aldonça has shuffled out of the room with the letter, I am flooded with remorse. I didn't sign out of fear. Out of shame. These are dangerous times, morality dictated by rigid men wrapped in righteous holiness, so my signature in the possession of others could incriminate me in ways I'd rather avoid. I don't want to run the risk of being accused of adultery or worse, yet by exercising caution and omitting my name, I've failed to be brave. I've failed Miquel, again.

I am tempted to hide his letter in my calfskin-lined chest, along with his other ones, but toss the paper into the brazier instead. Nevertheless, the contents of the chest call me, a siren song of nostalgia and regret. I open it, the hinges creaking with age, and dig under the folded papers until I feel the familiar binding of the old sketchbook. With care not to upset the stack of letters, I pull the book out and leaf through its brittle pages. My technique has improved a great deal since I sketched these portraits, yet I'm proud to note that the charcoal lines are sure and strong, the yearning in the beloved face dramatically exposed. Sighing, I return the sketchbook to its secret place and stroll to a window, where, by craning my neck just so, I can see the bells of Santa María del Mar and the seawall's Torre Nova. It was near the seawall that Miquel lived during his last stay in the city, on Carrer de Sota Muralla.

It's been almost two years since I dared to enter that building, two years since I last saw Miquel. Two years too long, and now an opportunity to remedy that. An opportunity to bear witness to a truth he does not know.

The following morning, I meet with Bernat Xirau, a muleteer whose name figures prominently in Jaume's ledgers. Jaume is compulsive in his record-keeping, and he keeps account books as prudently and with as much detail as a Genoese creditor. For once, this is to my benefit.

Xirau looks the kind of scoundrel one would cross the street to avoid, beard the color of red embers and a scary-looking scar the length of his left cheek. His *barretina* sits at a jocular angle on his head. When he meets my eyes, it is without the slightest intention of bowing his head, deference the first casualty of our alliance. He twists the ruby ring on his thumb with unusual relish, and it occurs to me that it's not nerves forcing this repeated movement but a desire to call attention to the beautiful piece. Payment of some gambling debt perhaps?

We haggle over a price for the journey, and once that's settled, he details itinerary and instructions. We are to travel disguised as pilgrims, no silk or satin or damask cloth, the better to fool the *bandolers*. No fancy leather footwear either. For provisions he suggests pickled sardines, salt pork, sausages, common cheeses, and the plainest of wineskins. No wheat bread, only barley, rye, or spelt: peasant bread.

He warns the roads are dangerous but also assures me his men, seasoned fighters, carry swords and *pedrenyals* at all times. I request his discreet loyalty, underscoring the importance of keeping his mouth shut around the other mule drivers who gather, sometimes drunkenly and noisily, around Carrer Gensana. He accepts this without question, which I take as a good sign. A well-placed word, a slip of the tongue, could stop our journey before it starts.

We depart three days later, without oil lamp or torch to light our way—a necessary precaution. The cobblestones glisten with dew, and the air remains tainted with the faintest scent of brine. Excepting for two night watchmen and one emaciated calico cat, Aldonça and I encounter no one in the shadowy stillness. We meet Xirau at Carrer de l'Argenteria without incident. He is dressed in black knee-high riding boots and a cape as substantial and dark as original sin. The silver hilt of a dagger at his waist glints a warning. With a gloved hand, he motions us to follow him, and ever so quietly we proceed to Plaça del Blat, where five mules and two men await us. Once astride the mules, we clop onward, past the somber Palau de la Generalitat guarded by helmeted soldiers with pikes and armor, through the narrow byways of the Call, and onto La Rambla, where the stench is such, from trash, urine, and the spoiling carcasses of animals, that breathing becomes an exercise in discipline. I cover my nose with the hem of my wool shawl, but this does little to mitigate my disgust. Then through La Porta de la Boqueria, we ride to Hospital, where our caravan grows by four more men and beasts. By the time we arrive at Portal de Sant Antoni, the rising sun glazes the sky, and fingers of gold and orange limn the few clouds.

I glance back at my cherished Barcelona as it awakens from sleep, a mosaic of stone and wood and brick. The air vibrates with the sounds of groaning wagon wheels, and I count the church steeples that interrupt the sky, my heart clapping hard against my chest as I don't know when I'll return.

"We're truly leaving," I say to Aldonça. "Finally! I can hardly believe it."

She glares at me and crosses herself twice. "May God shine a light on our crooked path and watch over our sinning souls."

I wince at the recrimination in her voice. No doubt she's hoping I'll change my mind. But I won't, I can't. If we return home, I'll lose my final chance to make amends. With Miquel so ill, I really have no choice but to do what I've long resisted. A reunion, and a frank conversation, must come now or never at all.

The great city muralla opens to a landscape of orchards and farms, greenery without end, and where land hasn't been scrubbed into measured lots, heather and thyme grow wild. As we distance ourselves from civilization, I try to strike up a conversation first with Aldonça, who pretends she can't hear me, and then with one of the hired men, the one they call El Musulmán. I suspect he's been assigned to ride alongside us because he's as large as the double doors of a church, his neck the size of a young girl's waist. His right eye wanders hither and yon, unable to remain focused for any length of time. And unlike the others, he's bareheaded and capeless. I ask about his experience on the road to prepare myself for what might come, but as he's about to answer, Xirau trots back to us.

"Make yourself useful somewhere else, Musulmán. I didn't hire you to gossip." He slaps the haunches of the giant's mule.

In a stern voice, Xirau tells me to resist socializing with his men—as if under normal conditions I would stoop to jabbering with servants. I keep these thoughts to myself, however. No use airing grievances.

We ride through Sarrià at the foot of our beloved Tibidabo before we continue on the gently rising passes at the edges of the Serra de Collserola, where we come across other mule trains on their way east, city-bound carts and animals laden with oil and hemp and wine. The mules are often adorned with tassels and bells, and the swish and tinkle of these prettifications herald them long before we spot them on a turn of the road. One particular convoy, chaperoned by a squadron of morion-helmeted soldiers, appears to be transporting silver coins because the iron wheels of the special wagons leave deeper than usual ruts. To protect from the inevitable dust kicked up by so many hooves, I tie my kerchief over my nose. I really wish I had my jewel-encrusted traveling mask, the one Xirau wouldn't allow me to bring. He insisted it wouldn't fit in with our disguise. Pshaw!

Sometime later we dismount by a stand of beeches for a lunch of smoked sardines and spelt bread, an unappealing meal that fits in perfectly with the strictures of Lent. Both the wine and water are warm from being lashed to the flanks of our animals, but I drink anyway, making sure to keep my eyes downcast. I'd give away a pouch of pearls to rub the inside of my thighs, grown sore already, but there's no privacy to be secured here, no sympathy. Except for a fellow journeyer, a wool merchant who's traveling as far as Saragossa, no one addresses us. We might as well be ghosts. Eventually, the other men wander off, alone or in pairs, to answer nature's call, and soon enough Aldonça and I follow suit.

When we're at a respectable distance from the group, I ask, "Is the saddle comfortable enough?"

"A little late to worry about that." She turns away from me and lifts her skirt to squat.

"How can you say that? I've been concerned about your welfare since the beginning."

"Pfft!"

"I didn't ask you to come. You volunteered," I remind her.

"True. Who else would watch over you? Who else would tell lies for you?"

"Not lies. Fibs, fabrications, and all of them necessary."

"Trickery tends to be discovered sooner or later. Have you thought of that?"

"I have. But we won't be found out, and if we are, I hope it'll be later rather than sooner."

"Hope doesn't always make for reality. You should know that better than most, Dolça."

Aldonça rarely uses my Christian name, but when she does, it grabs my attention. I understand her anxiety stems from a love no mistress can purchase.

"What you say is true, Aldonça, but I've little choice in the matter."

"We always have choices, but those choices come with consequences. This time your choice will mean sacrifice. Which you're not used to, I might add."

By the afternoon, my seat has grown unyielding and my back stiff. The undyed serge gown, a garment I'd be embarrassed to wear under different circumstances, feels scratchy against my skin. At one point we enter a forest dense with conifers and oaks. An eerie cold settles upon us, and the complaint made by leather rubbing against animals sounds ominously loud. My eyes take their time getting used to the dimness; I touch the scapular around my neck for moral support.

"Halt!" Xirau suddenly shouts.

I glance up and gasp. I can hardly breathe.

Just ahead of us, in a clearing striped by light filtering through the canopy of trees, three men swing from the sturdy branches of a cork oak, eyes popping, tongues lolling, faces blue and swollen. The threadbare black breeches of two are patched at the knees. The third man still wears his black cloak. All are missing their boots. The strangling ropes moan with the unbearable weight of death, and the fetidness, that miasma of finality, presses close, closer still. Soon the maggots will arrive, and the magpies and the vultures.

Bile rushes to my throat, and the regurgitated sardines of my midday meal leave a foul taste in my mouth. I'm choking on horror and revulsion. Though I shield my eyes with a hand, the harm can't be undone, the spectacle unviewed. Next to me Aldonça makes the sign of the cross and I do the same, my hand trembling as it touches my forehead, my chest, each of my shoulders.

"*Bandolers*," Xirau says, the disdain in his voice clear as a mountain stream. "And no more deserving death to them."

Hanging bandits from the nearest tree is common punishment, perhaps an expedient one, too, if you're in the hinterlands, but it's still upsetting to witness justice meted in this manner. Even thieves possess souls. Even the most despicable have parents, spouses, children. It becomes obvious to me rather quickly, though, that my traveling companions are not as bothered by this horrifying spectacle as I am: they barely glance up at the dead. Only the wool merchant, with his golden curls and effete gestures, mutters something under his breath, and I'm not sure if it's a curse or an invocation.

"Let's get on with it," Xirau orders. "We don't have time to waste."

We obey, and nothing else is said, neither prayer nor blessing, nor the mention of a proper Christian burial. When I pass under the three bodies, eyes firmly closed, fists gripping reins, I shrink into my clothing, hoping to go unnoticed by the vengeful spirits that lurk in the shadows. The terror blazing through my insides is fiercer than the one I felt when Aldonça and I hurried past the night watchmen a few hours ago. Be that as it may, I reason with fear, I bargain with dread. I tell myself that encountering this omen early in the journey is to our advantage. The worst is behind us. I repeat this as a chant, an incantation to ward off bad luck and evil forces. Yet . . . I draw little comfort from my own assurances.

After skirting the Llobregat for many hours, we cross the river on a flat-bottomed boat and eventually file into Martorell, best known for its proximity to the hermitage of Montserrat and for a narrow pedestrian bridge named Pont del Diable, or Devil's Bridge. As it is the conclusion of the workday, laborers in their short trousers and traditional waistbands known as *faixa* gather in groups along the road. They stop their conversations to watch us go by. Our entrance startles barefooted children at play and they run behind us, shrieking and flapping their arms. At the venta, the innkeeper wears an unkempt beard and a curdled expression.

When I begin to dismount, no one offers assistance, not even Xirau. Only at the last moment am I helped to the ground by El Musulmán. The giant aids my nursemaid as well. I'm unsteady on my feet after so many hours in the saddle, but Aldonça and I manage to carry our meager belongings inside as a young girl in a dirty white smock leads us through a large room furnished with several rustic tables and then up tight stairs that reek of boiling cauliflower. We are deposited like cheap cargo in a corner chamber that is as dank as it is dark. Without waiting to hear comment or request, the child leaves us, returning minutes later with an earthenware saucer and pitcher of water. I've never been more delighted for the opportunity to clean. We're covered in grime.

Our accommodations are sparse. A straw mattress on a rope bedstead hangs from the wall farthest from the lone window. Aldonça and I are to share this. Though we've brought bedding at the urging of Xirau, our supplies are abominable: a canvas sheet and coarse woolen blanket, both of which bring to mind the qualities of a hair shirt. I yearn for familiar surroundings, for the scent of burnt olive stone from the metal brazier in the corner of my bedchamber. For my Rennes linen sheets and ermine-lined coverlet. For the brocatelle curtains that keep out the sun when needed and the Persian floor carpets that lessen winter's bite. They are so far from reach.

"*Déu meu*, we've no pillows!" I exclaim. "Not even a sack of chaff. How do they expect us to sleep?"

"We'll sleep like the rest of this dim-witted country sleeps," Aldonça snaps. "What did you think? That they would bring out feather pillows just for you?"

Chastised, I complain no more, though there is plenty to protest. Our evening meal, brought to us on a wooden tray by the child in the dirty smock, consists of cheese we know as queso fresco and a stew notable for its absence of meat. I had hoped for small chunks of lamb or pork, at the very least. We eat in companionable silence, unwilling to speak of what we saw in the forest. After prayers and before bed, Aldonça brews valerian tea downstairs, a much-needed concoction for our nervous state, and I sink into the ghastly straw mattress, defeated physically but sustained in the knowledge that I'm one day closer to Miquel.

Awakened sometime later by the cock's crow, I'm overcome by a strange prickliness. The room is frigid, but the cold alone can't be blamed for my discomfort. Then, without warning, Aldonça throws off the blanket and jumps from the bed.

"Damn fleas!" she spits, her breath puffing into little clouds. She scratches with both hands.

I, too, scramble out of bed and strip off my nightclothes. My entire body is covered by tiny red dots, as is Aldonça's. I'm livid, but Aldonça, more attuned than I to such matters, dresses quickly and marches downstairs. By the time she returns, I'm again in the traveling garments of a poor pilgrim, faded shawl and fraying kerchief, but now I must remove them to apply an unguent that smells of honey and cinnamon.

Aldonça curses the fleas, and I feel a sudden surge of affection for her. She informs me of Xirau's response to her complaint. "He said, and I'm using his words exactly, 'Tell the *senyora* to grow acquainted with the smallest of our citizens.'"

I laugh aloud to avoid weeping and take myself downstairs to request paper and quill. I write a note to my cousin in Saragossa to alert her of our arrival in a few days. The terror of another night in the company of fleas prompts me to risk the chance she might send word to Jaume about our whereabouts. If she does, she'll have chosen her allegiance, as I have. As we all must. I've learned, perhaps too late, that we can't pretend to be above the fray. Our very existence is a treacherous voyage between security and menace, between loyalty and duplicity, between comfort and penury, and it's best to choose a shore early.

When we climb back onto our saddled mules, the muleteers mutter a deferential *bon dia*. I study the men as they joke among themselves. One resembles Xirau in his ruddy coloring and red hair, a relation of some kind, likely a brother. His name is Gerard. Another is missing a finger on the hand holding the reins. A third is speckled with freckles. All wear their swords close. I search for the firearms Xirau promised in our meeting, but these *pedrenyals* must be well hidden because I can't detect them under the men's cloaks.

Soon after we take to the road, we cross a rickety wooden bridge over the green-gray waters of the Anoia. A pine-scented wind blows hard against my face. From where we are, the mountain of Montserrat looks like a hand with many knuckles, each crag naked of vegetation. The monastery appears to float above the jagged precipice, defying perception and common sense. Inspired by the sight, I assure myself that clear and uneventful progress awaits us.

We spend most of the afternoon on a rocky path that threads through barren mountains of granite before descending into a landscape of emerald quilted together by the rich russet of soil. I'm lost in thought when a commotion pulls me back from a daydream. At first, I have no idea of what is transpiring, but then the noise . . . the shouts and screams. Battle cries echo around me. Such a racket. Disoriented, I turn this way and that in an attempt to figure things out.

"Follow him!" Xirau shouts, pointing to El Musulmán.

But as the dust from pounding hooves settles around us, the men close in. Thirty or forty of them, wielding daggers and short-nosed harquebuses. Mud-splattered. Dirty-faced. With unkempt beards and knotted hair. A few wear old hauberks, that high-necked jacket of mail once popular among those who went off to war, but most are in shirt-sleeves. Somehow the possibility of being sliced and slashed feels more menacing than taking a shot by pistol.

The reins quiver in my hands. My stomach churns. I sneak a peek at Aldonça, who remains expressionless and steady on her mount. Is she scared? Does she think, as I do, that she's at death's door? Thoughts tumble through my head without reason or measure.

One of the men, a lanky rider on a brown horse, snarls a question at us, but his words make no sense. He brandishes a flintlock in one hand, a *pedrenyal* in the other, and wears a coat of green damask that surely was stolen from some unfortunate soul. When no one responds to his gibberish, he takes aim at our donkey. The explosion startles us, and I jump, landing hard on my saddle. The donkey brays, staggers a few steps, and then tumbles to its knees. Blood pools around the fallen beast.

Again the bandit shouts, louder as if that might elicit a reaction, and Xirau responds to him in Catalan and then in French. After some kind of strange exchange, Xirau tells his men to hand over their pistols. Swords follow, a couple of beautiful silver-handled daggers as well. And I think: what use were they, these armed guards I hired, if we've been ambushed?

The donkey-killer demands something else. Xirau listens carefully. He appears calm, unafraid, but a vein pulses in the middle of his forehead. He issues another order, and the men fumble around their clothing before tossing pouches of gunpowder to the ground. The man in the green damask coat turns his attention to Aldonça and me, which makes El Musulmán curse under his breath. He must feel helpless too.

"And who are the two women?" the bandit asks in accented Castilian.

"They're pilgrims on their way back from Montserrat," Xirau replies.

"Pilgrims?" The donkey-killer stares at us with distaste. He studies our dress, our foot coverings, probably assessing the possibility of plunder—nothing more because at our age we are ill-pleasing to the eye.

After a few harrowing seconds that keep my heart at a gallop, the man loses interest in us. He asks Xirau, in that strange mix of Catalan and French, where our caravan is headed. Saragossa, Xirau lies. He never mentions Madrid. Of course, he must have a good reason. The bandit then orders his men to look through our belongings, and we're pulled off our mounts and made to stand in a line at arm's length away from each other. The ground feels shaky under my feet, and my flea bites begin to itch again, the unguent Aldonça applied this morning now useless. I blink my eyes several times in hopes that I'm dreaming, but too much of the world surrounds me. Too much, too much. Shards of light filter through the trees. The scrub brush takes on color, green and brown and the gold of ripening millet. A bird caws. The scent of wild-flowers drifts simultaneously sharp and sweet. If I were to die now, slayed by thieves, my body might never be discovered. Vultures would peck out my eyes, wolves would tear the skin from my bones, and my skull would be bleached white by the sun. I shake away the depressing image.

The *bandolers* rifle through our satchels and saddlebags, pocketing random finds. The bounty is small, and they express their disappoint-ment with florid cursing. I'm surprised they haven't made us strip to our undergarments, as other robbery victims have been forced to do. They seem to believe Xirau's story about our pilgrimage—and why not? We're poorly dressed and made even more unattractive by the dirt that has collected on our clothes. I steal a glance at Aldonça. She refuses to acknowledge me, but I recognize the determined jut of her chin. She's angry and disillusioned and probably wondering how she allowed herself to be put in this situation.

The bandits have almost finished ransacking our stuff when they discover the drawstring pouch where I've been keeping my notebook and charcoal. "Please, sirs!" I cry out. "They're my drawing supplies."

The men stop their work and stare at me. The donkey-killer guffaws. "A pilgrim artist, for true?"

Bringing these items now feels foolish. What was I thinking when I packed? That I would sit by candlelight at a venta and sketch our meals?

"Draw me then," the donkey-killer says. "A charcoal portrait in exchange for your freedom."

He grabs the notebook and trots over to me. I smell the man's sweat, the bitterness of it, and wish I had my pomander with me. I would be soothed by the scent of civet.

"I need to sit," I say.

He gestures to a flat-topped boulder. Once I'm seated, he settles himself at the other end, arranging the damask coat so the green fabric glimmers in the sunlight. He's like a peacock showing off its plumage. And I? I'm the frightened mole hoping to dig itself back underground. My hands shake so much that I can't manage a straight line. I take a deep breath. I shift my weight. I swallow hard—but my hands continue performing their little spastic dance. He snickers. I can feel the eyes not only of the *bandolers* but of Xirau and his men, too, and of Aldonça. Desperate and without a way out, I force myself to put stub to paper. I outline the hard contours of the donkey-killer's face, the receding chin, the misshapen nose, the thick brows. For a few minutes, I'm absorbed in the task, but then a rhythmic clamor forces me to look up. A rider is galloping toward us, and when he finally pulls up on his white horse, just a few varas from where I sit, he studies the scene with an intensity that unsettles my thoughts. He is square-headed and broad-nosed, with scraggly hair the color of gesso. His dress is fancier than one would expect here in the wilds, white satin shirt with slashed sleeves and freshly waxed boots. My eyes are immediately drawn to the stitched outline of a pig on his doublet. (As far as I can remember, our populace has been divided between the *nyerros*, who wear the badge of a pig, and the *cadells*, favoring the symbol of a puppy. Though the conflict originated with two families, the animosity has spread throughout the principality, nurtured by centuries of hostilities.)

"Who killed the donkey?" the man on the white steed shouts.

The donkey-killer squirms next to me, and before I can collect my wits, the man rides over to us and kicks the donkey-killer in the chest. The latter staggers backward and falls off the boulder.

"Imbecile!" the man shouts. "That's one less animal for us."

No sooner has the man in the green damask coat pulled himself up from the ground than the rider kicks him again. Then with unexpected agility, he yanks a leather-handled whip from his saddle and lashes the *bandoler* on the back and buttocks, around the legs and shoulders, each pop and snap accompanied by a volley of profanities. Dark blooms of blood begin to sprout on the coat, but the beaten man doesn't make a sound. I'm left speechless. From the corner of my eye, I see Xirau signal to his men, but I don't have a clue what that could possibly mean. Finally, the rider wheels his horse to face the others and screams at them to hurry. Though there's not much to pack away—we are truly traveling light and without luxury—the *bandolers* fill two sacks to bulging. As they do this, the man guides his white stallion around, issuing commands, cursing and insulting when needed. He finally makes his way to me and asks what I'm holding in my hands.

"A treasure map?" he taunts, and dips from his saddle to snatch my drawing.

"It's a sketch." But he can see that for himself.

"Quite a good one." He studies it with a slow admiration that makes my skin crawl. "You did this?"

I nod. He folds it and wads it under his shirt.

"I feel generous today," he declares when the men are done gathering the loot. "I have just come from praying to La Moreneta virgin in Montserrat, so thank those Benedictine monks for saving you from an unfortunate end. You're free to go."

Gratitude flutters in my chest, a bird taking flight.

"But," he continues, "in exchange for your lives, we'll take the mounts. Good thing God gave you two legs. Now you can use them as he intended." He roars at his own wit, but no one laughs with him.

After tying the mules to their horses, the *bandolers* trot away, kicking more dust in our faces. I notice Aldonça swaying side to side, face pale, shoulders slumped. Mercifully El Musulmán offers her his arm, and she takes it to steady herself. I take faltering steps toward them.

"That was a close one," she says tartly when we're face-to-face.

"Depends how you define a close one," I reply. "We weren't murdered, but we're in the middle of nowhere without transportation or supplies. Now we can die a slow death instead of a quick one."

"Don't be so dramatic. You're to blame for this anyway."

I turn away so she won't see my tears.

"Vilanova de Camí isn't far," Xirau announces. "An hour's walk if we hurry."

And so we begin our march, never once looking back at the dead donkey now covered by a cloud of flies.

The road slopes downward into a thinly settled plain typical of this part of Anoia. Our silence is interrupted only by El Musulmán's occasional whistling. He seems to be enjoying himself, unlike the rest of us. When we pass a roadside sanctuary that houses a crude figure of our heavenly mother, he makes the sign of the cross. The rest of us follow suit, wanting to ensure whatever safe passage we can still claim.

When we finally limp into Vilanova de Camí, my feet ache and my mouth is dry. Xirau exchanges pleasantries with some of the townspeople as he leads our group to a slate-roofed building behind the town's blacksmith, where we wait outside for him. I suppose he'll have to secure some kind of loan or credit here, in a place where he apparently has friends. He's already advised me that he'll arrange for money to be delivered to us by messenger within the next day or two. I worry that this may clue my family in Barcelona to our whereabouts, but I can't figure out any other solution to our predicament.

After this errand, we stop in a dark tavern, where we're served drinks, and then we follow him along a winding path to a house, where he rents three carts and mules from an old couple with no more than a dozen teeth between them. Packed into these vehicles that still carry the remnants of previous journeys, hay and dried buds of sorghum, we leave for Igualada, in a race to enter before nightfall. Never straying far from the shadows of the wooded foothills, we travel past fields of wheat, rye, barley, and maize, past scrub oak, myrtle bushes, and strangely formed outcroppings, past grazing cattle and fat sheep that look up at us with bovine interest, past red and yellow and blue wildflowers slanting into late-afternoon light. When we arrive at the gated city, Xirau pays the expected toll to the guards.

Igualada sits on the left bank of the Anoia. Its city walls are thick with bulwarks and crowned in battlements, but the traffic of merchant transports and fine carriages is lively. As we approach the center square, the tantalizing odor of roasting meat drifts over from an establishment. I'm hungrier than I thought, but the appetizing smell also reminds me of another kind of hunger, one you can feel not in your stomach but in your heart, in your very bones. Miquel suffered from its pangs, I not so much. Where he craved fresh beginnings and faraway lands, I preferred the known, the certain. Invariably I chose comfort and complacency, abundance and luxury, over his offers of exotic adventures. Security has always served as my compass—until now. But no use punishing myself for that, no. The throbbing in my calves and heels is enough. There's not a bone in my body that hasn't suffered some kind of insult from the bouncing cart.

We lodge at a venta where the rooms are larger than the last we experienced, but because we threw out our flea-infested bedding in Martorell, we now have to buy new provisions. When Xirau and his brother, Gerard, leave to purchase them—and to report the robbery to the cuadrilleros of the Holy Brotherhood—the rest of us congregate in the dining hall for a bowl of pottage and a carafe of wine. I can barely stand.

Our exhaustion is such that soon after nightfall, without even removing our filthy overskirts, Aldonça and I collapse on a bed that's little more than straw packed into a sack. My head, too crowded with doubt, too terrified by the events of the past few hours, weighs as heavy as a barrel of wine. Next to me, my nursemaid is uncharacteristically quiet. She hasn't spoken more than half a dozen words in the past few hours. I'd feel better if she scolded me. Defending myself would lessen the burden of guilt. She's far too old to have joined me on this journey.

"Aldonça? Tell me the truth. Are you angry with me?"

She clears her throat but doesn't speak.

I try to turn on my side to face her, but I can't. I have no energy to move my limbs. "Do you want to return home?"

"Not without you."

"I can't return. You know that." To return would be to surrender the possibility of reconciliation with Miquel. To return would be to miss the opportunity to cleanse my conscience. To return would mean an inevitable confrontation with Jaume, who's too often quick to judge and lacking in compassion.

"Then, Dolça, don't ask what I want. You'll do as you please, as you've always done."

In the silence that follows, a scuttling noise comes from the attic:

nocturnal creatures readying themselves for the hunt. I pull the blanket up to my chin. After several minutes I think Aldonça is asleep, but just as I'm slipping into a sweet slumber, she mumbles, "Together. We'll continue together."

That night I dream of my reunion with Miquel. The time and place are wrong, however. In my dream I'm a young girl of fifteen, Miquel a wanted man, my parents still living. And when I wake, the visage that appears before my half-opened eyes belongs to my lover's wife, or how I imagine her to be since we've never met. When I tell Aldonça about this apparition, she displays no pity.

"Serves you right," she says, as she helps me dress. "You shouldn't have taken what isn't yours."

Chapter 3

*In Which I Lose a Loved One
and Learn to Wait*

When we received news of the Christian armada's victory in November of '71, the city's populace broke into boisterous celebrations. People danced in the streets, and fireworks exploded over the midnight sky. At a Te Deum sung in the cathedral, the faithful filled the pews and spilled out the doors, such was our gratitude. My own celebration, on the other hand, was muted. Word from Miquel didn't arrive until January, and in those intervening months, I suspected the worst. Everyone had heard horror stories about the battle at Lepanto. Tens of thousands had been impaled by pikes, struck down by cannon shot, burnt in fires, and drowned in roiling waves.

So when his letter from the military hospital in Messina finally arrived, I was relieved he had survived—even as my hopes for a swift reunion were dashed, even as the memory of his lips on mine faded. The missive told, in a roundabout way, that Miquel was among those who had survived the carnage, only to be left mangled and disfigured.

Dear family,
May this letter find you in good health and in the protective
arms of Our Lord and Savior. I am healthy enough to finally be

able to write to you about the naval combat that has ended the treachery of the infidels. As you well know, I was assigned to the command of Diego de Urbina as a harquebusier on the galley Marquesa. A fine ship of sturdy build, with two masts, lateen sails, and five cannon mounted on the bow, it was propelled as much by the prevailing winds as the power of its oarsmen. Our orders were to sail out on the tenth of September with Don Juan's fleet, but vicious squalls stranded us in the harbor of Messina for four days and not until the sixteenth did we weigh anchor. In spite of this delay, our fleet created a spectacle worthy of our cause, more than three hundred ships headed to the Ionian Islands determined to avenge the atrocities of the Turks.

On the morning of the sixth of October, we entered the Gulf of Corinth, within sight of the Lepanto Channel. The men stood in awe of the outline of the Acroceraunian Mountains, but unfortunately, I did not enjoy this view. Felled by illness, I remained on my pallet, shivering and overheated, knowing only of the outside world from my brother. However, once it came time for battle, I could not allow a fever to thwart the completion of my obligations, and when Don Juan issued the final orders to his fleet, I did not remain below deck. The command "To arms! To arms!" was enough to power my heart and limbs. I raced to man my battle station, and none could dissuade me, for I would rather have died for God and country than hide as a child would in the galley's hold.

We moved toward the Gulf of Patras and then rounded Point Scropha. A necklace of ships, bearing the flags of the Ottoman provinces, sailed toward us, clasped by a galleass that flew the green flag with the yellow monogram of Koran verses belonging to that barbarian Ali Pasha. We lost no time to fear or wonder, throwing ourselves into preparation for battle straightaway. Water barrels were placed all around to fight the inevitable fires. Guns were loaded and decks sprinkled with sand for surer footing. Swordsmen oiled their weapons, and javelins were heaved to the top of the masts.

And then it began. Oh, dear family, if I could remember it all, but pandemonium was such that only after talking to my fellow soldiers have I cobbled together a depiction of this battle. How accurate a portrayal this is, I do not know. If I were to depend on senses alone, it is sound—terrifying in its power—that has left the most indelible mark on my memory.

The blood-curdling cries.

The clang of swords and the crunch of mace against skull.

The blasting of horns.

The crashing of cymbals.

The roar of cannon.

The thunder of artillery.

The crackling of fire riding the sea.

The splash of falling debris.

The creak of timbered hulls.

The howls of men in their last.

The shouts of boatswains in a dozen languages.

Oh, the din! And the smoke that enveloped it all.

The Marquesa *endured repeated assaults from the Turks, for we were in the thick of the fighting and the enemy boarded us before we managed to repel them. We dealt with them in hand-to-hand combat that cost us dearly, as I have come to learn that forty of my shipmates were killed in battle and three times as many were wounded. The fighting continued into late afternoon, blood and writhing bodies making the decks a slippery and tripping danger. Sixty thousand fighting men on both sides stabbing and slashing and slicing, shooting poisoned arrows and firearm pellets, flailing at whatever moved. We were aided by God, but also by the superiority of our infantry, by the revolt of thousands of Christian galley slaves aboard the Turkish vessels, and by the death of Ali Pasha. The latter event I did not witness, but it is said that he was wounded by a harquebus bullet and beheaded by a captive, his soul now in the hellfire of immortality. To the man, we met both Demon and Creator in those hours—but we made the world safe for Christianity.*

I am well, recovering from two harquebus bullets in the breast and a third that shattered my left hand. Infection has retreated. I am under the direct care of Don Juan's personal surgeon general, Don Gregorio López, who is here to supervise the care of the wounded. We are many, but we rest in the knowledge that we have achieved the unachievable with the help of Our Lord and for the glory of His Father.

With love and admiration,
Miguel

I read and reread that letter, and always my eyes lingered on that last paragraph. On one word: *shattered*. It sounded ominous, but what did it really mean to have a shattered left hand? The world I knew offered only one place to the crippled, and I couldn't imagine Miquel in that role. When I badgered Mother with questions, her answers were too curt to quell my anxious curiosity. "He's in the hands of God," she'd say. Father was no help either, preoccupied as he was with the imminent construction of a new warehouse for the storage of flour. Besides, the relationship between the two men had cooled since La Nit de Foc, and a letter recounting exploits was unlikely to get Miquel back in Father's good graces. As for Aldonça—well, she dismissed my concerns altogether.

"Worry less about a man without a future and more about your own person," she'd scold. "Look at your nails!"

She had a point. Though I scrubbed with a special soap made of barilla boiled with olive oil, paint seeped into my very fingertips, refusing to cede. However embarrassing this proved for my family, I was secretly proud of these marks. They were medals of honor, laurels of triumph.

That winter, Àvia began a steady and permanent decline. Her eyes dimmed, her remaining teeth fell out, and her wrinkles deepened. Swift to fatigue, she rarely railed at Castile's meddling in Catalan affairs or the hypocrisy of the Inquisition and spent her days ensconced in an upholstered chair next to Mother in the sewing room. At meals, if she felt sturdy enough to join us, she gummed her food like a goat cropping meadow grass. In spite of this, or maybe because of it, I never shied away from her company. She was, like me, stubborn, but in ways I had yet to understand or master. For example, when we recited the rosary on feast days, reverently fingering our prayer beads, she ended the Hail Mary with words I couldn't find in any prayer book: *Holy Mary, Mother of God and my blood relative, pray for us.* And every time she said this you could count on Mother, the ever-faithful rule-follower, to scold her: "Stop that, for the love of God!"

I was called to my grandmother's chambers the day my menstrual quarantine ended. The practice then, as it is now, was for a woman to be kept in seclusion for a week during her menses, and though I was excused from my lessons, this wasn't an occasion to embrace, by any means. The monthly courses still carried a fair share of shame and discomfort. Mother believed, as did my aunts, that each cramp or ache was a reminder of Eve's original sin and hence to be endured as penance. Moreover, the process of preparing the rags to absorb my blood was quite tedious. If on the rare occasion I had to venture outside the house during those days of mortification—most likely to visit one of the aunts—I had to carry a nosegay of sweet-smelling herbs around my waist to neutralize the odor of blood. For a heavy flow, which I experienced later, Aldonça prepared an elixir made of the powdered ashes of toad.

The one and only Regina Benaviste de Prat's rooms were on the west side of the house, which meant they were chilly in the morning and hot in the afternoon, but always redolent with the perfume of cut flowers and fresh fruit. The walls were covered with ageless tapestries, one depicting shepherds in the fields, another a hunting scene, a third showing something she called the tree of life. It was her bed, however, a short-legged, four-poster of mahogany, that I coveted, for it had the most beautiful carvings of nymphs along its frame.

She was reclining on pillows in her divan when I entered.

"I've saved something for you," she rasped. "Since your birth I've prayed to Adonai to grant me the strength to live this long."

"Adonai?"

She waved away my question. "Help me get up."

I did, and then, leaning on an ivory walking stick, Àvia shuffled to a corner, where a carved walnut wardrobe had been polished to a dull gleam. Atop this wardrobe sat a small coffer. She motioned for me to reach up to retrieve it, an easy feat as I was two or three heads taller than she was. Inside the box was a small gold amulet, wrapped many times over, first in plain linen, then in blue brocade, then in green silk, and finally in black velvet. It was in the shape of a hand.

"This is a hamsa," she said.

"Hamsa," I echoed. I took the talisman from its resting place and noticed, in the middle of the palm, a series of tiny crystals forming an eye.

"It represents the hand of God," she continued, "and it will protect you from evil."

"What evil? Why? How?"

"Shhh! Stop with the questions, girl. My mother gave it to me and before that her mother gave it to my mother and before that—"

"But you haven't given it to my *mare*?"

"No."

"Does Mother know you have this?"

"Yes."

I waited, hoping she would elaborate, but when she didn't, I pressed: "Doesn't Mother want it?"

"No."

"Why? It's lovely."

"She considers it a pagan symbol—and a danger."

"How a danger?" I gently placed the amulet back in its nest of fabrics.

"It is beloved by Jew and Musulmán."

I knew we were neither. Father often boasted to houseguests how he could trace his lineage to the earliest Catalan merchants, those who had plied the waters of the Mediterranean, hazarding past Sicily and onward to Athens. One of his ancestors had also served under Jaume I, when our Catalan king conquered Mallorca in 1229. And yet . . . yet.

"How come you have it?" I asked.

"It's been in my family for at least three centuries, or so my mother said."

"Three hundred years!"

"Yes, and it's a symbol of who we are and what sets us apart. That legacy makes the hamsa valuable, not the gold or gemstones."

Though I was well versed in history, including the tales of antiquity—Tutor Guillem had seen to that—I found it difficult to imagine that anything, and in particular this gold hand with two opposing thumbs, had survived the passing from one generation to the next. Had I been older or less self-absorbed, more knowledgeable of the world beyond my home, I might have questioned my grandmother. I did no such thing. I simply listened to what she had to say, without prodding for explanations. But don't judge my disinterest. The pressure to conform is much too strong, as binding as mortar, as durable as iron.

"Keep it near you at all times. And when you have your daughter, you, too, must pass it on to her."

I bent down and kissed her head.

Àvia died three days later on a cold March Tuesday of sullen skies and brutal breezes. After a requiem mass, we interred her in the family mausoleum, next to the grandfather I had never met, Joan Prat Ripoll, and for months I wept every day, much as I had after my brother Andreu's death. Her absence remained palpable long after the designated period of mourning. I expected to see her at supper, to smell the perfume of her pomander, to hear her humming in a darkened hallway.

Many years later I would show Miquel my hamsa and recount the exchange with Àvia. He didn't seem surprised by the story, only saddened. Long accustomed to the suspicion of old Christian neighbors and the inexplicable rejection of his applications to serve the Royal Court in the New World, he was already aware of the stain on our shared maternal line. For him, the idea of our grandmothers' grandmothers' grandmothers renouncing the faith of their ancestors to lead an outward life of piety was one more confirmation of this Spanish predilection for disguise and deception. He believed that we inhabited a world of shifting allegiances, where few could claim who they were or express what they thought.

"We, all of us, lead double lives. You, me, the entirety of Spain," Miquel said. "You're so sheltered you don't recognize it. You live in a gilded cage and think yourself free."

During that period of mourning, Miquel did not return to Barcelona. The separation, along with my grief, proved torturous, like tiny daggers pricking the skin. Much to my dismay, he reenlisted with the tercios, a final flourish of bravura that he would come to regret. He had recovered from the two harquebus shots that had struck him in the breast, but the injury to his left hand was permanent, though apparently not serious enough to handicap his military career. Assigned to an allied fleet under the command of Marco Antonio Colonna, he wrote letters that were as insipid as they were brief, bragging about the cities he visited (Sardinia, Palermo, Corfu, Tunis, Trapani, Naples) and about his promotion to elite trooper. I resented every word. Why hadn't he come back to claim me? Was there another woman in his life?

Offered no proof otherwise, I convinced myself that my dashing poet-soldier was faithful. How could I not? I suffered from two conditions without quick remedy: ignorance and inexperience. Some might argue, as Mother did later, that I was infatuated with a mirage, besotted by a man who did not exist in the flesh but only in my imagination. What's more, Mother considered romance superfluous. Marriage, she believed, had to be founded on a sturdier element than love. I didn't originally agree, though later experience would teach me different.

At any rate, in September of '75, Father received word from a ship captain that Miquel would return to Barcelona from Naples by month's end. Energized by such news, I became consumed by a flurry of preparations, my mood mercurial and my painting abandoned. The mirror became my best friend. I obsessed over my skin, my hair, every line, spot, and imperfection in my countenance. All for naught. I did not know then, or for a long time, that Miquel would be sidetracked, diverted to a life neither of us could have imagined.

At the beginning of my wait for Miquel, I was awash in expectations and hope. With maids in tow, I took to visiting the port under the guise of wanting to spend time with cousin Glòria, then recently betrothed. The constant bustle of the wharves proved jolly entertainment, from the squawk of seabirds to the reek of fish to the many-colored splendor of flags and pennons. Depending on the time of day, we would stop at a market stall on the way home to buy jellied fruit or a paper cone of cinnamon-roasted almonds, but the sweets never countered the bitterness of Miquel's inexplicable absence. Every once in a great while, I'd glimpse a man with the same chestnut-colored hair or a sailor with a similar walk, and my heart would leap, only to have that promise crushed like stone in a vise.

After twenty months of this almost daily ritual, those strolls became a procession of despair, more torture than diversion. Longing turned into a permanent ache below my breastbone, sometimes raking my breath, sometimes wresting hot tears from my eyes. I began to doubt Miquel's words, my own judgment. Eventually, our outings ended altogether when Glòria was forced to rest because of her pregnancy. Weeks of waiting turned into months, which added to seasons that collected into years, almost five, before I would learn what had happened to him in the waters between Naples and Barcelona. And by then, I was well established on the life path my parents had intended all along. My future felt inevitable, conventional, impossible to change.

In due time, I returned to everyday pastimes and preoccupations. Aldonça at my side, I once again made fervid rounds of Barcelona's churches in an attempt to study the masterpieces displayed in our temples. Oh, so many of them, and each more exquisitely executed than the next! In the cathedral alone you could lose years to awe, for wherever you looked, art seduced the senses. I especially admired Bartolomé Bermejo's *Pietà*, his stormy sky rendered in the Flemish manner. Also, a retablo of the Transfiguration by Bernat Martorell, and on one of the pipe organ's door, Pere Serafí's luminous *Birth of Christ*. Among these masterful expressions of beauty, I found tranquility, if no answers.

Mother worried that I'd insist on a future as a bride of Christ, thus removing the possibility of continuing the family name with a proper heir, but this fear had as much substance as her others. Which is to say, not at all. (Mother also fretted that my height—I was as tall as Father— would reduce my marriage prospects, a ludicrous notion even if the influence of my dowry was discarded.) She behaved as if her sole purpose in life was to find me a husband and regarded my general disinterest in the men of our social circle as a personal affront.

"You're getting too old to be so picky," she said every time I snubbed a suitor. "You need a husband. Then you'll have your own household and we'll have our *hereu.*" An heir, a precious heir.

If Father happened to be within earshot, he'd wave the notion away. "Let her be. She's still a child, and I have much to teach her."

Father appeared to be in no hurry to marry me off, and I was pleased by his support. Now, of course, I know he was simply taking his time doing what he knew how to do best: negotiating, laying the groundwork, making a deal with someone who would benefit the family's holdings.

So mired was I in my anxious thoughts—*Where was Miquel? Why had he not sent word? Had he dismissed me as just one more conquest?*— that I couldn't see my way beyond the minutiae of my small life. I would return home from the palaces of God to attempt imitation of the masters, but my perceived limitations, both in talent and in technique, only added to my despair. I once confided my misgivings to Frerik, the old Flemish painter who served as my tutor for several months. He smiled a slow smile that expressed a special intimacy with discouraging thoughts.

"You must strive for excellence nonetheless," he said in his choppy Castilian, the only language we had in common. "It's only in this striving that we're known to achieve great work."

My skill level was not the only doubt that beset me. I questioned my reasons for painting, too, as I foresaw no future for a woman in this art form. It was a favorite lament of mine, this lack of opportunity, and I bandied it about whenever Frerik assigned me a particularly difficult exercise to complete.

"I know of only one woman who has achieved recognition for her work," I complained. "What am I to expect for myself?"

"Only one?" he challenged.

"Yes, Sofonisba Anguissola, the Italian who served in our Spanish court. She was the queen's lady-in-waiting, but she was sent packing into marriage when Elisabeth of Valois died."

"Men are sent packing into marriage too," Frerik noted, an unmistakable slyness in his tone. "That said, my dear *senyoreta*, there are other women painters for you to emulate. Two of my compatriots, in fact. Caterina van Hemessen and Levina Teerlinc. Perhaps you can do less grumbling and a little more studying of history, sí?"

He arched a brow and directed my attention back to the canvas, where my attempt at painting a peasant and his donkey had led to an impromptu lesson on how to present volume and depth.

"You have four ways to create this illusion. First the basic technique of dark and light values. Like this."

Enthralled, I observed the confident movement of his hand, as brush and pigment adapted to his touch.

"You can also make use of color in the underpainting. Thus." A stroke, a dab, a smudge. "Or, we also have at our disposal . . ."

His lessons were master classes not only in how to *see* but also in how to translate what was seen. From the making of brushes to the grinding of pigment to the rendering of a vision delivered in a dream, they were a welcome change from the predictable sameness that was my lot in life. With Frerik I lost track of time, forgot where I was, and stopped thinking of Miquel, Miquel, Miquel. I like to believe I was his favorite pupil, as he always mounted a fierce defense of my choices in theme and content, encouraging me to follow what obsessed my eye: the prosaic texture of daily life, the simplicity of the common man. Paradoxically, this compulsion was made stronger by my unfamiliarity with the subject matter. Then again, is there not an allure to the different, the distant? Is it not better to depict privations rather than experience them? And so, with Frerik's support I grew assured of my preferences, even when Mother, easily scandalized, insisted I paint scenes of a more religious nature. There were to be no sacred apparitions for me, however. No still lives or formal portraits either. I gained a freedom on hemp and linen that I couldn't possess anywhere else.

Frerik was one of the many painting instructors Father hired over those years, their length of employment dependent on Father's mood. They included a stocky Valencian who preferred tempera to oil, a Barcelona gentleman who excelled at portraits of martyred saints, and a Florentine who was hard of hearing or pretended to be in an effort to press close to me. Unfortunately, none of them proved as inspiring as the Fleming with the pale skin and large ears. None of them turned out to be as tolerant and supportive.

In addition to this artistic instruction, I also continued learning the day-to-day operations of the family's mercantile trade under Father's tutelage. Several times a week, I accompanied him to a building on Carrer del Comerç, where assorted employees occupied the first landing, while the upstairs space, which echoed like a cave, was reserved for Father and his secretary. Maps and nautical charts overwhelmed the walls, with the only personal token being a small framed portrait of Andreu on Father's desk. Sometimes the scent of sandalwood drifted through the open window, but no one could explain from whence it came.

I'm certain Father would have preferred my brother at his side, but he wasn't ill-pleased with my presence or my efforts. Though a woman *mercader* was rare, I soon learned there were others like me, all of them widows governing their late husband's affairs. Usually, they were helped by a trusted assistant until a young son could take control or a daughter married. I didn't know of any unmarried women in my circumstances but suspected *pubilles* were more common with small estates and in rural municipalities. Too many sons had died in wars or challenged their fate in the New World. And for all of Father's jokes and jests—he complained of my pomander's scent and of the time it took for a maid to dress my hair—he was proud of me. I inquired incisively, assimilated knowledge quickly, and ignored distractions most of the time. I didn't match his long hours of labor, but I was an apt pupil, acquiring the skills to negotiate, to audit ledgers, to discern between a losing proposition and one that simply needed extra attention. I also gained an understanding of the dangers Barbary pirates posed to both our trade and our lives. I don't think a month ever went by without some report of a plundered seaside city or the confiscation of a merchant galley and the kidnapping of its crew.

Father also taught me the importance of luck and the necessity of courting its capricious favors. "Preparation and patience are important traits in business," he'd say. "That's what many confuse as luck."

It was in his office that I met the man who would become my husband. At first, I thought him one of Father's clients, nothing more than that. I didn't, until much later, look upon him as a suitable life companion; my romantic longings belonged elsewhere. Against my better judgment, I kept hoping for a message from Miquel. I even imagined the possibility of his family sending a letter to inform us of his whereabouts, an unlikely scenario since Mother had had no contact with these distant relatives after Àvia's death.

Also, during that interlude and without my knowledge or approval, my parents commenced the intricate negotiations that would seal my fate to the man they had selected. Did I notice this familial diplomacy? No. Was I blind to the purpose of my new *galant*'s visits to Father's office? Yes, for a while. In my futile wait for Miquel, I failed to realize how forces, known and unknown, can steer the future, much like a vendaval wind can pull a carrack from its course and into undiscovered seas.

Chapter 4

*When We Welcome True Pilgrims to
Our Ranks and Doubt Muleteers*

My head remains wooly this first morning in Igualada, and I'm relieved that, in order to replenish supplies, we won't be spending any time on muleback for at least one day. My bones wouldn't be able to bear more jolt and jostle. Downstairs in the dining area, Xirau is speaking to two representatives of the Holy Brotherhood, both identifiable by their green robes and leather chest armor. When he finishes, he approaches the table where Aldonça and I are breaking our overnight fast with a slab of dark bread and a wedge of goat cheese.

"I'm working on replacing our mules," he begins, "and this is going to take some—"

"What about the constables you were speaking to?" I ask. "Won't they go in search of our mounts?"

He waves the question away. "They're useless. The *bandolers* run circles around them, and many *pagesos* provide safe harbor for the outlaws anyway. We won't recover anything."

"What's the use of your men then? They did nothing to stop the assault."

"They saved your life, *senyora*."

"And how's that?" I stare at Xirau, but his face remains inscrutable.

I suspect I'm being deceived in some way. But how? Why? I know little about Xirau, except that his name appeared numerous times in our account books, leading me to believe that Jaume places great trust in him for the transport and delivery of goods. I can complain about many things dealing with Jaume, but not about his business sense. He's both a shrewd *mercader* and an astute judge of character.

"The price of a few mules," he continues, "is a lot less than the price of a few lives. Riera's band—and that's who it was, Bernat Riera, on the white horse—is the largest in these parts and that's why they overtook us. But I assure you that there are many smaller factions that dare not attack us when their scouts spot my men. And those groups, *senyora*, are much more dangerous. They've nothing to lose."

I don't respond, but Aldonça says, "Then out with it, young man. You're obviously preparing us for something."

Xirau smiles for the first time. "Indeed. As I said at the beginning of this conversation, we must replace our mules and our supplies."

"At what cost?"

"I've been to see a few mule drivers, men I trust, and they are willing to sell on partial credit, as they know me. The price, however, doesn't vary." He pauses as if to catch his breath. "A mule runs forty *lliures*."

"Forty!" Several men turn to stare at me. "That's highway robbery."

"I'm not asking you to pay the full price of each animal, but I can't shoulder the entire cost either. The price of the journey must be adjusted."

"It was exorbitant to begin with," I protest, even as I know that I have no choice.

"Commensurate with the risk. I'm not in the business of transporting old women nor of keeping secrets from one of my most important clients. The latter action, *senyora*, might prove an expensive gamble for me and I must be compensated accordingly."

So, he worries about Jaume. I wouldn't, or at least not a lot. I believe that in some ways Jaume is relieved I'm gone, out of his hair. I'm a burden, and a vocal, meddlesome one at that. Moreover, Jaume believes me incapable of any ingenuity. He could never imagine me using the ledgers for my own purpose.

"What else?" I press.

He ticks off the supplies we need, perishables we would have had to buy anyway, but he also must find a gunsmith to replace the men's weapons and a bladesmith for the thieved swords and daggers. Again, he claims these purchases are possible only because of his reputation and credit with merchants in various towns. "This'll take most of the day, maybe longer. But if all goes well, we can leave for Cervera tomorrow."

That night, after this exchange with Xirau, I'm plagued by a recurring nightmare. Miquel has taken a turn for the worse, and I am no closer to seeing him. He lies on a down mattress, propped up by pillows, his face wan and his hair damp with sweat. The wife sits next to him. There's an open book on her lap, and I spend the dream wanting to see its title. Is it *La Galatea*, Miquel's first book? One of his plays? Or his *Novelas Ejemplares*? Most likely it's the *Quixote*, which so insulted me.

The dream leaves me in a state of deep melancholy, and Aldonça blames this on a dramatic change in the levels of my four humors. "Too much black bile," she opines.

I say no more, for fear she might recommend a treatment.

From Igualada we labor over parched and uncultivated land, up switchbacks that climb, climb, climb until we reach the brow of a hill overlooking a valley that unspools like a luxuriant green carpet. On this ridge Xirau allows a few minutes for the new mules to catch their breath. On our descent we encounter many people and conveyances, more so than before, and the journeyers are a motley collection: priests and merchants, craftsmen taking their handiwork to town, stonemasons looking for employment, soldiers returning from war, and a troupe of thespians performing passion plays along the way.

When we stop to eat, the wool merchant sits with us. He tells us that Cervera is situated on a height, and once we enter it—the city wall has seven gates—we will be charmed by its many cheerful gardens. He describes this with much fanfare and dainty gestures, as if performing for an audience. I welcome the company, my nursemaid not as eagerly.

"How do you know this road so well?" asks Aldonça in an accusatory tone that doesn't seem to bother our fellow traveler.

"I travel a lot."

The wool merchant's name is Andreu, like my long-departed brother, and his assessment is on the mark. The terraced houses and gardens are as lovely as he predicted, but Cervera's main road coils and curls like a slithering snake. I find the town center, with its ancient castle and bell tower, as somber as a cemetery at dusk. At the venta, we are joined by three sisters who are on a pilgrimage to all the places Ignatius of Loyola visited. The Basque-born priest, they explain as if we did not know, was beatified a few years ago, but the Society of Jesus he founded has met with some controversy because it admits conversos, converted Jews, into the holy order.

During our shared meal that evening, one of the pilgriming sisters narrates that in 1527, a soldier stole a piece of *lignum crucis*, the cross on which our Lord was martyred, while serving in Rome. Upon his return, he gave it to the local priest assigned to this town.

"Though no one knows where this relic is hidden, it's one of the mysteries that inspired us to come here," the pilgrim says. "We do know there was an attempt to cut the lignum, but it resisted the blade."

"Resisted the blade," echoes Aldonça, her curiosity obviously piqued.

"Yes, oh yes," continues the woman. "Every time the priest attempted to cut it, loud thunder shook the earth and frightened the town. Every time."

"Really?" I say. I'm thinking of how my grandmother complained that Spain was blinded by religion, a condition that forced us into too many wars. Piety, she liked to say, was a Spanish quirk, a costly national defect. Not that Àvia ever expressed this in public. She was, like me, bold and brave only when it didn't threaten the advantages we enjoyed.

The oldest sister has a mouth that droops and a voice that grates. I've noticed she often talks to herself, though when I tell Aldonça this, she corrects me and says the widow is praying. The younger two are plumper and shorter than the eldest but also sweeter looking, with slanted brown eyes that appear to be smiling even when their mouths are not. They chatter like swallows on a tree until the older one, whom they refer to as *estimada germana*, dear sister, shoots them a reproving look. I'm grateful to have other women along on the journey and am curious about their lives, but I have no intention of making friends. I don't want them nosing around my business, asking questions, making judgments, spreading rumors. Silence, I'm learning, is the best shroud.

After Cervera, we cross the large plain of Urgell, where many fields await the spring planting of wheat and maize, and spend the night at Bellpuig. We bed outside the city in a Franciscan convent, which has a beautiful spiral staircase that climbs to a belfry. Then at dawn we take to the road again, eventually crossing the river Segre over an arched bridge and succumbing to yet another toll and search by customhouse officers. We enter Lleida, where we will remain for two nights in observance of Palm Sunday.

The following day Aldonça and I tend to our first duties of Holy Week by heading to the Church of Sant Llorenç. I'd rather go to the cathedral, but Sant Llorenç, she insists, is ideally positioned to watch the Passion Sunday procession. She is correct. At Plaça Sant Josep, where vendors have erected stalls laden with fronds, we take our place among the milling townspeople, and soon enough children in white robes approach, tossing boughs on the uneven street stones. The appreciative murmuring from the crowd grows like a wave cresting to shore.

"Hosanna! Hosanna!" shout the faithful as they step back to make room for the procession.

A swarthy, bearded fellow in a simple white tunic and rope sandals files past us on a donkey. He makes the sign of the cross, in keeping with his role as Jesus. As the hosannas echo around us, representatives from the trade guilds march by wearing festive-colored robes, each leader bearing a silk banner that flaps straight and strong in the wind. After the procession ends and our fronds have been blessed, we elbow our way through the church's heavy oak doors, hoping to get a good seat inside, but the throngs are such that we're relegated to one of the last rows, at a distance from the altar. We take our place next to a woman minding two children dressed in little more than rags and a sleeping baby swaddled in a dirty blanket. Mingling with the common people is stiff punishment, but it's an indignity I must endure. I kneel, bow my head, and mouth my contrition: *Forgive me, Lord. Forgive me for the sin of pride, the sin of lust, the sin of adultery.* I don't know if this confession qualifies for absolution, but acknowledging one's faults is a good start. After I finish my prayer and take my seat, I remind myself that this is the season of humility, of renouncing vanity and selfishness. However, when an old man in the pew ahead of us leans closer, giving off a rank smell, I abandon the thought. I cover my nose with my hand and press as far back as I can on my bench. What I would give for my family pew back home—or at the very least for my gold-plated pomander!

Before Mass begins, I survey the church. I espy the three sisters, their covered heads bent close together. The eldest, whose name we've learned is Adriana, looks straight ahead, as stiff as planed wood. My gaze wanders again and stops at another familiar shape. Xirau is seated just to the left of us. He and his men have had their beards trimmed. I'm surprised by their presence, but really, I shouldn't be. An absence would be noted unfavorably. In Spain, we know—and never forget—that the observance of religion is not a choice, but a lifetime obligation, a tax levied on the spirit. It overshadows whatever a heart might seek and a mind might question.

After Mass, we greet the sisters outside. Adriana is trying to convince the two younger ones to participate in an afternoon of contemplative prayer before the Eucharist, so our exchange is brief. I'm relieved we're not invited to join them. I can't think of anything I would want less at this moment.

Aldonça and I decide to make for the river. The day has turned springlike, and a mild breeze has swept the sky clean of clouds. Chirping birds gossip like women waiting their turn at the well. Our stroll on a grassy path near the banks is quite pleasant, and I remember, so many years later, what Tutor Guillem taught me about this city and its ideal placement on the declivity of a hill. Here the Carthaginians settled, as did the Romans, and then the Goths, who fell to the Moors. The Moors, in turn, were conquered by the last count of Barcelona, Ramon Berenguer IV, who had just ascended the throne of Aragón. I offer all this history to Aldonça, who responds to it with a yawn. When I ask if she finds the chronicle of our illustrious people boring, she answers that she is unusually tired.

Shortly thereafter we run into the sisters a second time. I guess the two youngest convinced the eldest to spend the afternoon outside, in a different form of prayer. We exchange pleasantries about the weather before Adriana recounts a story she heard at the inn, about a young hidalgo arrested two days earlier for stabbing his wife twenty-three times.

"He found her in bed with her lover," she says conspiratorially. "Imagine that."

I can well imagine it.

"The woman's lover was his best friend," Adriana adds, "so it's a betrayal twice over."

One of the younger sisters makes a tsk-tsking sound, and I ask what happened to the offending man. Barely clothed and shod after being discovered, he bolted from town and has not been seen since.

"I suppose the husband will hang for the murder," I say, wishing for the improbable.

"Why would he?" Adriana gawps at me as if I were unbearably dense. "Adultery should always be punished and treachery cannot be condoned. Besides, the husband defended his honor, as he should. Don't you know cuckolded husbands are legally entitled to kill their wives and their wives' lovers?"

Of course, I know this—who doesn't?—but to hear it so plainly told proves unsettling. I say nothing more.

On our way back to the venta, I mimic Adriana's haughty tone, the way she has of speaking to people with a mix of disdain and concern, but Aldonça doesn't laugh. In fact, she's unusually quiet when we again cross Plaça Sant Josep, still alive with the smells and sights of the festivities. Complaining of a dull pain in her head, she retires to the room before our evening meal, and I'm left alone to indulge in the many glum scenarios that adulterous lovers must inevitably suffer for their sinful union. An honor killing is but one of them.

We decamp Lleida at first light, and the tiresome landscape does little to brighten my mood. My dejection worsens when we pass the many roadside wooden crosses that mark the spots where unlucky journeyers have surrendered their souls. True to tradition, Aldonça adds a stone to the heap of rocks next to each of these miserable monuments, and thus encouraged, the sisters do the same. After several hours we cross a long row of small boulders that mark the Catalonia-Aragón boundary. Parched hills eventually give way to wide verdant patches, and trees sway in the breeze, thick as monks in prayer. After we enter Fraga, three men ride out to meet us just inside the gates. They appear to be properly commissioned *agutzils*, armed with halberds and protected by helmets and breastplates with the insignia of a cross. Following a short discussion with Xirau, they confront the wool merchant. I'm not sure what the argument is about, but when he refuses to dismount, two of the sheriffs pull him from his mule.

"What's happening?" Andreu cries out. "Why are you doing this?"

My legs quake. In front of me, two of the sisters hold shaking hands over their mouths, but Adriana is smiling, and when she catches my eye, she nods smugly, triumphantly. I avert my gaze. Regardless of the merchant's offense, what kind of person would gloat over someone else's misfortune? The same person, I suppose, who so gleefully recounted the tawdry finale of a fallen woman.

Andreu continues to plead with the lawmen, his voice growing shriller. Townspeople cast concerned glances our way, then hurry off. As he's dragged away, the heels of his boots squeal over the cobblestones. There is one last shriek in self-defense—"You have the wrong man!"— before he disappears around a corner.

Without explanation or hesitation, Xirau ties the spare mule to his own and waves us on. Aldonça weeps quietly. El Musulmán's breathing comes loud and ragged. I remain petrified and confused. No one, however, speaks. No one questions Xirau.

Later, when I can't find Xirau at our miserable inn, I ask his brother about the incident.

"He's wanted by the Inquisition," Gerard says of Andreu.

"For doing what?"

"I don't have a clue. I know as much as you do."

"Will we just abandon him here then?"

"What do you propose we do, *senyora*?"

I'm at a loss to offer a solution, and that sense of helplessness weighs heavy on my heart.

That night neither Aldonça nor I leave our small windowless room. The merchant's arrest has soured our mood, and I can't banish the belief that Andreu tempted the jealous hand of fate. Mere hours before he was taken, he had boasted of lucrative business dealings in Saragossa, likely provoking the greed of one of Xirau's men, who'll be rewarded handsomely for his betrayal if the Holy Office adds the merchant's holdings to its own coffers. I can't prove this, but my distrust grows the longer I spend on the road.

Our eventful overnight in Fraga is followed by more monotonous travel. Only when we draw closer to the Ebro does the land turn more hospitable with fields, vineyards, and orchards. This scenery, however, does little for Aldonça's disposition. Her head feels as if it is about to explode. "Like a petard," she moans. Sometimes she sees jagged lightning behind her eyelids, other times a spiderweb of color. Even a self-applied treatment of sage and bay hasn't ameliorated the pounding. When I ask if she needs to rest, however, she waves me away with impatience.

I don't know what else to do, but I get much-needed support from an unexpected quarter. El Musulmán is solicitous, going as far as ignoring Xirau, who seems discomfited by the pains of an old woman. The giant rides his mule next to ours and slows his pace to force the other men to do the same. For all his bulk, he's surprisingly gentle with the beasts, and I've seen him settle a wayward mule with only his voice. As an added benefit of his company, I also discover the reason behind Andreu's arrest.

"Was he Judaizing?" I ask.

"Worse."

"Then he's a disciple of Luther and they found a copy of the Ninety-Five Theses in his possession."

Aldonça groans, and I mistake the reason for her complaint.

"Well, it is possible," I say defensively.

"It's not Luther I'm moaning about," she snaps. "It's my head. I feel it growing larger and larger. Is it?"

"Let's stop to rest," I insist. "Maybe a tea of—"

"No!"

"If we stop for a bit—"

"No!"

"All this dust can only be—"

"I'll survive. We must get to Saragossa by Maundy Thursday. You heard what Xirau said."

Her whimpering quiets, and I return to the subject of my curiosity.

"If not for religion, then why was the wool merchant arrested?" I ask El Musulmán.

"He's a man-lover."

"I'm not sure what—"

"A sodomite, *senyora*. You know what that means, no?"

I gasp. I glance about me to see if any of the others are listening, but no one is paying attention to us. For a while I'm lost in my horror. It's common knowledge that such men are castrated or stoned. My thoughts then turn to El Musulmán. Spaniards of Moorish descent were expelled in years past, and yet El Musulmán is still here, a Morisco in this country of old Christians.

"Aren't you worried they'll come for you too?"

"Why do you say that? I'm as Catholic as you are."

"But your lineage."

He chortles dismissively and then tells me his story. His parents left him in the care of a Christian family when they were forced out of Granada in 1609. Four and ten years at the time, he had been baptized as an infant and raised in the Catholic faith, as were his parents and grandparents and great-grandparents before him. Spain was his home-land, the only one he had ever known. "But we weren't wanted," he says, "and that's always hard to accept."

"Where are they now, your mother and father?"

He shrugs. "They were on their way to Tunis last letter I received, with my six younger sisters."

"Don't you miss your family?"

After a short pause, he replies, "They are safe. In time my sisters will marry good men and have families of their own."

I want to ask why he chose the rending pain of separation to stay with his neighbors. Does he regret that decision? Is he fearful of inquis-itors? Those questions can't be voiced aloud, at least not in the fanatical climate of the land, but I now understand why Miquel often said we lived in an age of paradoxes, in a country of contradictions. Our love, it was just a reflection of that.

Chapter 5

In Which I Am Betrothed and Accept Fate

I can use many different words to describe Françesc d'Oms Calders. Charming. Chivalrous. Intelligent and handsome. A man who made me feel as if I mattered. These descriptions might explain my actions to those who would consider me a coward for choosing safety over true love, a life of comfort over an itinerant existence of hardship. Our parents were wise in pairing us. Not only were we suited to each other, but I never doubted Françesc's ability and desire to maintain the life that was our birthright. To this day, I don't regret our union. I grew to love him in my own way, even as Miquel's hold on my heart refused to wane. Cousin Glòria never understood this. She believed a woman—a good and honest woman, as I claimed to be—couldn't love two men at once. Yet, I'm proof that this is, if not probable, at least possible. There are no constraints on the love a heart can hold, but also no limit to the grief it can endure.

Françesc was prematurely gray and deep into his first score of years when we met at Father's office. My initial impression? His bearing was that of a man assured of what the world owed him. Yet he was neither boastful nor arrogant as many men of his station tend to be, and his smile was gentle and generously offered. He enjoyed playing games that tested his equestrian skills, including sortija, which allowed him to run his beautiful black stallion, Tibidabo, around the ring. He excelled as a swordsman, too, but it was his humor, his ability to brighten the day, that I most admired. Well-traveled and well-read, he was unafraid to voice his opinion but then was wise enough to let the topic rest. His low moods, however, could last for weeks, and the despondency that descended on our house on these occasions was enough to test the strongest among us.

The first time I saw Françesc, he was seated ramrod straight in a chair at the office. My primping and preening in front of the mirror had made Father late for his morning appointment, and when we arrived, he ran past the first-floor clerks and up the stairs, leaving me to struggle with my skirts on the steep steps.

"Françesc, so pleased to see you again," I heard Father say. "You're looking more and more like your father with every passing day."

"If that's true, I hope I've inherited his sagacity but not his baldness."

Father guffawed. "Have you been waiting long?"

"Enough for me to order my thoughts about this contract, Antoni. I do have some reservations."

"Let's hear them."

Just then, I entered the room and noticed our visitor's fine boots, which were the one feature entirely visible to me. He stood and turned my way, probably because he'd heard my dramatic sigh of annoyance. The figure he cut, the clothing he wore, the deep bow he executed when he saw me—it would have impressed even the most experienced woman (which I was not). Father made the introductions, and Françesc took my right hand and kissed my wrist, where glove met skin, but didn't release me right away.

"Finally," he said, stretching the word as if he'd been waiting a lifetime to be where he was. "Finally."

"I'm a man of my word, Françesc."

"You are, *senyor*, you are." Still holding my hand, Françesc brought his face closer to mine, indecently so I thought. "I dare say this may be the beginning of a mutually beneficial association."

"In more ways than one," Father added.

"What are you talking about, Father?"

I yanked my hand from Françesc's. How dare he presume to be so forward! Then I crossed the room, heeding my mother's admonishment not to slouch, and settled at my rosewood writing desk. I removed my kid gloves.

Father didn't answer. Instead, he began sifting through a stack of papers until he found whatever he was looking for. He handed the document to Françesc, who read it with a furrowed brow. Unable to contain my curiosity, I said in a rather self-important voice, "I don't like to be left in a state of ignorance."

Françesc laughed, and what a pleasant sound it was. "My dear Dolça, I live in a perpetual state of ignorance. I'm constantly reminded of how little I know and how much I still have to learn. It's humbling."

Those words, so sincerely spoken, made me look at him in a different way. It allowed me to see past what was immediately visible. That's not to say there was no pleasure in what my eyes encountered. Françesc was, as I mentioned, an attractive man, with expressive hazel eyes and a strong nose in a face that tapered down to a beard absent of gray, unlike his hair. His right cheek dimpled when he smiled. He was tall, taller than Miquel, though not nearly as thin, and as he grew older and our lives turned more sedate, heft colonized his waist. But this was a long way off. That morning, as he and Father discussed trades of iron from Ripoll and exports of tanned leather from Olot, I stole long glances at him. At first, he didn't notice, but once I turned more brazen, he met my stare with a raised eyebrow. Maybe he meant it as an invitation, but that's not how I read it. I felt he was making fun of me, and I looked away.

At midday Father and I left the office, with Françesc tagging along, and during the short walk home I couldn't help but remember similar promenades with Miquel. My heart ached for his company—but also with the pain of his betrayal. How could Miquel forget me so easily? As we strolled up Montcada, Françesc tapped my shoulder to show me a blue parakeet perched on a clothesline off Flassaders. I gasped in delight. He chuckled. Something in me gave way after that. Though Father invited him in, Françesc excused himself, saying he had other business to attend to. I wasn't upset to see him leave and didn't wonder if we would see each other again. Hope for Miquel's return still burned fiercely.

After that initial meeting, Françesc turned up everywhere, but it took me a while to catch on. I confronted Mother in the sewing room about these "spontaneous" encounters, and she confirmed my suspicions with a shrug and a smile.

"Your father tells me the two of you get along well." Then as if to ward off my resistance, she added: "Whether or not you appreciate our efforts, we've done you a favor by making sure you share an affinity with your future husband."

"Husband? What are you talking about, Mother?"

"Oh please, Dolça, don't play naive with me."

"I'm not playing at anything."

"Then, I don't understand how you can possibly be surprised."

"Surprise is the least of it, and who says we share an affinity?" I imbued the last word with a heavy coat of mockery and contempt.

"Your father. And Françesc."

"An affinity for what?"

"For art. For books. I understand you even had a lively discussion about some shipment from Sardinia."

"I can have that same conversation with any of Father's clerks!"

"But you didn't, and you wouldn't have enjoyed it half as much anyway."

"I don't love him."

Without flinching, Mother completed her stitch, stabbed the needle into the fabric, and set her embroidery hoop to the side. She peered over her spectacles at me, and I noticed, not for the first time, the fine lines that spread weblike from her lips and eyes. "What would you know of love, dear child? The love you read about belongs between the pages of those silly books. It's not real life and hardly a reason to marry."

"Mother, I know what love is."

"You do, do you? Because you're such a woman of the world." She made an exasperated sound. "Love is more than a passing fancy. Or a foolish infatuation. It's not an invention of your imagination either.

Love is what grows slowly through the years and binds two people who are appropriate for each other."

I didn't know how to respond to this and was wise enough to keep my mouth shut. I wondered if Mother had ever speculated about my feelings for Miquel. I had been asking about him every week—indeed, almost every day, as insistent as a weed in a flowerbed.

Mother reached out to take my hand. "Dulçie, Dulçie, I was young once too. I understand you. Your yearnings, your longings. But I assure you that in due time you'll learn to care deeply for Françesc."

"I do care for Françesc, Mother, but not in that way."

"That will come, but you have to be patient and you have to work at it. Think of love as an egg. It needs time, warmth, and attention for the chick to hatch."

"Not all eggs hatch."

"Yours will." She patted my hand. "Most do."

"How would you know?"

"Do you think your father and I loved each other when we married? We'd met only three or four times before our parents—"

"That was hundreds of years ago, Mother. It's 1579! I don't want to settle."

She waved her hand. "You're not settling. And I'm quite sure, knowing Françesc and knowing his family, this arrangement will be quite advantageous for you."

"And for Father."

She ignored my statement. "He's a handsome man, isn't he?"

I nodded.

"Kind, too, I'm told. And he has a good head for numbers."

"So did Tutor Guillem."

Mother laughed, but I willed my face still. After a bit, she took up her embroidery again and said, "I know you'll not want for anything with Françesc."

"What's that supposed to mean?"

"It means, *maca*, that whatever fantasy has crossed your mind is nothing more than a youthful illusion. Life with a poet-soldier guarantees you of one thing and one thing only—penury. A poet-soldier can't feed and clothe and entertain you in the manner you deserve."

I knew exactly who she was talking about but volunteered nothing to counter it. What could I say? Miquel hadn't even bothered to return to Barcelona. And anyway, at that moment I fixated on the trivial—that is, the realization that Mother knew, or had hazarded a very good guess, about my most secret feelings. If she had seen past my feeble attempts to disguise my emotions, Father had too, and perhaps everyone else as well. I was mortified, embarrassed. Why had I overestimated my talent for hiding what I felt so deeply? How could I have shortchanged my parents' wisdom and intuition?

After that conversation with Mother, my future seemed inevitable. I had my doubts, of course. Those never quieted completely. Even so, on those occasions where Françesc held my hand under the watchful eyes of many, I was sincerely touched by his devotion, by a gratifying awareness that, in his eyes, I was essential, irreplaceable. Also, he always brought a small token when he came calling, and these keepsakes, however small their packaging, tended to the rare and the expensive. An opal ring that had belonged to his grandmother. Poetry by Joan Boscà Almogàver, the Catalan who wrote in Castilian. And of course, my favorite: a Venetian-published copy of *The Golden Ass* with its woodcut illustrations of Apuleius's tale of a young man accidentally transformed into a donkey. It was impossible not to compare them to Miquel's gifts, and those traitorous thoughts filled me with a sense that it was I, and not my missing beloved, who had played someone false. What if I felt no quickening of the heart or obsessive hold on thoughts that Miquel's presence had once elicited? There was so much to recommend Françesc.

Mother was right in her assessment. Over time and with exposure, I grew to love his many fine qualities, to appreciate his words of encouragement for my painting, to admire his quick and astute understanding of how Father wanted to develop the business. Our encounters moved from the second-floor office on Commerç to more familiar settings, festive but intimate dinners that initially included only his parents and then grew to grander affairs with our extended families and circle of friends. There were new gowns, and new jewels, and new shawls and gloves, and for once Father didn't object to these expenditures. Even Mother, who usually managed to rein in my most outlandish whims, seemed quite content to allow them. Only Aldonça—and Àvia's niggling voice in my head—attempted boundaries. However, a nursemaid's reproaches, delivered with an expressive grunt or a roll of the eyes, changed nothing, certainly not the self-importance I wore as easily as my cape of lynx. As a result of my new possessions and busy schedule, the heaviness in my heart eased. At the time, I believed I had made peace with an idea that two years earlier would have proven impossible to accept: Miquel wasn't planning to return for me. Now the reason for his abandonment didn't matter. Whatever the explanation or excuse, it had no place among the gems and jewels and gowns filling my chests. Later there would be guilt and regret—but not at the beginning, never then.

To complete the complex transactions required for a mutually beneficial alliance of the d'Oms and Llull families, we spent several summer days at the d'Oms' sumptuous *masia* north of Barcelona. We arrived there after a long and bumpy ride in our carriage, which was drawn by a team of four spotted horses, the better to impress my future in-laws. Mother, who didn't like to travel, was out of sorts by the time we got there, pale lips trembling in a face washed of all color, but Aldonça, who had managed the entire trip seated on the hard bench next to one of our armed escorts, coaxed her into a better mood. Mother was then able to greet our hosts with her usual grace. Françesc met our carriage, resplendent in muted-gray breeches and matching hose, a multicolored gilecuelo over his wide-sleeved shirt. I knew by the twinkle in his eye that he was pleased to see me. As I him. I was immediately taken by the physical similarities between d'Oms *pare* and d'Oms *fill*. While Françesc had inherited his mother's eyes with their faint speckles of green, his other features came entirely from Carles d'Oms, including the endearing right dimple. Their personalities, though, were quite different. I would eventually come to know my father-in-law as an arrogant, often insufferable man who drank too much and smiled not enough, a master who was as cruel to his peasants as his son would be considerate of our servants. Françesc's mother, on the other hand, was soft-spoken (when speaking at all), a delicate, self-effacing creature who blended into the drabbest room. She spent most of our visit in a perpetual state of nerves, constantly fingering a brooch. Golden-haired and fair, María seemed out of place in her family of dark men, but it was her kindness that she passed on to Françesc. Through the years I thanked our Lord for this.

I had visited many fine country houses, and was oblivious to the merits of our own, but the thick-walled d'Oms castle was in a different category altogether, as much for its trove of precious furnishings as for the dim coolness of its chambers during the hottest months of the year. The massive structure, several varas from the tallest watchtower I'd ever seen, stood on a verdant promontory overlooking a small vineyard and endless hectares of wheat. Two blooming wisteria trees perfumed the entrance, and inside, the polished wood ceiling beams gave the rooms a touch of refinement. The furniture was beautiful, too, most notably a painted Italian cassone and a long, blue-veined table carved from a single marble slab. The well-fortified property had a communal oven, its own blacksmith and barber-surgeon, as well as a *corder* to make rope, a *candeler* to supply candles, two *fusters* for carpentry work, and a small church (in addition to the family chapel) with a sad-looking altar. Beyond the farmland and the peasants' hovels, the d'Oms lands stretched into woods of pine and oak and were populated by a variety of beasts, the most important of these being the boars. These wild pigs were held in high esteem, as hunting them was a popular pastime for the d'Oms men. It would become a favorite activity of Father's too.

Roasted boar was served that evening, though it was somewhat overshadowed by the endless parade of dishes. The meal began with fresh fruits, followed by a plate of mixed olives, and later the choice of the boar or rabbit stew or hens stuffed with raisins and pine nuts, accompanied by almonds and the finest white bread I had ever tasted, and then finalized with a sweet dish of apples baked with rosewater, ginger, cinnamon, and cloves. I might mention, too, that the wine was from the d'Oms vineyard. When I complimented our hosts on the apples, María said she often served a similar recipe using pears, but without the ginger, and that it always was well received.

"Françesc," I said, "which do you prefer, the apples or the pears?"

He smiled, and next to me Mother stirred, probably satisfied that I was taking my impending domestic role so seriously. "Both, dearest. I've got a hearty appetite."

Everyone laughed. Françesc winked at me.

I was seated between my parents on one side of the banquet table, and Françesc, with his relations, across from me. With a smile firmly pasted on my face, I spent the night vigilant of how I chewed and where I placed my hands, mainly because my bell sleeves were so cumbersome that they threatened to flop right into my food—a lapse I had managed at home at least once, much to my parents' consternation. By the end of the meal, the effort to avoid embarrassing Mother had given me a headache the size of a wagon, and I was happy when we retired to our chambers early.

Those rooms were impressive too. Mine was in the same wing as my parents', but smaller, with a carved bedstead and a thick mattress overwhelmed by a profusion of pillows. I discovered a red velvet pouch resting on one of these pillows, a cream-colored paper under it. I unfolded the note. *My little Dolça* (no one had used "little" as an endearment in a very long time), *I hope your stay is the beginning of many. Fondly, F.* Inside the pouch was a lovely black pearl held by a simple white-gold band. I'd never seen anything like it, and when I slipped it on my right pointer finger, it fit as perfectly as if it had been sized. The maidservant who had joined us on the trip noted the ring's beauty with a wistful sigh. As she helped me into my nightdress, she said, "Your intended is a handsome man. We pray for your happiness."

Humming, she brushed my unruly black hair until my scalp tingled.

Later, if passing thoughts of Miquel disturbed my sleep, they were only of his disloyalty. He had broken his promise to return, and I couldn't be expected to forgive such an offense, could I?

During that first visit to the country, we also met Françesc's brothers. Martí, the youngest, was about my age, a youth who bumbled his words and wouldn't meet my eyes. At the time he was considering the church as a career, but about a year after we married, he left for the Indies and became a valuable contact for Françesc's dealings in that part of the world. Gabriel, the heir, was fourteen months older than Françesc, and perhaps because of this proximity in age, the two shared the same laugh, the same breadth of shoulders, the same prematurely graying hair. He also was as gallant as his brother, bowing at our initial meeting as if I were a queen or a duchess.

"When Françesc told us about you, I thought you were one of his fevered hallucinations," Gabriel said, holding my hand in both of his, much as his brother had on our first meeting. "However, you're truly as beautiful as he said."

I giggled, entranced by so many compliments. But when I turned to greet Joana, Gabriel's wife, I recognized that these words were more about ingratiating himself than about the truth. Joana was a vision of true beauty: large brown eyes in a perfect oval face, a nose so small you doubted its purpose, and a beauty mark to the left of her rosebud mouth. Though vanity and shallowness would have been excused in such a woman, Joana didn't suffer from either fault. Unlike my cousin Glòria, who tried to dominate every conversation, Joana proved to be a patient listener and amiable companion, asking questions as needed and, perhaps more important, keeping her counsel when it was essential.

She greeted me with a sisterly hug and whispered in my ear, "I'm so happy you're joining the family. I think we're going to spend a lot of time together." Prophetic words, those. Though she wasn't particularly interested in books or brushes, we spent the next few days talking about my desire to paint and her hope for a son—she was just recovering from a miscarriage—while María entertained Mother. When the men hunted, she and I walked the gardens early in the morning, marveling at the birds and the impressive collection of roses the d'Oms gardener tended. It was over an afternoon merienda of *orxata* made from the d'Oms' own almonds that I discovered an unexpected and not-so-hidden secret about a family I thought to be impervious to ridicule and gossip.

When one of the maids brought us the drink, I remarked, without pausing to think, how much the young girl resembled my future father-in-law. Joana cocked her beautiful head just so and looked at me as if I had grown a second nose. She scooted closer to me. "Can't you tell?" she said softly. "She's Gabriel's half sister."

I still didn't quite understand and asked, rather stupidly, "And Françesc's too?"

"Of course."

"You mean . . . Don d'Oms . . . he . . ."

"He has several other children, our dear father-in-law. Some work the orchards or the fields. The girls, they're all house servants."

I opened my mouth but no words came. Joana stroked my arm. I think she wanted to console me. At that moment, and for good reason, I accepted her as the wiser and older sister I had long wanted.

"You're so very young," Joana said.

"No more than you," I replied, and then compared ages with my new friend. She was only two years older. "This must not be a question of youth but of ignorance."

"Not ignorance, Dolça, but innocence. There's a difference. I didn't know many things until after I married. And I'm learning still."

"Is there anything else I should know?"

Joana shook her head. "Not immediately."

"Does the *senyora* know?"

"María? How can she not?"

"She doesn't care about his infidelities? How they exist right under her nose?"

"We've never spoken about it, but from what I've observed, she appears to accept the behavior. Or maybe a better way of putting it is that she's resigned to it."

"I wouldn't. I couldn't."

"You'd be surprised at what we women can accept."

"It's a betrayal of the sacred marriage vows!"

Joana laughed. "You truly are an innocent. I wish I weren't the one to tell you this, but men take those marriage vows lightly. Our father-in-law's behavior is hardly uncommon."

"Not my father!"

"Oh, dearest, I've upset you! That wasn't my intention. Your father most likely is the exception." She hugged me.

"And your husband?" I asked, her collar muffling my question. When she didn't answer, I persisted. "What about Gabriel?"

She sighed and covered her face with her small delicate hands. "He's a man, with a man's desires."

I was confused by her words but chose not to question her further. She would tell me when she was ready, when she knew me better and trusted me more. In the sociable silence that followed, I was thankful for Françesc's kindness and integrity. I knew my husband-to-be was different from his father and elder brother. I knew it with all my heart, and when his journeys to the interior eventually took him away from our home for long periods, I did not turn suspicious, for he gave me no reason to be chary.

As was customary, Françesc's courting visits were chaperoned, but Mother and Aldonça played blind when he kissed me in such a way that I felt a stirring between my legs. He remained considerate of my reputation, however, and never behaved inappropriately, not like the rogues women whispered about. Joana once asked me if I was curious about how Françesc spent the evenings when he left my house, but it had never occurred to me that he did anything but sleep or play cards. He didn't look as if he patronized the houses of ill repute. When I demanded to know why Joana would ask such a question, she assured me she didn't suspect him of anything. "Françesc," she said with conviction, "is the best of the d'Oms men. Treasure him, Dolça." And I did, as best I could.

Our betrothal lasted more than a year, which was unusual. Many reasons were given for the delay—Françesc traveled for business, Father was in Madrid for several months, and a suitable house needed to be found and furnished—but I wasn't concerned, not at all. Mother fretted, yes, but I didn't ever doubt Françesc's intentions or his feelings for me. A collection of trinkets filled my coffers as a testament to his commitment. Besides, I was busy enjoying Joana's company, anticipating my mornings in the office with Father, and working with a new painting tutor. There also were, as always, the duties to family: weddings and christenings and funerals, visits to cousins and ministrations to the elderly aunts and uncles. Who had time for worry?

At the cusp of a new decade, did I stop to think of Miquel? Of course I did, but I understood, as any practical woman would, that I couldn't pine for the unattainable—the nonexistent, really—unless it was misery I preferred. I can't deny that, if I allowed my thoughts to wander, I relived the small moments we had shared, but quickly enough, the knowledge that I had been nothing more than a passing interest dragged me back to earth. More to the point, I was perfectly content to be carried along by the tide of well-wishers and the promise of a bountiful life with Françesc.

Fate, however, is a demanding taskmaster, as callous as a slave trader and as complicated as the rendering of shadows on canvas. It excels in temptations and ironies. A week before the wedding—a small event that was to include only family, followed by a larger *convit*—a mysterious missive was delivered to me by a new maid. Quite fortuitously, Aldonça and Mother were out on a wedding errand, and because I didn't recognize the script or the seal, I set it aside until that evening. When I read it by candlelight in the privacy of my bedchamber, I was paralyzed with anger, fear, and indecision.

So wrote Miquel's brother:

Esteemed Dolça,
   I beg forgiveness for the delay in writing this letter. In August of year past, I was ransomed from the clutches of the corsair who

had kept both my brother and me imprisoned in Algiers, along
with numerous other Christians taken in September of 1575 from
the galley Sol. Unfortunately, Miguel there remains. His captivity
was, and continues to be, a tragedy my family must suffer, but we
persist in our hope for his return.

Upon my release Miguel begged me to inform you of his situ-
ation, but I have been remiss in the mission he so earnestly begged
of me. I regret my lack of action, for I never intended to forsake my
brother or his desires. He thinks of you often and with the deepest
of feelings. Also, we remain indebted to your father's generosity
and invaluable help.

Forever in your debt,
Rodrigo

Stunned, I sat on my cushioned stool, unable to move. Miquel
hadn't abandoned me! He hadn't forgotten me! In a dreadful turn of
fate I had never foreseen, he was rotting in some pirate's dungeon. I was
horrified that I had misjudged him. But . . . but what did Rodrigo mean
by Father's invaluable help? Did Father know about Miquel's imprisonment? Did Mother? If so, why hadn't they told me? Would he ever
be released? Many, many questions, but the most vexing was one only I
could answer: what would I do now with this information?

Though I climbed into bed at some point in the evening, I didn't
sleep at all, haunted by the deep tenor of Miquel's voice, the desire in
his eyes, the crookedness of his smile. The memory of his hands on my
breasts left an imprint of heat and passion. Ironically, for every remembrance of Miquel, there was a corresponding pleasant impression of
Françesc, making my confusion and ambivalence that much deeper
and distressing.

With Father, though, I was unforgiving in my recriminations.

Chapter 6

Regarding an Unexpected and Punishing Loss

Our first stop in Saragossa is my cousin's house, on Calle del Coso. I've not seen Núria in ages, and when she greets us in the courtyard, I'm taken aback by how the passage of time has shown her no mercy. Her shoulders are rounded, and her luxuriant hair, once the color of sable, has turned the white of a communion wafer. A small woman with piercing dark eyes in a chinless face, she's clothed in plain black, and this austere style doesn't favor her—but then again, she's always been indifferent to her looks. When we were children, she preferred to spend hours talking to our *àvia* or reading alone, mainly history tomes. Sometimes she'd plead to be taken to the Call to see the converted Jewish temple and shops, a habit Mother declared eccentric and unsafe.

Upon seeing Aldonça, she orders the servants to carry my nursemaid inside. Aldonça's headache, which abated earlier in the afternoon, has returned with a vengeance, and every clop and jostle of the mule have resulted in agony for her.

"She'll be well cared for," Núria assures me when I try to follow.

Once the muleteers ride away, my cousin opens her arms to me, and though I'm covered in dust from the road and hardly pleasant company even to myself, I step into her embrace. The comfort of seeing family cannot be overstated.

"I thought we'd never get here," I say. "The road has been so tedious."

"You will have a restful end of the week here. But now I have something to give you." She reaches into the pocket of her skirt and produces a letter. "This was delivered on Monday."

I glance at it and immediately recognize the penmanship. Of course, he'd guess that I would stop at my cousin's on this journey. I glance up at Núria and realize she's waiting for me to reveal the identity of the writer, but I won't. I can't. I remain cautious even here. She continues watching me as I slash the wax seal with a ragged nail. The words are few and the script strangely imprecise.

Dolça,
> *Hurry. I am waiting.*
>> *Miquel*

There's no date.

"What is it?" Núria asks, her curiosity getting the better of her.

"Business, just business." I don't elaborate, hoping to imply this is also the purpose of my trip.

Without further comment, she ushers me into her spacious home. We pass by small lounges and large rooms, most of them invested with wall-sized tapestries and gold-trimmed leather hangings, a few exemplary paintings too. The coffered ceilings are high, and the furniture is of mahogany, walnut, and oak—not a block of pine among these noble woods. And yet in this bounty of armoires and chests, what surprises me most is the profusion of crucifixes and niches housing saints. I don't remember Núria as particularly pious, though of course many find religion later in life.

"I'll send someone with a basin of hot water and fresh linen cloths," she says as we climb the staircase to the living quarters. "Then you can rest."

After a thorough washing and a late merienda of a ring-shaped anise pastry, I change, with the help of a young maid named Anna, into a royal-blue gown that has been set out for me. The silk is so soft that my eyes water with happiness. Oh, how I've missed the comforts of home! I then venture down the hall to see Aldonça. She's sleeping soundly in a bed not as spacious as mine but with fresh sheets and sturdy pillows. A bowl of fruit and a pitcher of watered wine rest within arm's reach on a round table. I'm relieved to find her breathing normally. When I touch her forehead to feel for a fever, she stirs and blinks open her eyes.

"Dolça," she says, "we must talk. There's something I want to tell you."

"It can wait. You need your rest now."

"You'll come back soon to talk?"

"Of course." But I forget my promise within minutes.

When I wake on Good Friday, sunlight streams bright and hot around the edges of the brocade curtains, and I realize I've wasted the morning. As soon as I ring for service, Anna enters and reminds me that a hot bath awaits me. It is a luxury that I appreciate more than ever after so many days of grime and dust. Toilette done, I ask after Aldonça and am told she's doing better. Yet when I visit later, my nursemaid's voice doesn't rise above a wheezy whisper. She feels too weak to attend the Good Friday procession but insists I go on without her. I leave her to the house servants, and as the day's activities overtake me, I don't think of her again.

In the afternoon, before the evening's pageantry, Núria insists on a tour of her home. It has four floors, including a basement and a loft. As in other residences, the storeroom also doubles as a wine cellar and stable. Much to my surprise, this is where she insists on taking me, and we descend steep stairs shadowed by the flickering light of our lanterns.

At the landing, she throws open a heavy oak door. "Here we are. I hope you'll be impressed."

What I see then is so strange, so out of place that I cannot find words to express an opinion. Instead of the storeroom I expected, a small table bedecked with silver candelabra is set for dinner.

"Our Shabbat," she announces.

"Our what?"

"Our Sabbath."

I recognize little of what's before me, but I gradually arrive at a vague understanding of how the flurry of preparations earlier in the day— the bath, the house cleaning and linen changing, the supply of olive oil instead of lard in the kitchen, the greens drizzled with vinegar—are part of a tradition lost but also of a ritual hidden. There's a good reason for concealment, however, a good reason for secrets.

"I'm so happy to share it with a loved one," Núria continues. "Your presence makes tonight even more special."

"This is too dangerous." Alarm has turned my voice shrill. "Do you know what can happen to you for this . . . this . . ."

"I do. That's why I perform the rituals of our faith in solitude."

"But your servants . . . your neighbors. Betrayal can come from so many places."

"I trust my help, as they trust me."

"I wouldn't be so certain." I'm thinking of Andreu the merchant, of course, denounced by someone who must have known him well enough.

She allows herself a mirthless laugh. "You remind me of Saül."

"Saül?"

"My late husband? You knew him as Pau. He waited too long to be true to his heritage and to our ancestors."

I head for the stairs, but she grips my elbow and leads me to a small cabinet, which she unlocks and opens.

"Do you know what this is?"

"An animal horn of some kind."

"This is a shofar. From a ram."

She takes my hand and guides it over the ridges and curvatures, the spots of polished smoothness. "It's sounded on Rosh Hashanah and Yom Kippur as a call to look inward and repent," she says. "Those holidays, the most sacred ones, are in the fall."

After she returns the shofar to its place, she retrieves a leather-bound book emblazoned with gold calligraphy in a foreign alphabet.

"Our great-great-great-great-grandmother's prayer book," she whispers. "Can you believe it? The only heirloom I have as a reminder of who I am."

I think of my grandmother's hamsa hidden in a coffer, under my other jewels, but I reveal nothing of my own secret. I hate myself for this. For my conventionality. My predictability. My insatiable need to be what others will accept and not what I could be. And yet, as I scold myself, I also consent to sit at Núria's table when she pulls out a chair for me. Buried in the ground as we are in this storage room, I know no one will see us. A crime concealed is no crime at all, I tell myself. Besides I'm curious.

The food has been arranged on silver trays, and the lusterware goblets and plates are painted with delicate vines. After she lights two candles, mumbling a strange prayer over them, we eat. She explains she's banished pork from her kitchen and has foresworn ham as well. (I couldn't possibly do such a thing. A good ham is a staple of the Spanish table, and a delicious one at that.) Koshering, she continues, must be done carefully and with much privacy. Hence, she tends to this herself, first trimming all the fat from the meat, picking out the sciatic vein from a joint if needed, and then soaking the meat five or six times in salted water before hanging it to dry in a wicker basket. She's hired a special butcher to dispatch the animal—calf, lamb, goat—in the particular way of her religion, by bending back its head and using a special knife to cut its throat in a single stroke.

For this dinner, there's no fish, as there should be on all Fridays, but especially this one, the holiest in all Christendom. Instead, we savor a beef-and-mint stew with chopped cabbage served in bowls. A mysterious side dish consists of eggs boiled with onion skins, olive oil, and ashes, which give the eggs a strange vermilion coloring. Huevos haminados, Núria calls them. The meal closes with a selection of seasonal fruit and azuquaque, delicious sugar candies made of almonds and rosewater.

"How long have you been doing this?" I ask.

"Since Saül sickened."

"This is reckless."

"Reckless?" She sets down her fork and regards me with obvious disappointment.

"Why pretend to have converted? Why not go to a land where your kind is accepted?"

"My kind? You come from a long line of conversos, Dolça, as I do. Don't forget that."

"I'm Catholic," I protest. "Baptized, confirmed, and married in the Roman Catholic faith. As were my parents and grandparents and great-grandparents. If we had an ancestor who—"

"Àvia Regina was Catholic by convenience, and I suspect you know that better than most."

I recoil at her words and wonder if I've done the right thing by seeking her out on this journey. I wish there was a way to remove myself from this compromising tableau. She seems to guess my thoughts because she places her hand on mine.

"We're too old to think of our differences, Dolça. Let's not focus on the separate paths we've taken. What matters is that we remain family. We come from the same stock."

"And answer to the same God," I add in a gesture of conciliation. My discomfort does not abate, however. I cannot entirely dismiss from my thoughts the potential horrors that might befall her. What Spaniard has not witnessed or been told of a torturing, a flogging, a burning for blasphemy?

After our meal we rush out the door to attend Saragossa's Procession of the Holy Burial. I find this the height of hypocrisy and tell her so, but she assures me, with a bitter laugh, that I shouldn't worry so much. She's mastered the art of keeping appearances, of acting one way and thinking another—and haven't we all? She pronounces these words as you might spit out the seeds of a custard apple.

The holy march to the cathedral is nothing like I've ever seen. First and foremost, there are the drums, so many and so loud and so insistent that I'm relieved Aldonça didn't come with us. Their booms thunder upward from the ground, reverberating through the soles of our shoes.

Spectators line the old city center three and four deep, and all around me women dress in mourning black, lace mantillas held fast by jeweled hair combs. They bow their heads and murmur prayers.

"Look!" My cousin points to a drummer's bleeding hands as one of the robed cofradías, or brotherhoods, files by. She makes the sign of the cross with such an exaggerated display of devotion that I stare in astonishment until she elbows me to do the same. I do as directed.

All the Nazarenos wear long, solid-color tunics and contrasting capirotes, pointed hoods that cover their faces, with only eyeholes to allow sight. Other men, the more corpulent ones, carry flower-strewn floats bearing a paso, the wooden figure depicting a grieving Mary or a suffering Jesus in some horrifying point of the Via Crucis. Following the drums' rhythmic beats, the penitents wend their way through the cobblestone streets and into La Seo. When we enter the cathedral, my cousin makes sure I note the building's exterior brick and glazed tiles, a very Moorish touch.

"The Mudejar influence, even here," she says under her breath.

Seated in a front pew, I admire the dazzling light created by the tiny flames of thousands of white wax tapers. My cousin tells me that tomorrow, during Easter Vigil, church bells will peal to proclaim the miracle of the Resurrection, and the music of those chimes will be followed by a general hurly-burly on the streets as the populace celebrates the end of Lent. Everyone will then return to their unholy ways.

"Godliness doesn't last long, does it?" I say. She doesn't respond to my sarcasm.

By the time we return to the torchlit grounds of Núria's home, I can barely keep my eyes open from the exhaustion. I stop in at Aldonça's room, but she doesn't stir when I put hand to forehead. Her skin is cool and dry, and I can rest without worry.

This relief proves misplaced.

On Saturday Núria wakens me, and at first, I'm not sure where I am. The softness of the linens and the seductiveness of the bed are unfamiliar, and I burrow deeper under the covers, reluctant to give up such comfort. I must be dreaming of this splendor. Where are the straw sacks? The fleas? The mice scurrying in the walls? The dangerous strangers lurking down the hall?

But then my cousin shakes my shoulders not so gently. "Aldonça is calling for you."

I bolt upright. The candle she holds is barely enough light for me to make out her face, but her expression speaks for itself. I throw off the blanket, and my exposed skin tingles from the cold.

"Aldonça—is she feeling better?"

No answer. The silence is overwhelming. Anna pops out from behind Núria holding a housedress and I slip my arms into its sleeves. She then coaxes my feet into slippers, and the three of us, yawning, partially dressed, and reluctant to speak, rush to Aldonça's room. There we find my nursemaid buried under wool blankets, her face flushed, her brow creased. Beads of perspiration gleam above her lips. I call her name, but she's oblivious to my voice.

I hurry to her bedside to feel her forehead with the back of my hand, just as I did the evening before. I gasp. She's hot as Hades!

"Haven't you applied cold cloths?" I demand of her attendant, an older servant.

"We have. All night, *senyora*."

"Why have you stopped then?"

"She asked us to."

"Don't you see that she can't think for herself with such a fever?" I shake with anger.

"We tried to apply the compresses, but she was thrashing around so wildly that she knocked the basin out of my hands."

I dismiss the excuse with an angry wave. I can't imagine Aldonça, strong and mighty Aldonça, in such a state. Anna, however, nods in confirmation of the attendant's words. I turn to my cousin in a desperate appeal. Núria signals to the servants and both hurry out.

"How long has she been like this?" I ask.

"I think the fever worsened recently. They came for me just before I woke you."

I sit on the edge of the narrow bed and lean closer to Aldonça. I search for her hands under the covers and find one curled in a loose fist. I place it in my own.

"I'm here. You're not alone."

She doesn't stir. The older maid returns with a new pitcher and basin, squares of woolen draped over an arm. Once moistened and wrung, I apply these to Aldonça's nape and brow. She doesn't move, but neither do I. I'm afraid to leave. If she calls for me again, I want to make sure she sees me, hears my voice, draws solace from my presence. I don't trust the old maid to be so responsive. Or the young Anna, for that matter.

Over the course of the next few hours, Núria comes bearing food and drink, a change of clothes, even a rosary of polished ebony. I remain seated in a chair, beads between my fingers but without inclination toward prayer. When my limbs stiffen, when my back aches, when the blood pounds my temples, I tell myself these bodily mortifications are necessary. Aldonça wouldn't be in this situation if it weren't for my selfishness, so my suffering should serve, in some small way, as a form of penance. Yet even as I tend to her, another concern crowds out these thoughts: her illness will surely delay our departure from Saragossa. While there's no predicting how many days her recovery will require, postponing this journey again is unthinkable. Miquel's latest letter carried a desperate urgency in its brevity. I must get to Madrid at the soonest. But how? I can't possibly leave Aldonça behind in my cousin's care, in a foreign city so far from home. She needs me. Is there any way to reconcile these conflicting responsibilities?

As the day advances, I fret over options but find none worthwhile or convenient. I'm ashamed of my venal interests, by how they consume me to the detriment of everything else. What am I to do? If we remain in Saragossa, Xirau might continue without us. I doubt I can locate another willing muleteer or find a way of sending word to Miquel without alerting those who might be looking for me.

Sometime later, the fever subsides and Aldonça wakens. She's pale but calm. I ask if she's hungry, if she's thirsty, but she refuses all offers.

Gently I prop her up, supplementing her sacks of chaff with pillows Anna has brought from my bed.

"You look better." I say this more for my benefit than hers.

She doesn't nod in agreement—but neither does she deny the statement. She appears content to stare ahead or to turn her attention, every once and again, to where I sit, slouching with weariness. In a voice hoarsened by disuse, she suggests poultices and potions, unknown herbs and unfamiliar spices. I call for Anna and order her to follow these directions to the letter. We must concoct whatever Aldonça desires. However, by the time these potential cures are ready, she has again surrendered to sleep. We use them anyway, guessing at their possible applications. Before long, the room smells like an apothecary shop.

I allow myself to hope, though there's neither logic nor substance behind it. I can't imagine this journey without Aldonça. She's been at my side for the entirety of my existence, and my earliest memories are of her hovering presence. As a child, I resented her reprimands, the many times she chided my willfulness, and then later I begrudged her quiet but unmistakable opposition to my relationship with Miquel. Yet, I've long depended on her, on her complete and irrefutable loyalty.

After the sun sets, Núria joins me, bringing a plate of leftovers from yesterday's meal. I'm not hungry, but I don't want to offend her, so I eat.

"I blame myself for what's happening to her," I say.

"You think yourself too powerful then, Dolça."

"She wouldn't let me travel alone, but I didn't fully consider how difficult it would be for a woman of such an advanced age to be on the road."

"She must have had her reasons for agreeing to accompany you."

True. She loves me.

I sleep the night in a makeshift bed that Anna has set up for me on the floor, a pile of blankets and quilts and little more. In her sleep Aldonça whispers and shouts, makes guttural sounds that are half-human, half-beast, but it's only nonsense that she speaks.

By early Easter morning, Aldonça's condition has worsened. She begins to convulse with such strength that I can barely hold her down in bed. She claws her pillows and sheets, complaining of a terrible quaking in her head. Moans turn to screams, alerting the rest of the household. Anna runs into the room, followed by my cousin. It takes the two of them to settle Aldonça, though this calm is short-lived because she tosses her head from side to side. I'm desperate to give her the relief she needs, but I don't know what to do, and with an impending sense of doom, I pray, pray, pray. I recite dozens of Ave Marias and implore for our Lord's intercession. What possessed me to cajole an old woman to do something against her will? If she doesn't survive this illness, her death will be another dark mark on my soul.

At daybreak, Núria sends for her physician, a measure I castigate myself for not having ordered sooner. Moments later, Aldonça opens her eyes and calls my name.

"I'm here," I tell her, making room for myself on her bed. "Here I am."

She doesn't acknowledge my words. I stroke her damp hair, touch her sweating face, though the room is not warm by any measure. Suddenly she clutches my hand, and her grip is astoundingly strong.

"I . . . I need to tell you something," she whimpers, pulling me closer.

"Shush now. You must rest."

"No." She gasps and closes her eyes. "I . . . I need . . . your forgiveness."

"Oh, my dear Aldonça, it's I who must beg your forgiveness. I've dragged you over mountain and plain."

She takes a long breath, then allows it to leave her body in labored gasps. "You are . . . you are like a daughter to me."

"And you like a mother." I want her to be quiet, to be still. She can't afford to waste her energy.

"I haven't . . ." She cringes, probably in reaction to a stab of pain because she raises both her hands to rub her temples.

"Whatever you want to say isn't important right now."

I ring for the maid, but it's my cousin who glides to my side in silent footsteps. When Núria sees the agony writ on Aldonça's face, she whispers in my ear, "The doctor should be arriving soon. I sent a horse along with the messenger."

Slowly Aldonça's face relaxes, the hard line of her lips slackens. She sleeps, and I redouble my heavenly entreaties. Halfway through our Lord's Prayer as I appeal for daily sustenance, she blinks open her eyes again and turns to face me. Her stare is vacant and without direction.

"Where's the light?" she asks.

"Should I open the curtains? It's a bright morning."

"I see only darkness."

I hold my hand up to her face, but I know the answer before I ask the question. "Can you see my fingers?"

Tears brim over, both hers and mine. She closes her eyes and sighs. I stand and pace the room, then sit after a few minutes. Desperate, hopeless, helpless, I watch her chest rise and fall, rise and fall—until she wakens and calls my name.

"I don't want you to think less of me," she cries.

"Never, never, never."

"Don't judge me harshly."

"How could I?"

"I did what I did . . . I couldn't . . . it was necessary . . ." She gulps hard and coughs once, twice.

"Don't say anything else, Aldonça. Please."

"Because I thought it best for you."

She raises herself on her elbows, a herculean effort that wrinkles her forehead and turns her face crimson, but then collapses in defeat. I rearrange the pillows and kiss her cheek. She manages a smile. Or a grimace. I can't be sure of which.

I hold her hand and wait for the physician, for help, for succor, and in the waiting I don't notice her last breath, only a deathly cold spreading to her fingertips.

On Easter Monday, while others without sin enjoy their delicious mona de Pascua cakes, I submit to the torment of mourning. Núria has sent Anna to assist me, and when the young maid opens the bed curtains, I spot all the essentials lined up along the dressing table. Shuddering, I close my eyes tight. If I could return to the oblivion of slumber, I would. I don't want to face the world. I don't want to face myself.

Anna helps me sit up in bed. I lift my arms, and she tugs off my bedclothes and slips a linen shift over my head. Wordlessly she adjusts my black brocade bodice, flattening my already sagging breasts with the too-stiff stomacher and bombast, and then helps me step into the under-skirt and verdugado, positioning the hoops so she can attach the outer skirt to the bodice. To finish, she ties the pleated sleeves to the bodice at the shoulders and folds over the ornamental cuffs scalloped in lace. Before we leave for the cemetery, she'll fit me with a white mourning linen cap that stretches down over my forehead.

"Preference?" she asks, pointing to two pairs of footwear from Núria's collection: jewel-encrusted chopines and the cork-soled pantofles.

I choose the latter for their comfort, knowing no one can see anything under all my hoops and skirts. Frankly, no one should care. Thus shod, I make my way to the cushioned stool in front of the dressing table, and Anna begins folding and rolling my hair, and then fasten-ing each section with metal hairpins. She holds up the silver-handled mirror, and brown eyes that once sparkled like sea glass now reflect back at me without shine. Finally, I have nothing else to do, no other excuse to postpone what I dread. My silly, useless interest in clothing and hair-dressing has served only to avoid the rock in my chest, the singe of tears in my eyes. Now I must acknowledge death. I must acknowledge my errors and blunders, no more delays.

When my stomach grumbles loudly, I exhale in relief. Breaking my fast offers one last reprieve, however brief, from obligations. I'm not proud of my shallowness. No, not at all. But it's the one sure way I know to protect myself from the spear of self-reproach.

Our funeral procession wends its way down narrow streets to the cemetery adjoining a plain stone church. The funeral cortege is small, in keeping with Aldonça's rank, but I'm grateful to Núria for her help in arranging it. To supplement our meager numbers, she recruited enough mourners from the convent of which she is a benefactor. Her regular almsgiving has resulted in a respectable procession, and at a short distance from the creaking wagon that carries the body, half a dozen nameless women in white follow us, shuffling, weeping, and praying for my nursemaid's soul. Each carries a tall taper meant to symbolize tenets of our faith: resurrection, immortality, triumph over death. (How I want to believe this lofty creed!) Like me, Núria wears a heavy black gown and mourning cap, not because she must but because she wants to accompany me in my grief.

Church bells ring briefly, then stop, and thank goodness for that. Having slept so little in the past two nights, every sound is like a hammer knocking inside my skull. And though I wish for silence, I also realize that noise, however mundane, assures me of one thing I don't deserve: I am alive. I am alive. I am alive. Still.

I'm in a fog too. Faces, buildings, beasts—all appear hazy, without defined edges.

I wish this were a dream. I wish I could awaken in another time and place, anywhere I bear no responsibility for someone's death. Is that even possible? I can't say. I'm devoid of drive and determination. Even as I walk toward Aldonça's grave, I'm not sure whether I should continue this journey or turn back for home. For now, the best I can do is take one step, then another and another, my feet moving of their own accord as if they belong to someone else. I count each worn cobblestone that leads to an ending I wouldn't have ever chosen.

This disorientation is familiar, even if unwanted. After Françesc's death, I didn't know where to turn, how to move forward, or what would happen to me in a world that too often proves unbending in what it expects of widows. But I went on, step after step after step, one day at a time, until life took its course, as it invariably does. I bore no blame for his passing, though. I could turn myself over to grief with abandon. Now, sorrow is clouded with guilt.

Aldonça is to be buried in a simple grave, wrapped in a simple shroud.

There's no family pantheon, no vaulted chapel for a maid, only a return to earth. I don't think our final resting site matters, though. We all end up in the same place anyway. We come from dust; to dust we return.

And still, I despair. Such words offer no reassurance.

Our procession trudges a sad path to the very back of the cemetery, past the church with the small belfry, past a rusted gate, past crooked headstones and marble monuments, past a tiny chapel with Doric columns. We arrive at an isolated field, notable for its freshly dug mound of dirt. I spot a priest in a black cassock, and next to him, leaning on shovels, two men in heavy boots and dirty garb. As I draw closer, my mind begins to play tricks on me. It's not a man of God waiting for us but Death itself, in priestly costume. A reaper with a scythe eager to wrench breath from our breast and life from our very arms.

"I can't," I cry out.

Núria turns to me. "What is it?"

"No! No! I can't leave her here."

"Come now, cousin." She makes shushing noises. "You're doing what you need to do."

I lean against her. I close my eyes. A bird tweets. The scent of hay arrives on a gust of wind. Is there a celebration of the Eucharist graveside? I don't remember. Is my nursemaid's body lowered into the yawning maw with care? I don't remember. Do shovels scrape against earth, the grating sound a reminder that life is, as Miquel wrote, nothing but a shadow that passes? Again, I can't remember. But I do recall, for Núria assures me of this: Aldonça is buried under a Judas tree and according to custom, parallel to the church, east to west.

This offers me scant consolation. She will rest, until the Last Judgement, far, so far from her beloved Barcelona. She deserves better.

A carriage waits for us at the corner. I can't feel any part of my body, and I weep and hiccup inconsolably. Núria and Anna scoop me up into the vehicle, and I sit on the upholstered bench. Someone closes the carriage door. Someone dabs my nose and eyes with a handkerchief.

I say aloud what has tortured me for two days. "I failed her."

Again Núria attempts to quiet my qualms, but I can't forgive myself for an exile Aldonça would have never chosen for herself. For this and for my negligence in summoning a priest for Extreme Unction, I bear endless blame. Regardless of the benevolence of our Lord, some acts are unforgivable. They stain our souls forever.

The carriage lurches forward. I hear a great keening then, a howl so mournful that it would pierce a soldier's armor. The sound rings straight and true from the excruciating depths of an anguished heart. So close, so very close to my ears, and so much a part of me.

Xirau and El Musulmán come to see me that very afternoon. Though the men offer their condolences, they don't express surprise at Aldonça's death. Maybe their judgment wasn't as confused as mine. I misled myself—worse, lied to myself—about her health all the way to the end.

"*Senyora*," Xirau says, "you must decide what you want to do now."

I stare at him. Do what? Decide how?

"If you want to continue with us to Madrid, we leave at first light."

Xirau's blue eyes search mine, but I'm distracted by the way his scar slithers across his left cheek. It appears so defiantly red. I wonder how he got it in the first place. In a fight? At war?

"*Senyora*." El Musulmán's voice forces me back from my ruminations.

The muleteer reviews our itinerary—from here to Calatayud, then descending through Guadalajara into Madrid—but that's not the guidance I seek. Should I return home, where I can grieve in peace and among my own, or continue alone in hopes of a timely meeting with Miquel? If Aldonça were here, she'd offer sound advice. Her very presence would temper my doubts, especially when it comes to the outcome of this trip—there is, after all, no guarantee of success in Madrid.

"I need your decision by nightfall."

I rise from my chair to dismiss the men but fall back, disoriented. El Musulmán rushes over and kneels by my side. I hold his stare, but the erratic movement of his wandering right eye makes me break into a honking laugh.

"You're in a bad way, *senyora*," he says. "You must rest."

I do, and later arrive at a decision that requires courage and fortitude to carry out. I will return to the road, continue on to Madrid, to Miquel, to whatever form of atonement is still available to me. Though Núria would prefer I stay, she offers me the services of her quiet young maid, and I assent, for I truly do not know how to be alone. Yet when I look at Anna, at a face as round as an embroidery hoop, she appears terribly young, her skin too smooth, her hands too small, her manner too timid. She can't possibly be more than three and ten. Truly, who will look after whom?

Chapter 7

In Which I Officially Assume the
Responsibilities of a Woman

I stormed into Father's library, eager for a fight but also anxious for explanations. If indignation were a color on canvas, I would have painted it carmine and outlined it in carbon black.

"How could you, Father? You lied to me. You lied!"

Father looked up from a ledger. "What are you talking about?"

"You know exactly what I'm talking about! You've known all along!"

He put the quill down with maddening calm and attempted a smile. "Can you offer a clue?"

"Miquel. You've known for months—for years!—that Miquel was taken prisoner by Barbary pirates."

His smile disappeared and for a moment I thought he would deny everything, but he didn't, and instead motioned for me to sit. I settled at the edge of a chair.

"I didn't know what had happened to him until the Trinitarians came to me for help, when Rodrigo was ransomed."

"And you—"

"Let me finish." He paused, then resumed. "When I heard from a Valencian merchant that Rodrigo had returned, I tried to assist with Miquel, but it's no easy matter, this ransoming. The price continues to go up, and when the friars think they're close to an agreement with the corsairs, there's another demand, another impossible request."

I took a deep breath. I didn't want to sound like a hysteric. "And where is he now?"

"I believe he remains in Algiers."

"And you thought it wise not to tell me? When I kept asking you and Mother about him?"

He stared at me without guilt or remorse. "I didn't want to worry you with a situation you couldn't change."

"But at least I would have known he hadn't . . ." I almost used the words *abandoned me*, but realized such an admission was neither in my best interest nor in Miquel's. I was about to be married to Françesc. Our families had come to an agreement, one that seemed to be amenable to both sets of parents. Mother was so obsessed with the bridal trousseau that she rarely complained about the hours I spent in front of a canvas. Was I willing to ruin this? And for what, exactly? Miquel had not declared his intentions, in so many words. He might never.

"We must have faith that the friars negotiating his release will succeed."

"How can I believe you?"

"Do you think your father would forsake an innocent man?"

I hung my head. A cloud passed over the sun, and the room grew dim. The brazier puffed a small sigh of heat.

"Dulçie, you know well the risks of taking to the seas, and so did Miquel. Our very shores are always in danger of attack. Our towns can be sacked and our ships—"

I held up both hands. I wanted no more justifications, no more excuses. "Does Mother know?"

He nodded. I closed my eyes to keep tears from spilling, but the pebble of resentment had already made its home in my belly. Over time it would grow, a boulder impossible to dislodge.

"Will Miquel ever return?"

"I don't know. No one can predict the whims of those barbarians."

I staggered out. It occurred to me that Miquel might be suffering in ways no man should be asked to endure. The cruelties of the Moors were well known. I only needed to recall the horror stories Quirze and Ferran had recounted when we were children, the better to frighten the younger cousins into obedience.

Later that morning Mother came to me in a place she rarely visited. Though she admired the luxuriant light of my studio, she loathed the smells, the implements, the very desire that pulled me away from the life she desired for me. In ignoring my work, she was like a crab boring through sand to hide from whatever didn't conform to her vision.

"I've spoken to your father," she began, standing stiffly in the doorway yet managing to look beautiful in an aquamarine gown with silver-thread embellishments. "I know what you're thinking."

"Do you, Mother? If you did, you would have acted differently. Or at least might have tried to persuade Father that I should have been informed of Miquel's whereabouts. I only asked hundreds of times."

I rose from my stool and set the palette and brush on a low table next to the easel. I knew the colors would congeal and the brush would stiffen, but I could fix that problem easily enough with a slow fire of charcoal later. Miquel's future had no such solution.

"You should know, Dolça, that he could be ransomed tomorrow. Or next year. Or never. Many have died in the clutches of those pirates."

"Why are you telling me this?"

"You want to know the truth, and I'm giving you the benefit of its possibilities."

"Why, thank you for that generosity."

Mother didn't take the bait. She instead studied the canvas, which unfortunately was facing the door and thus open to her disdain. "Why must you devote yourself to such pedestrian subject matter?" she said of my ill-clothed peasant woman at the communal well. "If you insist on painting, and if your father is so blind as to allow it, the least you can do is focus on more worthy themes. Perhaps the Virgin ascending to heaven? Or Jesus blessing the children?"

With that, she left me to my heartbreak.

But then as now, I didn't forget Miquel. Even as I prepared for the life I deserved, even as my affection for my husband-to-be deepened, Miquel remained close to my heart, a puzzle to be solved, a prohibition to be tested. I could no more stop loving him than I could change the essence of my art.

I admit to many tears on my wedding day. Tears of anxiety. Tears of joy and tears of sorrow. Never, however, of doubt—odd as that may sound. The wedding mass was celebrated in Françesc's family chapel with only the most immediate relations in attendance. Along with my silk-and-lace gown, its simplicity no reflection of its cost, I wore my father's mother's mantilla and my parents' gift of new earrings of gold and rubies from New Spain. Françesc presented me with thirteen gold coins, the *arres*, to symbolize his commitment to support me, and in the manner of our Catalan forebears, I exchanged gifts with the groom. From my new husband, I received a purse made of gold brocade, fringed with pearls and embroidered with gems; I gave Françesc a Baudelaire sword, selected by Father, with a jewel-encrusted pommel that winked in the sunlight. The festivities grew by several hundred people and lasted well into the following day, and there was so much food and drink that I was told by Joana, an astute observer and witty storyteller, that some relatives stayed more than two weeks, unable or unwilling to return to their own lives. After our first night together, we spent several days in the d'Oms *masia*, the country house where our families had finalized our union. Crickets sang us to sleep and birds chirped us awake.

But . . . that first night.

I had secreted a small kitchen knife under the bed as a necessary tool to ensure Françesc would never learn I was not the chaste maiden he had expected. I did not want him to feel cheated, and I feared that, if he discovered my impurity, he would tell his parents or confront Father. To avoid such a situation, I had to take drastic measures. In truth, I didn't know what awaited me or what I was expected to do. It had been several years since I had lain with Miquel, and Mother had been vague about what she meant by "wifely duties," averting her eyes when I pressed her for details.

My bedchamber in our new house on Ample had been furnished with some tapestries from my childhood home and with books I had begged from Father, but a lot of it was new: the four-poster bed and its brocatelle curtain, an ebony dressing table imported from Antwerp, and a carved chest my mother-in-law had gifted me once our engagement had been announced. Amid this luxury, Carme, the young maid I had taken with me from Father's, tittered like a fool as she brushed out my hair.

"Your husband will be pleased," she said, giving my tresses one last hard brush-through. "You look so beautiful, and your nightdress is of such soft linen."

"What will it matter? It'll be too dark for him to notice anything."

"Oh, miss, don't believe that. Men are like cats. They can see in the dark."

Her giggling exacerbated my unease, but not for the reason she might have guessed. I dismissed her with an angry wave and climbed into bed, making sure my fine nightclothes were displayed at their best, even as I prepared for the worst.

"You're a sight to behold."

I jumped, startled by Françesc's voice. In another setting, I might have chided him for creeping in like a cat, but dread had left me speechless.

"I didn't mean to frighten you," he said.

He had removed his doublet as well as his collar and wrist ruffs, but was otherwise still clad in the fine velvet from the wedding. The rounded toes of his black shoes reflected the light from the lantern in his hand. He approached the bed and sat on the edge, offering a hand to help me sit up better. I took it, but not without trepidation. He leaned over to kiss me full on the lips.

"My bride," he whispered, and set his lantern next to my candle. Then with the lightness of a bird, his fingers caressed my face and tickled my chin. "Now, what would make you comfortable?"

I shrugged, and he tapped the tip of my nose with his finger, smiling all the while. When he stood, I thought he planned to leave the room, but he did no such thing and instead unclipped the buckles and slipped off his shoes. He then removed his breeches and his white shirt. I kept my gaze on his eyes as he clambered onto the bed and settled next to me, adjusting the pillows so we both could rest comfortably. He took me in his arms and held me tight for a long while, or at least until I stopped shaking like a criminal condemned to the noose. He kissed my closed lids, the space between my brows, my earlobes free of jewels, my quivering chin, and my bared neck. He didn't stop there either, halting only long enough to remove my nightdress.

"Tell me if I hurt you," he said into my ear, but of course I admitted to nothing, terrified as I was of a more pressing danger.

Once he fell asleep after our lovemaking, I slipped out of bed, snatched the kitchen knife from its hiding place, and tiptoed to the window. I opened the curtains to allow a ribbon of moonlight and, gritting my teeth, sliced the inside of my middle finger before hurrying back to where my husband lay. I spread the oozing blood on the sheets and hoped—prayed and pleaded with a forgiving God, actually—that this pretense would be convincing. It apparently was, for he didn't say anything to me in the morning. He simply nuzzled at my breast and groaned with pleasure, a sound I would learn to appreciate many times over. After that, he returned to my bed almost every night he was in the city, and I never failed to welcome him.

Five weeks after we were wed, Françesc set off on a business trip, and I was left alone with a platoon of servants and a cavernous house that was not yet a home. Mother visited and I still helped Father in the office, but I was surprised by how much I missed Françesc's lively conversations. He did write often, though, and left instructions that an east-facing room on the second floor be furnished with benches, easels, counters, and brushes, whatever I needed. In truth, he spared no expense in pleasing me.

Joana was, as always, reassuring. "It is difficult at first, Dolça, but you'll get used to your own company," she said. "You'll have your friends and confidantes, your needlework, your charities, and the running of your household."

"Yes, of course." I laughed to disguise my concerns. My immaturity, really.

"And soon you'll have many little ones to occupy your time too," Joana added, elbowing me gently.

We were walking back from the cathedral, where we had attended a Te Deum in thanksgiving for our victory in the Battle of Alcântara, which was said to have ensured King Philip II's ascension to the Portuguese throne. Though it was unseasonably warm for September, we remained in good spirits and were already preparing for Advent.

"I've given no thought to children," I admitted. "I can't imagine how I'll behave once they come." Unlike my female cousins, I didn't find bawling infants attractive, though I knew it was my job to produce many.

"We all have our doubts, but then we rise to the occasion."

I squeezed her hand, knowing she was eager for motherhood. "I know you'll be an excellent and loving mother, dear Joana. Any reports on that front?"

Her delicate features rearranged themselves in a display of sadness. "Nothing."

"Yet."

"Gabriel," she began, then stopped to glance around. Our maids were walking a few steps behind us, absorbed in their own conversation.

"What about Gabriel?"

"He spends far too much time at the family estate."

I couldn't understand why my brother-in-law would choose to be away from his beautiful wife. Joana's hair shone like spun gold in the sun, and her easy nature turned any setting into a welcoming place. "Why not go with him then?" I suggested. "The country air would do you good."

She stared up at me in disbelief, and I pressed no further.

When Françesc returned—and he always would, no matter where he went or how long he remained away—his ardor exhausted the two of us. Sometimes we would linger in bed, pretending to sleep until the footfalls of servants or the sobering chime of church bells announced the noon recital of the Angelus, and only then would we rise to begin our day, the indolence providing as much enjoyment as the warmth of each other's tangled limbs. We attended family dinners and danced at the viceroy's masked balls (Françesc was quite adept at the pavane and the allemande), played cards with cousins, and cheered at the cane tournaments in El Born. Whereas I would paint every day during his absence, if only for a few hours, I rarely stepped into the studio when he was home. With him, I grew pleased with myself, with the power of my own body. Mother noted with wry amusement that I strutted like a peacock in the courtyard of a marquis.

Then, with little advance notice and a vague return date, Françesc left again, just as the evenings had begun to lengthen. It was during this time I learned about a family matter that disturbed me greatly. Our marriage, it turned out, had been delayed not because of the reasons I had previously imagined. The wait had been a result of Carles and María's demand for proof of purity in Mother's line. As Joana told me this, I thought of Àvia, of the jeweled palm she had given me before her death, and I was angry and offended, insulted by the gall of my in-laws, but also curious about how our parents had resolved this issue—or better said, curious about what Father had conceded to escape public humiliation. He had much to gain from my marriage. Entry into the d'Oms family meant Father at last would get the title, and privileges, of nobility he so desired, not necessarily for himself but for a future grandson.

Because my sister-in-law was wracked with remorse after divulging this not-so-secret secret, I swore I wouldn't speak of this to anyone, not to Françesc, not to Father or Mother. In fact, Joana would take that story—and many of my confidences—to her early grave.

Six days into November, Aldonça interrupted my work to deliver a sealed note:

30th of October, 1580

Dearest Dolça,
I have been freed by the Algerian pirates, thanks to the ran-
som raised by the Trinitarian friars. I am not far, currently in
Valencia, and wish to meet with you.

Yours always,
Miguel

I looked up at my nursemaid to see if she could guess what I had just read, but her features betrayed neither approval nor dismay. None-theless, I tore the paper into tiny pieces, my hands shaking all the while. Then in a nervous frenzy, I put away the pigments and cleaned my brushes, removed my apron and the thick-weaved linen shoe coverings. Aldonça watched without helping. In a tone as flat as wine in a goblet, she announced, "I've already sent word to him that you're married."

He came anyway.

He was thin, the hollows under his cheekbones shaded in a way that would have required great skill to draw. His hair had lost its luster and his beard demanded attention. Only his eyes, still lively, still inquisitive, were unchanged.

"I hadn't expected you to come," I said when the maid showed him in. We didn't kiss or embrace in greeting.

"Why would you think that? I made my intentions known in the note I sent."

"I offered no encouragement."

"I needed none."

Knowing Miquel, knowing his pertinacity, I should not have expected different. I motioned for him to sit, and we took our places on opposite ends of the room, he on the edge of a wingback chair and I mirroring his stiffness on the settee. This salon was where I met callers and also where, when Mother visited, I could pretend to labor over a needlework project.

"You're married now," he stated, and the hint of accusation was impossible to ignore.

I nodded. He surveyed the room with an appraising eye, and I was happy I had chosen to make the atmosphere here subdued. A small vitrine, which housed a few glass and ceramic pieces, was my most obvious conceit, but I had also rewarded myself with a *barguenyo* mounted on wrought iron and with a front that hinged out to create a writing space. It was inlaid with ivory in the Moorish manner.

"Beautiful house."

"Yes, it is." I didn't add that it had yet to feel like home.

"What's your husband's name, may I ask?"

"Françesc d'Oms Calders."

The surname meant nothing to him, for there wasn't even a flicker of recognition. I wanted to ask about his imprisonment in Algiers, but I didn't know how to pose the question without reviving the nightmare. Then I remembered my manners. "Would you like something to drink? To eat?"

"No, thank you."

"Have you called on my parents?"

"Your father at his office, but not your mother. He's been very helpful."

"Helpful?"

"In obtaining a position. As you might imagine, it's difficult after . . . after all this time. I'm a man with no assets and few connections."

"I understand," I said, but in reality, I didn't. I had no idea how one would go about looking for employment. And I wondered how helpful my father truly wanted to be. He had a long memory, and surely he had not forgotten our argument before my wedding. Or the many times I had asked about Miquel. Or that long-ago evening when he had found us embracing.

"I plan to remain in Barcelona for a few months to see what might come up."

Even to my naive ears, the imprecision of this scheme had little to recommend it. Aside from Father, who else could help him in Barcelona? Maybe Quirze. But wouldn't it be better to seek work where his family could provide support, in whatever form that might take? I didn't voice my opinion, however.

"This is a city with much to offer, Miquel."

"And not just in the way of jobs."

"But your family must want you to come home, no?"

"I'd like to think someone else might want me to stay here."

The air crackled. He shifted in his chair, and I crossed my ankles to keep my legs from shaking. This was a reckless game to be playing. Just a few minutes earlier, I had heard the rustle of a maid's skirt as she walked down the hall.

"Well," I said, standing suddenly. "It was good of you to visit."

Miquel frowned. He probably hadn't expected such an abrupt dismissal, but he also had to know that I couldn't just return to the past, to the coy coquetry of years ago, as if I had no husband. I had certain responsibilities now, not the least of which was unassailable behavior.

"I'd like your permission to come calling again, Dolça."

"Miquel, my situation is—"

"I know your situation, but please also understand mine. I didn't choose to waste the past five years of my life. Nor did I choose to be away from you."

If his intent was to provoke discomfort, he certainly accomplished that. I felt obligated to say, "As long as you know where I stand."

For this he had no answer.

Our next four meetings were no less awkward, but he never overstayed his welcome. I saw to that. I was well aware of how his presence might arouse the servants' suspicions, and I imagined rumors already circulating in the kitchen and servants' quarters. I even thought of inviting Mother for his visits, perhaps because Miquel hadn't seen her yet, perhaps because I didn't trust myself, perhaps because . . . oh, I can come up with so many excuses! In the end, however, actions are what matter, and those speak loud and clear. I didn't tell Mother or Father about Miquel's visits. Nor did I write Françesc about them in my weekly letters. I did mention Miquel's stay to my cousin Glòria in passing, and I recounted his visits to Joana but never once referred to the jumble of emotions that knotted my stomach and kept me awake at night. Telling two friends absolved me, or so I believed. Otherwise, did I feel any guilt for these not-quite-clandestine encounters? Was I so willfully credulous that I didn't foresee the inevitable? Did I not take into account how his presence would affect me? No, no, and no.

Our relationship, this new one, was built on an unsteady foundation, and we trod with care. During those first visits, he told me of his imprisonment, of his four failed attempts to escape, and of how he had kept his wits about him in such trying circumstances. ("I thought only of the future. Of you. Of us.") But Miquel was at his most animated when he spoke about his writing and how hardship had informed it. On one occasion, we argued heatedly when he claimed I couldn't paint commoners or a simple scene from ordinary life because I had no point of reference on which to base any such image. I was insulted. This was precisely the motif threaded through all my work! I invited him on a tour of my canvases, proudly refuting his accusations. Impressed with my *Washerwomen*, *Men at the Mill*, and *Thrashing Wheat*, he showered me with compliments. At the time I hungered for his approval, for any remark that noted my effort and talent. But I also was oblivious to how my cosseted existence served as a wedge between us, and how it would continue to do so for years to come.

And then on a nippy November Tuesday, I woke out of sorts, irate even. I longed for Françesc's company, for his silly jests and small kindnesses—but I was also beginning to resent his long absences. Was this to be the pattern for our marriage? Maybe because I was nursing this grievance, maybe because I was frustrated by my inability to correctly capture the dappled hues of a yew tree in the shade, I answered the knock on my closed studio door more brusquely than the interruption required.

"What is it now?"

"*Senyora*," a maid announced timidly, "your cousin is here. Shall I tell him you're indisposed?"

This was the recurring strict order I had given the house staff in case of unexpected visitors, but it didn't apply to Miquel, of course. "No, no. Bring him in, Roser."

As her footsteps receded, I removed my apron, washed my hands over the basin in a corner, and tried my best to tame my hair. I thought of moving the easel because I didn't want him to witness my struggle, but I ran out of time when he was shown into my studio.

"My apologies for interrupting," Miquel said in a formal tone intended, I assumed, for the help.

"I'm sure, dear cousin, that you have a good reason."

Roser asked if she should bring refreshments. After I declined, she closed the door behind her, an unusual move as it was far from customary to host a man unattended, a convention I was skirting already. But the maid was young and as innocent as a foundling. I, on the other hand, had no such justification.

"I must apologize for . . ."

"Coming without an invitation again," I finished for him.

"I don't like it when my own work is disturbed."

"What's done is done, Miquel. Let's not worry about that now."

He insisted on inspecting my new work, a mortifying situation for me, to be sure, and because of this request, we found ourselves in close proximity as I explained the process, from preparing the canvas to grounding the pigments to mixing the hues. I was in midsentence when he reached for my face and kissed me.

"Dolça, I think of you constantly. I can't imagine my life without you."

I didn't reply, and he didn't back away. Arms wound tight around my waist, he explored my mouth with his tongue, and I responded in kind. No longer could I question the purpose of his visits—or my motives for accepting them. That morning I crossed through a portal that could only lead to trouble and heartache.

I know, I know. I should have resisted Miquel. I should have rejected his advances. I should have exiled him from my home. But I did none of those things. Rather, I allowed him to press against me until I was conscious only of his smell, his labored breath, his lips on the hollow of my neck and the swell of my breasts. In hurried, hungry movements, he undid the ties and buttons that encumbered my frame, and once free of such deterrence, he marked my nipples first with his fingers and then with the suckling pressure that was a sweetness like no other. Murmuring in my ear, he hiked my skirts, and I undid his breeches. He traced a line from my chest to the border of my pubic hair, and then how effortless it was, the sudden slip to that mysterious wetness inside. From there it was no more than a small step to surrender, a yielding that was as much physical as mystical. Around us colors faded, canvases disappeared, and all that existed were hands and lips, thrusts and nibbles and rubs. Skin, glorious skin. He could not stop, nor did I want him to stop. In the desperate attempt to make up for lost time, we discovered no need for mattress or bedstead, only for each other's caresses. How simple it was to mold myself to his body, how fated this dance of tender touch.

That November morning wasn't the only lapse of judgment. I eventually became the willing initiator, the one who used her knowledge of family habits and her city's secret places to plan our trysts. In turn, Cousin Quirze, now married but with a wandering eye himself, became Miquel's most trusted accomplice once again. What did this say about me as a wife, as a woman, that I so blithely cuckolded a husband who had been nothing but loving and considerate? What drew me to a man who could never provide the life I wanted, who would never be approved by my parents? I couldn't explain it then, though later, much later, I would arrive at an answer that justified my recklessness: Miquel was the proverbial forbidden fruit—and my behavior an act of disobedience. The risk of our illicit relationship simply magnified the natural attraction.

When I finally confided in Joana, among the many things she asked was how I was able to divide my affections between two men, how a heart could be halved without damage to the whole. I had no answer, only the understanding that I was capable of both a mortal sin and an untenable love. That much I could admit, no more.

Françesc was home for the Christmas and New Year festivities, and consequently, I saw Miquel only a couple of times during those holidays, always from a distance. I should add that my two loves, husband and paramour, once ended up next to each other at a family gathering, but their conversation was so brief that I'm certain Françesc wouldn't have remembered his rival had I questioned him about it. I, in contrast, choked so pitifully on my *torró* that Mother had to palm my back until I was able to dislodge the almonds of the nougat bar from my throat. After that, I made myself ill by drinking too many of Aldonça's calming concoctions. But Françesc didn't suspect, I don't think, and was, as ever, attentive during the weeks he remained in Barcelona. At home he would sit in a chair, remove his shoes, prop his feet on my bed, and tell me all he had seen during his journeys. He talked of orange groves in Valencia, figs in Vilafranca, walnuts in Vic, and the Muntanya de Sal in Cardona, a salt mountain so wondrous he believed it had been created by a whimsical god. His conversations always lifted my spirits, and I was able to bear the occasional whip of remorse without any outward display of such. No small accomplishment, but also nothing to brag about.

On New Year's Day, Françesc and I joined the family at the Ninou Fair for glassmakers in El Born, one of my favorite traditions. We began the day's festivities at the Basilica of Santa María del Mar and from there enjoyed the cavalcade of dignitaries as they paraded to Plaça Sant Jaume, led by the bishop, our *conseller en cap*, and various grandees. These were followed by lesser representatives from church and government, but also by the consuls from the Llotja de Mar, each marching row so magnificently dressed, their banners so colorfully displayed, that even the sourest citizen was forced to believe, at least temporarily, that the New Year would usher good tidings. My brother-in-law Gabriel doted on Joana, who had recently discovered she was pregnant, and that day he purchased every glass item she fancied. Françesc soon followed suit, and we had to send for two servants to carry home our loot. All in all, the day was pleasant, and the warmth of family helped soften the bitter winter wind. With Françesc at my side, I vowed to end my association with Miquel. I couldn't bear the thought of hurting my husband, and I knew if he ever discovered my betrayal, our relationship would suffer a great, if not final, blow.

Only Joana appeared distracted that New Year's Day, and I attributed this to her condition, though her cheeks were rosy and her step lively. As we walked home arm in arm, I tried to cajole her into a better mood, but she would have none of it.

"Come on, Joana," I insisted, "look at all the beautiful glass you'll exhibit at home. The little camel alone is a work of art."

"Yes, but I wish you would worry about yourself more, dear friend."

"What do you mean?" My muscles tensed.

She lowered her voice. "I think Gabriel suspects."

"Suspects what?"

"That something's going on between you and Miquel."

I gasped and leaned on my dear friend. "Did he say something to you?"

"He made a passing comment the other day. Said you and your cousin were awfully friendly."

"In those words?"

She nodded.

"Do you think he's mentioned something to his brother?"

"I don't know."

She didn't bring up the topic again until the following afternoon at our usual merienda when she made me promise to stop seeing Miquel. Too dangerous, too immoral, she insisted, and then reminded me of all that could happen to an adulterous wife. Glòria also warned me to tread with care and admonished Quirze to stop abetting my shameful behavior. "The scandal of it!" she screeched. "It will affect us all." As a result of those well-intentioned warnings, I spent weeks consumed with worry and studied my husband for any sign that would signal his knowledge of my duplicity.

Right before our *carnestoltes*, Françesc left again—and with him my New Year's vow of marital fidelity. I spent much of carnival in Miquel's company, the debauchery of the pre-Lenten holiday simplifying whatever furtive meetings we planned. In public, we danced with cousins but never with each other, the better to confuse our companions. We laughed at the satires performed on makeshift stages and avoided as best we could the volley of oranges mischievous boys aimed at passersby. But in private we held each other in a reverent study of our bodies. Several times Miquel begged to spend an entire night with me—"To know you in your sleep," he explained—but that was one boundary I refused to cross.

I bridged the chasm of guilt with the ease of a practiced negotiator, a skill Father had taught me well. Joana was not as forgiving, though she guarded my secret willingly.

"I just don't understand why you're doing this."

"I love him."

"Do you, really? Or do you love the opportunity to rebel against your parents? To thumb your nose at all the rules we're forced to obey?"

"That has nothing to do with it."

"I think you're lying to yourself and you don't realize it yet."

"I'm very careful."

"That won't matter for long."

"Do you speak from experience?" I teased.

"I'm far too cowardly to seek my own pleasure, though I'm not ignorant of the joys that could bring. Plus, I know that while men can do as they please, women are judged differently. Surely you know why Gabriel visits the country house so often? He has at least two lovers there, women whose presence I must endure every time we visit. On the other hand, if I were to behave in that way . . ." Her voice trailed off.

My eyes widened.

"So, I settle for all of this." She gestured with her hand to encompass her well-appointed salon. "But mostly for this." She rubbed her growing belly, the precious baby for which she had longed.

"But don't you want love?"

"Love!" She snickered, and I immediately remembered the conversation I had had with Mother about two years earlier. "What does that purchase? What true comfort can it provide? In the end, men take their gratification wherever they can and we women are left to care for the consequences."

Shortly before Ash Wednesday, Miquel announced he would be leaving for Madrid and then Cádiz. He had been commissioned for a special mission to North Africa, specifically Oran, with no return date yet set. I was stunned. Somehow I had believed (stupidly) that his stay in Barcelona would never end.

"Come away with me, Dolça," he pleaded. Seated across from me in bed, he took my hands. "We can start a new life together."

"In Oran?"

"No. You'd stay in Cádiz with friends, until I return."

I stared at him in disbelief. "You've lost your mind."

"I've never felt saner."

"You forget I have a husband. I'm a married woman. My obligations are—"

"You wouldn't be the first woman to flee a marriage."

What could I say to such an invitation? It was pure folly. I envisioned my scandalized parents, my brokenhearted (and perhaps vengeful) husband, my shocked friends.

"I know it would mean a big sacrifice on your part, but with you by my side, I could conquer the world."

I cared nothing about world conquest. I was happy with my house, my servants, my jewels and gowns, my parties and meriendas, and I was neither willing nor prepared to surrender them. What would life with Miquel really mean? I'd have to cook my own meals. Clean my own house. Wash my own clothing. None of the chores I knew how to do.

He drew me closer. "I know it sounds sudden, but I've been thinking about this for some time. Consider it please."

I didn't want to follow Miquel into a life of sacrifice, but I didn't want to lose him either. I confided in Joana again, and again she insisted I break off the relationship. "This is the perfect opportunity," she said. "A clean break."

While it was difficult to ignore the advice of a person I admired and loved, I did just that. As Àvia would have said, *Entrar-li per una orella i sortir-li per l'altra.* In one ear, out the other. Advice most needed is the least heeded.

A few days after Miquel departed for Madrid, still hoping I would change my mind, I woke to nausea that made me queasy in a way I never had experienced. My breasts were tender, my sense of smell keen. When I realized I had missed my monthly bleeding, I wanted to bury myself in the cellar, in a dark corner where no one could find me, where my sin could remain hidden, but that of course proved impossible. Instead, Mother and Aldonça, elated by the much-awaited news, immediately jumped into action. They cared for me day and night until Françesc, notified by Father, cut his trip short to hurry home. I know of no man who expressed such joy on learning of his wife's condition. Yet I could not know if he or Miquel had fathered my child, as both had been recently enough in my bed to claim the title.

But pregnancy did not become me. I spent eight weeks feeling miserable and had no compunction about making others around me equally so. Then one late evening, cramps plowed me over and blood painted the insides of my legs red, so much of it, so foul and sticky and thick. The miscarriage scoured me clean, and I wept with pain—and relief.

For weeks Mother and Aldonça appeared at my door daily, bringing with them the undisputed weight of order and routine. Every morning I was dressed in a clean plain shift, my hair braided and adorned with whatever my mother found scattered among my coffers. In addition, I was bathed several times a week, regardless of the weather or my own desire, though this unconventional practice was much criticized by my husband's family, who believed that water, regardless of temperature, could affect the delicate balance of the body's humors. Mother ignored this basic medical precept and insisted that Àvia and, before that, her mother's mother, had kept such rituals both at the birthing bed and during the lying-in period. And so, we would be served well by doing the same. I thought it ironic that she'd honor Àvia in this fashion, too late, too late.

In spite of my protests and his own father's reproving comments, Françesc didn't leave my side. He brought in a physician, a stoop-shouldered man who blamed the loss of the baby on one of two causes: a fright or a violent jumping up and down. I hadn't suffered a scare or hopped around like a crazed rabbit, but my dear husband couldn't be persuaded otherwise, and he took every precaution to ensure I experienced no surprises, no sudden or bewildering events. In other words, he attempted to build a fortress around me.

"We'll have other children, *maca*, many others, as many as you want," he assured me.

I stared ahead stonily. For sixty-six days I had lived a tormented life, conflicted by the possibility that my child would look like Miquel instead of the husband who would give him home and title. I couldn't confide these feelings to anyone, so my sense of being spared remained my secret, my sin, my shame.

Chapter 8

*Concerning a Uniquely Spanish Paranoia
and the Inexorable Weight of Truth*

There are many shapes to sorrow, many ways to grieve. I learned this after my brother, Andreu, died, after the passing of Àvia, Mother and Father, and Françesc too. But one sorrow can't prevent another, and I rediscover grief's punishing whip on our way to Calatayud. While I mourned others with a deep and steadfast woe, no guilt layered that heartache, no remorse colored my longing. This doesn't hold true of my grief for the woman who loved me as her own. I feel to blame for Aldonça's death. I'm convinced the journey I imposed on her, the strain of the road, contributed to her sudden ill health.

And yet once again here I am astride a fresh mule. Once again, and until we reach Madrid, I've taken up this tiresome trek and stifled my qualms. Still, I wheel around on my saddle half-expecting to speak to my nursemaid—only to be greeted by the childish face of a borrowed maid who rarely speaks more than five words at a time. Even the three pilgriming sisters keep to themselves more than usual. In fact, when the younger two offered their condolences this morning, Adriana made it a point to cut that short, probably not wanting to show kindness to people she considers impious. Only El Musulmán has the occasional tenderhearted word or gesture, maybe because he knows the vagaries of rejection. Nothing encourages sympathy more thoroughly than familiarity with misfortune, and this bull-necked giant with the wandering right eye can probably summon a litany of calamities.

When we first leave Saragossa, the road crosses a plain dotted with well-cultivated farmland. There are olive and fig trees, a few cherry trees with swollen buds but no blooms, and vineyards braided by fields of maize and hemp. Soon enough, however, we enter a land parched and naked, interminable heath, and ascend a stony path that challenges even the most sure-footed beast. The soil colors strangely, from white to sand to pale ginger, and then the arid hills give way to blue mountains and black massifs.

By the following morning, my ears thrum. I attribute this to our steep climb and the delicate frost that hangs on spindly trees. At the summit, where it's even colder and the wind bracing, we're able to admire a small dell of fields below, but Xirau quickly herds us through a narrow byway in single file. We then descend into Calatayud, on the banks of the Jalón. Though the town provides satisfying accommodations, I only manage a few bites of the night's stew. My throat is sore, and unlike my departed nursemaid, Anna can offer no remedy.

Back in our room, no sooner has Anna begun to undress me than the innkeeper's wife bangs on the door. The stout woman informs us that a decree from the Holy Office mandates our attendance in the town plaza for an auto-da-fé tomorrow. I stifle a groan.

"What does that mean?" Anna asks when we're alone again.

I explain that an Edict of Faith was probably issued several months ago, encouraging people to report heretics in their midst, and now the entire town has been invited—nay, ordered—to bear witness to the results of this investigation.

"Is this where they burn people?"

"I don't know," I say, though of course I do. But why not spare the child for a few hours?

In the milky light of dawn, Anna and I line up with the muleteers along the main road that fronts the town square. I search the crowd for the three pilgrim sisters but can't find them. They've probably secured a better spot; this is, after all, an event that would be to Adriana's taste, and she'd want to get an unobstructed view. I'm grateful for their absence, though. I'm ill-disposed to the pinched piousness of that woman.

The townsfolk are somewhat rambunctious, with a nervous energy that can be blamed as much on curiosity as on fear. The uncovered tiered seats on the east and west streets are full, and on the balconies of buildings fringing the plaza, there's no mistaking the stylish figures of the dignitaries. El Musulmán, whose height allows him to observe what most of us can't, is thoughtful enough to describe what's going on. Much of the plaza, he says, is occupied by a makeshift amphitheater, part of which is decorated with banners of every color. Stairs lead to two boxed standing areas, one for the Inquisition officer who will read out the sentences and another for the condemned who will hear his or her fate. Just below these boxes are rough-hewn benches for the prisoners.

A fife and drum contingent strikes up its funereal march as the gentlemen of the court parade to their places of honor on stage. The crowd stirs in hopes of getting a better view of the royal representatives and their splendid ceremonial dress.

"The marquis is wearing a midnight-blue cape with gold buttons," El Musulmán narrates. "And the count is in all black . . . The mace bearers, six of them . . . in suits of gold thread. You'd be impressed, *senyora*."

"Any women among them?" I ask, expecting none, but El Musulmán holds up two fingers. Wives who, I suspect, would rather be elsewhere. After the burning's done, their gowns will reek of smoke and charred flesh. They will never sleep well again.

The archbishop and attendants follow in their scarlet vestments, taking their places on the stage, and then the green-robed familiars of the Holy Office and representatives of the Council of the Inquisition itself. They're joined by four men who aren't easily identifiable.

"Important men," El Musulmán guesses. "Maybe from the city council."

Would Françesc have accepted an invitation? Or Father? Would they have regarded it as part of their duty to church and country to witness vicious punishment and cruel death? I'd like to think not, but pressure to conform is a great motivator.

"If I were one of the dignitaries on that stage," says Gerard, "I wouldn't want to be so close to the flames. An escaped ember . . ." He makes a sound like an explosion.

Xirau's men titter. Next to me, young Anna shudders.

Once all dignitaries have taken their places, the crowd breaks into applause as if a great entertainment is about to take place. Jubilation dims into a solemn buzz as word spreads that the procession of prisoners is headed our way at last. El Musulmán describes a man on horseback carrying the standard of the Inquisition, its embroidered coat of arms with the inscription EXURGE, DOMINE, ET JUDICA CAUSAM TUAM (Arise, O Lord, and judge thine own cause). Then two brown-robed friars parade past, one waving a standard bearing Pope Paul V's gold-and-blue coat of arms with a black imperial eagle and the other carrying a wooden cross draped in black cloth.

Shortly after, a contingent of merchants armed with pikes marches by, followed by a few men lugging blocks of wood and charcoal. They are the tradesmen who have provided the essentials for the burning of the criminals. When the heretics appear, the crowd erupts in jeers. The first group, El Musulmán relates, is condemned to burn for the gravity of their sins or for their refusal to recant their religious beliefs. They march two by two, barefooted and wearing nothing but tall pasteboard caps and sanbenitos, the penitents' tunics painted with flames and monsters. Some are in chains, others wear ropes around their necks. Many can barely walk and are assisted by guards. The men, more numerous, are separated from the handful of women, but all, regardless of sex, carry unlit white candles. As they draw nearer, the prisoners' howling becomes louder and more strident, their wails burrowing into my head.

When the man in front of us crosses himself, his friend says loud enough for everyone to hear, "They won't be getting any pity from me, hombre. These swine have chosen their lot. And anyway, you should know that before the cock crowed, they were fed like kings. Bacon. Bread. Soup. Eggs. My brother's one of the guards and told me about their last meal. When did you last eat like that?"

Four more men on horseback, lances pointed at the sky, direct a small chorus of tonsured monks as they chant a hymn barely heard above the din of the crowd. Trailing behind them, past the hissing and hooting masses, come the prisoners condemned to lesser sentences— those who have made anticlerical statements, or robbed churches, or disrespected sacred objects, or committed bigamy, or practiced sodomy or bestiality. My thoughts turn to Andreu. Where is he now? What has been done to him? Is he marching in a similar procession, stripped of dignity and hope?

The parade of prisoners has ended, and all are now seated in their box. An Inquisition officer begins to read the name of each accused, many of whom must be assisted by a guard or a friar as they stagger to the box to learn their fate. The process is interminable, and the verdicts a litany of horrors.

Burning for those who have not been reconciled.

Strangulation before flames for those who have expressed repentance.

Wearing a sanbenito for life for those with minor charges.

Public flogging for the thieves and the bigamists.

The scourge of hemp cord on a bared back during the next six feast days for those who blasphemed.

Ten years in the galleys for a collection of other offenses.

The judgments, all one hundred and three, grate in my ears. I think of my cousin Núria, of what might happen to her if she continues her secret customs, and I shake my head hard to dislodge the thought. No good will come from my useless worrying. I reach out to steady myself on El Musulmán's arm. He places his hand over mine. "You must fortify yourself, *senyora*. The worst is yet to come."

I feel strong enough to weather what may transpire, but Anna is weeping, a child's hiccup-and-sob kind of cry. I draw her close. She is small and thin, nothing more than a waif, and I find myself weeping along with her. Not for her precisely, nor for the prisoners on the plaza, but for myself, for the emptiness that my nursemaid and others have left behind. When I close my eyes, I can see Aldonça's face, but also the faces of Françesc, Miquel, Father, Mother, my brother Andreu, Joana, and all those I've loved and lost. I'm so consumed by self-pity that I'm startled when El Musulmán tells me the condemned prisoners are being led to the stakes. I still refuse to open my eyes, and El Musulmán continues to describe how guards tie each heretic to a post, first hands and then feet. How several men pass lighted torches close to their faces in warning. How the executioner strangles those fortunate enough not to suffer the torture of being burned alive. How the torchbearers set fire to each pyre of brushwood and charcoal.

Then the shrieks of agony rise over the crackle of the blaze, and Anna stiffens in my arms. My eyes fly open of their own accord. Flames the color of hell rise skyward. I tell Anna to cover her ears as I cover my own, but that only serves to muffle the shouted prayers, the calls for mercy, the bawling. There's no way to avoid the putrid odor of burning flesh that fills the plaza, no way to dispel the ashes and smoke. The bonfires last an eternity, and it occurs to me that while witnessing cruelty is altogether different than being felled by sorrow, both can haunt in a way that destroys the soul.

When it's over at last, when the fagots have burned down, when the ashes have settled, when the dignitaries have filed back to their fiefdoms, when the crowd has thinned and the children have resumed playing with rocks and sticks, when I've dried my tears and hardened my resolve, a chill creeps into my bones. No matter how tight I pull shawl to body, I can't warm myself. I can't stop thinking that my cousin's trusting nature will be her downfall.

The spring sun hangs low in the opaque sky, and soon the remains of the heretics will be gathered in large sacks and scattered in fields, hardly a proper burial. In the lingering smoke, I imagine the stolen breaths and filched dreams of the dead. Though it's past the hour of the midday meal, none of us wants to participate in the celebratory feast held in the courtyard of the cathedral. We return to the inn instead, walking slowly, for Anna is still shaking and crying. Xirau's men appear as distressed as

I am, and this may be because we, all of us, are but one informant away from a ruined life.

Late that afternoon, with Anna on the floor next to me, I seek the comfort of bed before the sun sets, and I sleep the deep slumber of the weary, slumber that stitches together memories of this unfinished journey. The bandits. The wool merchant. Friday night dinner at cousin Núria's. My dear Aldonça's fevered face. Also, tilled fields and green hillocks and muddy riverbanks, the flap of bird wings and the bleating of sheep, the scent of birch and pine, the heat of the noon sun and the bracing slap of cold before sunrise.

And all, each and every scene, licked by orange-and-yellow tongues.

A while later I wake with a start, neither rested nor relieved. My mouth is dry, my eyes scratchy. I realize the dream isn't what disturbed me but a rapping at the door. Maybe it's the innkeeper's wife. Or Xirau, with details for our departure in the morning.

I don't move quickly, as I'm of that age when limbs are no longer nimble, and so the knock turns impatient, belligerent. Anna jumps up, and though I warn her to ask for identification, she flings open the door to the last person I expect to see in this miserable town. His face is wind-chapped, the pox scars red and furious. His hair, the chestnut color of his father's, is tousled, but his garments speak of quality, without mind to the mud splatters of the road: a long cape of black merino wool, russet hose, boots of a leather so rich and supple you want to press cheek to them. One large hand, still in Córdoba kid gloves, holds his hat as a cat might clutch a mouse between its paws, and the other rests on the jeweled pommel of his sword.

I sit up in bed, my hair in certain disarray. As he takes in the room, every detail of scarcity and inferiority noted, his nose wrinkles in distaste. And still, there's a sweetness to his face that I know well, and love more.

"Mother," Jaume says.

"Son," I reply.

If I were younger, I'd bolt downstairs, running toward a future I've failed to make my own. If I were stronger, I'd flee by climbing out the window. But alas, I'm neither young nor strong. I'm an old woman, marked by the brutality of time in much the same way a river gouges a path through mountains. And while my brief nap has alleviated some of the fogginess of thought, my head remains heavy. A debilitating doubt washes over me. How did he find me? What will he force me to do?

Jaume doesn't wait for me to invite him in. "Who's that?" He points to Anna.

The child curtsies but doesn't respond. Apparently, he doesn't expect an answer, for in less time than it takes to draw a breath, he begins to bark orders.

"Let's go, Mother," he says. "We're moving you to decent lodgings."

His mouth has hardened into a straight, unforgiving line. Sometimes I think my son, whom I love above all else, doesn't know the difference between servant and kin.

"What are you doing here?" I ask, and pat my hair to recover whatever's left of my dignity.

"I've come to bring you home."

"I'm not going. I'll return only after I've done what I need to do."

He ignores the statement and waves his right arm in a gesture that encompasses the entirety of our surroundings. "Look at this room. Look at this bed. There isn't even a proper chair for me to sit in."

"Jaume . . ."

"You're not to stay here a moment longer. This is an embarrassment. I can't understand what would prompt you to live like this." He paces the tiny room, sword clanking at his side. "The family has been sick with worry since your disappearance. Your grandchildren have missed you. They ask Elisabet about you every day."

"I'm not going home," I repeat. "I'm needed in Madrid."

"Needed?" He snorts.

"How did you find me?"

He throws his hand up in exasperation. "I'm not answering any silly questions until you gather all your belongings."

"It's not a silly question."

"Very well. I'll answer with one of my own. Do you realize how simple it is to bribe *pagesos* from Barcelona to Calatayud?"

And well, of course. A coin here, a coin there can open the mouths of many peasants, perhaps even Xirau's or that of one of his men. After all, poverty is widespread and betrayal cheap.

"I'll come with you only if you promise me one thing," I say.

"I won't make promises I can't keep."

"Then I'll stay where I am and tomorrow I'll continue on my journey as planned."

Jaume sits next to me, and the bed creaks under his weight. He's a big man, with a predilection for fine wine. Gray has filigreed his beard, and furrows have spread like cobwebs around his eyes. At three and thirty, hardly an advanced age, he appears older than his contemporaries.

"Mother, I'm tired. I've traveled day and night to get here, so your stubbornness doesn't help my mood."

"I'm not being stubborn. I'm simply doing what I must."

He remains silent for longer than necessary. I want to hold my son's hands as I did when he was a child, but they're too large in comparison to mine, too controlling, and moreover, such a gesture might be accepted as a concession. Under no conditions am I returning to Barcelona before I see Miquel.

Jaume stands. "Fine. I've not covered all these leagues to get into an argument. We will discuss Madrid after we've rested."

"But the arrieros I've hired . . ."

"I've already spoken to Xirau."

"Was he the one who betrayed me?"

"Betrayed?"

"Someone must have been informing you of my whereabouts."

"Mother." He pauses for effect. "I won't speak to any of this now. We'll have time enough later."

"Then I'd like to thank Xirau for his service."

He assents and only then do I ready myself. However, it's not Xirau I seek nor his brother Gerard, but El Musulmán, who listens to my dilemma with an open heart. He understands.

Back in the room, I find the innkeeper's wife demanding something of Jaume. Both fall silent when I come in, and she doesn't even lift her gaze to meet mine when she slithers back into the darkened hallway. I wonder about her price and if the bribe will be shared with her husband.

"Where are we spending the night?" I ask.

"You don't know the family, but the lodgings will be more than adequate."

"I have no doubt. You aren't one to sacrifice comfort."

"But you have. The innkeeper's wife said you brought only a saddle-bag and your leather satchel."

I point at them. His expression is inscrutable as he slings each over an arm. "So very light, your belongings. I'm surprised you've managed this far."

Jaume has arranged for us to stay with the brother of a friend, a wealthy merchant whose palatial home is so well lighted by sconces and torches that I feel I'm at a street celebration. Though our host is alone—his wife is visiting family in Valladolid—his hospitality is flawless. I'm shown to one of the bedchambers, beautifully appointed with an inviting canopy bed, but I don't dare caress the linens for fear that my resolve might wane. Servants heat copious amounts of water for a bath, a surprise pleasant enough to make me forget my tender throat and creaky joints.

"Now isn't this much better?" Jaume asks when he comes to bid me good night.

"Of course, it's better, but it doesn't solve the problem at hand."

"Which is?"

"My journey. I can't afford to lose any more time."

"Your only trip now is back to Barcelona. I'm hiring a carriage."

"I'm not going with you."

"You don't have a choice, Mother. Not anymore."

I consider, albeit briefly, confessing why I must continue to Madrid. The conditions for such an admission have never been so favorable. We're alone and together. No clerk is asking for help, no ship captain is demanding attention. Yet . . . yet. I look into Jaume's face, a countenance that still possesses traces of Miquel's own, and my confidence wavers. A revelation of this sort would be devastating, for him and for me. I cannot open myself to questions—or worse, rejection. He would likely consider me a harlot, a traitor, a woman of few scruples who does not deserve the love of her family.

In the end, I'm robbed of the choice because he walks out of the room without explanation. After several minutes, he returns, a sketchbook in his hands. My heart drops at the sight of it. I'd recognize it anywhere.

"I found this in your chambers."

I force myself to slow my breathing, to steady my hands.

"I was desperate to know what had happened to you," he continues, "so Elisabet and I searched your coffers and chests. Your painting studio."

I remain silent, for good reason.

"We found some interesting items, ones that I imagine you wouldn't have wanted your son to see. Or anyone, for that matter. But understand that you gave me no choice. You and Aldonça disappeared. No note, no message."

I continue to stare at him, determined not to cede, but this simple act proves exhausting.

"You behaved cruelly and without regard to our feelings," he adds. "We were sick with worry."

"I'm sorry about that."

"We thought the worst."

He takes a seat next to the bed. He opens the sketchbook, the one so carefully hidden in my calfskin-lined chest.

I will not look at it.

I will not look at the charcoal portraits on each page.

I will not look at the features that he cannot fail to recognize.

I will not.

"I know who this man is, Mother."

He studies the first sketch. I remember it well, remember where we were, what was said, why I drew it, even how Miquel teased me about my efforts. Jaume turns to the second page. Then to the third page, the fourth, the fifth, each a different pose, a varying angle.

"So many images of one man, but not any the same."

My head throbs from a growing dread, but mostly from the shame I've long tried to avoid. I hope for deliverance from what I know is coming.

"Were these sketched on different days?"

I must respond in some way, so I shake my head.

"Are you proud of them?"

"In a way."

"They're quite good. I would even say they were sketched with great care and feeling."

I would rather not defend myself. He's correct anyway. I meet his gaze. It reveals nothing.

"How old are these?" he asks, riffling through the pages. "The paper is quite brittle."

"Very old. Older than you."

"A long time to keep sketches—unless, of course, they have special meaning."

I hold my breath, waiting for him to elaborate. Surely he must see that he shares a resemblance to the model in the drawing. Surely. And then I know he does, he absolutely does, for he hurls the drawing pad across the room and stands abruptly. The chair falls back with a loud thud.

"How could you?" he asks through gritted teeth. "Saving those sketches. And those letters . . . those letters!"

"Jaume—"

"At first I didn't want to believe it. I refused to believe it. My own mother . . . I couldn't imagine . . . it didn't make any sense."

"Let me explain."

"There's no explanation for immorality."

Jaume's large hands are balled into fists, and the rage in his voice could slay an armored knight at ten paces. I, in contrast, feel nothing but a growing numbness.

"I have been living a lie my entire life."

"I did it for your own good."

"Really? You expect me to believe that?"

"Yes! Think how different your life would be if I . . ."

"Don't insult me, Mother. I'm not a fool. I can well guess at your motives."

"I've had to live that lie too."

"To save your own skin. But now . . . now, to chase down your lover like a common . . . like a . . ." He flushes with the effort to find the right word.

It's best not to add anything to the argument. I tell myself he will calm down once he has spewed out the hurt.

After a time, he asks, "Did Father know?"

"No."

"But he suspected. I'm sure he did. Why else would he have teased me about not looking like anyone in the family?"

"He didn't know, Jaume. I'm sure of that."

"Does my Oncle Gabriel? Did my grandparents?"

"No one ever said anything to me."

"But they thought it. They think it."

"Maybe. It doesn't change anything, though. We can keep our lives as they are."

Jaume glowers at me in disbelief. "Only you would believe that."

Heat spreads across my face, which I imagine to be splotchy with embarrassment. He strides to the door and turns back to me. If only I could hide under the covers.

"We will leave as soon as I secure the carriage tomorrow."

He slams the door. I call out for him, but he doesn't hear me—or he chooses not to. In the stillness that follows, a whimpering rises from a corner of the bedchamber: Anna.

"Come out from there, child," I tell her.

She creeps into the flickering candlelight, unwilling to lift her head to look at me, but it is I who is mortified that she witnessed such a horrid exchange. I ask her to help me ready for bed, and she assists with discreet efficiency. My voice gentle, I suggest she go back to her corner to sleep, and I, still shaken, crawl into bed. After what feels like an eternity, I hear the crack of a pebble on the window and quietly, quickly slip into my drab pilgrim attire. I must hurry, but when I grab my belongings, Anna materializes next to me.

"Go back to sleep!" I whisper.

"Where are you going?"

"Nowhere that you can come."

"But you are leaving, and I must go with you."

I consider my options and, recognizing I have none, motion for her to follow me. We tiptoe into the hallway, down the darkened stairs, and out the front door. I'm out of breath and trembling. My heart hammers in my ears, but the chilly air strengthens my determination. When the night watchman stops us, I use my best anguished voice, "Good man, we are on our way to church. I've found that only prayer can relieve my sleeplessness."

He appears skeptical and takes a menacing step toward us, but I soon realize he simply wants to get a better view of our faces. For once my wrinkles and gray hair save me, as I'm too old for a romantic tryst or for whatever other prohibition is imposed on young women these days.

"Be careful," the watchman warns me. "Evil spirits lurk in the dark."

"Bless you for those words of caution, good man."

And before he can change his mind, we disappear into the shadows. I drag Anna by the hand, knowing this is a moment I'll remember with both wonder and pride. I'm attempting something that no one, myself included, would have expected me to do. But there comes a time in every woman's life when she must dismantle the present to determine the future. It is a choice that isn't imposed, a choice she doesn't stumble upon, but one she makes knowing full well the consequences. This is such a time.

Leaning on a wall, lantern in hand, El Musulmán awaits me with two sad-looking mules.

"Ready, *senyora*?" the giant whispers.

"Sí."

"She's coming too?" he asks when he spots Anna cowering behind me.

"I can't leave her behind. What if she alerts the others?"

"I have but two mounts."

"We'll make do."

"Are you sure?"

"*Res aventurat, res guanyat.*" Nothing ventured, nothing gained.

Yet, even as I say this, I scold myself—not for what I'm doing now, but for what I could have done in my youth. How different my life would have been had I taken a single risk, had I dared to trade comfort for unsanctioned love.

El Musulmán helps me and then Anna onto a mule, and after giving the guards a generous bribe, we pass through the city gates, out into darkness. On to Madrid, on to Miquel. On to redemption. Maybe it's not too late to rediscover the curious girl I once was. To become what I might have been.

Chapter 9

1582–1590

In Which I Become a Mother
and Suffer a Surprise

Soon after I had resumed my social obligations following my miscarriage, Françesc sank into a deep melancholia, displaying an overwhelming sadness and fatigue that would haunt our marriage from time to time. During those weeks of endless despondency, he shed weight and lost interest in business matters. He locked himself in his study, and we were forced to leave his meals outside his door, meals that often went uneaten. I had no idea what to do, but in keeping with the family's commitment to appearances, I pretended nothing was amiss when I visited friends and relatives.

One morning I found him in his bedchamber, still in his nightshirt, hair disheveled, eyes swollen and bruised.

"Husband," I said, caressing his face, "you can't stay like this forever."

"Why not?"

"Because you—we—have a life outside these walls. We must tend to it."

He made no reply, and though I was fully dressed, I climbed next to him in bed, careful not to wrinkle my silk. I kissed his neck, stroked his beard, declared my love. When he remained silent, I redoubled my efforts.

"We must make another baby," I said. "You promised."

At this bold invitation, he didn't smile or take me in his arms but continued to stare at the beamed ceiling without acknowledging my words. His manservant entered several times, as did Cook herself when supper had again been sent back untouched. Both clucked and tutted at the sad scene, but they also looked scared for him and, I suspect, for themselves. That day no amount of encouragement prompted him to dress, and I didn't leave him alone until my neck grew stiff and my lower back ached.

Desperate, I finally told Aldonça what was happening, and at her suggestion I fed him a gingerroot tea with mysterious herbs she claimed would improve the melancholy. His mood did not change, however. Father, who eventually guessed what was happening when my husband abandoned his work, urged me to speak to his older brother, but I didn't want to embarrass Françesc. Or maybe it wasn't embarrassment that kept me from acting, but a niggling suspicion that I was to blame for his disposition. My own heart was burdened by guilt, my stomach churning with loyalty divided. I hadn't expected my shamelessness to take a toll on the people I loved, and certainly not on people who did not deserve punishment.

Then, when I was at wit's end, when I was certain he'd wallow in low spirits forever, he came back to me, the husband I knew, jovial and erudite and eager to please. Just as suddenly as he had descended into gloom, he soared into cheer. He visited me in the painting room to offer encouragement and to ask if there was anything I might need. And he listened with rapt attention whether I was explaining how to use a pumice stone or how to prepare the canvas with a porridge made of flour, cooking oil, and honey. I glowed with pleasure at his interest.

We also returned to our public life, at first only with family because that's where Françesc felt most at ease and then with a wider group of friends. Though I found my mother-in-law to be fatuous and my father-in-law lacking in morals, these traits were offset by the laughs I shared with Joana. At the time, Joana, beautiful Joana, was again in full bloom, her belly round and hard as a melon. In contrast to my own short, tormented pregnancy, she radiated a happiness that was contagious, and everyone, from the Moorish enslaved girl to the stable grooms, longed to satisfy her every whim. As for her husband, Gabriel, he was still arrogant and inconsiderate, and I viewed his gross infidelities as terribly injurious to Joana's tender heart. Of course, I never mentioned any of these partialities or antipathies to Françesc. How could I, when I myself was tainted by sinful choices? Was it Matthew or Luke who warned us in the Holy Book that we were to take the plank out of our own eye before we could remove the speck from our brother's?

Eventually my husband, fully recovered, took to the road once again, and though his departure saddened me, I was, as Joana had predicted, getting used to our separations—separations made easier to bear by his affectionate missives and the occasional pouch of gemstones delivered to my door. Also, once Françesc set out, my time became my own, to do as I pleased. In his absence I turned into another person: an unapologetic schemer, comfortable with personal contradictions and adept at intrigue.

By the time shadows lengthened and leaves fluttered to the ground, Miquel was back from his mission to Oran, and without thought to consequences, we revived our relationship in a matter of days. To justify the indefensible, I told myself that love was not meant to be finite. It couldn't be constrained like the strings on a vihuela or foreordained like the seeds in a pear. As creatures made in the image of God, we had no need to limit ourselves to a prescribed number of passions; our affection could be boundless, inexhaustible. In short, love expanded to accommodate circumstances. And it was this distorted logic that allowed me to reconcile my two warring halves, to make peace with whatever scruples I could still claim. I never sought absolution behind the confessional grill either, believing acknowledgment of this mortal sin to our family priest would destroy my life. The religious weren't above sharing—or blackmailing—as they saw fit.

Miquel and I seldom met in public, unless there was a plausible explanation for it, usually a joust or tournament at Plaça Fra Menors, where guild representatives flourished their damask standards and clergy paraded in their richly colored chasubles. For obvious reasons, we preferred the privacy of his small rented room, a natural choice for new lovers, especially adulterers. (Let's not mince words here. Our trysts, though not impossible to arrange, required deception, lying, and the duplicitous assists of the always willing Quirze.) When we were alone, far from the threat of spies and wagging tongues, we enjoyed discussing his writing and his unwavering hope for its success. He'd occasionally read to me from his work, acting each part in a way that might have served him well if he ever decided to perform on stage. During those years, he worked on two plays, both of which provided insight into his captivity in Algiers: *El Trato de Argel* and later *Los Baños de Argel*. That he chose to devote so much of his talent to a past that had stolen his youth proved that Miquel was tormented by this experience—and plagued by an unbecoming cynicism as well. Once, when he was sitting for me, we fell into a conversation about the residences lining Ample, particularly those of the dukes of Cardona and Sessa and the count of Santa Coloma.

"What braggarts!" he complained. "What gasbags!"

"I don't understand why you're so obsessed with those houses. They're just homes."

"Just homes?" he mocked "That's what you think?"

"Hold still. I want to make sure to get your mouth right." I ignored his deprecating tone and pretended to be engrossed in my drawing. I had told him that I needed to practice my burgeoning skills, but this was just an excuse to sketch his portrait. I wanted to make sure I had some record of his likeness when he left for Castile.

"You approve of excess and profligacy? You think that everyone lives in one of these grand palaces?"

"I think no such thing."

"Yes, you do, because you know little beyond your experience."

"I'm sure those residences can be found in Madrid too. They're hardly unique to Barcelona." I shaded his brows with quick, short strokes, trying to recreate how they provided shelter to those deep-set eyes that sent my heart aflutter.

"That's not the point, Dolça."

"What is the point then?"

"Their extravagance. Their flamboyance. And the contrast to the hunger of the hordes outside their doors."

I put my notebook and charcoal to one side and raised my head to face him without affectation. "You know what I think?" I said as sweetly as I could. "I think you speak from a place of envy. That's why you can't stop talking about them. I think that if given a chance, you would love to claim a *palau* as your own."

He glared at me. "Who wouldn't want to live in a palace instead of in a hostal where drunks constantly interrupt one's sleep? But in this world only those born into the right families have that privilege. The rest of us, we're nothing but cannon fodder, expendable, disposable, superfluous."

"The people who reside in these homes are deserving of them! They didn't steal them. Who do you think lives in such places?"

"Men of power and money."

"Like my father."

"And your husband."

"Miquel, is that what this is about? My husband? His family and his wealth? His ability to provide for me?"

He blanched, but in a quiet voice, he continued, "Without their patronage men like me, poets and playwrights, painters and sculptors, wouldn't be able to eat. Wouldn't be able to create, period."

"*Déu meu*, Miquel, that's an exaggeration, to be sure."

"Is it?" he said, raising his voice again. A vein pulsed in his neck. "You lead such a privileged life, every desire fulfilled, every want satisfied. You can no more recognize reality than a deaf man can hear a cathedral choir sing."

I was stunned. He had never spoken to me with such rancor. When I recovered my voice, I retorted, "How dare you! You don't even know what my life is like, and for your edification, señor, it isn't just carriages and masked balls."

Then I burst into tears. He hurried to my side and drew me close, kissed my lips, my neck, the inside of my arms, and slowly, with the tenderness conciliation inspires, took me to bed. He settled me on pillows and undressed me. There was a fury to our lovemaking that morning, a desperation that allowed us to overlook the chasm that divided us, the chasm that always would. But after that exchange, and for years to come, I wondered if his lengthy stays in Barcelona were as much about the potential for patronage as for the pleasure of my company.

That argument about extravagances would not be our only row during those almost two years Miquel resided in Barcelona. When, absent the possibility of a steady job, he finally decided to make his way back to his family, we quarreled again.

"Come with me, Dolça," he begged. "We can make a life together."

"You've asked that already, before leaving for Oran, and my answer hasn't changed. Cannot change."

"Why?"

"I'm married!"

"So? You wouldn't be the first or last woman to leave a marriage. My grandfather lived with his mistress for years."

"That's what you want? For me to live away from my family and in constant fear of legal and religious reprisals?"

He threw his hands up and then paced the room, an exercise that, despite the force of his steps, looked simultaneously comical and desperate, as the space was small and cramped. I was determined for him to understand my reasons, however. If I explained it as a matter of survival, perhaps it would be less of an affront.

"How would we survive, Miquel?" I asked, my tone gentler. "We must eat. We must bed somewhere. We must clothe and shod ourselves. And with what? You're destitute."

He stopped midstride. Bitterness rearranged the features of his face. The studious Miquel turned into a man I didn't know. "You underestimate me, my dear lady. I won't always be a poor nobody."

"Of course not, my heart. I'm simply being realistic about the present. Anyway, we don't have a lot of time before you leave. Let's not waste it in argument."

He didn't reply for a few long moments. And then this: "No relationship can survive selfishness."

"What do you mean? I'm being practical, not selfish."

"No, Dolça. You prefer the luxuries of the flesh to the comforts of the heart."

He might as well have clubbed me over the head. I shouldn't have been surprised, though. We wound those we love in varied ways, by outright betrayal, yes, but also with our words and with our silences, and by disappointments large and small. I've come to believe that the pain we inflict on lovers is unavoidable, the damage predetermined.

Miquel departed on the first of October, three days before Spain abandoned the Julian calendar for the Gregorian, a reform that saw the city feverishly preparing for famine and plague, for fires from the earth and lightning strikes from the sky. Nothing of this sort came to pass, but it wasn't until November that I, distracted by these superstitions, realized I was once again with child, once again sentenced to suffer through uncertainty.

My family could not have guessed at my anguish. Father was ecstatic at the possibility of an *hereu*, and Françesc immediately hired the city's best midwife, keeping her abreast of my progress to ensure her presence when needed, for she was much in demand among the wives (and mistresses) of the grantees. Mother was pleased by the selection because the old woman's reputation was impeccable—in other words, her name had never been linked with a single report of witchcraft use of the afterbirth. In addition, she had a birthing chair delivered to my home days before I retired to my bedchamber to await childbirth. Though it looked like a torture instrument, it had been in the family for at least three generations, and the adjustable arms and footrests were in surprisingly effective order. Not to be outdone, María gifted me a small wooden crucifix that had been carried by a crusader to the Holy Land, and Aldonça presented me with a silk pouch containing strands of hair from a saint.

None of this lessened my fear, though. Nothing could. When the contractions began early one morning, a nervous and excited Françesc sent word to the midwife and our mothers. He then took my hands in his.

"Be brave, wife," he said. "I know God and His Blessed Mother are here with us."

I smiled, though unease clouded my head. It was not the kind of preoccupation most mothers-to-be entertained. What if the babe resembled Miquel, if not at birth, then soon after?

Mother and Aldonça were the first to arrive, their plain attire and undressed hair a sign of their haste. They shooed away my husband and together began hanging tapestries of pastoral scenes over the windows to block out light. Soon enough the air had turned as suffocating as a tomb. Aldonça placed a small plaster statuette of Saint Margaret of Antioch, the patron saint of pregnant women, on a table and wrapped a prayer roll around my midsection to help with the delivery. Then she visited each corner of the room, murmuring prayers to ward off evil spirits. Mother felt my forehead and pronounced me free of fever, though later when my body shook with the spasms of labor, sweat would dampen my brow and soak right through my plain chemise.

"Your father is with Françesc downstairs," she said. Knowing they were nearby provided immeasurable comfort.

My nursemaid approached. "Try to relax, *maca*. God willing and with His Mother's grace, you'll do just fine."

María, Joana, and Glòria arrived later, and they echoed more prayers and petitions—but it wasn't enough. I screamed, and writhed, and cursed. I begged for death, but instead of deliverance the midwife forced me to sip from a bitter potion that tasted of vinegar and pomegranate seeds. Aside from the pain, the memories that surface now and then of those hours are like dabs of unused pigment on an easel, rich in hue but disconnected from each other. The shimmer of oil on the midwife's hands. The yellow of an amber stone placed on my undulating belly. The aroma of fennel from the ointment that eased the throbbing in my back. The susurration of orders. *Breathe. Blow through your mouth. Slow. Hold. The head is crowning. Now push*, maca, *push.*

The midwife sat on a low stool and arranged her hands to catch the child. Another push, and another, then a convulsion so fierce that I couldn't stop the overwhelming desire to shit.

"A boy! A boy!"

The child bellowed as if the world already belonged to him. The midwife held him aloft, all bald dome and flailing limbs, and with a knife she pulled from the leather sheath at her side cut the umbilical cord with one strike. When she placed the child on my breast, prayers rang around me, a chorus of gratitude. I stared with both awe and dread at his misshapen head and his slitted eyes, the pink bow of his puckered mouth, the balled fists, the dull gloss that filmed his body. His breathing echoed my own. And then just like that, he was taken away, washed in a basin, swaddled in strips of linen, and delivered to the wet nurse waiting in a room equipped with a cradle built by the *mestre* who was employed by Françesc's family. Before the week was up, my son was baptized, but as was typical of the day, I didn't attend the short ceremony. Joana described it for me in minute detail, though: the sound of my boy's lusty wails and the morning light as it striped the font with a radiance that meant God was smiling upon us.

I didn't leave my bedchamber for a month and saw my son only as Mother deemed appropriate, when I stopped bleeding and color had returned to my cheeks. Perforce my life changed. I didn't pick up chalk, charcoal, or brush for more than three years, which pleased Mother, who liked me more when I assumed the role she had always envisioned for me. My transformation, if I may label it so, proved effortless. I was entranced by the beauty and bounty of my baby. After the first six or seven months, his face turned cherubic and plump rolls creased his doughy flesh. I enjoyed inhaling his milk breath and insisted on observing the nursemaid as she powdered him with wood dust after changing his linen diaper.

Françesc was equally enamored of him. Then and again he would ask, "Who do you think he takes after?"

My jaw would clench, my stomach somersault. "It's too early to tell, husband."

"Doesn't he resemble me?"

Françesc appeared certain of the answer, so I'd quietly smile and hide trembling hands in the folds of my skirt.

In the spring of 1585, after the publication of *La Galatea*, Miquel reappeared in Barcelona—rather unexpectedly, I might add. During our separation, we had exchanged only two letters, and I hadn't answered his third, as I had suffered two miscarriages and was particularly disconsolate the second time. Françesc was, as usual, supportive and tender, never speaking a cross word or accusation, but I couldn't help but feel inadequate after each calamity. The bloodied sheets, the lying-in after the cramps, and the fever—all were a form of celestial judgment that would have been avoided had I been more virtuous, of that I was certain. At any rate, Miquel's missives could never have been mistaken for love notes; every page lacked intimacy and emotion. I think he wrote—and I answered—out of a sense of obligation and shared history. With characteristic eloquence, he detailed his brother Rodrigo's soldiering adventures and his delight that he had been contracted to write two plays. He also mentioned his move to Esquivias, though he gave no reason for this unusual relocation from Madrid. I would discover his motive later, and it would wound me deeply. But really, how could I fault him for wanting to forge a life for himself?

To Miquel's first request for an audience, I answered curtly, as Françesc intended to remain home until Easter, which arrived late in April that year. From Mother, however, I knew Miquel already had visited them, impressing my parents with his travel tales and his new cosmopolitan apparel. I supposed that Father had forgiven him for that moment of indiscretion so long ago. (Or maybe, knowing the prevailing thought of the day, I had been blamed for tempting a usually upright and judicious man.) Regardless of that revived relationship, I behaved on my own accord, without consulting anyone. When Françesc departed for Valencia, hoping to establish new trading partnerships in this southern city, I waited a respectable two days before sending for Miquel. I told myself that I was doing this only because I owed him an explanation about Jaume.

Mother was right: Miquel looked different. When a maid showed him into the formal chamber where we entertained guests, I couldn't help but notice his new boots and the doublet of expensive green brocade. He, in turn, examined the room, which was filled with impressive furnishings: a small trestle table of lustrous walnut with a hexagonal tile top, a gilded cabinet inlaid with ivory, a settee with a carved back, and several sgabello chairs imported from Naples. Best of all, or at least my favorite item, was the hand-woven rug from Alcaraz, with its bright yellows and deep reds.

"Are you still painting?" he asked, when we sat across from each other, I on the settee and he in one of the chairs.

"No. It's been many months since I've even tried. I'm a mother now."

"Oh yes. A boy child. Congratulations. How old?"

"Two years, this month next."

I imagined him counting backward and expected a smile of recognition. None was forthcoming. I reconsidered my idea to tell him about my concerns over Jaume's parentage, but he interrupted my thoughts with the unexpected: "Well, I have news of my own. I married this past December."

I felt the blood drain from my face. Had I not been seated, I would have fainted. Thankfully my dove-gray damask hid my shaking legs. "Congratulations to you as well," I mumbled.

"Her name is Catalina. She's twenty years old."

Miquel, at eight and thirty, was old enough to be her father.

He then added, in a rather caustic tone, "She's an old Christian."

"Beneficial for employment and patronage then."

"I also have a daughter."

At this point, words abandoned me. I stared at my hands, the gems on each ring winking in the morning light. Perhaps the marriage had been arranged hastily, forced. "An infant still?" I asked.

He guffawed. "In a sense. My Isabel was born in September to Ana Franca de Rojas and her husband, the trader Alonso Rodriguez."

I started, the meaning of his revelation striking me all at once. If this was true, his daughter had been born to his married mistress three months before his nuptials. Was he interested only in wedded women then, since they required no responsibility? Did my son, if the boy was Miquel's, have a half sister?

"Catalina is a fine woman," Miquel continued, oblivious to my dismay. "We've settled in her family home in Esquivias."

"It's bitterly cold there in the winter, no?" I knew I was babbling but couldn't think of anything else to say.

Before he could answer, one of the maids entered the room to ask if I needed her to serve a platter of cheeses and bread. I leaped at the chance to extricate myself from what was becoming an increasingly awkward conversation.

"That's not necessary," I said. "My cousin is getting ready to leave."

Miquel eyed me with surprise, but he stood anyway, his new boots squeaking at the effort. "As always." He bowed deeply. "It's been a pleasure."

"Mine as well." My sarcasm was barely contained, and I couldn't resist one last volley. "I'm sorry you didn't meet my son. He'd remind you of Françesc."

The truth was my son looked like no one but himself. At that age his complexion was pasty, his hair sparse, and his body so squat some might have mistaken him for a court dwarf. No one could have guessed his parentage, no. But I did entertain some very private doubts.

I wouldn't see Miquel again until several weeks later, on the Thursday of Corpus Christi. In Barcelona, this is a holiday of great rejoicing, and while the solemnity of Easter can be inspiring—churches decorated with rows of white wax tapers, penitents bearing crowns of thorns— our observance of the festival of the Holy Sacrament is endowed with a different beauty altogether. Consider the carpets of flowers that color the streets of villages like Sitges. Or the *gegants i capgrossos* with their giant papier-mâché heads. Or the majesty of *consell* members and priests as they escort the Host to the cathedral. Such ritual, such performance!

As custom demanded, acolytes in the cathedral had decorated a cloister fountain with seasonal flowers—carnations and common borage, roses, lilies, and weaver's broom—to prepare the setting for *l'ou com balla*, or the dancing egg. This beloved tradition calls for an egg to be emptied and sealed with wax, then placed atop the spray of the fount, where it twirls and tumbles on the spurting water. This fascinating little trick is a favorite of the faithful, and I wanted to introduce my son to it. I never considered we might run into Miquel. Thankfully we were surrounded by people, many pushing to get a better view of the dancing egg, when Miquel approached. He was the first to speak.

"So, this is your son." He addressed me loudly, the better to be heard over the raucous throng. "Two years old, you said."

"Two and a few weeks," I replied curtly. I could feel Mother's stare on me, and those of my aunts.

Miquel observed Jaume with an unreadable expression, but my son, in the arms of his sturdy nursemaid, didn't even glance his way, preferring to play with Joana's eldest son, who was amusing him with a dragon puppet.

"He takes after you."

"That seems to be the case," I lied. Thankfully, the always perceptive Joana interrupted our chance meeting with a distraction of some kind, and by the time I realized it, Miquel had disappeared into the crowd. I sighed with both relief and regret; Mother had not stopped observing me.

But our desire for each other could not be tamped down as easily as loose soil over seeds. It was inevitable we would become lovers again, though my surrender would require time. In the beginning we struggled through a reacquainting period, our affection limited to shy touching and sly smiles and lively stories, always stories. Mostly these were about his travels, people he had met, and events he had witnessed. As a raconteur extraordinaire, Miquel was generous in describing friends who supported him—Fortuny, a Valencian, and a favorite niece, Constanza—but he reserved a biting disdain for the dramaturge Félix Lope de Vega y Carpio, a man as famous for his illicit liaisons as for his growing oeuvre.

"He's overrated, puffed up, and egotistical," Miquel ranted, then and again.

I, however, never opined about my competition, the famous painters of the moment, as I had never met any of them, nor did I feel my limited work to be worthy of recognition.

Our conversations were always garnished with cheap jug wine, the only kind he could afford to serve and which I therefore learned to tolerate. As in his past visits, I resumed my attempts to sketch him, and I was able to finish several portraits, capturing with accuracy the receding hairline, the squinting eyes under uneven eyebrows, the sensual mouth set between mustache and beard. When I expressed frustration, he replied reassuringly, "Mastery's a long process and ever so elusive."

I didn't glance up from my paper to read his face but understood he was speaking from experience.

We had moments of great physical passion, of course, the pleasure so exquisite that to recall them now is to experience the heat and tremors again, but there also were times when we settled on the familiar in perfunctory service to our bodies. My favorite times, to be sure, came after lovemaking when we lingered in bed without speaking, without thinking, touching, touching, touching, fingers like feathers, breath the warmth of a hundred braziers. My head on his chest, I could hear his heartbeat, a cadence both exotic and ordinary.

Make what you'd like of all this. Judge as you please. After all, opinions are as common as fleas in straw. I acknowledge that many might think there was no justification for my actions. Certainly, I could no longer claim the forgiving mantle of inexperienced youth. So why did I risk my good name, my place in polite society, for a married man who had scant to offer? And more: why didn't I tell Miquel about his son when it became obvious to whom Jaume owed his looks?

I can answer those questions in so many different ways—mostly with convoluted rationalizations and laughable lies. Only now do I understand the convenience of self-deception, how its continual exercise can legitimize what is indefensible. But truly, the abiding reason for what I did, the most relevant one was this: I loved Miquel, and loved him in my own way, with a strange kind of greed and not just because he was what I could not have. I loved the excitement he brought into my life and the sense, however tenuous, that I was free to do as I pleased.

My behavior did not go unnoticed, though. How could it, in a city where everyone knew my family? Soon after Jaume turned five years old, my parents requested I come to their house alone. I worried they would deliver unpleasant news about my father's health as he had been nursing a cough for several weeks. But when we convened in Father's library, I quickly surmised that the topic of our conversation would involve a different kind of unpleasantness.

"It has come to our attention," Father began, as he shut the door firmly, "that you have sought out a type of entertainment unworthy of your station."

"Unworthy of your marriage vows as well," Mother added.

I had not yet been asked to sit when these words were uttered in a most matter-of-fact tone, and my knees buckled. I would have toppled to the floor had my father, on his way back to his desk chair, not scooped me up and set me down on a bench. Stricken, I searched my mother's face for some form of reprieve or mercy, but the sternness writ there was its own message. I opened my mouth to deny their accusations.

"Stop!" Father said. "Don't lower yourself to lying."

"Your behavior is shameful enough. It's beyond embarrassment. You must end this . . . this . . . abomination immediately."

"Before your husband gets wind of it."

"D-d-does he . . . he know?" My voice rang faintly.

"If he doesn't," my mother retorted, "he soon will."

I buried my face in my hands, hoping one of them would provide a few words of comfort, but this act of contrition did nothing to change the bitter disappointment and resentful anger that hung in the air. I tried a different tack.

"How did you—"

"That's not important now, Dolça," Father said. "It matters only as proof that you're not fooling anyone."

"You're lucky that we've managed to contain the scandal."

"Contain the scandal?" I straightened my shoulders. "What do you mean?"

"Again, it doesn't matter. But it's fortunate we intervened when we did."

I didn't know what kind of intervention Mother meant, and I didn't dare ask. So many possibilities, and all of them frightening. The frantic pace of my thoughts was matched by my racing heart.

Mother motioned for me to stand, and when I couldn't, when my legs refused to cooperate—such was my paralyzing disorientation—she marched over and yanked me up by my arms. She then dragged me to Father's desk as if I were nothing more than a slothful maid. He pushed the inkpot and a sheet of paper over to me.

"You will write a note and we will have it delivered to Miguel immediately," Mother said.

"And you are to never see him again."

"But, Father, that's impossible. Miquel's part of our—"

Before I could finish, my father jumped up from his seat and slapped me. I was so stunned I felt no pain. I couldn't even manage tears. Father had never struck me. Never.

With a trembling hand, I wrote what Father dictated: *Miquel, I can no longer see you. Do not call on me. Do not write me. Dolça.*

When the ink had dried and the note was sealed, Father turned to Mother: "Get her out of my sight."

Though humiliation weighed heavy on my chest, I felt fortunate that Jaume's parentage had not been questioned. That . . . that would have done me in.

I did not visit my parents for several weeks after that meeting, not until we were invited as a family to a celebration of Mother's birthday. The strain between us lasted for years, and our relationship, I believe, never truly recovered. To this day that has been one of my greatest regrets. As for Françesc, I observed his every gesture and clung to his every word, fearful that my mother's prediction would come true. But if my husband had any inkling of how I had spent my time during his travels, I could not tell. He continued being his affable self, an exemplary gentleman. I, on the other hand, could barely get out of bed, as much from shame as from the disillusionment I had caused my parents. I lost my appetite, refused social invitations, and did not set foot in my studio for months. Troubled by my listlessness, Françesc arranged for us to visit his family's country home with Joana and Gabriel. Spending time with Joana and watching Jaume ride his pony and play with his cousins brought me a small measure of consolation but no self-forgiveness.

I kept true to my word and didn't see Miquel again for almost a decade. Within days of my meeting with Father and Mother, he left suddenly for a surprise commission in Sevilla and was later assigned to Écija, where he served as a commissary. This must have been an unenviable job as people always resist paying taxes, especially with fanegas of wheat that can feed their families. Quirze confided that Miquel rarely went home to his wife and that excepting his *Dos Odas sobre l'Armada*, he didn't write or publish during that time. In spite of my request for no contact, he penned letters to me, ones I never answered but that I kept—foolishly, as it turns out—in a coffer hidden in my room. If anything, I think our long separation fueled his fantasies instead of quelling them. As for me, that estrangement reinforced a lesson I had learned from my husband's travels: absence is the handmaiden to longing.

As in my own life, those last years of the eighties were fraught with strife for my compatriots. The pirate Francis Drake sacked Spanish ports, our enemies in the Low Countries proliferated, and the English defeated King Philip's invincible armada in an embarrassing days-long battle. These calamities were followed by inflation, a scarcity of basic staples, and disease. Death, death, and more death. In a span of weeks, la peste decimated my family. Mother and Father succumbed first, and then Joana and my mother-in-law, along with most of Glòria's brood.

And while losing one's parents is devastating, an unmendable culling of the past, the death of a trusted friend is a savage stab-and-twist to the gut. Joana had been a sister, an ally, the woman who loved and counseled me without judgment or self-interest. Forever generous, she had offered me refuge, humor, and wisdom. She was irreplaceable, and I wept knowing that a confidant is worth more than all the gold in the world. I miss her still.

I must note that we survived the plague because Françesc, ever quick-thinking, shuttered the house on Carrer Ample and transported us all—furniture, crockery, chests, and bulging saddlebags—to the family *masia*. After that endless, terrible year, I would always associate the countryside he so loved with the crushing pain of loss.

Chapter 10

From Calatayud we travel all night, guided by stars and a generous slice of moon. Darkness doubles as a velvet cloak, both concealing and welcoming. I'm surprised by this because I rarely venture out late anymore and never into the wilds, where the menacing grunt of a nocturnal creature is far more common than a watchman's friendly warning. Though I was quite fatigued when we started, the rhythmic drumbeat of hooves has invigorated me, as has the tight hold of Anna's thin arms around my waist. I'm wide awake now, sight sharpened and hearing keen. My hands remain strong and steady on the reins. The growing stiffness of my body, the soreness in my throat are easier to endure, if not to ignore altogether. We're but five days from Madrid, no more than six, and knowing I'll soon see Miquel, knowing I'll finally unburden myself, is like a magical elixir. Now all we must do is elude my son—no small feat. In this vast country, he already has succeeded in finding me once.

El Musulmán is never farther than a whisper. We rarely speak, however, maybe because he's fearful of being overheard by bandits, maybe because he's a man who understands this is not the time for trivial conversation. When the giant does talk, it's to give instructions with a voice that blends into the shadows around us. "Go right," he'll say. Or, "Watch that boulder."

We follow a path guided by the sloshing sounds of a creek, not the royal highway that tracks the Jalón, and we rise and descend on gravel and rocks until we settle into a vale. I suspect he's chosen this seldom-used route the better to avoid attention. At first, I can discern only bare mountains in the distance, a jagged outline against the opaque horizon, but when the moon shines especially bright, I spot the outline of vineyards and farms, fruit trees and fields, and an occasional unidentifiable animal sitting on its haunches with luminous yellow eyes directed at us. Eventually, this valley becomes broader, or at least it feels so, and the creek's gurgle grows louder, gains strength. We pass over a bridge of three arches, not far from a lofty tower that inclines to one side, before returning to our hidden trail. Then we cross into another valley, this one carpeted with mysterious undergrowth, and spot two men running past us like jackrabbits fleeing a fox. Though I'm unsettled by their sudden appearance, I don't ask about them. Anybody traveling in darkness is hiding from someone, as we are.

As the night progresses, my strength wanes. My legs and arms turn heavy and my muscles ache. Breath rattles in my chest. I think Anna has managed to fall asleep, the slumber of the young, because I can feel her head on my back. I consider requesting a few minutes of rest but settle instead for a gulp of watered wine. We need to put as many leagues as possible between us and those who'll make chase from Calatayud. I don't doubt that Jaume will be in rabid pursuit as soon as he realizes I've fled. My son hates being defied, and he doesn't take well to being fooled. He'll storm about the venta, his anger echoing like thunder. He'll question Xirau, the innkeeper's wife, perhaps even the other muleteers. But if copper coins purchased information on my whereabouts for Jaume, they can also ensure secrecy for us. El Musulmán has seen to that.

After passing several signs of civilization—church spires jutting into the sky, wreaths of white smoke curling from homesteads, shepherds sleeping with their flocks—El Musulmán halts our lonely progress and helps us down from the mule. I struggle to recuperate my balance, and my hips creak as I totter over the wild grass. Anna, on the other hand, is as spry as a deer. He brings out a chunk of black bread and more wine, and the three of us sit in silent communion, listening to the crickets' cacophonous song. He says we're near Alhama de los Baños, a village well known for its salutary hot springs.

"If only we weren't renegades of the road," I jest, pressing one hand to the small of my back. "Those curative waters would be of help to me now."

"And for me, no doubt." He groans in sympathy and then smiles. "The Moors built those baths and what, alas, was the result? Yet another fine deed forgotten."

I chew on the gummy bread in silence. If I possessed any energy, I'd remind him of the history lessons that date as far back as the ancients: conquerors take without asking and display neither gratitude nor humility, only greed. But no use expending effort on what can't be changed.

We climb back on our mounts and head into the awakening horizon. Fantastical colors—vermilion, orpiment, glair, and honey—streak the sky as it lightens into day. Soon after the sun has climbed high enough to insult our eyes, we make camp in an abandoned farmhouse infused with the stench of horse dung and piss. We bed for a few hours, but I'm not used to sleeping on a dirt-packed floor and hardly rest. Amazed at her adaptability, I observe Anna curled into a tidy ball, oblivious to the sounds and smells that make my skin crawl. I envy her detachment. At the moment I don't realize this roofless structure will be the best accommodations on our way to Guadalajara.

On the second night, the trail leads into woods so impenetrable that El Musulmán must hack away at branches with his sword to secure a wider passage for us. Sometimes we halt completely because we can't see beyond our mules' muzzles. Pressed against my back, Anna vibrates with fear.

"Are there evil spirits here, señora?" she asks, her voice barely above a whisper.

"No, child."

"But I feel something following us."

"Your imagination is playing tricks on you."

"Are you sure?"

"Of course."

I'm not sure of anything but know that if I do not lie, if I display weakness, it will frighten Anna even more. The forest with its shadows and murmurings feels like the perfect site for a satanic cult or a witch's coven. Even El Musulmán senses danger, for he rides with his back as straight as a blade. At one point, he lights a small torch and has me hold it up to illuminate our path. The effort is more exhausting than I might have imagined, and I worry about setting the trees on fire. The air reeks of smoke and something metallic, like blood. Brambles cling to our clothes. But then at last the tangled boughs give way to a clearing, and the three of us exhale an audible sigh that sounds like wind through leaves. Anna even breaks into song, and the giant and I surprise her by joining in on the refrain: *Fa la la lan, fa lan, fa la la lera. Fa la la lan, de la guarda riera.* We've turned giddy with relief.

This diversion is short-lived. Soon enough the tips of my ears burn; my face tingles. The horizon sways. My eyes refuse to focus. As we approach Medinaceli, having crossed from the kingdom of Aragón into New Castile without fanfare, chills wrack my body, and before dawn, with still a few hours left to ride, we're forced to seek shelter under a copse of leafy trees. Though a magpie screeches in protest, I fall asleep, insensible to the hard ground, head resting on a thick root. I can smell my own sweat.

I awaken at dusk, feeling slightly better. Anna insists I fortify myself with food and drink and offers a heel of bread and a wedge of cheese from our supplies, but the mere thought of chewing exhausts me. Her little hands shake as she carefully tips the wineskin to my mouth. Tears prick my eyes. Though Anna is ever attentive, I miss Aldonça, her skills and her knowledge; she would have been at the ready with a tonic to cure what ails me. Such a good and faithful servant! But I must not think of her. I should not, cannot, if I'm to continue this journey.

Remarking on my paleness and puffy eyes, El Musulmán asks if I feel strong enough to ride through the night. I insist we do, with more vehemence than necessary. So at the first failure of light, we take to the road again, following a winding path up a mountain that El Musulmán says is part of La Sierra de Cuenca. The treacherous terrain is made worse by the difficulty of clearly seeing what lies ahead, but he lacks no confidence, and I trust him. Once we have achieved the summit and entered a parched plain, however, my feverish shivering begins again.

"She's not well," Anna calls out in alarm. "We should stop."

El Musulmán wheels around. "*Senyora?*"

I wave away his concern. We've already suffered too many delays, and the specter of Jaume in chase is reason enough to make me want to forge ahead, though I'm uncertain how long I can stay upright. We continue into the darkness, every step a small torture. Mercifully El Musulmán assures us that we're very close to our next resting place, but I have no energy to inquire about the exact distance. Before us and around us, the landscape spreads out into barren hills, distant mountains, flatland destitute of trees, all shaded by the faint shine of the waxing moon. I lose track of time, unable to perceive the movement of the stars. My head feels so large and my neck so weak that I lean over the saddle and rest on the mule's mane. Anna leans in with me. The animal smells of hay, of life hard-lived. My clothes smother me, but when I try to throw off my shawl, Anna fastens her arms around my shoulders, effectively pinning me. El Musulmán shouts something I can't puzzle out. He's never used that tone in my presence, and thus I'm forced to suffer the heat, my body a crackling fire fueled by all this unnecessary wool.

We cross a river. The Henares, El Musulmán says. Why is he shouting when we should be discreet? The moon disappears. Light the color of ashes seeps into the horizon. In the distance the leaves of young wheat plants wave; a farmhouse darkens the horizon. The mules' hooves pound the red clay. My back throbs. My joints hurt. My heart pounds against my chest. My hands slip from the reins. I can't breathe. I can't see. But I hear Jaume's voice, his reproaches flung in my face.

The world dims and then darkens into nothing.

A woman addresses me in Castilian. I don't understand a single word. Such nonsense she speaks.

Anna clings to me. Furrows of concern climb her forehead.

A man flings my saddlebag over his shoulder, but I can't find my voice to protest. How dare he take my belongings so brazenly!

El Musulmán—he knows what I need. To Madrid, to Madrid. We mustn't stop. Not to eat. Not to rest. Not for Jaume or Aldonça or the rising sun. Not for death.

Miquel visits first, just as thunder explodes inside my head, a sound so violent my teeth chatter. He's young, bobbed hair the color of roasted chestnuts, beard a burnt gold. He smiles in the beguiling way he once had, before we . . . simply before. *Before expectations. Before spouses and children. Before demands and interferences.*

"Dolça, I've been waiting for you!"

"I'm here. I've kept true to my promise."

"I'm surprised."

"Why?"

"Because you've never kept a promise before."

"With good reason, Miquel. I was not free to make a promise of that kind."

"Or so you claimed. How many times did I not plead for you to join your life to mine?"

I ignore the barb and change the subject. "I've come to tell you something important."

"What could be more important than your presence, the loveliness of your face, the music of your voice?"

"Enough with your pretty words." I blush, and since there's no other way to declare this, I say it straight: "You have a son."

He doesn't appear to understand: "A daughter, dearest. A daughter named Isabel, and not a fine one at that."

"But you also have a son. He goes by Jaume Françesc Carles d'Oms Llull."

Disbelief erases his smile. "Always I've wanted a son, an heir. Now you stand before me to say this is true, yet he bears the name of another."

"I didn't know he was yours until . . . well, until long after he was baptized."

"And you've not said a word of this to me for all these many years?"

Do I detect an accusatory tone? Or is that inflection disappointment? Both. I touch his arm. He reaches for my face.

"Does he know I'm his father?"

I look away. I'm well aware of my cowardice, but to have someone else recognize it is a different matter altogether. "Until recently I . . . I thought it best for him and for you that neither should know."

"Best for me?" he scoffs. "I'd say it served you and only you."

"What do you mean?"

Though I rush to hold him close, Miquel vanishes. He has left, he is gone, and my heart is rent by his rejection.

A cloth rests on my forehead, another along my nape, both so cold, so cold. Oh, my head! I'm not certain if my eyes are open or shut. I cannot make out my surroundings, but it appears as if I've been laid to rest in a hole as deep and black as a crypt.

"A tavern wench!" I shout. "How could you! I'm the laughingstock of Barcelona."

Miquel winces at my words, his face a mask of horror. "It's not true, not true at all."

"What's not true? What part of your book?"

"Dulcinea is a character, nothing more. Readers know that."

"Says you. Everyone I know whispers about me behind closed doors."

"Dolça—"

"Don't touch me. Don't come to me with excuses and explanations. What good are they to me now? The world knows who I am, what we've done."

No improvement, no, says the woman with a voice as thin as a reed. But she keeps calling out a name in her delirium. Over and again she calls. Same name. Who could it be? Her husband?

Should we send for the priest?

I lie on a cold, uneven floor, face up, legs outstretched, arms at my side. Paralyzed. My eyes, however, beam through the dark, and there, in the spectral light, Françesc's children hover above me, their cherubic faces perfect reflections of his. They have come for me. The babes I miscarried, the babes I couldn't save. The babes I might have raised if not for the unforgivable iniquity I chose time and again.

I crave their silky skin, their downy heads, their warmth on my chest. My babies. But I refuse to go where they want to take me.

Hush now, hush. All is well. You're hallucinating. There are no babies here.

I move. A hand. My leg.

Señora, you must drink. Try a drop, a sip. This potion will do you good.

We are to host a party for Aldonça, her upcoming nuptials long delayed. It will rival a royal celebration. Forty hams. Twenty casks of wine. Thirty partridges, five-and-twenty hens. No stinting on the pine nuts or raisins. Oranges, pears, grapes, and melons too, fresh and candied. Bread, the best and whitest.

She asks for pa amb tomàquet? *Bread with tomatoes? How absolutely pedestrian, but if it pleases my nursemaid, so be it. Purchase the olive oil from Siurana. No other place produces such quality.*

Give her a pomegranate tree too, and four of fig. Her bridegroom, whom I haven't met, will receive a silk levacap, *the better to cover his bald head.*

Who's this Aldonça she asks for?

Isn't there anything else we can do? Surely there is. A poultice? A brew?

Françesc opens his arms. I hurry to him and bury my face in his embroidered doublet the color of fresh cream.

"Dear wife."

"Françesc, I'm aflame. The heat, it doesn't let me breathe. I'm burning for my sins. Françesc!"

He takes a step back. Behind him . . .

"Mother? Father? Àvia!"

I'm a cold mountain stream, running headlong through gully and gorge on my way to a finale that is more majestic, more infinite than anything I could have imagined. Only in retrospect do I see the full story of my days, beginning to end, only in review can I appreciate how decisions I made, whether in haste or in leisure, whether out of conviction or out of convenience, have molded the life I now leave. So bittersweet, this leaving, leaving, leaving.

And then I return. I am of this world again because of a familiar voice, its timbre so dear that I want to dance with joy. But I cannot move my limbs, only open my eyes, lift my head.

"Be still, Mother. Don't fatigue yourself. You must rest."

My son is here.

My son is here to fetch me.

My son is here to fetch me back to Barcelona. I cannot go.

"Where am I?"

"The fever's broken," he says in response. "Thanks be to God."

"Jaume?"

"Shush! Close your eyes now."

I do as I'm told and slip into a world that is neither here nor there, neither past nor present, real or imagined. I am surrounded by memories. The tinkle of a tambourine, the honk of a goose. The weight of a lace mantilla on my head. New grass, warm wind, slanted afternoon sun as clear as chicken broth. A laugh that froths like breaking waves. On my cheek the scrape of beard stubble, in my grip the yield of a new charcoal stick. The scent of civet and the stink of cod in Cook's kitchen. A plate of green olives. Colorful stains on my painting smock. Fleeting impressions they are, and not mine to keep.

A chair scraping against the floor wakens me, and now I'm fully conscious. I don't know how long I've been asleep.

"I'll be back, Mother. I'm going to bring you something to eat."

After my son leaves, I open my eyes again. Weak light filters under and around the window curtains, a warrior skulking into battle. Morning or eventide, I'm uncertain of which. I don't recognize my surroundings. The bed is comfortable, its pillows firm and the linens as smooth as those I left behind at home. I attempt to sit up, only to realize this ordinary effort is much too difficult. My heart flutters and I must rest before trying again. Finally, I balance on my elbows and examine the bedchamber.

The room is spacious and the furniture pleasing without resorting to extravagance: a brazier, a large carved trunk, a fine desk with three small drawers, and a lovely prie-dieu. Delicate flasks of perfume sit on a dressing table, next to a silver hairbrush. A large tapestry of snowcapped mountains hangs on the opposite wall. A woman's room, that much I can guess. But whose? Where? How did I end up here?

Dizzy with exertion, I lower myself onto the pillows and consider those questions. I feel as if I've emerged from a fugue state. The last I recall is a canopy of stars and a stone bridge over green river waters. The moon like a scythe. A whiff of hay and an insufferable heat. Beasts baying in the distance. And somewhere in the recesses of those vague recollections, the jowly face of a thick-browed woman speaking nonsense to me. I know these experiences to be real, but they exist far away, in an unreachable dimension. Confused, I sink further into the pillows. What's that foul smell of rot? I sniff and then realize I'm the one who smells of death. My face burns with shame. And in a trice it comes to me, the reason I am where I shouldn't be. I swallow hard, recalling my intimacy with death.

There was a fathomless depth, but also light so brilliant my eyes were blinded. Dark-light, light-dark, days sliding one into the other. I remember the sensation of having left my body, a realization that I was one with both light and dark, and that light could not be separated from the dark, nor exist without an opposing presence, much in the same way a reflection cannot be removed from a mirror. Am I making sense? Has illness robbed me of reason? Also, this place of dark-and-light was crowded with people, those I've loved and those I've long forgotten. They were draped in the most exquisite silk, leather as buffed as a royal saddle, and velvet so plush it would have incited a queen's jealousy. Together we floated, side by side. And though they were there, everywhere, around and above and behind, these people who had populated my life, they couldn't be touched. They were the glimmer of a candle and the shadow of a cloud, ephemeral. Together and alone, they were specter, spirit, ghost. I might have remained with them if not for a duty unmet. I knew then, as I know now, that I was expected in Madrid.

Yes, Madrid! I can't continue to dawdle here. However many days I've spent abed have served only to delay my reunion with Miquel. Newly energized, I call out for El Musulmán, but try as I might, no sound comes out. Instead, I emit a kind of scratchy rasp that claws at my scorched throat. My second attempt is like a dog's bark, unintelligible. I fear I've lost the power to speak, or at the very least, my speech has weakened along with my limbs. This diminished strength frightens me more than the unfamiliar surroundings. Location one can change, but to be silenced, to be . . . I shudder. Goose bumps make me look like a defeathered fowl.

I call again for El Musulmán. Silence echoes in response.

Within a day, perhaps two, the giant with the wandering eye does pay me a visit. By then Jaume has explained that I've been ill for a week with a mysterious fever that led to delirium.

"I have failed you, *senyora*," El Musulmán laments. "We didn't reach Madrid."

"That is not your failure, good man. I took ill. My health, and perhaps my age as well, defeated us."

Seated in a chair across the room, he glances over at Anna in the corner and then stares glumly at his riding boots. He's avoiding my eyes, that's clear to see. Though still in bed, I'm freshly washed, dressed in a white high-necked shift bordered in lace. Anna has drawn my hair back in a simple braid and sprinkled it with lavender water. I want for nothing; Jaume has seen to that. Nevertheless, I look like a faded copy of the woman I once was.

El Musulmán fiddles with a red *barretina*.

"I see you've adopted the head covering of my people," I say, hoping to ease his discomfort.

"Oh, this?" He grins sheepishly. "It's not mine. It's Xirau's."

I recall the muleteer's first visit to Carrer Ample, how the *barretina* sat on his knee while we negotiated the terms of the trip. How long ago that seems! A lifetime at least!

"How did it come to be in your possession?"

"Xirau gave it to me. Those of us who make our life on the road believe that any day might be our last. He meant the *barretina* as a blessing for our journey. He was worried about the ordeals we might confront traveling at night."

I'm confused. Did El Musulmán confide in Xirau about our escape from Calatayud?

"You will forgive me?" El Musulmán insists.

"Forgive you? Whatever do you mean?"

"When you fainted after crossing the Henares, I sent for your son. I was fearful of how God would punish me if you died far from family and faith. We pass to eternal life but once."

"You need no forgiveness from me. You did what was true to your heart and by doing so you probably saved my life."

He dares to meet my eyes. "I hope your search is fruitful in Madrid."

"I'm certain it will be."

He stands to take his leave, but I motion for him to retake his seat. His visit has raised questions and doubts, and he may be the only person willing to divulge the truth. After he sits, I fold my bony hands in my lap.

"So Xirau knew we would leave Calatayud without him and the rest of the men?"

"Yes, of course. I told him. You must understand that I owe much to this man. For me to flee without a word is not fair repayment."

"He didn't attempt to stop you? Counsel you to warn my son?"

"Of course not. You hired him, not Don Jaume."

I fidget, rearrange the bed covers, and consider this concept. For some time now, I have considered Xirau and his brother, Gerard, as the men most likely to have informed Jaume about my destination, facilitating his untimely intervention after that horrible auto–da–fé. The brothers had much to gain by keeping my son versed on our whereabouts. My one payment for this godforsaken trek could not possibly match the promise of future employment and pay.

"I'm puzzled by what you've told me," I say.

"*Senyora?*"

"You say Xirau knew we would flee from my son and did nothing to stop us. But then . . . then . . . oh my thoughts are so jumbled."

"You must not trouble yourself with these worries. They'll cloud the mind and impair the spirit."

"But I must know. It's a matter that has concerned me since Calatayud. How did my son know where to find us? He said bribes led him to us, but I doubt that. And I made certain to not breathe a word about our trip to anyone in Barcelona. Was it one of the men who informed on me?"

El Musulmán laughs. "Not I. Not the others. Truly you do not know?"

"Of course not. Why would I be asking?"

"Oh, my dear *senyora*, it was your nursemaid. She sent a message to him from your cousin's house. She knew she was dying and wanted to make sure you would be safe when she passed."

My breath catches. "Aldonça?"

"Yes, the very same."

"That's not possible. She would never betray me. She was like my mother. No, more than my mother. A friend. My conscience."

"Therein you have your answer."

Baffled, I gawp at him.

"She didn't betray you," he continues. "She protected you, *senyora*, as I did when your skin was afire and you could barely breathe. She understood the danger you faced, the danger you refused to consider, and did what you wouldn't do."

"But . . . but . . ."

"She loved you. She was devoted to you. She gave her life for you. You must count yourself fortunate in that way. Twice saved, in Calatayud and now in Guadalajara. Best not to make it thrice."

I don't know what to say. I don't know what to think.

El Musulmán stands again. "I am to meet up with Xirau in two days," he says quietly. "We are to return to Barcelona. I wish you luck in getting to Madrid."

"I will need more than that, I think. A miracle. Divine intervention."

"And you will get it."

Once he leaves, I slip under the covers, dizzy with El Musulmán's disclosure. Aldonça, Aldonça, I never would have suspected. Alas, how little we know, or understand, of the people we love.

Chapter 11

*Regarding the Many Faces
of Loss and Change*

On a bright, balmy day in October of '95, Jaume began complaining of a pain that shot down his legs, an uncharacteristic complaint for, unlike other children, he was not one to bewail afflictions. At that time, he was three and ten but not particularly tall or strong for his age; the brawn would come later, in young manhood.

"Where does the pain start, *Pastisset*?" Françesc asked. My husband had chosen that affectionate nickname because the boy's sweet nature reminded him of the jam-stuffed fried cakes Françesc liked.

Grimacing, Jaume pointed to his lower back.

"Are you well enough for your lessons?"

He nodded, so I didn't give the symptom another thought. That night, however, we noted a rash on his face, and by the following morning, the small hard protuberances had filled with an opalescent fluid. His fever spiked. Imagining the worst, I wrung my hands in lament, but Françesc had the presence of mind to summon the physician who had long tended to his family. After a thorough examination, the old man confirmed our fears, without bothering to soften or disguise the news: my son had come down with the pox.

He asked for some clean cloths and a large bowl from the maid and, using instruments he took from his pouch, performed a bloodletting that he said would improve my son's condition. Then as quickly as he arrived, he ran off, leaving behind detailed instructions for the care and quarantine of the patient.

Françesc and I were devastated, as both of us had known many who had succumbed to the dreaded disease. But Jaume, he looked at the lesions on his skin, sighed, and then promptly asked for a cup of chocolate sweetened with sugarcane, not a trifling request because we had to send a servant to the Sant Pere de Rodes Monastery for cacao at an expense best forgotten. When at last he sipped this luxury, he smiled, and for a moment too brief, I thought all would be well, that the pox would disappear just by the very fact that we wished it gone.

As we were fortunate not to be diseased—no small miracle—we took turns making sure one of us was always at his side. Following the physician's orders, we inducted vomiting and administered enemas, all treatments Jaume hated—with just cause. We also sent alms to the monasteries and donations to the churches, as we were desperate for intercession of any kind. Yet the pustules spread, denser in his extremities than on the body proper, but no less alarming to observe. During those interminable days and nights, I blamed myself for my son's suffering. Suddenly and with complete clarity, I realized I was being punished, albeit delayed, for my wanton conduct and defiance of the holy marriage vows. After every fervid recitation of the rosary, I promised more charity and a renouncement of my conspicuously self-centered ways. Anything and everything to spare Jaume. I was sincere in my words, never more so, and at that time I was convinced I'd stay strong in the face of temptation.

Early on, the pox pustules appeared like small beads embedded in the skin, but with time they leaked a turbid, foul liquid. Once deflated they scabbed black, and though these crusts eventually flaked off, raised scars remained, nowhere more noticeable than on his face. Silently I was grateful that disfigurement was the only result of this disease. I also was confident that these marks would not blemish him inside as Jaume had never been particular about what he wore or how his hair was combed. He didn't bother with mirrors and preferred to play with his cousins, their favorite pastime a gruesome reenactment of the more notable battles of the Crusades.

The pox changed all that, however. His world contracted and he turned inward. He couldn't pass a reflective surface without glowering at what he saw. Before the pox marked his face and transformed his temperament, he had been polite to strangers, pleasant with servants, obedient to his tutor, and even-tempered with his relatives. Afterward, he became imperious, ireful, a boy who cared only for his own company. In the immediate years that followed the disease, he read more than even I had at his age, and he displayed a penchant for literature, penning short plays, which he performed for us with much emotion and verve. As doting parents, we applauded those attempts until Françesc made it a point to take Jaume along for business meets, effectively discouraging him from an occupation my husband thought was worthy only of dilettantes. In the eyes of the law, as well as in the hearts of the family, both fulfilled their roles to perfection, Françesc as father, Jaume as son.

Yet even though Jaume favored my own father in certain features— the breadth of his shoulders and the way laughter rumbled straight from the belly—it was impossible for me to ignore the telltale traits my son shared with the man who had been my lover. The shape of their noses and the color of their hair—these were the more comparable features, but the two also possessed the same wide forehead and a way of holding their heads when talking, tilted slightly to the right as if favoring the left ear. I never commented on any of this, but Françesc was fascinated by it, though not in a suspicious way.

"Our son is his own little self," my husband liked to say, a playful pride in his voice. "He resembles no one."

This wasn't true. Françesc simply didn't recall Miquel in any significant way because their connection had been brief.

As a result of his facial disfigurement, anger held Jaume firm into his early twenties but thankfully no longer. Self-aversion succumbed to confidence in his skill as an *home de negocis*, heir to the Llull fortune and the d'Oms lineage. He didn't lack for female interest either. Many a woman was willing to overlook his pocked face for a comfortable existence.

Yet having endured his own trial, Jaume refused to accept weakness in others, and he was steadfast in his opinions. One particular incident comes to mind as an example. Françesc was still alive then, so my son would have been six and ten, no older. A fierce spring levante had swept in from the sea like a fire-spitting dragon, damaging buildings by the port as well as two ships anchored in our waters, one of which we had insured. It came to light that the ship's goods hadn't been transported to a warehouse as Françesc and Jaume had been assured and that the crew had done nothing to secure the shipment when news was received of the impending storm. When the owners came around with outstretched hands, there was considerable debate about what, if anything, was owed. Françesc wavered, as he had known the men for several years, but Jaume refused to award them any compensation and, young as he was, stood his ground.

"Word spreads we've paid out on a claim without merit and they'll think us weak," my son insisted.

Françesc deferred to Jaume's intractability. It wouldn't be the only time. Françesc trusted Jaume's judgment, and I heard him once remark to his brother, *"El peixos grossos sempre es menjaran els menuts."* And indeed, over time my boy proved that in the world of commerce, a large fish always devours the small.

I don't know if this has brought Jaume happiness, though.

"You're the most beautiful woman here," Françesc said as he glanced around the grand ballroom festooned with banners and flowers.

"Don Françesc," I replied, squeezing his hand, "you're resorting to exaggeration."

It was impossible not to be enchanted by the summer evening. Thousands of candles burned in iron chandeliers, and women were bedecked in jewelry and silk. The men—oh, they, too, looked so handsome in their finest embroidered brocade!

When the flabiolist of a three-member cobla ensemble played the introductory notes of the *introit*, we took the first steps of the *tirada de curts* for King Philip III and his new wife, Margaret of Austria, who sat in high-backed carved-oak thrones. The choice of opening with a sardana was, as Françesc explained, "prudently deliberate." This most beloved of Catalan dances was intended to remind the king that, while we swore allegiance to the crown, we weren't under his thumb entirely. We remained an independent principality, loyal first and foremost to our own laws. Whether the visiting royals understood this was anyone's guess. I suspect the king, ruler but a year, couldn't have known much about this particular dance or its significance, for in Castile the preference was for pavanes, galliards, alta danzas, even the more difficult canario. Or so we were told.

"I'm not exaggerating, *senyora*," Françesc continued, his voice rising above the music. "I speak only truth about your beauty."

I rewarded his gallantry with a flutter of eyelashes and a teasing laugh. Though I was far from the flower of youth in 1599, that night I felt particularly elegant in my crimson gown embellished with gold thread.

"You mock me, dear lady."

"Husband, please be kind enough to pay attention to what we're doing. The king is watching."

"Your beauty attracts his eye."

"I'm old enough to be his mother." As I said this, we raised our arms for the longer steps of the *llargs*.

After our sardana, a performance that seemed to please the royals because they applauded enthusiastically, we made our way to one side of the ballroom, where we mingled among our friends as we waited for the dancers of the *ball de bastons*. Gabriel was present with Joana's replacement, the not-so-new wife who had borne him a set of twins and two other children in rapid succession. Also in attendance were several d'Oms cousins and a smattering of my own relatives, at least those who had managed to snag a coveted ball invitation.

"We must make the best of the king's visit," Françesc was saying to Gabriel and two other men. "It may be the city's only opportunity to push for the construction of our own armed galleys."

Gabriel nodded. "Persuading Philip shouldn't be difficult. He knows perfectly well that we must protect the coastline. These intrusions by Barbary pirates are a danger to commerce and to the lives of his subjects. Who, by the way, pay his taxes."

"Speaking of taxes. I think we need to push for the taxes in arrears to be discharged," opined Bernat, the oldest of the d'Oms cousins, a man known as much for his shrewdness as for his long nose. "The countryside is suffering."

And indeed it was. The decade had been marked by unusually cold, wet weather and, as a consequence, poor harvests. Françesc was well aware of the *pagesos'* troubles, but his intentions for this particular royal visit tended to the personal. He hoped to be rewarded with a title of some kind, in consideration of his generosity in extending much-needed capital to the crown. I wasn't interested in men's politicking, and my thoughts kept drifting to Jaume, who several days earlier had informed us that he wanted to learn to play the *sac de gemecs*. I had expressed my dismay roundly, but Françesc had reacted just as he had done with Jaume's childish attempts at playwriting. In other words, he did nothing. Françesc was confident that Jaume would come to his senses when he realized he hadn't the least bit of talent for bagpipes.

Françesc tapped me on the arm. "Dolça, you're frowning and there's no place for that here. I'm determined to have a good time."

"I'm thinking of Jaume and his bagpipe."

"Forget about that nonsense. You worry too much about the boy. He will be just fine. Tonight is for fun and celebration."

I was pleased with his words, as the past two years had seen my husband's melancholia return with a vengeance. His spells of despair had grown longer and more frequent, and the gloom felt deeper with every onset of this unpredictable malady. The anguish of witnessing his sadness, of knowing one was helpless to pull him out of it, was exhausting. It also sent Jaume into bouts of anger, which he exhibited not by locking himself up or refusing to eat but by shouting at the servants, a young ogre with a fluctuating squeak in his voice.

Françesc drew my attention back to the center of the room, where two dozen *bastoners*, red sashes binding white breeches to their waists, faced each other in double-row formation. As the music rang out, the men jumped into their steps and began striking their canes together. The rhythmic clacking echoed throughout the large chamber, punctuated by the audience's encouraging claps and the shouts of the dancers themselves. I forgot about Jaume, about the king and his new queen, about the possibility of an elevated title, and my heart expanded to the joy of the music.

My husband leaned closer and said, "You're my one true love, wife. I'm blessed to have you."

I smiled up at him, silently swearing to pamper him more, to love him better. Françesc deserved that of me. I didn't know it then, but I would treasure his words in the future. To this day, when I'm lonely or indignant, desperate or saddened, the memory of that magical evening lifts my spirits in a way few other memories can.

Soon after the ball, Françesc departed for a three-month trip to Castile, a journey he had been planning for a while. Unfortunately, and without our knowledge, it would coincide with la peste's reappearance in the plains and mountains of that region. Though the plague of 1599 showed mercy on Catalonia, it didn't spare my family. I would be widowed before Christmas, and as a result of this tragedy, my life, with all its grievances and pleasures, would be altered drastically and forevermore.

Mourning, stricken by remorse, I turned down food, grew gaunt and weak, irritable. I declined to receive kinfolk and friends who wanted to help me through this terrible darkness, and refused to leave the house for months, finding it impossible to complete the most basic acts of washing, dressing, even rising from bed. I couldn't think past the idea that my husband had died far from home, far from the comfort of his wife and family, though his Madrid procurador assured me that he had received the best care possible. In the capital, with the most current medicines available, he had been treated by a renowned surgeon who had attempted several remedies, including purgatives, sudorifics, bloodletting, and herb concoctions, as well as a new treatment of borage distilled in sorrel water with lemon syrup and dittany leaves. Not that any of this helped, and it might have even caused my dear Françesc unnecessary pain.

Horrid images invaded my dreams, phantasmagorias of the great pestilence. In these nightmares, boils swelled to the size of a common apple and, when lanced, oozed enough vile fluids to flood my room. I saw myself drowning in this overflow, sputtering and flailing for life. To ease these night haunts, Aldonça prepared a bitter potion composed of ingredients best left to the imagination. This tonic, however, had the unfortunate effect to render me unconscious, and she allowed only sparing use of it. Jaume took to sleeping on the floor next to my bed in order to fend off my demons, and that period, I now believe, marked our role reversal, the passage of authority from parent to child, from one generation to the next. Slowly, almost imperceptibly, he assumed the duties of business and household and proved adept at the administration of both. He became the only other person, aside from Aldonça, that I allowed in my chambers.

"Mother, I'm here," Jaume would say again and again when I woke in the middle of the night screaming. Then he'd embrace me until I shook no longer.

Though I should have drawn comfort from the few words Françesc had dictated on his deathbed—

My dearest Dolça,
  Whatever happens when I depart this valley of tears, know that I always have loved you.

  Yours in this life and next,
  Your Husband

—I only grew more distressed by my inability to conjure up Françesc's face. (Memory punishes us in that way, providing us with too much of one remembrance and not enough of another.) No matter how desperately I tried, his features blurred, his voice dimmed, and the warmth of his hand on the crook of my elbow faded. I forced myself to hum the tune he liked to whistle in the bath and to preserve the musk he left on my linens after days of gracing my bed with his presence, but even those precious details were difficult to call up over time. My life had become a series of subtractions, of people lost and opportunities fallowed, of gifts squandered in the pursuit of selfish diversion. Or so I thought then.

When at last I tiptoed back into a life I didn't deserve, troublesome whispers reached my ears. Many in the family were of the opinion that I should follow my cousin Glòria's footsteps into a convent, a drastic step she had taken when most of her family had succumbed to the plague of the past decade. Gabriel's wife, my not-so-dear sister-in-law, had the audacity to suggest that a woman of my age and condition—a matron of some means, in other words—might find solace in religious sister-hood. She would have bound my hands and feet, gagged my mouth, thrown me onto a cart, and wheeled me through the heavy portals of Convent dels Àngels. Not that this retreat from the world was unusual for widows, but it wasn't a path I wanted to take. A tiny blaze of desire for life, for happiness still burned, and it was, I now think, this quiet rage at others' assumptions for my future that eventually forced me into the realm of the living. I came to learn that even in the darkest times, we possess a will to continue and a hunger to thrive.

I eventually tried as best I could to reapply myself to painting, but my attention was haphazard and my hand unsteady. My drawing skills had stagnated over time, and my ease in preparing pigment had declined as well. Still, just as shadow requires light, the gloom in my heart needed contrast, and I discovered that by simply sitting in the studio, among the smells of siccatives, surrounded by a visual feast of colors, my thoughts quieted. The plain weave of the linen, or the sturdiness of the loom that would bear it, or the way a brush whispered on an empty palette was enough to soften the litany of self-reproach.

But such reprieve was temporary. Recriminations always returned: Why hadn't I stopped my husband from leaving for Castile? Could I have bid him a more loving farewell? Was my licentiousness the reason behind this punishing blow?

As to add more distress to my remorse, a letter from Miquel arrived that first spring of the new century. In truth, the missive was not unexpected. Though Miquel had continued to travel extensively for his work as a royal commissary, mostly to villages of no consequence, he never desisted in his attempts to communicate. In one letter, he had even composed a poem for me, one that years later would make its way into his *Quixote*, the book that usurped my name. I remember its first lines still:

> *Ah me, Love's mariner am I*
> *On Love's deep ocean sailing;*
> *I know not where the haven lies,*
> *I dare not hope to gain it.*

His condolence letter contained no rhyming, but it did carry an unnamed hope:

11th of April, 1600

Dear Dolça,

On his recent visit to the capital, cousin Quirze informed me of your most tragic news. It is with sincere sympathies and concern for your well-being that I pen this letter. I know well what Françesc meant to you. By all accounts he was a fine and generous man who met his Creator too soon. With the luxury of distance, I can acknowledge him as a worthy rival.

I hope you will accept this letter in the manner intended and think me not presumptuous or hypocritical, particularly as I have not received word from you in a very long time. The past years have been challenging. As Quirze may have mentioned, I spent time in the royal prison on Calle de las Sierpes in Sevilla for embezzling funds I neither stole nor possessed. I thought God had abandoned me there, such were the unspeakable conditions and systemic cruelty. The inhumanity I witnessed, however, did not break my spirit. Rather, it sharpened my wits and inspired the idea for a story I now pursue. Once wrong was righted and justice

*rendered, I sat at my desk again, and now, with nib in the ink
pot, I spend most hours writing, thinking, and writing again.*

*Perhaps you can find similar succor for your grief in the act of
painting? The creation of art alleviates, however temporarily, the
torment that gnaws at the soul. And it is in this way that one can
endure an hour, a day, a week, a fortnight, a year, decades—as I
have survived your absence.*

*Again, my heartfelt condolences. Remember that you are al-
ways in my thoughts and in my heart, without regard to the many
leagues that separate us. I have not forgotten you. I aspire to a life
in which your feelings and intentions match my own.*

Always yours,
Miquel

As with his previous letters, I did not reply to this one, though
my recalcitrance turned out not to matter. The following year Miquel
returned to Barcelona and immediately sent a message that he had taken
a small apartment on Sota Muralla. Stomach aflutter, hands trembling,
I read the note announcing his arrival—and promptly tossed it into the
brazier. I had neither the interest nor inclination to revive a relationship
that had rewarded me with both trouble and pleasure. Age had made
me wiser, and it had also quieted the needs of the flesh.

Yet when he showed up at my door without official invitation, I did
not turn him away. Nor was I surprised by his presumptions. Of course,
he would view my widowhood differently than I, or others, would. For
him, it meant opportunity.

"Time's been kind to you," he said by way of greeting, and bowed
as if at court. "You look as I left you, the same."

In contrast, the years had left their mark on Miquel. The lines around
his eyes and mouth had deepened, helped along by scowl and squint, and
his thinning hair was highlighted by gray. His dress remained simple, but
very much of Sevilla in the vividness of its fabrics. All this I took in with a
sweeping glance, and I admit that my heart leaped at the sight of him, for no
reason other than emotions are true only to themselves, not to their owners.

Our first meeting was initially uncomfortable. I received him in my studio, an unusual move as now, in widowhood, I considered it a haven, an inviolate space, one best kept from the prying eyes and pointed questions of others. Part of me, I suspect, also thought the stone bowls, the pigments, the spirits, the oil, the scrapers and trowels and brushes, even perhaps the muslin used to protect a completed work, would somehow smooth the inevitable awkwardness. Seated across a low table, we quietly assessed each other, but once the maid left us alone after serving refreshments, we both attempted to connect beyond vague generalities.

"How have . . ." he began, and I said, "It's been a . . ."

We laughed, and after that our conversation flowed as briskly as a mountain creek. We were two friends establishing common ground again. He asked what I was painting, and I walked across the sun-kissed room to turn my easel toward him.

"Windmills?" he asked, surprised.

"Why not? They are everywhere, and what can be more of our place and people than that?"

"Windmills," he echoed.

Encouraged by the intensity of his interest, I explained how I sized and primed the canvas. How I checked the proportion on a scale model drawing, enlarging the image with a grid. How I sketched my subject and then dead colored (in this case with gray tones) the underpainting. How I smoothed layers and blended hues and forms. I prattled on and on, as much out of nervousness as pride. So far I had been extraordinarily pleased by my work on this piece, and once finished, the *Ruta de Molins* would end up becoming a personal favorite.

After I had exhausted the topics of siccatives, varnishes, chalk, and glue, he told me of his travels and his work, also of the horrid week he had spent in jail, accused of illegally seizing three hundred fanegas of wheat.

"Lies! Trumped-up charges. And to add insult to injury, I was forced to Madrid for a hearing that—"

"But these false charges were dropped, no?" I kept my voice low enough not to offend or incite.

"Of course. Pedro de Izunza—he's the commissary general—testi-fied on my behalf."

His sudden smile erased the consternation that had creased his face, and I seized upon that pause. "And your family, Miquel? Your mother, sisters, your brother Rodrigo?" What I meant to probe was his other relationships, the unmentionables of wife and bastard daughter.

Turns out his personal life had not fared any better. He saw his wife, Catalina, seldom, confirming what I already knew through Quirze, and of his daughter, Isabel, he spoke not a word, leading me to believe this was a relationship marked by strife. Only his brother Rodrigo, who still soldiered for the crown, merited a laudatory comment or two. He also spoke enthusiastically about the character of a knight-errant that he hoped to develop into a book-length manuscript. He did not once inquire after Jaume, however, and I, in turn, said nothing about our son. Once we reached the end of these safe subjects, we fell silent for a bit.

Finally, I asked: "Why are you here, Miquel?"

"Is it not obvious?"

"What do you mean?"

"Dolça, I'm here for you. How can you not understand that?"

"I am widowed—"

"And free."

"But you cannot say the same about yourself."

Another long silence, another long study of what our eyes might betray. I looked away first.

"I am here to plead my case," he said softly.

"You have no case, Miquel. You're married and nothing can change that."

"I've never stopped loving you. Never, and you know that. I suspect you have feelings for me too. If it hadn't been for your parents, our lives might have been different."

I gaped at him, incredulous, but he appeared not to notice for he continued to advocate for himself, for this shared existence he had long envisioned. "It's not too late for us, Dolça. My economic situation has improved. I've met with some success, enough for a comfortable living."

"Too much time has passed. Years and years. We are different people now, with different priorities. I have a son, you a daughter. We have obligations."

"We've always had those! Who doesn't? But we can overcome such difficulties."

"They're not petty responsibilities."

"To me they are, in comparison to the reward of love."

I couldn't help but consider the luxuries to which I had grown accustomed: the imported rugs, the feather pillows and soft mattress, the silk and brocade robes, the platoon of servants, the jewels and leather shoes, the furniture and tapestries and books. The many prospects for Jaume's future. But also, and not least, the time and funds that allowed me to pursue my painting without worry or thrift.

"Miquel, we must be truthful with ourselves. We cannot deny who we are and what we want."

"Precisely. I know what I want. What I've always wanted. And if you can look me in the eye and tell me you do not love me, then I will leave right now and depart this city at first light."

How easy it would have been to say what I needed to say. How much simpler it would have been to lie. But when I uttered nothing, not even a word of dismissal, he allowed himself a slow smile of satisfaction and vindication. I wept quietly then, and though I wasn't sure at the time what had brought me to tears, I now believe it was a sense of failure. When you cannot do what you've been trained to do all your life, when you're unable to accomplish the most basic requirements of decorum and decency, personal disaster is the most likely outcome.

"My dearest, I do not want to cause you more grief," he continued. "I know what I ask of you is not easy. But promise me you will think about what we have discussed."

He stood, walked to where I was seated, and kneeled. He tucked a knuckle under my chin and lifted my face so that we were as close as two people could be without kissing. His breath smelled of the tea we had just sipped.

"I love you, and nothing will change that. Not the passage of years, not leagues of distance, not the strictures of society."

He kissed me lightly on the lips, then rose and walked out the door. I did not move from my chair for a very long time, the burden of choice paralyzing me for hours. Jaume found me in this position in the late afternoon, and though his frown revealed concern, he asked no questions and instead verbally castigated the servants for leaving me alone. I feared one of them might reveal that Miquel had stopped by, but none did. Most likely they were too intent on staying out of my son's way. Only Aldonça remarked on the visit, her tone one of both worry and admiration.

"That is one obstinate man. As stubborn as an ass."

Following Miquel's social call I clung to my routine with unwavering resolve, which meant that I spent most mornings in the office with Jaume and the afternoons investigating potential marriage candidates for my son. (Yes, he was nearing that age.) I needed habit to anchor me to reality, though I admit that Miquel's silence during those weeks—no messages, no notes—was discomfiting. It added to the confusion that had settled in my heart like a hen squatting on her eggs. Do not misunderstand. I was relieved he stayed away, but I was also insulted that he could manage such a feat. If he loved me as he claimed, if his need to be together was so overwhelming, how could he resist the separation?

As it turned out, we would come together again but not by his machinations or mine. An ingenue would consider that chance meeting coincidence, but I thought it fate. We may live under the illusion of personal choice, that we are the masters of our destiny, but the script of our lives has been written long before we set foot on this earth. How else to explain the constant calamities, all the grief I have caused and suffered myself?

At Jaume's insistence and Aldonça's encouragement, I decided to join several cousins at a May Day poetry contest. A sizable crowd was expected at the plaza, as announcements had been distributed all about town at a time when we Barcelonans desired, and needed, distraction. In late March more brutal winds had caused catastrophic damage to buildings near the port, and three families, including more than a score of children, had been buried alive under collapsed roofs. These gales had also sunk several anchored ships, taking more than a few souls to their Maker, which was one reason Jaume did not accompany Aldonça and me to the competition, so busy was he keeping our merchant accounts in good order.

"All of Barcelona will turn out for this," I told my cousins Assumpció and Alba as we strolled through the crowded streets. "It has been a while since we've had such a contest."

"At least two or three years," Alba added. "And this literary joust is offering a sizable purse too."

"Really?"

"Yes, three silver spoons."

Alba was Glòria's eldest daughter, a homely young woman who, according to Jaume, was destined to follow her mother's footsteps into the convent. I considered his judgment harsh, however. Alba had some outstanding qualities. She possessed a vivacious personality, a keen mind, and more than enough humor to make up for her unexceptional looks. In fact, had she been a few years younger, I might have considered her for my own son.

"I would enter the contest if women were allowed to compete," Alba continued. "I'll have you know that I've tried my hand at verse."

"I'm sure you possess talent," Assumpció said. "You're clever that way, but don't be too public about it. Men don't like that."

"They fear our skills," I teased. "They know who has the power and the talent."

Alba tittered at the irreverent comment, and Assumpció gave my shoulders a quick hug. "I'm happy you're back among us. Our outings were not the same without you."

"It has been a very difficult time," I replied demurely. Though the official period of mourning had long past, I still wore black in public, which encouraged a certain deference from others. The drabness of my dress, I should acknowledge, was overdue penance, my secret admission of sin.

I hadn't enjoyed a walk in many, many months, however, and the luminous spring day was perfect for one. As expected, the square was lively with people, and the aroma of sausage and onions filled the air. Silk streamers draped every balcony in sight. From stalls along the perimeter, hawkers sold cloth, hides, flowers, and tatted lace as well as pickled pigs' feet, fruit, and pastries. On the easternmost edge of the plaza, a platform had been erected, and eight wooden chairs, now empty, were lined in two rows on the stage.

We searched the crowd for the others who were expected to join our group, stopping to exchange pleasantries with neighbors and acquaintances. For the first time since Françesc's death, I sensed the possibility of normalcy, and I was glad to have agreed to this excursion. As was her way, and recently more than ever, Aldonça did not leave my side, not when we bought wild berries from a stand or admired the bobbin lace on display. It was she who first spotted Miquel, for she tensed next to me and tried her best to steer me in the opposite direction. No fool, I immediately guessed at her motive and turned around to see him for myself.

He stood with Quirze, Ferran, and their wives, laughing at what must have been a funny anecdote, and then, as if sensing my stare, he raised his head and met my eyes. My heart thumped hard against my chest. He said something to his party, and they all waved in greeting, then together the five of them pushed through the throng to reach us. It was inevitable that, after initial pleasantries, Miquel and I would drift away from the others and closer to each other. Inevitable, too, that we would fall into polite conversation.

"Cousin," he said, "I'm delighted to see you. I keep thinking about your windmills."

"Just the windmills?" I teased.

"What do you think?"

"I should have known you would be in attendance," I said, hinting at a motivation best left hidden.

"And I had hoped against all hope that you would also make an appearance," he parried.

"It's a beautiful May Day to do so, no?"

"Indeed, made even more enjoyable by your presence. I expect you have given some thought to our last conversation."

Before I could reply, my nursemaid stepped between us. "*Senyora,* the contest is about to begin. Shall we move closer to the stage?"

To prove her observation, the shrill flourish of horns quieted the crowd. I couldn't help but recall what Miquel had once told a young relative about such contests: *"These competitions are platforms for the deluded, the arrogant, the entitled. True poets, the men who compose a poem with the skill of the greats, don't stand a chance against the dabblers who use their rank to versify. So always aim at the second prize, for the first will be awarded through favoritism. The second, on the other hand, is gained on merit."*

On the platform a finely dressed man announced the names of the three judges and the rules of the contest. Then eight contestants of varying ages climbed the steps and took the stage. They settled in their chairs to much applause.

"Now we will see what kind of literary talent your city can claim," Miquel whispered.

"We have plenty of talent, Miquel. You should know that."

He chuckled. Despite Aldonça's efforts, he had not budged from my side. Quite the contrary: he now stood so close I could feel his breath on my neck. The flirtation was difficult to deny. My cousins stared at us, but then politely averted their gazes. I'm not sure why. Perhaps they preferred to pretend ignorance. Perhaps they were embarrassed by our brazen behavior. My nursemaid was, certainly.

"Please!" Aldonça hissed. "Can you not be more discreet?"

"Why?" I asked. "Will I be reported to someone?"

"I can't imagine who," Miquel countered. "You have no parents, no husband, and—"

"Ah, but I have a son."

"A son. And how can he stop you from enjoying yourself? From claiming what is rightfully yours?"

"You'd be surprised."

By this time, Aldonça's face had turned a bright red, and her lips pursed in anger. She attempted to recruit Alba to remove me from what she obviously deemed a compromising situation, but the poor child did not understand what she had been called upon to do.

"Are you brave enough to guess who might win?" Miquel asked Alba.

"How can I? They have not yet recited their verses."

"Verses have nothing to do with it, Albita. To prove my point, I will pick the winner." He paused to scan the contestants and then gestured at an older gentleman whose dignified demeanor bespoke his station in life. "There. He will take first place. Mark my words. Would either of you ladies care to wager?"

Alba shook her head emphatically, and Assumpció insisted she was not a betting woman. I placed my hand on Miquel's arm and nodded. "You name the stakes."

"Delighted to do so."

He said nothing more. He didn't need to; we understood what hung in the balance.

One by one each poet approached the center of the platform to state his name and poem title before launching into an impassioned recitation. Voices rose and fell on the appropriate lines; gestures embellished a phrase here, a word there. Some contestants even stalked the length of the stage as if the wood floorboards of the scaffold weren't long or wide enough to hold their fervor. Most poems were about unrequited love, and by the fifth of these, Aldonça whispered in exasperation, "What a waste! Such passion should be applied to more practical matters." Her contempt was expected. Aldonça had never married, never expressed an interest in doing so, not that I knew of. And without the memory of a lover's touch, without the experience of physical tenderness, a love poem added up to nothing more than a collection of empty words.

When the prizes were at last awarded, Miquel's prediction proved true. He smiled knowingly at me.

"I suppose you will honor your wager."

"Of course. I'm a woman of my word."

"Is that so?" He arched a brow in contradiction, which annoyed me. I had not once promised him what I could not give.

The crowd dispersed, but my cousins lingered, chatting and planning for a gathering at the closest family home. Alba enthusiastically accepted her Oncle Quirze's invitation for pastries and wine, but Assumpció begged off with a headache and the two of us agreed to head back to our own residences. Sensing an unexpected victory, Aldonça tugged at my arm to create space between Miquel and me. He refused to be outmaneuvered, however, and remained by my side.

"Shall I contact you about a convenient time for me to collect?" he asked as we headed in the direction of Carrer Ample. "The wager you lost."

Suddenly nervous, I asked, "Is that wise?"

"I don't think judiciousness plays a significant role here."

I felt the force of censorious stares and glanced in the opposite direction. Several varas away stood Gabriel with Joana's replacement. They were leering at Miquel and me. Miquel followed my look and cursed under his breath, but I nodded and signaled in greeting. When we drew closer to my in-laws—it was impossible to change our path without being obvious about our avoidance—Miquel bid us all a curt farewell and hurried away. My conversation with Gabriel was mercifully brief, and Assumpció and I were soon on our way home again.

But once we were alone in my chambers, Aldonça lost no time in scolding me. "This is why you should be careful. Gossips are everywhere, and they're ready to pounce at the slightest excuse. Today you gave them more than they could have dreamed."

What she did not say but what I already knew: people talked regardless.

I will be brief in recounting how the poetry contest wager was settled: Nothing came of it. Nothing. Nada. *Res.* I did not reply to Miquel's messages or Quirze's intercessions, and when both men came calling at different times, most likely to arrange a rendezvous, they were sent away with the message that I was indisposed. Asked for how long, the servants followed my instructions to the letter and explained that it would be for an indeterminate time. Distance had made me reconsider my coquettish behavior. I had been unduly influenced by the loveliness of the afternoon, by the excitement of the crowd, and by what I thought was my newfound freedom. Once alone, however, I recognized that I had no such freedom, for what had bound me to my role had not been sacred vows but fear and complacency. I was more faithful to my husband in death than I had been during the early years of our marriage, though such belated devotion tempered neither my guilt nor my longings.

A month later Miquel left for Castile again.

Chapter 12

*Wherein My Recovery Turns into
a Frightening Experience*

During my recovery, I pass many hours alone in a well-appointed bedchamber, reading when I'm awake and resting when I fatigue. I don't want for company. Carmeta, the mistress of the house, comes by every morning as if she were making a social call instead of keeping company with an ailing stranger. A handsome lady with a pointed nose and a wide, generous mouth, she sits by the window with her embroidery hoop, angles herself toward the sun, and begins to talk about the weather or her children, five in all. She turns out to be a good storyteller, but I don't return the favor with anecdotes of my own. Occasionally she will ask to "borrow" Anna for assistance downstairs, but I think this is more to get the clingy child out of the room than any real emergency. Carmeta makes no inquiries of me unless they're related to my health or culinary preferences. I'm thankful for this. Then again, I don't invite confidences. When she offers to provide something other than a book to while away time—"Cross-stitching?" she asks. "Knitting needles and yarn?"—I'm polite in my refusal. I see myself as more of a charity case than a guest, though I wouldn't be surprised to learn that Jaume has rewarded her husband in some way, as their extended hospitality can't possibly come without strings, particularly when offered to strangers.

The two men do share a common venture: both have employed Xirau for their respective trading businesses, which is the reason a desperate El Musulmán brought me here when I grew delirious. José Ignacio del Pino is a client of some note, from a family to be trusted in time of need.

In addition to Carmeta, I usually entertain one other visitor during the day. Shortly after the hour of noon, a kitchen maid with three long black hairs on her chin tempts me with the hearty aroma of a heavy stew or thick soup. My favorite dish is her *salpicon*, minced veal with onion, tomato, and garlic, but like the other meals she offers, I can consume only a few bites at any one sitting. When I stop after the requisite nibbles, she clucks like an exasperated hen. The sound always agitates Anna, who has become increasingly skittish over these past few days. Though I encourage her to get fresh air, to take a walk outside in the lovely garden, she refuses these suggestions, preferring to skulk in the corner. She even takes her meals sitting cross-legged on the floor. What a difference from the irrepressible girl who broke out in song after our passage through those dense woods! I can't guess the reason for this change. Is she ill? Is she fearful? Is she homesick? Does she worry about what might happen if I'm displeased with her service? I've plenty of time to devote myself to these inconsequential worries and do so with abandon, as they're a better alternative to dwelling on the grief that chokes my heart or the fear that I won't reach Miquel in time.

I'm eager to return to the road, and I would like to speak to Jaume about this, but I don't know how best to approach him. We didn't part on the best of terms back in Calatayud—I ran away, for heaven's sake!—and surely he's furious about this latest defiance. Probably the only factor delaying his outburst is that we're living among strangers, and he has never been one to air the family laundry with outsiders. Though we take every evening meal together in a small adjoining room set up to accommodate our dining, I find myself tongue-tied in his presence. I'm careful of what I say and how I say it, and hence our conversations have been civil but also stiff and formal. He speaks to me as if I were a relative he just met, telling me of his discoveries in the city in a matter-of-fact way. So many beautiful sites, he says. And so many potential business partners among the local merchants. I study his words, his gestures, his tone for clues to his mood. He is relieved at my recovery, of that I am certain, but also angry at the knowledge he now possesses of his true parentage. Balancing these conflicting emotions makes him cautious, withdrawn, resentful. He'll have to work out those complicated feelings by himself. The question is: do I have time for him to do so?

Finally, on a rainy night, I sense an opening. He has received a letter from Elisabet in Barcelona, and he is as close to jovial as I've seen him in a long while. I seize the opportunity.

"Françesc and Margarida miss you," Jaume says.

"And I them."

"They ask Elisabet about you every day."

"Do they want me or the jellied fruit I always bring them?" I joke.

"Both, I suppose." He allows himself a smile, and I answer with one of my own.

"And Elisabet, how is she?"

"She is well, and with good news."

"Yes?"

"She's with child again."

"Oh, Jaume, I'm so happy! That is definitely good news. We must celebrate."

I pour him another glass of wine, but when I look up, he's staring into the distance, pensive. I know not to break that reverie.

"It'll do the children good to see their only living grandparent," he says finally.

"Of course," I agree. "We'll see each other soon."

He then tells me he has rented a carriage for our return and thinks we'll be able to leave in five or six days, perhaps sooner, depending on my recovery. He doesn't want to rush it.

"The carriage and the guards don't come cheap," he adds, then lowers his voice. "These Castilians are born swindlers."

I laugh conspiratorially. My son, he is Catalan through and through. "But I'm sure you negotiated the best deal possible. You're not without skills."

"Maybe. Not many were willing to see a carriage all the way to Barcelona."

I look down so he won't see my disappointment, but I must speak my mind now or surrender entirely to his plans. I take a deep breath to muster up courage. "I'm not going back, son."

"What? What do you mean?"

"I'm not returning to Barcelona, not until I first go to Madrid."

He bolts from his chair, rattling the plates on the table. "I don't understand you. Why, in the devil's name, are you so determined to go there? After all that has happened."

"To see a dying man."

"Your lover," he spats.

"Your father."

"No, Mother. My father was Françesc d'Oms Calders. He was the one who raised me. Who loved me and fed me and made sure I had a roof over my head and a business to run when I became a man. Have you forgotten that?"

"I haven't. How could I? He was my husband too."

"Whom you betrayed."

I have no words to fling back at him. Told plainly, truth can be neither denied nor defeated. When at last I find my voice, it's a quavering, pleading one.

"Let's at least finish this meal, Jaume. Our hosts have been so generous in providing it. We can discuss everything else later."

"There's nothing to discuss now or later," he sneers. "Besides, I've lost my appetite. I'm done here."

And once again my son turns his back on me. Once again I'm left alone to ponder how long-ago decisions burden us in ways that only a seer could have predicted.

The following morning, angry shouts startle me awake. The commotion is clearly coming from downstairs, though I can't make out who's speaking or what they're saying. Anna and I quickly change out of our night shifts, and she asks if I'd like my hair pinned and dressed. I agree, only because one must face emergencies properly prepared. But as she brushes out the tangles, heavy footsteps thud on the stairway, and before we have time to collect our wits, there's a banging at our door. A man bellows out a name.

"Anna Galindo Salas!"

My young maid freezes. I, too, tense.

"Is Anna Galindo Salas of Saragossa in there?"

I don't respond but turn around on the bench and reach up to snatch the brush from an ashen-faced Anna. Her eyes are wide with terror. She shakes so hard her teeth chatter. I scoot to one side and pull her down next to me.

"Anna Galindo Salas, housemaid in the previous employ of Núria Ripoll Masso, widow of Pablo Salvat Déulosal!"

I consider dragging one of the chairs against the door but realize that won't hold off whoever is on the other side. Besides, such a move would only trap us in the room, with no other means of exit except jumping out a window. And to flee what? To run where? I set the brush down on the vanity and take a deep breath. I signal for Anna to return to the corner of the chamber, her usual place, then rise to face the loud menace. Every step requires effort, and when I finally cross the room and stand before the door, it's as if I've walked leagues and leagues, all uphill. I remind myself that Jaume is here. Whatever this disturbance, he will deal with it. Whatever the misunderstanding, he will know how to resolve it.

As I fumble with the latch, my fear succumbs to worry. What if something tragic has happened at my cousin's? A terrible accident? A death? The spread of plague? After several bungling attempts with the bolt, I manage to open the door.

Three men of impressive bulk stand before me. Two are young and bearded, with swords sheathed at their sides but no other weapons or armor. They flank an older man wearing the ascetic habit of the Dominicans, a white ankle-length scapular covered in part by a black shoulder cape with a hood. A leather belt with a rosary attached to it cinches his great waist. The friar isn't very tall, but his stoutness makes up for this deficiency. Though he's mostly in shadows, his outsize nose stands out, made more noticeable by its large round tip reminiscent of a mushroom. I squint past these strangers and spot Carmeta, her face contorted in panic. She's trying to send me a message with the rapid movement of her eyes, but I can't decipher what that might be. I glance past her, hoping to find some form of reinforcement. There is no one. Not her husband. Not Jaume. Not a single servant.

"Señora," says the Dominican friar, "we are looking for a maid of—"

"I heard you, Brother."

"Is she here?"

"Who's asking?"

The friar takes a step forward across the threshold and into the room. He leans on the door. Such a bold move into a woman's chamber is hardly appropriate, especially by a religious man, but he doesn't behave as if beholden to propriety. I know he means to frighten me, and it works. But I pretend otherwise, refusing to cede space. Again I demand to know his identity.

"We are members of the Aragonese Inquisition and as such are representing the Holy Office." He lifts his chin as he speaks, a hint of self-importance.

At least I don't need to worry about some fatal calamity at my cousin's household. But on the heels of that relief comes a string of sinister thoughts. What do they know about Núria? Did someone denounce her? Has a spy followed us here? I shudder and hope the friar doesn't notice my discomfort.

"And who are these other two?" I motion with an imperious wave at the two younger men, hoping to give my nerves time to settle.

"They're representatives of the Holy Office, as I said."

I regard them with exaggerated disdain, but my show of defiance doesn't change their stiff pose. I turn back to the Dominican. "Well then, how can I help you, Brother?"

"We are here to question a young maid. I believe she is now in your employ. Her name is Anna Galindo Salas."

"What do you want her for?"

"Is she here?"

"It depends."

"Stand aside, señora. We are here to take the prisoner."

"Prisoner!" Behind me Anna whimpers. "How can you take a child prisoner?"

"She's a witness."

"A witness to what?"

"Señora, I will not warn you again. Stand aside."

"But I'm entitled to an explanation. Not only am I her current employer, I am also her unofficial guardian. Her well-being is—"

"Señora," pleads Carmeta, tears rolling down her cheeks. "Do as the Brother requests. My husband is not here. Your son is not here. There's nothing we can do until they return."

I hesitate. To hand over young Anna to the clutches of the Holy Office is a horror in its own right, but I recognize that the Inquisition's interest is not the young maid, who owns nothing other than the clothes on her back. They must be building a case against Núria. Did I not warn that fool? She was far too lax, far too trusting.

"What will you do with her?"

The Dominican exhales testily. "I don't need to answer any of your questions, but I will do so to soothe your concerns. As I mentioned, she is a potential witness in a case out of Saragossa. We must question her."

"She's a child. Are there no provisions in the law for her age?"

"Now, señora, do not make this more difficult on us or on yourself."

Something in me gives way, a sense of futility yielding to hope for a possible resolution. Best not to irritate the friar further. We will likely need his goodwill later. I turn to face Anna, who lies crumpled on the floor, head tucked into her knees. "Come now," I say, making every effort to sound soothing. "You must go with these good men. I will come for you as soon as I can."

But Anna doesn't move, even when I call out to her again. The friar grunts, and because I'm no longer facing him, I don't sense the men's movements until it's too late. They push past, knocking me against the door, and rush across the room. I have no time to react as one of the guards lifts Anna, throws her over his shoulder, and runs out. She howls. The piercing wail echoes down the stairs and out the door and into the courtyard, its desperation equal parts horror and fear. We hurry behind them.

"We will come for you, Anna!" I shout, but I have no faith in my promise. What can I possibly do?

Carmeta holds my hand tightly as the guards throw the girl across the saddle like a sack of flour and then tie her to the stirrups. They disappear before we think to ask where they're taking her. I can barely gather my thoughts.

"I can't believe this is happening. I don't understand anything."

"I'll send word to my husband," Carmeta says, patting my arm. "He will know something—or somebody."

"What will they do to her? She's just a girl."

"We can't think of such things, señora."

With a tug at my skirt, Carmeta leads me back inside. A couple of the servants slink out from the kitchen. She sends one of them to her husband's office and then asks if I know where Jaume might be. I have no idea. After last night, my son wouldn't think of entrusting me with his plans, but of course I'm too embarrassed to admit this. She seems to guess at my discomfort, for she suddenly remembers that he mentioned something about going to the ayuntamiento. She dispatches the second servant to city hall.

The wait for both men is interminable. Though Carmeta insists I break my morning fast with bread and a hot drink, I turn down her offer. I'm not hungry. What I feel is insurmountable exhaustion, as if the fever were still a menace and my recovery doubtful. By the time José Ignacio appears, I've drooled and dozed off in my chair, an embarrassing situation I try to hide. He is a tall man, heavy-browed, thick-lipped, and stoop-shouldered. His high-pitched voice does not do his good manners justice. Now he's asking so many questions of his wife, speaking so quickly, even angrily, that she grows flustered.

"So, in summary," he says, "you don't know where she was taken or the name of the Dominican friar who came here. You don't know what she's being charged with."

Carmeta hangs her head. Neither of us considered any of these inquiries. How could we? We were stunned by the presence of the Holy Office representatives. Everything happened so quickly.

José Ignacio turns to me and regards me with wary interest. There is no mistaking his suspicion. "And you, señora, can you not at least enlighten me as to why the Inquisition visited us? We've never had an issue with the Holy Office. Not once, not one single relative or friend has crossed paths with these authorities. We are good Catholics, both from old Christian families who have lived in this city since it was a one-mule hamlet."

"I . . . I think it has to do with my cousin from Saragossa. And the men who came, they didn't provide us their names but claimed to be from the Aragonese Inquisition."

"And they're here in Castile? From Aragón?"

"That's what they told us. Is that usual?"

"Did they show you a warrant from the local inquisitor general? Any papers with official seals?"

Carmeta and I trade worried looks. "We didn't think to ask," she says.

"Of course not." He sounds more annoyed with us than with the intruding friar.

"But surely there is a way to make inquiries?" Carmeta implores. "At the local inquisitor's? Or a church? Perhaps Father Carmelo can help."

"I'll have to find out what's going on. It seems highly irregular that the officers, or at least the friar, wasn't local."

José Ignacio tromps over to the other side of the room and sits next to a window. Harrumphing loudly, he rings for a servant. None of us speaks, but I catch the guarded glances husband and wife exchange. I wish Jaume had not insisted we stay so long. These good people must be ruing the day they welcomed a fevered, delirious woman into their midst.

After several minutes, a maid enters the room with a tray of cheeses. Behind her is a disheveled Jaume, worry plain on his face.

"They took Anna?" he asks, without bothering to greet anyone.

Before I can answer, José Ignacio jumps in, detailing what he knows. He suggests the men meet alone to plot a course of action, a proposal I find encouraging. Between the two of them, they'll find a solution. Jaume is a great negotiator, more persevering than a plague of locusts, and José Ignacio must know many influential men in town.

"Can we help?" I ask as they walk out of the room. "There must be something we can do."

Jaume swings around so quickly that he nearly falls into José Ignacio. Once recovered, he glowers at me as if I've committed an unpardonable deed, uttered some unreasonable request.

"Mother, you can start by staying put. Knowing where you are is one less thing for me to worry about."

My face grows hot with embarrassment, and I escape to my chambers as soon as it's polite to do so. I'm so chagrined I can't even look at Carmeta when I take my leave. What must she think?

They come for me in the afternoon, when the men are in town and Carmeta and I are alone with the servants. We do not expect any visitors and, in fact, have just sent an errand boy to the apothecary for a headache remedy. Carmeta rests in her chambers and I in mine, both of us nursing our pains, when a maid shouts out like a town crier, "They're back! They're back!"

And they are, the Dominican friar and his two bearded guards. Within minutes they're tramping up the stairs, creating such raucousness that my initial concern is for Carmeta and what she might be forced to do. After so many disruptions, she might consider throwing me out, and for good reason.

"Dolça Llull Prat!"

I bolt up in bed, an instinctive recognition of my family's long-held surnames. My head feels heavy, my limbs numb.

"Widow of Françesc d'Oms. Of Barcelona proper."

"Who is this?" I ask, pretending ignorance. "I am resting."

"We are representatives from the Aragonese Inquisition tribunal."

"You again. What do you want?"

There's a shuffling of boots, followed by hurried whispers. I force myself to walk to the dressing table and peek at my reflection in the mirror. Without Anna's help, I've done a poor job with my hair. It's more bird nest than crowning glory.

"Please step out into the doorway."

"I'm not going anywhere until I get a proper explanation." I try to sound forceful.

"We request your presence downstairs, doña. A simple matter. Just open the door."

The ingratiating quality of the friar's words repulses me, but I do as requested, and there they stand, in the same spot they were mere hours ago. I'd like to slap the smugness from the friar's face but turn my attention instead to Carmeta, who hovers to the side, a guardian angel, or at least a rescuer of last resort, motioning for me to join her. Head held high, I sidle past the three men and lean on her proffered arm, knowing that nothing in this situation bodes well. We take each step with deliberate measure, but halfway down the stairs, a queasiness overtakes me. The air around me thins as if instead of descending we are climbing, climbing, climbing. I gasp for breath. My ears ring. I rest against the cold stone wall as the world spins. My legs refuse to support me, and the two young guards reach out to stop me from falling. Carmeta calls for help, and a maid appears suddenly at my side. She smells of fried onions. She helps her mistress hoist me up by the elbows, and together they guide me until I'm seated on a blue velvet settee in a room awash in sunlight. A yellow-haired girl appears from somewhere and pours wine into a goblet that has been set out for me. I sip; the liquor's heat settles my insides. I feel suddenly alone. Abandoned. Shipwrecked. How long before Jaume returns?

"On the dates between Friday, the first of April, and Monday, the fourth of April," begins the friar, "you were reported in Saragossa, visiting a woman by the name of Núria . . ."

Of course, this is again about my cousin. How I now lament my stay there! And all because I yearned for the luxuries of home, because I could not bear the discomforts of travel.

The friar drones on, but my senses are so dulled that I hear him as if from a great distance. His words make no sense. His gestures seem exaggerated. The room tilts, shapes blur, and then the colors around me—the red of the window curtains, the blue of the settee, the yellow of the maid's hair, the white of the friar's scapular—fade into black. I fall into a depth as silent and cold as a catacomb.

I don't know how long I'm out, but when I finally open my eyes, supported on either side by servants, Carmeta is positioned in my line of sight. But no Jaume. No José Ignacio.

"She's recovering from the fever," Carmeta is saying. "She's still weak."

"She barely eats," adds one of the maids. "And she's an old woman."

The friar is not moved by these words, however. He looms above me, a menacing grin plastered on his face.

"What is it that you want with this woman, Brother Tómas?" Ah, so Carmeta has followed her husband's advice and now is in possession of a name.

"We're making inquiries related to a case in Saragossa. As I've explained."

"And what does that have to do with my guest?"

"Plenty."

"I don't understand how just this morning you took a young maid from this house and now you accost an ill woman. Are the religious now tasked with the persecution of the old and the weak?" Her indignation is unmistakable. If only I could hug Carmeta, applaud her bravery! But as it is, I struggle to keep myself upright.

"We're making inquiries, nothing more than that."

The friar explains that the tribunal has received a report of Jewish practices in the Saragossa home of my cousin Núria. His account, delivered in a monotone, is succinct and far too vague for me to assess how much he knows—or to even reach any conclusion as to the source or the status of the case. However, it's enough to give me a sense of what they suspect. I wonder how much of this information was obtained from Anna, or if she has merely been a corroborating witness.

"I know of whom you speak," I say, "and I can tell you that your informant is mistaken. She's a deeply pious woman."

"And you know this how?"

"I arrived at her house on the eve of Good Friday and departed after Easter. I witnessed firsthand her devoutness. Let me assure you her faith is unassailable and for anyone to make an unfounded accusation is slander. Pure and simple. It would behoove you, dear Brother, to investigate the motive of the accuser. Most likely it's someone who wishes her ill."

I'm breathless by the time I finish my speech, but the Dominican's face registers no emotion. I'm unsure of what else to say, and I know I must be careful that my own words aren't used against me in some way.

"You're related."

I nod.

"You know her well?"

"Of course. And as I said before, her piousness is unquestionable."

The friar tugs at the rosary dangling from his belt and then stares at me as one would observe a bug swimming in one's soup. I don't avert my gaze. I won't honor his suspicions. I also fear asking after my cousin, fear the possibility of incriminating myself. After all, I did observe her lighting candles and reciting strange prayers. Wouldn't that be guilt by association? And who knows what information they've managed to obtain from Anna. If that poor child has been tortured, what will prevent her from singing as prettily as a finch? I wonder how she might be tolerating what is perhaps the most frightening experience of her short life.

As if guessing my concern, Carmeta inquires after the young maid.

"She will remain in custody as long as our investigation is active," the friar replies.

"I suppose we're done here," I say dismissively. I rise with great effort and move toward the stairs.

"Not quite." The friar sidesteps to block me.

I stop and look away. The fewer facial expressions he observes, the less he can conjecture.

"I am fatigued, Brother. I must get myself some much-needed rest."

"That will have to wait. We are here to take you in for questioning."

"What?" I exclaim, and Carmeta demands, "By what authority do you issue such an order?"

"You know well the authority invested in me by both Crown and Church. The tribunal must conduct its business as it sees fit, for the safety of the realm and preservation of the one true faith."

I open my mouth to hurl insults, to damn him to hell and beyond, but change my mind. Prudence is sometimes better than defiance.

The friar signals to one of the guards, and the bearded man leaps forward, handing him a document, which Brother Tómas unrolls. He proceeds to read it in its entirety, stumbling over the longer words and sometimes losing his place altogether. I'm unable to speak. This is . . . this is impossible, a nightmare. How can this be?

I am to be arrested immediately.

I am to be questioned by the Holy Office in the matter of an open case.

I am to declare the truth or face a potential death sentence.

Flanked on either side by a guard, I'm led out the door and hauled up onto a donkey that has been waiting between two bay horses. Shaking, I endure the short ride to a building with shuttered windows and double oak doors, both of which are decorated with giant iron studs. One guard helps me down from my mount, a gesture I consider thoughtful until he slips a hood over my head.

"Follow me," he says. A calloused hand grabs my left wrist.

I tread forward carefully. I hear the creaking of a door, then the scuttling of heels across the stone floor. The sudden cold of the place reminds me of a wine cellar. More steps and I smell the reek of unwashed bodies, of feces and vomit and pus and putrefaction. The deeper we walk into the bowels of the building, the clearer—and more distressing—the sounds: moans, faraway screams, anguished pleas, shouts of damnation. My knees soften, but the guard holds me up as if I were no heavier than a doll.

"Steady, señora. We're almost there."

Another door groans open and shut. The guard removes the hood. I blink to adjust to the sudden light. The room is large. The walls are bare except for a large wood cross. In the center, placed to command attention, the Dominican friar sits at a table, his big nose redder and rounder than I remember. A ledger is open before him and next to it is another leather-bound book. To his left, at a smaller table, a bald man hunches over a stack of papers, quill and inkpot at arm's distance. Probably a clerk of some sort. There are no torture implements that I can see, no straps, no spikes, no ropes. A bubble of hope gurgles up in my chest.

The friar adjusts the short black cape over his shoulders. He motions for me to come closer and then mumbles something to the clerk. After explaining that he's responsible for keeping official records, he asks my name, my age, my permanent address. As if he didn't know them already! Every time I answer, the clerk scribbles something. Following the volley of questions, the friar falls silent for a long time. It's so quiet in the room that I can hear the uneven breath of the guard next to me. My thoughts race in nonsensical circles. I wish I had a chair, anything to rest my weary bones, but there's no other furniture in the chamber except for the writing tables. During this interminable pause, the Dominican coughs a few times before spitting into a handkerchief he produces from somewhere. I've never despised someone so fiercely or so quickly.

"Were you at the house of Núria Ripoll Masso, widow of Pablo Salvat Déulosal?"

I nod.

"Speak up so we can hear you."

"Yes," I croak, the sound as small and insignificant as I feel.

"What days were you present?"

"We arrived on Maundy Thursday and I departed the day after Easter Monday."

"We?"

"My nursemaid and I."

"And where is she, this nursemaid?"

"Dead."

The clerk stops his scribbling and stares at me as if doubting this easily confirmable truth. That gesture makes me nervous and hopeful at the same time. The information these men have is obviously incomplete. Aldonça's death was the biggest event to transpire at my cousin's house during the holy days, and an informant would have passed this on. Moreover, Anna certainly would have provided such a detail.

"The cause of death? When?"

I close my eyes, feeling the pang of loss afresh. "I don't know the cause of death, but it was on Easter Sunday."

"Propitious for resurrection."

I stare at him uncertain how, or if, I should respond. The Dominican looks through some papers. I lean closer to the guard and ask for something to sit on. A stool, a chair, a crate will do. This prompts the friar to look up and demand, "Did you say something?"

"I asked for a chair."

Sneering, the friar pounds the table; no chair is brought in. The questioning continues. He asks why I was at the house, how often I visited my cousin, the purpose of this particular visit, also if I had noticed anything unusual.

"Nothing unusual," I say without hesitation.

"Nothing? You observed nothing?"

I recount our attendance at the Procession of the Holy Burial, the beauty of the Nazarenos in their tunics and capirotes, the inspiring beats of the drummers, the dazzling light of the cathedral's tapers. The details are such that no one can doubt my sincerity.

"And that's all you saw on Friday?" he demands.

"Only that. As I told you before, my cousin is a very pious woman. She has her own pew at the cathedral and she's extremely generous with the Holy Mother Church. She's even the benefactor of a local convent."

"As she should be."

"Of course. As we all should be."

"Yet, we received a report of Judaizing by this esteemed cousin of yours. That she koshers her meats, refuses pork, keeps the Sabbath."

"From whom?"

"I'm not at liberty to reveal that."

"A false report, I can assure you. A malicious report. I can't understand who would lodge such a falsehood. Núria's beyond reproach in her observation of Catholic teachings. In fact, I'd add that her life is exemplary, and maybe because of this, others are jealous. It wouldn't be the first time envy turns to slander. To say she lights candles, that her kitchen . . ." I stop. I worry that he might ask how I know so much about these Jewish rituals.

Again, I grow dizzy. I'm not used to standing for so long, and the midday fare I ate was light. A stabbing pain shoots up my back. If the Dominican keeps me in this room any longer, if he continues with his endless questions, I'm afraid I'll slip up in some way. Or . . . or since I've not told him what he wants to hear, I'll be imprisoned for days, stretched on the rack or hung from a strappado. I wonder if those horrors are happening to Anna or Núria at this very hour, torture so brutal they'll confess to anything.

"And you, as you stand before me, swear you didn't see this woman, your cousin, observing the Jewish Sabbath."

"Yes, I swear."

"Under penalty of death you swear?"

"I swear before our Lord Jesus Christ." I cross myself with the same enthusiasm Núria displayed during the Good Friday observances. This profane lie, I believe, is no worse a sin than loving two men.

"Very well," the Dominican says with an air of finality.

He consults with the clerk, and I'm optimistic about being dismissed. I tell myself that I've been convincing in my testimony. I've performed in a way that leaves no room for doubt. I've acquitted myself in an exemplary manner. And as soon as I return to the house, I will demand we leave this godforsaken city, ride as far away and as quickly as Jaume's hired carriage can travel, though of course I know the tentacles of the Holy Office stretch far and wide and no one is immune to their grasp or greed.

Then a disturbing thought creeps in: Anna. I cannot leave Anna behind, regardless of the outcome of my inquiry. Once she joined me on the road, her welfare was entrusted to me. Yet I don't know where she is or what she has said—or even how much she knows. At this point, I can only hope that Jaume and José Ignacio are successful in finding her.

"Brother?"

"Yes?"

Though he's obviously irritated at the interruption, I press on. "There's a young maid you took this morning. I'd like to know what has happened to her."

"You would, now?"

"Of course. She's just a child."

"I'll keep that in mind."

"But where is she?"

He shrugs, and it's such an obvious lie that anger overtakes my dread. Still, I hold back words and instead pray that his body will be consumed with boils. I pray he develops leprosy, that he grows blind with the sickness of whores, that he is flogged, starved, decapitated, burnt to a crisp.

Oblivious to my thoughts, the friar returns to his papers. After a brief interlude, he addresses the guard: "Take her to the cell."

"What? No!"

The last words I hear are mocking, pitiless: "The old bat seems to have a knack for fainting, doesn't she?"

I come to sometime later. My first notion is to call for Jaume, he who has always been able to solve any problem, large or small. But then the events of the past few hours rush back to me all at once: the friar, the guards, the arrest, the questioning. I fight back tears, knowing hopelessness will only make me weaker.

Where is my son? Does he know where I am? Will he come for me? Of course he will. I cannot, will not doubt. In the meantime, I must remain strong. I survey my surroundings. The cell is dimly lit by a weak light pouring through two barred windows. The stench is atrocious. Rats squeak and scuttle. A half-dozen other women sit in shadow, slumped against the walls, clinging to the very oppressiveness that troubles the air.

I search for Anna, and when I see a small bundle pressed against a corner, I immediately know it's her. I call her name; she sits up, looks around.

"Señora!"

The surprised delight in her voice serves as a magic potion for my flagging energy.

"Come, child. Come over here."

And she does. I search her face and limbs for cuts or bruises, for any trace of torture, but find no marks. She assures me that "the fat man," as she calls him, asked lots of questions, most of which she couldn't answer. She begins to cry and folds herself into my arms. We remain in this embrace for a very long time, or until something grazes my shoulder. I scream, dragging Anna with me as I crawl backward on my hands and heels to get away from whatever has attacked me. But nothing has. It's only the young guard who stood next to me during the interrogation. He jiggles my shoulder again, demanding my attention.

"You've been released," he says in my ear.

I shake my head in disbelief. This is a trick, a ploy to entrap me.

"Hurry." He pulls me up. "Before Brother Tómas changes his mind."

"And the child?"

"No one said anything to me about her."

"She's coming with me."

"For God's sake, woman, don't be a dupe."

The guard's torch provides barely enough illumination for me to read his face. "Why can't she come with me?"

"Look, we don't have much time to argue, and I only have permission to release you. No one else."

"Why? What's happening?"

As I ask these questions, the guard continues to pull at my sleeve, and I, in turn, keep dragging Anna by the arm. I have no intention of leaving her behind. Perhaps he doesn't notice, perhaps he doesn't care, but together we trail after him, staggering through the cell's creaky iron gate, down one torchlit corridor and then another before coming to an abrupt stop in front of a narrow door. At first, I suspect it leads to another chamber, one where the terrifying work of the Inquisition is done.

Where confessions, true or not, are extracted. Where we'll learn that everything we've experienced thus far has been a preamble, a formality.

"Don't worry," he reassures me as he thumbs through a key ring. "You're one of the lucky ones. You have wealthy protectors willing to donate to the cause."

Before I can ask him to clarify, he throws the door open and shoves Anna, then me. We tumble out into the night and the cool wind slaps our faces and Anna yelps and I gasp as we plunge into the waiting arms of Jaume and José Ignacio.

"Mother!"

"Jaume!"

"Thanks be to God!"

Jaume snatches me close to his side and José Ignacio lifts the wailing Anna off the ground. We laugh and we shriek and then run. We run and run and run, we run through the darkness, through alleyways and one broad street, past a dog sleeping in a doorway, along a winding road lit by torches. And the silence of the late hour is interrupted only by our footsteps and the stuttering inhalation of my sobs.

Chapter 13

1604–1606

Concerning the Use of My Name and the
Consequences of Fame on My Reputation

On a blustery January day that stiffened limbs and made hair stand on end, Miquel appeared at our office on Carrer del Comerç without warning or previous invitation. It had been a frigid winter thus far, a devastating season for anyone who took sustenance from land or sea. Commerce had come to a halt in many areas as the roads, particularly to the north in the Pyrenees and to the west in Castile, had turned inhospitable to travel. Hence, we expected no visitors until a general thawing blessed us—which, I might add, didn't arrive until late spring, for temperatures only grew more bitter with every coming week. At the time we didn't know we had entered a decade-long period of harsh winters, unusual snowfalls, and damaging windstorms, not only in our city but also along the Costa del Maresme, from Caldes d'Estrac to Sant Pol de Mar.

In the back room of the upper floor, at the desk Father had equipped for me so many years earlier, I heard the front door open downstairs but paid it no heed as I was consumed by the task my son had assigned me. Though he had proven himself quite capable of running the business after Françesc's death, the files were in desperate need of organization. In addition, Jaume had become suspicious of some questionable bills of lading and suspected a particular clerk of petty embezzlement, a charge he didn't make lightly because the man had been in our employ for some time. My son, for all his rigidity and occasional abrasiveness, was loath to dismiss someone who, until then, had been dependable and loyal. He possessed a compassionate side, too, though some might have found it well concealed.

Protected by columns of empty crates and cocooned by the esteem of employees, I toiled in relative privacy and comfort. The scratch of quill on paper, the sight of Jaume bent over his ledger, and the familiar smell of wool and leather provided the consolation I couldn't find in my household. I also felt relevant, essential.

When one of the clerks announced I had a visitor, I thought him confused. No one I knew would ever think to visit me here.

"It can't be for me." I furrowed my brow in consternation. "The caller must be for Jaume."

The clerk shook his head. "No, *senyora*. The visitor requested you specifically. He said Aldonça sent him."

I regarded my ink-stained fingertips, not the presentable hands of someone ready to accept callers. "Jaume, have we forgotten an appointment?"

"No, Mother. You heard Manel. It's for you, but if you'd like for me to accompany you, I'll come." The last words carried a current of irritability. Jaume hated interruptions.

"I'd like that, yes. *Gràcies*."

Yet as soon as we had walked the necessary paces, navigating the steep stairs and then the serpentine path that led to the room fronting the street, I rued my decision to ask Jaume along. This was one visitor I should have handled alone.

Miquel stood at the counter, looking weary and lost. Snow dusted his gray cape, and he had trudged mud into the premises. My knees knocked against my skirts.

"Miquel, dear cousin," I said in a greeting that was, to my ears at least, overly friendly. "I didn't know you were in Barcelona."

"Dolça," he replied, his voice weighted by caution, "I'm pleased to see you."

For what seemed an eternity, we stared at each other as if the world around us had been suspended in an eerie void and we were the only two people in it. Then Jaume cleared his throat, and everything around me became animated again as if suddenly lit by thousands of candles.

"Is there something we can do for you?" Jaume asked.

"Miquel, this is my son. Jaume, this is my . . . your . . . my cousin from Madrid."

"Now from Esquivias."

Each man took the measure of the other. Did they recognize themselves? Did they suspect kinship? Though Jaume had retained Miquel's coloring, as well as the shape of his nose and the breadth of his forehead, the resemblance between the two was no longer as strong as it once had been. Also, time and circumstances had exacted a brutal toll on Miquel; he looked older than a man of four-and-fifty years.

"Are you visiting our fair city?" Jaume asked.

"For a time, yes. I'm in the process of finishing a book."

Jaume pursed his lips; it was as close to a sneer as politely possible. Like Françesc, like Father, like any good *mercader*, he possessed a strong disdain for poets and painters. "Your first, sir?"

"No, no. I'm a published poet and playwright."

Jaume seemed unimpressed by this accomplishment, and hoping the conversation would develop no further, I announced, "Miquel is a busy man, Jaume, and I'm grateful that he stopped by, but we shouldn't delay him. He and I can catch up later." I smiled at Miquel, pleading with my eyes for him to understand my message.

Oddly, Jaume was unwilling to go along with this abrupt dismissal. "Haven't I met you before?" he asked, cocking his head. "I feel as I have."

"I think not," Miquel answered.

I interfered, "When you were very young, Jaume, barely weaned."

"I must have not made an impression, if Cousin Miquel can't remember."

Miquel laughed good-naturedly, and Jaume surprised me by offering to show him the premises. Much to my relief, Miquel begged off, claiming an appointment. But at the door, before he opened it to the midmorning cold, he turned and said, "I hope to see you soon. At Quirze's?"

I was surprised by the brazenness of his invitation. So, apparently, was Jaume.

"My mother doesn't socialize as much as she once did," my son replied. His words were clipped, the inflection curt. "The loss of my father has been immense."

"Of course, of course." Miquel's cheeks colored, and he hastily escaped into the frozen streets.

Though I expected Jaume to bring up this conversation later, he never did. With so many other preoccupations, he probably gave our unexpected visitor no more thought. My son's lack of interest, however, didn't change the incontrovertible fact that once again Miquel had entered my life—and I had no idea why. I thought our chance meeting (and unpaid wager) at the poetry joust had settled matters between us.

I didn't see Miquel again until Candlemas, more than two weeks later. As with all Catalan customs, this holiday was observed in both secular and sacred fashion, for it arrived after Christmas and before the spring equinox, marking the end of one cycle and the beginning of another. Tradition called for us to store away the crèche—ours was carved from beautiful Sienna marble—but also to entertain ourselves in the forecasting of the remaining winter weather. There were many ways to do this, none of them entirely accurate, but they were beloved by the populace and harmless enough for the ecclesiastical authorities to ignore. According to folklore, if it rained on Candlemas Day, winter was nearing its end, but if the day remained dry, the cold would persist well into April and May.

On that second of February, no rain fell on Barcelona, but the sky served as a stage for ominous clouds, giving hope to those of us who yearned for warmth. Bundled up in our finest wool, we went to El Born to watch the procession of young women as they carried candles for the blessing at church. If not for Alba's participation in this event, I might have remained at home, next to the brazier, spiced cider in hand, but I felt it was my duty to provide support. As expected, most of my relatives attended the Candlemas procession, including Quirze and, at his side, Miquel.

We avoided each other, or at least I made it a point to not meet his eyes, though I often felt his stare on my back, boring, questioning. Jaume and Miquel did speak, but very, very briefly. I had hoped that one of them would show more than a passing interest in the other after that encounter in our office, but it was obvious this connection was not to be. Jaume probably thought of Miquel as a poor relation and therefore of no use to him, and as for Miquel—who knows how he viewed our son. By then, I had given up on the idea of revealing to either of them the secret of their relation. The truth served no purpose, quite the opposite, and the acceptance of that misbelief granted me peace and justified my complacency.

After the procession, Quirze, the ever-accommodating host, extended an invitation to continue the festivities at his house, and though Jaume declined, I accepted. Quirze's would be a safe and acceptable venue to continue my furtive examination of Miquel. For all my pretensions, I remained drawn to him like a magnetized needle in a compass. I think he knew this; I think Quirze did too, as did the gimlet-eyed Aldonça.

My cousin had grown fat and gray over the years, and his stomach often strained the seams of his finely tailored clothes. Though he had been successful in business, Quirze's personal life had been a series of tragedies and mishaps. A son had drowned, his first two wives had died in childbirth, and his current one had survived the pox a few years earlier. None of these tragedies, however, had affected his desire—or talent—to entertain. His home was not far from mine, and it was often the site not only of family gatherings but also of bacchanalian festivities during carnival and La Nit de Foc. In such a setting, with wine liberally poured and consumed, it was inevitable—nay, natural—that Miquel and I would drift toward each other and eventually fall into conversation. Wasn't that what we inevitably did, time and again?

Initially, Miquel spoke of his book, about a character crazed by too much reading, and how the idea had developed during his time in prison. He spoke, too, of his literary successes, though his tone carried a lingering disappointment. Sadly, the financial rewards he so diligently sought had not matched his triumphs.

"Do you ever question your most deeply held beliefs?" he asked.

"What do you mean?" I gulped down my wine, sensing that our tête-à-tête was suddenly taking a serious turn.

"We all live by a code of principles and expect that our devotion to these principles will result in a particular kind of existence."

"Such as?"

"You care for your children and your children will care for you."

"True. Jaume is devoted to me, as I'm devoted to him." I didn't elaborate, however, as I intuitively understood that his relationship with his daughter was fraught with problems. He never spoke of her. "But what else do you have in mind?"

"The Christian principles. That the meek will inherit the earth and the persecuted will possess the kingdom of heaven."

"Hmmm. So far I've seen none of that."

"Precisely." He drew closer to me, so close I could see the stubble on his cheeks, the circles under his eyes.

"I don't know what you're getting at."

"Be patient. I'm going to give you another example—society's assumptions. That the talented will achieve success, that those who have served the king will receive just remuneration, that—"

"Miquel," I cajoled, uncomfortable by his sullen tone, "it's unwise for a man of your years to hold those tenets as gospel. At the risk of sounding cynical, everyone knows they're only platitudes."

"But I've held them as truth my entire life, and nothing has come of it."

"Nothing? Such harshness."

"No, I'm realistic, and that's the difference between the two of us. You've been coddled from birth." I grimaced, but he went on: "My opportunities, on the other hand, have been few and are even now narrowing. I'm limited in everything: money, prestige, stability."

"I wouldn't put it that way."

"How then would you describe my circumstances, my Dolça of the pampered life?"

At a loss for what to say, I squeezed my goblet of wine so hard that my hand and arm began to throb. Thankfully, Alba and Assumpció wandered over to us right about that time, happily chattering about the upcoming nuptials of another cousin. The mood lightened and Miquel was temporarily distracted. Just the same, he left our group as soon as he could, as soon as it was appropriate to do so, and we did not speak again that evening. As I watched him move away, however, it occurred to me that life truly had cheated him, and he was well aware of this. That aura of invincibility, that conviction of inevitable success—what I had so admired in him when we first met—had been chiseled away by war, imprisonment in Algiers, false accusations in his own country, and a series of jobs for which he was ill-suited. My refusals to his proposals had probably contributed their own blows as well. However, I also knew better than most that, though he might waver, though he might doubt and stumble, in the end, he was not one to abandon hope or lose heart. No, not my Miquel. He would soldier on.

Over the course of the next few weeks, when we came face-to-face in public, we were courteous but spoke no more than a few words to each other. This strained relationship proved more painful than the years of separation to which I had grown accustomed. Something was suddenly gone from my life, and I couldn't name the source of my loss, much less admit to it. Eventually, I blamed this feeling of privation on an immodest reality: I was hungry for the touch of a man, for the caresses only a lover can offer. I longed for sweet words whispered in my ear, for the admiring stares of a beau, for the knowing smiles of a beloved. Five years had passed since Françesc had provided me with those blessings, and though I was no longer a young woman, I was not stonehearted.

There was more to it, of course. After seeing Miquel again, knowing he was in my city, within walking distance, made me miss him specifically, not just any faceless man. We were two of a type, he and I, driven by what we couldn't possess and haunted by what we did. Aware of the extent of my deception, the depth of my guilt, he also understood me in ways family couldn't, and didn't. He knew my shadows, my grays, my darks, that which I hid from others. Ours had been a complicated union from the very start, made more difficult by our disparate stations in life but also by his doggedness and my intractability. The truth was I missed our arguments as much as I missed our conversations.

So, when Miquel sent a messenger with a plaintive plea—*Please meet me before I leave for Castile. I have much to tell you.*—I went without considering implications or consequences. Quirze accompanied me to the door but no farther.

"You two are among the people I love most," Quirze said.

"I'll take that as a compliment," I replied.

"But I will also count you as my most frustrating failure."

Before I could ask what he meant, Miquel opened the door and my cousin left the premises. I followed a formally attired Miquel into a room bright with light and smelling of wet wool and smoke. It was outfitted with two claret-color wingback chairs, a low bedstead with a thin mattress, and a desk that was no more than a slab of dark wood on spindle legs. Heavy blue curtains decorated the windows, but the walls were bare except for surprisingly beautiful brass sconces. I could feel him watching me as I took in my surroundings.

"Not much of a place," Miquel admitted with a self-deprecating chuckle, "but it's an improvement from the hostals."

"It does have a good view," I said. My tone was cautious but conciliatory.

Together we walked to the open window, and the charms of the address were obvious. From this perch, one could smell the brine of the sea, hear the creaking of ships' masts, and admire wooded slopes in the distance. After a few moments, he said, "Will you do me a kindness and take a seat?"

I did, and he sat on the other wingback chair. He took several shallow breaths, and I braced myself for . . . well, for an accusation. I thought he had finally grasped what appeared to me as obvious: Jaume was his son, the fruit of our long-ago union, the secret I had been keeping from him. And this meeting would allow him to take me to task for not telling him.

I couldn't have been more wrong.

"I asked you here, my dearest Dolça, to plead my case before I leave."

My heart stuttered, but I didn't speak.

"I know you love me. I know that as well as a bird knows how to fly or a flower knows to grow toward the sun. So, I'm trying to understand your reasons for rejecting my overtures."

"Rejection is a strong word."

"What other would you use then?"

"Words are not my business, but I think rejection implies a wholesale refusal of . . . well, of everything. Of your company. Of your stories. Of your humor. That's not what I want."

"What do you want then? Because truly I'm very confused."

Sensing my ambivalence, he rose from his chair and collected me in an embrace. I didn't speak and he didn't press for a reply, but I allowed him to eventually steer me to bed and we made love that day for the first time in many, many years, a quiet and slow process that had little to do with the ardor of our youth. Later, the curse broken, our legs entwined, I turned on my side so he wouldn't see my tears. I feared he might judge them as regret, not gratitude. That's when I spotted crumpled papers scattered under his desk and asked him about the mess.

"The writing," he confessed, "has been difficult. I think I've taken on more than my skills and experience can manage."

I was amazed that he had admitted to such doubt. Miquel had never expressed any hesitation about his talent—only frustration and anger that it wasn't duly recognized. I was at a loss for what to say.

"Every day I write until my hand cramps or my inkpot runs dry. I can't pull myself away from this flood of words jumbled in my mind. I can't escape. On the contrary. It's as if I'm enslaved. The more I suffer, the more this manuscript grows in size."

He paused for breath, and I took advantage. "Maybe you should take a week or two away from it. Give it a rest."

"Don't you think I've tried? I'm haunted by this story, by this errant knight and his lowly squire. Haunted! Consumed!"

"Do you have a working title?"

"That's the one thing of which I've been certain all along. *The Ingenious Gentleman Don Quixote of La Mancha*."

"Quixote?"

He nodded but didn't elaborate, though later I would discover he had adapted the surname of one of his wife's relatives. Of course. I'd discover many more details about the book once it was published, particulars that were hurtful and insulting and that, in consideration of our relationship, never should have met paper or press. That, however, would come later.

"Sometimes," he added, "the ideas pop into my head in the middle of the night, when I can't sleep. The scenes arrive fully formed and I do little but transcribe what appears before me. I'm held back only by the speed of my own hand in directing the pen, and that never seems swift enough."

"And other times?"

"But other times—most times—I struggle to find the correct word or scene to forward the plot."

"Do you have a publisher?"

"Yes, Francisco de Robles. And a printer, Juan de la Cuesta. I have several meetings with them next month."

"In May, then. That's good news, isn't it?"

"Good news? Is there such a thing? Both de Robles and de la Cuesta are well known, but together they drive a hard bargain."

I put my head on his chest and reminded him of what he had once told me about my own attempts at mastery: *Do you love painting? Can you imagine your life without it? Those should be your only concerns.*

He nuzzled my neck. "Thank you for that sensible advice because this book will likely make me no more than a few ducats."

And then . . . and then, eight months after he left Barcelona, eight months after we made love for the last time, *El Quixote* entered the world, all 664 pages of it, fifty-two chapters of irony and adventure and cultural criticism disguised as comedy. The first edition was printed on cheap paper made by the Jesuits of El Paular and not on the fine rag paper Miquel had expected. It went on sale in Madrid on the sixteenth of January, 1605, for 290.5 maravedis.

I would have burned each of the four hundred copies of its first edition in a bonfire to betrayal.

When Quirze returned from a business trip to Castile, he wasted no time bringing *El Quixote* to my attention.

"Have you read the book?" he asked, as soon as the housemaid left us alone.

I looked up from my desk, where I was writing a letter to Gabriel, my still-very-much-alive brother-in-law. "Book?"

Quirze held it up with two hands. The title appeared atop in large letters, along with Miquel's name, including the Saavedra surname he had added a few years back, in a smaller type. There was a detailed illustration, but from where I was sitting, I could only distinguish the outline of a bird.

"Miguel's book about a crazy hidalgo. I brought it home for you."

"Thank you, cousin."

"Before you thank me, you should read it."

Such words from Quirze foreshadowed trouble, so I proceeded with caution. "Last year Miquel told me it was about a knight and his squire."

"True."

I motioned for him to sit. "What are you trying to tell me?"

"The hidalgo's muse, this man named Quixote, is a character that should rouse your interest."

"Muse?"

"His woman. His queen. His lady. His inspiration."

"I'm not understanding you."

He looked down at the thick, ivory-colored book cover, in no hurry to answer. Whatever he was about to say, I suspected he had already discussed it with others. How many others and how close to me, I didn't know.

"Spit it out, Quirze."

"The woman bears your name."

It took me a moment to figure out what he was saying, and when I did, I jumped up from my seat, hitting my knees against the desk. "Dolça? The character in Miquel's book is named Dolça?"

"No, no."

I sat again and sighed with relief—too soon.

"He named her Dulcinea," my cousin continued, "and she's central to everything this Quixote lunatic does. Her beauty is described as—"

"Why would he do that? Why would he use my name?"

"Are you listening to me?"

"Yes, of course I am, Quirze."

"Stop worrying about what and why Miquel did or did not do. Focus on the ramifications. That's what has brought me here."

"Dulcinea," I said to myself. "Dulcinea."

"Dolçie, listen! You need to know something else. Don Quixote refers to the character as Dulcinea in his hallucinations, but her true name, her Christian name, is revealed as Aldonza."

Aldonza! There would be no mistaking, no skirting around our connection now. Thank goodness Aldonça could not read, for she would have been mortified. I leaned back in my chair and covered my face with my hands. I wasn't sure what to think. I must admit to an initial satisfaction, a small pleasure at the thought of my influence on Miquel's work, but that feeling quickly gave way to an awareness of more sinister implications. Now everyone would know about us. Suspicions would be confirmed, rumors would be revived. There would be snickers, there would be gossip and condemnation and whispered words behind cupped hands. I blushed at the mere thought of certain repudiation from family and friends.

I don't know how long I remained in this state of shocked silence, but out of nowhere I felt a hand on my shoulder. Annoyed, I brushed it away.

"*Senyora*, you must drink." It was one of the new maids, Ermessenda, holding a glass of *orxata* for me. A fruit platter had been placed on the desk. I shook my head in dismay. I couldn't recall asking for any of this.

"I rang for her," Quirze said. "Now drink up."

I sipped the drink, but the thought of eating turned my stomach, such was my distress. Apparently, Quirze entertained no such reservations. He helped himself to the food without qualms or encouragement. I watched him with a growing sense of doom. He chewed like a cow. How had I never noticed this? Once satiated, he dabbed at his mustache and beard and then turned his attention back to me.

"It might not be as bad as I suspect," he said. "Few will read the book and by summer it will be forgotten, just as his others were."

"And you call yourself his friend."

He laughed. "It's true what I say, and Miguel himself would be the first to admit to his failures."

"That's not my concern right now. But if it's published here in Barcelona . . ." I couldn't finish the thought.

"Even if it is, and that's a big if, not many will read it. That's a reality."

"But those who will are people I know." I winced.

"No need to lose sleep over a distant possibility. For now, I thought it best you should know. As they say, *avís és avantatjat.*"

"Yes, forewarned is forearmed."

"Read it and judge for yourself. I may be making more of it than I need to."

"Did you speak about it to him? When you were in Madrid?"

"No."

"Why not?"

"I hadn't read the book then. I wasn't in the capital on holiday, you know. I was busy tending to business."

Quirze's defensiveness was a bit excessive, and I eyed him with skepticism. Had he come here on Miquel's behalf to scout my reaction, to measure my anger? I decided not to pursue the matter. What good would it do to challenge his version of events, to question his allegiance? He had been kind enough to stop by immediately after arriving from Madrid, had he not?

With a pat on my head and a kiss on each cheek—no matter our age I was still his *cosí preferit*—he left the book, still smelling of glue and pulp, next to the fruit platter. I spent all day and night reading it. I laughed, I wept, I seethed, and perhaps most confounding of all, I admired. Yes, I cannot deny that I turned each page with a growing respect for Miquel's talent, the skill with which he had created his characters, his settings, his theme. Don Quixote was a man for our age.

This, however, would not save me from all the tittle-tattle produced and consumed by the vapid. In September, at a family dinner at Cousin Ferran's house, his wife, a hard-faced woman with beady eyes, couldn't stop talking about the book. A month earlier the *Quixote* had been published in Valencia, and several of my intimates had already commented to my face on the coincidence of names. I suspected worse was said behind my back.

"Did you know Cervantes would do this, Dolça?" Sofia asked me, practically shouting from her position at the head of the table.

"No. Why would I?"

"There must be a reason he chose your nickname from so many others."

Other relatives dropped their own conversations to eavesdrop on ours, but I pressed on, "If there is, Sofia dear, I'm not privy to it."

"Both of you have known each other for so long."

"Yes, we have. Since I was very young."

"And you've always been close, it seems. Thick as thieves when at the jousts and the festivals."

"We are indeed," I said stoutly, deciding to confront her insinuation head on, the best way to quash rumors. "We're as close as any two cousins with common interests can be and I value that relationship, as does he."

"Yet he shows this by doing something so crass," she insisted, "so lacking in class."

"If someone used me as writerly inspiration, I'd think it an honor," Quirze interjected. "It's a form of immortality. Dulcinea is famous and will be so for a long time. I wish somebody would versify about me or give a character my name."

I smiled at him in gratitude, but his spirited defense didn't hold long, not with Sofia's unrelenting attention. "You'd think that, Quirze, because your morals are so low," she said. "I wouldn't like it if my name was used to denote an ugly character with vulgar manners. This Dulcinea is a woman of easy virtue with nothing to recommend her."

"And you developed this opinion from what? From reading the book?" Quirze retorted. "I can't imagine such a feat. All the years you've been married to my brother I've known you as an *estúpid* woman whose only interest is her looks. Which are pitiful to begin with."

For several long moments not a slurp or a champing was heard in the hall, but then my youngest aunt—who was nearly blind but still possessed excellent hearing—broke the spell: "Are we so desperate for a topic of conversation that we must discuss a book? Why not talk about the birth of the new royal heir? Or about those evil English?"

The laughter that followed sounded forgiving, or at least I wanted to believe it so, and as I returned to my meal, I was thankful that Jaume wasn't present to witness the exchange. But surviving one case of innuendo meant little in a longer timeline of aspersions. Tracts anonymously published in Barcelona and Tarragona, even in the village of Sitges, spread gossip and amplified rumors. For instance, a one-page newssheet known for its specious comments about several wealthy Barcelona families included this gem:

> Talk in Madrid, Sevilla, Bilbao, and as far as Lisbon points to a certain Barcelona matron as the inspiration for Dulcinea, that not-so-maidenly wench in the unforgettable adventure story penned by a former royal commissary, Miguel de Cervantes Saavedra. Wagging tongues say the flesh-and-bones Dulcinea is a widow well-born, from a distinguished lineage of warriors and merchants. Wagging tongues also reveal that unrequited love is not only the message of this tale but also its motive. Could there be more similarities between Aldonza de Lorenzo, the sturdy peasant girl, and the Catalan-speaking lady of refined bloodline? Is there a secret the Castilian writer will divulge in the much-awaited but not-yet-written sequel? Curious readers await answers.

There was no way to quell the talk, no manner of salve to soothe my embarrassment. Miquel's fame, so awaited, brought me only humiliation and heartbreak. And while some women, Quirze's third wife among them, believed that serving as a muse was proof of importance, I didn't subscribe to this line of thinking and to this day consider any such correlation crude, an achievement reserved for those who lack a good name.

As soon as Miquel returned to Barcelona in late autumn, I lost no time in confronting him at the Sota Muralla address. My anger had waxed and waned since my meeting with Quirze, but as the popularity of the book grew—by then two Madrid editions, two in Lisbon, with a second edition for Aragón—so did my sense of offense.

"How could you?" I shrieked when Miquel answered my knock. "You've deceived me in the worst way possible. You've betrayed my family, my nursemaid, everything I've offered you."

Miquel pulled me into the room and slammed the door shut. I blinked several times to adjust to the dimness, but once that happened, I allowed my wrath full rein. "You're the lowest of the lows. An opportunist. A Judas. A—"

He put a hand over my mouth and made shushing noises, but I had no intention of stopping. I'd been waiting to confront him for a very long time. Barely had the morning church bells pealed than I had slipped out of the house and hurried through the streets as they filled with laborers and carts. I was eager to expend my fury on the one person who deserved it. I wanted to strangle Miquel, shake him, slap him, insult him, belittle him. Harm him in the very same way he had hurt me. This was, after all, a man I had welcomed into my bed only a year earlier, and that weakness had cost me dearly.

I pulled away from his grasp. "This Dulcinea in your . . . your . . ." I brandished the book in front of his face, not an easy gesture by any means since it was a bulky tome without the reinforcement of parchment binding.

"Why did you give that simpleton . . . that peasant . . . my name?"

"It's not your name. You don't own Dulcinea. Furthermore—"

"Everyone, my entire family, my circle of friends, all of Barcelona society knows it is my name. Do you think them blind? You've made it even more obvious with the reference to Aldonza of Toboso. And how you describe her! The insulting words you use! How you ridicule and disparage her!"

"Dolça, you're exaggerating. You shouldn't consider the name of a character an insult. I would think it a compliment."

"A compliment?" I sputtered. "Are you mad? I feel used. Exploited, manipulated. I've been nothing to you but . . ."

I reached into the air, gesturing wildly. He grabbed my shoulders and forced me into a chair. I stared at a spot of ink as it settled into the crevices of his desk and was inordinately pleased to witness its spreading stain. The brazier grumbled, and a pigeon pecked at the closed window.

"Dolça, I never intended for you to be hurt by Quixote's Dulcinea. In fact, I thought you'd be pleased. She is his one true love, his guiding light, his—"

"She is not! All those imaginary qualities are stewing in that crazy man's head, nothing more than fantasies, and you know that well enough."

"But is that not true of all loves?" He took my hands in his. He kissed each knuckle one by one. "Can one truly love, give completely of oneself, without idealizing the person loved? That's what Dulcinea represents."

The floor shifted beneath my feet. I took a deep breath to calm the dizziness.

When I didn't answer, he continued, "Dulcinea, Aldonza, whatever her name, whatever her role, wasn't meant to represent you in a cruel way, dearest. When I created that character and settled on that name, I did so with a heart that ached for you, a heart that desired nothing more than your presence, your attention, your love. I thought you'd be impressed. Please accept this explanation. It's the true one."

"You take me for a fool?"

"No, not at all."

"I'm a laughingstock."

"How can you say that?"

"Your writing . . . your tone. Why is it that Dulcinea is brawny and can throw a bar as far as any lad? Why does she have hair on her chest? Why is she so loud and common that she can summon men from the bell tower just by yelling?"

"You're missing the point."

"I think not."

"So, what would you like me to do?"

I was taken aback by his question. My anger was such that I'd given no thought to what might be done to limit the impact on my life and reputation. Could the editions in circulation be destroyed? Was it too late to change the character's name for future editions? I didn't know about such things. But then at that moment, I convinced myself—wrongly, as it turned out—that this book would go, as Quirze had predicted, the way of his others. Which is to say, into oblivion. In that case, I'd be foolish to draw attention to it. If its popularity soon dissipated, there was no reason to create a spectacle. At that moment, silence appeared to be the best solution.

"My dearest, I would never ever do anything to hurt you," he insisted. "Believe me, please."

"No. You would want revenge."

"Revenge? What are you talking about?"

"All those times I've refused your invitations. You're angry that I've not wanted to leave Barcelona with you."

"Oh, Dolça, Dolça, Dolça. You misunderstand." His voice sounded pained, but I couldn't allow myself to feel anything beyond indignation.

"I think I understand all too well."

"Trust what I say, please. *Please.* I did it to honor you."

"And you expect me to believe that?"

"Yes, because it's the truth."

"Truth? You want to know the truth? Well, here it is. I am the talk of Barcelona. My reputation is in shambles. My friends think I'm—"

"Exaggerations."

"Are they? And how do you even know this? You only arrived yesterday."

"Your reputation will be just fine. Quirze has assured me of that."

Aha! They had spoken, the two men. They had worried. They likely had considered how best to stanch the insinuations they heard. "You don't understand society, Miquel. You never have."

"Oh, but I do, because I've always lived on the outside looking in." He laughed, and it was not a pleasant sound.

"Don't minimize the consequences of your actions. You've not been on the receiving end of those whispers."

"I haven't, that much I'll admit. But I also think you're ignoring the advantages. You're not seeing a fuller picture."

"What's that supposed to mean?"

"It means you'll live for all eternity."

"Who cares about that? I live in the here and now. I'd rather remain unknown."

Our conversation continued like this, running in circles, bumping into dead ends and arriving at no conclusion, so I eventually left, slightly mollified. Once I was alone with my thoughts, however, his words lost their power, and in their place the reality that he had appropriated my identity, the notion that he had tarnished my standing festered like an untreated wound—even as I found the book and its demented knight sadly hilarious.

In the end, Dulcinea—with her hair of gold, her forehead Elysian fields, her eyebrows rainbows, her eyes suns, her cheeks roses, her lips coral, her teeth pearls, her neck alabaster, her bosom marble, her hands ivory, her fairness snow—became the woman who drove us apart. Not Miquel's wife, not his daughter, not the mother of his daughter. What truly distressed me was his refusal to protest the falsehoods propagated by critics in pamphlets, tracts, newsletters, and booklets. These offended deeply, and our relationship, survivor of both physical separation and social convention, suffered its most rigorous beating in the latter half of the new century's first decade. I wouldn't see him again for five years, nor would I answer a single letter or ask Quirze about him, and at the time I didn't feel the slightest remorse for this estrangement.

Chapter 14

27TH OF APRIL TO 15TH OF MAY, 1616,
ALCALÁ DE HENARES AND MADRID

---

*Concerning the End of a Journey and a
Failed Mission Unexpectedly Salvaged*

We await dawn, the deliverance of daylight, in a room near the kitchen, five of us in varying states of disquiet. Carmeta and José Ignacio, Anna, Jaume, and I huddle around a table, next to the brazier. We are wide awake, animated, even jittery. Sleep feels superfluous. We cannot stop talking. We cannot stop from reaching out, from touching. We appear possessed by an urgent need to reassure each other that we're all here, undamaged, whole. We move from gleeful recounting of our reunion to the more sober assessment of how the Dominican intimidated two innocents. How he might have gotten away with who knows what if he had not been so susceptible to worldly goods. The men have their theories about what transpired but refuse to share them. They claim we should not trouble our thoughts with such matters—as if we haven't already been frightened out of our wits. My son provides an inkling of his suspicions when he refers to the fat friar as "the rogue Dominican" and our interrogation as "irregular." He speculates, and José Ignacio concurs, that the Aragonese tribunal—if Brother Tómas is truly acting on its behalf—has not communicated with its Castile brethren to coordinate efforts. I'm not sure what all this means, or if this mattered in our release, but I have little inclination to push for details. I'm happy to be safe, and what concerns me is only this: Brother Tómas had a respectable amount of information about my cousin, and regardless of motive or circumstances, he appears to have the power to use that information for his own interests, whatever those interests might be.

"There may be more competition than we think," Jaume says. "A rivalry of sorts between the regional tribunals."

"I don't understand such things." Carmeta shakes her head. "But it makes no sense to come into a good Christian household and threaten the family. For what?"

"We may never find out," Jaume says.

"So much of life is inexplicable," I say. I dread the possibility that someone at this table might ask about my cousin, so I quickly add, "Why would that friar want to talk to Anna or me?"

"Whatever the reason," José Ignacio continues with a wry smile, "it didn't seem to affect negotiations. No one turned down our offer."

I ask what he means.

"A bribe, Mother," Jaume snaps. "A payoff. As Father would have called it, *suborn*."

The men guffaw and my host slaps his knee, but Carmeta and I shrug in confusion, for though we know the exact meaning of a bribe—our lives are made better by the ability of our families to proffer these inducements—neither of us can figure out what is so comical about the situation.

The night wears on, darkness deepening. Hoots echo in the distance. Since the maids are asleep, it is Carmeta who pours the wine and serves us cold leek pottage and generous chunks of ham. The aroma of the food brings tears to my eyes. Famished, I consume my serving quickly, without stopping to talk. But Anna, who sits at my feet stiffly upright, refuses to eat. She also refuses to go to bed even after we gently explain that a makeshift mattress of straw has been arranged for her in my bedchamber. No amount of coaxing from the sweet-tongued Carmeta can convince the young maid to leave my side. She remains mute and blank-eyed.

"The fright has affected her here," Jaume whispers, and taps his head.

"For good reason," Carmeta adds. "She's but a child."

"Maybe with time she'll recover. It's amazing how one can prevail over embarrassment, humiliation, even betrayal."

I look up from my bowl and study my son. His words surprise me. Is he referring to himself, to the realization about Miquel that has upended his view of the world? I'd like to ask but know this isn't the time or place.

At last, the rooster's crow rouses the servants, and Carmeta orders water to be heated and a bath to be drawn. I am overjoyed by the thought of soaking in the tin bathtub (such a prized rarity), for I need a good and thorough scouring. After this refreshing ablution, I succumb to sleep, but my slumber is fretful, almost fractious, and I awaken several times entangled with the covers. Much later that same day, as the sun slides behind the rooftops, Jaume and I dine together. As has become customary during our stay in Guadalajara, we take our meal apart from our hosts, but it is, as always, quite savory: roasted partridge, turnips in bacon, and cardoons. Enjoying every morsel more than usual, I steal glances at my son and note how much he has aged in just a few weeks. The lines around his mouth have grown more numerous. Gray has gathered at his temples, and a certain weariness has seized his shoulders, pressed them down in resignation. I don't express my dismay at these changes, however. Instead, I listen drowsily as he makes small talk about the weather and the city. But when he suggests, seemingly out of nowhere, that we send Anna back to Saragossa, I'm pulled back to full attention.

"Send back? What do you mean?"

"You don't agree?" He appears perplexed by my reaction.

"It's not about agreeing. It's about the responsibility we owe the young maid."

"She can't be of service to you now. She's more encumbrance than help."

"True, but what exactly do you mean by sending her back? Are you planning to—" I glance over to the corner where she sits on the floor. *Can she hear us? Does she care?*

"She can return with one of the merchant caravans. José Ignacio has offered a few dependable ones."

"The child would travel alone?"

He nods and then adds, obviously for my benefit, "She wouldn't be the first or last to do so."

"But what is she returning to? We don't know what has happened to Núria!"

"Anna should be home with her people. Or at least in familiar surroundings."

"You've made up your mind, I gather."

Again he nods.

I don't like the idea of sending the maid off on a hard trek with strangers, but I also recognize that I must focus attention on my own journey, my own mission. I must still find a way to continue to Madrid. As if guessing my thoughts, Jaume grins enigmatically. He raises his goblet and takes a long sip, then pats his mouth and whiskers dry with a serviette, rather daintily, I might add. He fixes his eyes on me. I brace myself for a reprimand.

"Why didn't you tell me before, Mother? Why did you keep the secret for so long?"

I have no need to ask for clarification. But how do I answer him without revealing the extent of the lie and my timorousness?

"I wanted you to have a good future," I say. "You deserved what Françesc was eager to give you."

"That isn't the whole truth."

"No."

The sound of my honesty reverberates in the room, yet I know its simplicity is not enough. Jaume wants, and deserves, more than a one-word answer. We're talking about his identity here, his place in the world.

"Do you love him?"

Now, *that* is unexpected. I don't know how to explain, not to my son at least, what it felt like to be enamored of a man so different from all those I had met, to be infatuated with his words, his adventures, his life with all its complications. After all, Jaume is fond of custom and tradition. He likes how they provide structure to our lives.

"Yes, I do love him," I say finally. "In my own way."

"Are you sorry?"

"Sorry?"

"For betraying Father. For loving Cervantes."

"I should feel regret, shouldn't I? But I can never regret actions that produced the person I love most."

He frowns, and I'm uncertain if he accepts that explanation or considers it self-serving. I lean over the table and place my hand over his. He doesn't pull away, and a strange hope billows in my heart, if only for a moment.

The following morning I'm surprised by Jaume's request to see me. Usually he's out and about the city before I dress, always the businessman on the hunt for a deal. I presume this meeting must mean he's ready to send Anna on her way to Saragossa, and as soon as we greet each other, I plead with him to dispatch a messenger to Núria's. Jaume, however, dismisses my appeal, adamant that forwarding any message would be unwise in light of my brush with the Inquisition. It would only draw the attention of the Holy Tribunal, or its vast network of spies. When he puts my petition in this context, I'm in total agreement. The last thing I want is another encounter with a Dominican friar.

Obviously pleased with the outcome of that short debate, he shows me to a chair near a beautiful escritoire and then proceeds to tell me he has mapped the journey to Madrid with the driver of the hired carriage. We will leave in two days, when Anna is sent in the opposite direction.

Madrid? Madrid! He either doesn't notice my stunned reaction or chooses to ignore it and, without further explanation, gives me an ink-on-paper rendering of the journey, sketched in his tidy script. Though he has never traveled as assiduously as Françesc once did, Jaume is familiar with this route. The map is obviously more for my peace of mind than for his. I want to ask him dozens of questions, but they're all variations of one: what led to his change of heart?

"Your persistence is to be admired even as it grates," he replies to my inquiry. "I am not immune to it, Mother."

I stifle a chuckle.

"Nevertheless, I want you to know there are rules to follow, *my rules*," he continues. "I don't want to rush. We will travel only as many leagues as your weakened constitution can endure, and not a league more. Do you understand?"

"Yes."

"There are several business matters I must tend to in the capital while we're there. That said, we will not linger in Madrid. I'd like to get home to Elisabet and the children at the soonest."

"Of course, of course. It's always good to return home." I smile, but my mind is plotting how I can use these altered sentiments to ask for a favor. I don't want to challenge this newfound goodwill—but why not? I walked with death, and it did not yet want me. I came face-to-face with the Holy Office but was rescued. If such experiences don't infuse me with determination and courage, what else can?

"Son," I begin, "there's one more thing I need from you."

"More? You want more?" He shakes his head.

Is he affronted by my audacity or is he teasing? Maybe he's holding his power over my head to ensure obedience. I can't guess his motive, and I'm not going to try.

I jump right in: "I'd like to stop at Alcalá de Henares."

"I thought you would," he replies without missing a beat. "Look at the map I gave you. It's the unidentified dot just south of here."

I gape at him with both disbelief and delight, but don't pursue the subject further.

Night surrenders to gauzy sunrise when I bid Anna farewell. I try to reassure her that someone will greet her when she arrives at Núria's, but her eyes speak doubt louder than words ever could. Though we've entrusted her to a caravan of tanners, a family long-known to José

Ignacio, I am uneasy about the arrangement. She is far too young, too innocent—and now too frightened—to be left alone among strangers, but I am without a voice in this matter. I can't insist she come with us to Madrid, not in her state, not without endangering what I consider a tentative truce with Jaume. I'm doing everything I can to maintain my son in good spirits, or at least in a generous mood. When her huddled figure disappears around a corner, I quickly blink back tears that I prefer Jaume not to see. He'd consider me a sentimental fool, and I'm not ready to acknowledge that might be true.

Soon after the little maid's departure, we take leave from our hosts, making sure to express our gratitude and respect. Their hospitality—and their support in time of need—has become the high point of this long and arduous trip.

"You've proven to me that there are indeed people of exemplary character left in this world," I tell Carmeta. "In many ways you've restored my faith."

"You're much too kind," she replies. "But when you encounter the Judases of the world, and you will again, I hope you'll remember us."

I cling to her until Jaume taps my shoulder and helps me climb the carriage steps.

As promised, the carriage is a fine conveyance, and its sturdy frame keeps the jostling to a minimum. I'm pleased by the comfort of the ride and by my son's attention to detail, from a basket of fresh bread to a wool blanket in the event of a chill. However, I miss the cold wind and the warm sun, the pleasure of the landscape unfolding like a quilt of many colors. There are, it seems, certain advantages to the limitations of poverty as experienced on muleback.

We make a formidable procession, the carriage protected by three armed men, dressed all in black as if it were a funeral procession. One sentry leads our small cavalcade, another sits next to the driver, who is also armed, and a third rides alongside Jaume, who at the last minute informed me he preferred to travel on horseback, in this case a black-spotted steed. I expressed disappointment at doing without his company, but he insisted our caravan would be more secure if he had firsthand knowledge (and view) of the road. There may be other reasons. On horseback he can avoid me, or better said, he can avoid whatever conversation we would engage in before our arrival in Madrid. We've not discussed, for instance, if Jaume would like to speak to Miquel alone or in my presence. We've not discussed how he would like to be introduced, what he might say, what questions he'd ask. There are so many possible scenarios, all of which should be planned, all of which should be assessed for their potential pitfalls, but I think Jaume would rather refrain from any debate. It would require another, more acute level of discomfort.

We will travel four leagues to Alcalá de Henares, where we will spend the night instead of continuing to the capital. This is to be a short day, as Jaume wishes not to tax my strength. If it were my decision, I'd head straight to Madrid after our stop, casting not a single backward glance, but I remind myself to be thankful that we head southwest instead of northeast to Barcelona. What's more, our stop at Miquel's birthplace will satisfy an abiding curiosity, at the very least.

Along the road we encounter other travelers because I hear the driver greet them in his lispy speech. (Castilian, such an ugly tongue. So much spitting and hissing and popping.) At some point, long after we've left Guadalajara and before we've stopped for a meal, I open the leather curtain to gain my bearings. The sky is pale, the wind brisk. There are farmhouses and orchards as well as a gray river threading through the brown-and-green of land. In the distance low-lying clouds crown jagged mountains. When we stop for a light meal, I ask Jaume to ride with me.

He gives me a sidelong glance, heavy with reluctance.

"I could use the company and the conversation. Time spent with my son always lifts my spirits."

"But I could use the fresh air, not to mention another pair of eyes to help on the road."

"Jaume, please."

In the end he agrees to join me in the carriage. I waste no time in bringing up the potential meeting that has worried my thoughts for these many hours. I don't ask, however, in the straightforward fashion

I'd prefer. With Jaume it's best to circle around, consider the lay of the land, and then ambush.

"Do you have plans for our stay in Madrid?"

"Of course. Mother. When have you known me to go anywhere unprepared?"

"What would those plans be?"

"I've told you, business, and I've sent word to Don Pedro as well."

"The procurador, of course."

"Always. First and foremost. But seriously, I want to take advantage of this opportunity. A month ago I hadn't expected to be on my way to the capital."

"There are other opportunities that have nothing to do with business."

"I'm well aware."

When he doesn't add to this statement, I, too, remain quiet, feigning interest in his saffron-hued hose, a ridiculous color that is much in fashion. The bump-bumping of the carriage wheels and the groaning of the upholstered bench provide a strange, almost musical background to my thoughts. I'm tempted to own up to my feelings— that is, to tell him he should accompany me to Miquel's so he won't later regret what he could have done. But, alas, candor is not always the best policy. I can't predict how he would respond to my suggestion, what he might do if he feels forced to act against his interests or preferences. I could arrive in Madrid as planned and still be impeded from seeing Miquel. Jaume could very well obstruct any reunion. This journey has opened my eyes to the infinite ways my son has learned to get what he wants.

After a time, Jaume mutters, "I know something is troubling you. You've been chewing your lip as if you were a starving peasant."

"Chewing my lip?"

"Yes. It's a habit you have when you're worried or upset. You may not be aware you do this, but I've watched for it since I was a child."

I laugh. All these years, and I've not been cognizant of what he describes. Do I lack such self-awareness?

"Anyway, out with it, before you bloody your lip."

"You wouldn't think it appropriate, what I want to tell you. What I *should* tell you."

"Don't think for me, Mother." He shifts his position on the carriage bench, but his gaze doesn't waver from my face. "You underestimate me."

And with this invitation, I confide my concerns, leading him in the direction I think he should take without being obvious about it. It is a fine line, this narrow chasm between guidance and command. In the end, though, he makes no firm commitment to visit Miquel, not in so many words, but he nudges my foot with his boot and chuckles, "Oh, Mother."

Just those two words, to be taken in whatever way suits me. "Oh, Jaume," I rejoin, "son of my heart."

I'm confident he will want to talk to Miquel. Though Jaume is a mistrustful sort, a man who keeps his emotions in check—traits that have served him well in business—he can be quite benevolent. And curious.

Miquel's childhood town lies at the foot of craggy hills and a fair distance from the Henares, from which it takes its surname. As we enter the city through the northeast portal, I keep the carriage curtain open, the better to familiarize myself with the place that molded Miquel as a young boy. From what I can observe on our route, the town's edifices are well built and the streets clean. People scurry about, both in the plain attire of servants and in the adornment of hidalgos. I've given the driver—through Jaume, of course—the directions I once guarded so well in memory, and as soon as the carriage stops, I throw open the door.

One of the guards pulls out the steps and helps me down. Though it's been but a few hours of journeying, I'm much more rested than I would have been after a mule ride, and for this I am thankful to Jaume. He also has seen to our lodgings; we will spend the night with a relative of Elisabet's, a young lawyer who has made his home in this city.

"This was once your fa . . . Cervantes's home," I explain when we stand before a house that is trying hard to keep itself from crumbling.

As soon as the words leave my lips, I realize there's no need for me to state the obvious.

The modest two-story structure isn't worthy of special attention. The peeling walls need new mortar, and one of the downstairs windows has a crack. The bottom quarter of the front door is rotting. I imagine Miquel as a child, running around the ground level, through the kitchen and dining room and a barber-surgeon's office, as that was the profession of his father. In the upper floor, he probably shared a bedroom with his younger brothers, Rodrigo and Juan. At what age, I wonder, did he become aware of the family's limited means? When did he compare his surroundings and opportunities with those of his better-situated friends? Certainly, the sight of this sad house provides me with an appreciation of both Miquel's frustrations and ambitions.

I express none of this to our son, though, and at first, Jaume offers no commentary of his own. But as we walk back to the carriage, he harrumphs like an old man vexed by a capricious wife. "*Abocador*," he mumbles disparagingly. Dump.

Now I worry I've pushed him in the opposite direction I intended. I don't want him to think less of Miquel, to be shamed by the circumstances of his father's family. I should have left well enough alone. Sometimes imagination is better than reality at providing details and filling the gaps of what we don't know.

The following day, on a clear, cool morning of birdsong and jasmine-scented breeze, our caravan leaves Alcalá de Henares. Jaume consented to send a messenger to Miquel's house on the corner of Calles de Franco and León to announce our arrival, but now as we near the inevitable moment of truth, I feel my resolve flagging. I'm tormented by indecision and wonder if including Jaume in a reunion is advisable. There's no predicting how either man will respond to the other, and considering Miquel's delicate state of health, this could be dangerous. Moreover, there's the matter of that wife of his, Catalina. I have no idea what she knows about me, if anything. In all our years together and apart, Miquel has rarely spoken about his wife or daughter, and whatever information I own of his life beyond Barcelona's city walls is scarce and, as experience has taught me, unreliable.

To ease my agitation, I try to banish all thoughts of Catalina and of Miquel. Instead, I entertain myself by staring out the carriage window, holding a handkerchief over my nose and mouth to ward off the dust. I catch sight of the winding Henares, its banks shaded by trees. A short time later, we cross a stone bridge over another waterway, the Tojote, and travel past the town of Torrejón and other insignificant villages and hamlets surrounded by farms before we encounter yet another bridge. The motion of the carriage eventually rocks me to sleep, and I miss our entrance into Madrid, an unforgivable offense as I had my heart set on examining the city that is, for better or worse, Miquel's home. (I'm curious, of course, to compare it to my own beloved Barcelona.) It's only when the carriage halts that I bolt to attention. We've stopped in front of a fairly new building with green shutters and red geraniums in its window boxes. Unlike the depressing residence of the previous day in Alcalá, this is quite presentable.

After knocking on the door, Jaume returns to me, mouth set in a grim pout. He tells me Miquel's wife is expecting me. I hesitate, then remind myself that an ill man cannot possibly come to the door to greet a traveler, no matter the distance traveled.

"Is he well?"

Jaume's reply is muffled or perhaps I'm in too much of a hurry to listen properly. At the entrance, he says, "Mother, I need to see to our lodgings. I'll leave the carriage here with the men."

"Don't you want to see Miquel?" I ask. "A visit will lift his spirits."

Jaume coughs, clears his throat, and then looks over my head at Catalina. "It's best you do this alone."

"I thought . . ."

I realize I had pinned my hopes on a grand meeting between father and son, but apparently, Jaume has thought otherwise all along. Perhaps he believes such an audience a betrayal of Françesc, perhaps he cannot imagine how Miquel's presence could benefit him. Whatever the reason, he has reneged on his implied promise. But before I can protest, he mounts his horse and gallops away. I'm left alone with Miquel's other woman.

We walk through a dim vestibule, past a central staircase, and to a side chamber as she explains that they rent the quarters from a royal scribe who occupies the second floor with his wife, four children, and a servant. She guides me to a chair and takes a seat on the other side of a low table. Surreptitiously I study her face, the strong cheekbones, small mouth, and dimpled chin. A scar in the shape of a quarter moon interrupts her smooth forehead. If I were to come across her at church or a street festival, my gaze wouldn't rest for longer than necessary. Yet I must admit her manner is courteous and her smile kind.

"So, you are Miguel's cousin," she says, apparently at a loss for how to begin a conversation. "From Barcelona."

I nod.

"A long trip, sí?"

"Long and dangerous."

"You have found lodgings?" As if she were truly interested.

"We will do so later."

"We have some fine establishments in Madrid. You should have no problems finding something appropriate."

"No, of course not."

A defiant silence follows. Catalina stares at her hands. They're short-fingered and ringless. In fact, there's not an item of jewelry on her person. No earrings, pendant, or brooch. Only a small pomander hangs by a simple chain from the waist of her black gown. Whether this lack of adornment is the result of financial circumstances or personal choice, I dare not guess.

But . . . where is Miquel? I've not come all this way—fended off dangers, endured deprivations, and suffered sorrows—to be met with such little courtesy. I shouldn't be made to wait.

"Have you been to Madrid before?" Catalina asks.

"Never."

"Do you like it?"

"I've not yet seen any of it. We came here straightaway."

"It has its charms, as all capitals do."

The city may claim some allure, but my surroundings cannot make such an assertion. I sit in a wing chair of threadbare crimson damask, my back as taut as the strings of a vihuela. Catalina holds court in an equally frayed seat. When I scan the chamber hoping to glimpse a hiding Miquel, I note it is as sparsely appointed as the woman before me: three small tables pitted with use and a long, upholstered bench under the window. The gold of the rug has faded. There are neither tapestries nor coverings of any kind on the walls, and the decorations tend to the utilitarian, namely lanterns, candleholders, a vase, and such.

"Miquel sent a letter requesting I come visit," I say. "That is why I'm here."

She hides her obvious surprise by looking away toward the dim hallway we traversed minutes earlier.

"His note expressed urgency. I think he has an important message for me."

"Everything in life is important. Everything urgent."

I ignore her cryptic words and press on: "He explained he was very ill and—"

"Did you know we moved here recently?"

She faces me again, her brows knit and her mouth puckered, and I sense she's avoiding something. Perhaps she knows about us? I have no idea, though it's likely Miquel has been as tight-lipped with her as he has been with me.

Maybe Miquel is upstairs with his landlord. Maybe he's out running an errand, tending to the last-minute matters of his books.

"He should have received a note in the past day or two that I was on my way. I sent it by courier from Guadalajara." How many times must I repeat myself?

At that point, a young woman, tall and of regal bearing, glides into the room, the black of her gown matching Catalina's. If a smile can serve as a reflection of temperament, she must be friendly and sweet-natured.

"I didn't know we had a guest," she says. "Should I bring refreshments, Cati?"

Miquel's wife offers no response, and the lack of such can be explained in one of two ways: she would like to see me leave quickly or she has little to offer a guest. Neither bodes well. Then another explanation occurs to me: Catalina's deficient hospitality may have to do more with her own inadequate manners than anything else. I like this version better.

"No need," I say as dismissively as I can muster. "I'm not here on a social call. I've come to meet with Miquel."

The two women exchange a look difficult to interpret. Then Catalina tells the younger woman, "This is Miquel's cousin—"

"Dolça? From Barcelona? Oh my! I thought you had changed your mind."

"What? Change her mind about what?" Catalina demands.

The young woman pays no attention to Catalina's confusion, and it occurs to me that Miquel's wife knows nothing of our correspondence. Most likely she read neither his notes nor my reply.

The young woman addresses me: "I'm Constanza, Miquel's niece."

Ah. My former lover's favorite relative. He loves this Constanza more than his own daughter. That much I've gleaned from his few anecdotes of family life.

"He wrote to me asking I come."

"I know," Constanza says, and sighs.

"Considering his delicate health, I'd like to see him as soon as possible."

Constanza walks to the bench under the window and collapses there. I'm uncertain if either woman understands the gravity of my situation, but I persist: "I can wait for him if he won't be long."

Constanza's eyes widen. "Oh, dearest, you haven't heard, have you?"

"Heard?"

"I've not had the opportunity," Catalina interjects hurriedly. "We were just getting acquainted."

I look from one woman to the other. Like a blind woman who has been granted sight all at once, I notice Constanza's mourning attire and the color of Catalina's gown. I feel a tremor in my knees. No. No. Nononono! There must be a misunderstanding. This can't be, no.

"He passed, señora," Constanza confirms. "He passed into the arms of our Lord and Savior. I'm so sorry you've come all this way to hear such devastating news."

Too late. I'm too late. I bury my face in my hands, tears brimming slowly at first and then in a flood. Oh, Miquel! So many leagues traveled, so many lives altered, and all for naught. I cannot do what I came to do.

Catalina observes me in stony silence, the spectacle I have become. For a recent widow, she is surprisingly dry-eyed.

"May I bring you something?" Constanza asks.

"When?" I ask, waving away the young woman's concern. "When did he die?"

"Six days ago."

I dab at my tears with the embroidered handkerchief tucked in my sleeve. "I . . . I . . ."

The two women allow me the comfort of another bout of weeping. Constanza crosses the room to bridge our divide. She crouches to embrace me. "I know how difficult this is. It's been trying for all of us."

If only Miquel had sent for me earlier. If only my journey had been faster, his health stronger, my obstacles fewer.

We spend a fortnight in Madrid, and I call on Catalina thrice more. She invariably receives me with a practiced smile, but one absent of warmth. I suspect she suffers my presence and my questions only out of obligation to her deceased husband. Her circumspection doesn't bother me, however, because during these visits I learn more about Miquel's illness as well as his most recent successes.

"Were his last days peaceful?" I ask, overwhelmed by the need for details that might assuage my guilt. "Did he suffer much?"

"He was in pain and always thirsty," Catalina replies. She is sparing me no discomfort.

Constanza quickly adds, "But these past months were ones of great triumph for him too, and he took delight in that. I've drawn comfort knowing he was happy with those successes."

Yes, my Miquel is quite famous in Spain, and also abroad. But what do those professional accolades matter now? He died without learning about Jaume, without the forgiveness we owed one another. I'm tempted to divulge the truth about Miquel and me, all of it, about what I've held in my hands and heart without ever owning it outright, but I resist the impulse. No good would come of that.

"As I've said," Catalina continues, "he suffered from dropsy and he was willing to try various treatments, but none worked and he knew . . ." Here my lover's wife stops to draw a deep breath. "He knew his days were numbered. So, he spent much of his time and energy finishing what he wanted to leave behind."

"You mentioned a new book," I prod.

"Yes, *The Labors of Persiles and Sigismunda*. In some ways I think the effort of finishing it is what killed him, but he believed this would be his one great achievement."

"Not the *Quixote*?"

She frowns. "Oh that. Too experimental, he thought."

"But readers love it. It's very popular all across the continent."

"It was the *Persiles* he considered his masterpiece," she repeats, rather vehemently.

"Have you read it?"

"No! I'd never ask to do such a thing. And he wouldn't have allowed it either."

I'm scarcely able to contain my glee that Miquel never gave her a peek at his early drafts. Obviously, such intimacy he shared only with me.

"To whom did he dedicate *Persiles*?"

"Count Lemos."

And well, of course. The second part of *Quixote* had also been dedicated to him. The man who had rejected Miquel for a Naples government post had later turned into his most generous benefactor. Miquel wouldn't have failed to acknowledge that. He knew the importance of a magnanimous sponsor, even as he found the need for such a relation-ship demoralizing.

"Despite his growing weakness, he also was intent on settling other outstanding matters." Catalina stares at her lap for so long I think she's forgotten what she planned to say, but then she continues. "When he felt strong enough to travel to Esquivias, I harbored the hope of a mira-cle. Now in hindsight I see that it was only desperate determination that kept him going. No more, no less, because when he returned from Esquivias, he felt worse than ever. But at least we were blessed that he had renewed his relationship with our Lord. I think this provided solace for him in the end."

"What do you mean?"

"He had taken orders as a novice in the Tertiary Order of Saint Francis. Were you not aware?"

My Miquel, religious? I disbelieve, but perhaps Catalina influenced him in ways I didn't previously understand. Perhaps she provided what I couldn't: a faith that kept doubt at bay, a home without reminders of what he lacked.

"He took his final vow on the second of April, Easter Eve, thanks be to God." Another pause, another pious drawing of breath. "On the eighteenth, a Monday I believe, the almoner of the Trinitarian monas-tery came to administer the Last Sacraments. Miguel asked for Extreme Unction and it was only then that I began to accept the inevitable."

Where was I on this date? I try to calculate the number of days we've been on the road, the ones squandered to banal distractions and the ones consumed by illness, but of late my mind is like a peasant's stew, a mix of everything without regard to quality.

"And the funeral?" I ask.

"As I mentioned," Catalina looks past me and her voice softens with reverence, "he was a Franciscan Trinitarian, so he wanted to be buried according to the order's rites. He wore the brown habit, but his face remained uncovered, ready to meet his Maker. The brothers carried him in a plain pine box to his grave in the convent."

"Is there a stone or a cross to mark it?"

She appears distressed. "That wouldn't be appropriate."

Not appropriate? For someone who, more than riches, more than comfort, desired recognition? I want to admonish this woman for her lack of understanding of the man I knew, but discretion wins out. And anyway, who am I to judge? How can I lament guaranteed obscurity for my son's father when I myself failed to award him the attention he sought?

"I'm so sorry you suffered through his suffering." That is the best I can do.

"I wasn't willing to give up hope until the last, but what we wish is immaterial, isn't it? We're but instruments of God."

And he's a capricious, distractable God, I'd like to add but don't. Sorrow should never be undermined by fact.

On my last visit to Catalina, I propose an idea that has refused to loosen its hold on me. As she is the executrix of Miquel's estate, only she can give permission to accomplish my goal. The chance that she will agree is low—I sense she knows more about me than she lets on—but I intend to try anyway.

That morning she greets me at the door with a black veil covering her face. She doesn't bid me enter, explaining that she's expected by Juan de Villarroël, a bookseller who is interested in purchasing the publishing rights to Miquel's *Persiles*. When she asks that I return the following day, I inform her of our forthcoming departure, though I'm vague about the date. Jaume still has business meetings scheduled, and I—well, I have business of my own. Do I hear a sigh of relief when I tell her we're leaving? Do I see a crinkling of satisfaction in her eyes?

No matter. She leads me inside somewhat reluctantly and lifts her veil but doesn't remove her gloves. Though I hurry through the proposal, my words are eloquent, passionate: I want to publish the two parts of *Quixote* in one tome.

"It'll make Quixote and Sancho even more famous," I conclude.

"And your Dulcinea as well."

I allow one beat before I counter, "Maybe."

"There's no maybe in that, Doña Dolça." She places a peculiar emphasis on my name.

"For the sake of your purse, I hope you're right."

Ignoring my barb, she muses, "I suppose Miguel would want this."

"I think he would. And I know just the right person in Barcelona for this project."

"Well, he did love Barcelona and spoke highly of the city. I always thought he anticipated his stays there too enthusiastically. Now it's obvious to me why."

She stares at me without blinking. Though enticed to rejoin, I judge it best not to add to the debate and take my leave soon after we agree to terms.

When Jaume returns to our lodgings, a small estate rented to us by a widow who, according to my son, is in "dire straits," I tell him about my fruitful morning. He asks for particulars, and pleased by his interest, I explain my vision of creating one special Barcelona book by combining the 1606 Valencia edition of the original *Quixote* and this year's edition of the second part.

"Will you change anything in the books?" Jaume asks.

I hesitate, not because I haven't considered the possibility. I hesitate because I know I cannot do as I've long wanted: replace the name of a character, the one who matters most to me. That much I owe Miquel. But my hesitation carries something else too: a release, an acceptance, a shift in perspective. After the hardships of the road and the privations I've witnessed, after the wily defeat of scoundrels and the unexpected generosity of strangers, I realize how my own journey was not unlike that of the deluded Quixote. Was I not on a quest too? Did we not both imagine an alternative reality? Were we not vanquished by our individual obsessions, by our own lies? Moreover, in light of Aldonça's death, my indignation over an invented Dulcinea has proven trivial, inconsequential, more froth than substance. The aspersions were minor insults, not enough to change my world, and I can't cite a single incident in which

I felt my way of life imperiled. I was embarrassed, yes. Mortified, of course—but in this great, broad canvas that is life, the innuendos will not outlast the creative genius of the book nor outlive the charm of a knight and his squire. Miquel knew this, did he not?

"Thank you for allowing me to come," I tell Constanza. "I think you'll understand why I asked to meet with you alone."

"Your note truly intrigued me. It's not often I get an invitation for a clandestine meeting." She laughs with genuine self-deprecation.

These past few days have allowed me to recognize why Miquel held Constanza in such high esteem. She's a gemstone embedded in rough rock. Today, though still clad in black, she has managed to offset the monotony of that color with a tiny opalescent brooch of a butterfly. Attached to her neckline, it appears ready to fly up and into her hair, which is the chestnut color of my son's. Also, there is a lightness in her step that complements the gravity of her well-polished manners. When she looks at me with both skepticism and compassion, as she does now, she reminds me of a young Miquel, of the irrepressible man I first met when he returned from Rome.

Constanza pours almond milk into pewter goblets and urges me to choose among the cream-filled pastries I bought from a vendor two streets down. She seems little bothered by the lack of maids to help her with guests.

"Surely you must be wondering why I've traveled so long and so far in hopes to see your uncle one last time."

"No, actually I'm not."

I draw back at the frankness of her response.

"You look surprised, Dolça, but let me explain. I was the one who wrote the postscript for you to hurry here. I was the one who made sure his first letter went out in the post."

"You, then. I knew the penmanship belonged to a woman."

"I also posted his second message, the one delivered to your cousin's."

At the reference to Núria, I feel a jolt of guilt; I've not given her situation a second thought since our arrival in the capital. I don't know if she's safe at home or rotting in some Inquisition dungeon. I have no news of Anna either. But I push away those worries for now.

"I received both messages, of course, but what prompted me to make the journey wasn't just your uncle's deathbed request."

"No?"

Then, without any other encouragement except my desire to be rid of the millstone that has weighed me down for too long, I reveal the truth about Jaume. I release the secret into the world and there's no one better to receive it, no one better to enfold it in love, than Constanza.

Her eyes widen, her mouth falls open. Shock gives way to tears, but she expresses no recriminations, no hostility, nothing of that sort. Instead, she puts me at ease by clapping happily and then declaring, "So I have a cousin! A new one I didn't know about!"

"You do, yes."

"Is he the young man who brings you here?"

"The very same."

"He resembles Tío Miguel, now that I come to think of it."

"Sometimes he does. Other times I see my late husband in his gestures, in the way he thinks and in the way he sees the world."

"I wish my uncle had lived long enough to know about him. He would have been pleased."

"I'm sorry I didn't tell him. I should have. It might have eased the adversities he faced."

"How so?"

"In one of our last meetings he seemed very concerned about his legacy, about what he would leave behind. A son—"

She touches my arm, and the pastry flakes that were on her fingertips now dance on my sleeve. "Don't torture yourself."

"He had a right to know about his son."

"Some would certainly argue that, but if I'm to be as candid as you've been with me, I must speak my mind. Truly I don't think having a son would have changed his life much. Writing was his alpha and his omega, his reason for being, his only ambition, especially toward the end. Everything else was secondary, and I'm convinced that he wanted to be remembered by and through his work, not by the number or name of his progeny."

My chest tightens with gratitude. It's as if Miquel himself has granted me the gift of dispensation from beyond the grave. I squeeze her hands in appreciation; her assurances have somewhat salvaged my journey.

Chapter 15

1614

Regarding Our Last
(and Most Familiar) Disagreement

I possess one last and lasting image of Miquel, one final encounter, and it weighs as heavy as a royal indictment. In the autumn of 1614, he arrived at my house glassy-eyed and unexpectedly drunk. His hair was a nest of tangles, and thumbprints smudged his spectacles. I had never seen him so.

"This is what I was th-thinking," he slurred. "Let's book passage to the New World."

"The New World?" I was astounded by this opening salvo. We had seen quite a lot of each other during the four years he had been living off and on in Barcelona. I had forgiven, though not forgotten, the injury of his *Quixote*, and our relationship had turned friendly, almost intimate in the way of two people who have known each other for decades. There was nothing, however, in our most recent interactions that could have encouraged him to proceed beyond that. Now for a reason I couldn't fathom, he was reviving an old disagreement, a traditional and forever dispute that would never be settled to his liking.

"I heard at the market that a large fortress is being built at the entrance of the harbor in one of the islands of the Indies," he continued. "An island named Cuba with the new capital of Habana. You've heard of it?"

I nodded. Jaume spoke about it often enough. He was eager for trade with the Indies, a challenge for us since other Spanish ports were better positioned than the east-facing Barcelona.

"They're looking for laborers, tradesmen, scribes, all kinds of workers. There we can start over, as unknowns but with a future."

"Miquel," I warned him testily.

"Men are making their fortunes in trade."

"I won't go, Miquel. Not at my age."

"Where there is will and ambition, age doesn't matter."

"Tell that to my dimming eyesight and creaking joints." I laughed more begrudgingly than the subject warranted.

"Age is your current excuse. There have been so many others that I could make a list as long as my arm."

"Not excuses, but reality. Barcelona is my home. I can't abandon my son, my grandchildren." Nor, truthfully, could I leave behind such expensive essentials as canvases and painting supplies.

"If not the Indies, we can stay in the capital then go across the border to Portugal. What about a little hamlet in the Pyrenees? Anywhere that we can be together."

"I can't."

"You mean you won't."

"That's not true. Don't twist my answer to suit you."

"We must seize the opportunity, Dolça. We're no longer so young that we can afford to delay."

"Nor are we young enough to throw away our lives and reputations. Can you not understand what the stench of scandal would do to my family, to Jaume whose life is but beginning? Such a transgression would be ruinous to the business."

"You lie to yourself. What you can't leave, what you refuse to leave, are your luxuries." He threw his arms out in surrender or dismay, maybe both.

"Miquel, please. Why aren't you content with what we have?"

"You're free, freer than ever," he argued, ignoring my question. "You're no longer married. You're a woman of independent means. What is the obstacle?"

"Must I remind you yet again of your current matrimonial state?"

"I've spent more time away from my wife than I've spent with her. I come and go as I please."

"You may, but I can't."

"Again, can't or won't?" His voice thundered with anger.

"The rules and expectations for women are different. You know that."

"Now that's a convenient excuse."

"It's not a matter of convenience. My life is here, Miquel. It's always been."

He slit his eyes, and I thought he would dismiss my suggestion, but then he said, almost joyfully, "Our opinions diverge on this and—"

"And on many other matters."

He began to pace. I followed his tottering gait in hopes that he would tire and leave me alone, but he patrolled the room up and down, up and down, so many times that I was sure he would wear grooves into the floor. All the while, he carried on about the many ways he could achieve the fortune that eluded him. Then, as if his energy had been suddenly renewed, he stopped, turned, and aimed a finger straight at my heart.

"You care only about yourself, about your pleasures and your comfort. You're—"

"How dare you say that!"

"—neither willing to sacrifice nor willing to explore something different. You're so absorbed in the ridiculous pomp of your small life that you can't recognize good fortune when it's offered on a silver platter."

"I'm well aware of the generosity and sacrifice of your offer." It took enormous willpower to keep my voice level. "I even appreciate the—"

"Appreciate? You appreciate nothing. You've treated me as you've treated your talent, with fickle passion and shallow interest. All this"— he gestured to include the fine furnishings around us—"are but props in a life of pretension. There's no depth to you, Dolça, no substance beyond your petty desires. Have you done anything that would require you to think beyond yourself?"

"I can't just leave my family and my entire life. I've told you before, and still you refuse to accept my reasons."

"Those are excuses. Women like you, women of your rank, fret about appearances and nothing beyond the surface. You care only about what others might think of you. You wouldn't give a starving child a piece of bread if you thought it might contaminate your good name."

Though my face remained as immovable as a mountain, the insult hurt me deeply. I offered no challenge, however, for I was desperate to appease him. I worried that the servants were eavesdropping just beyond the door and that the details of our row, his impassioned accusations and my spirited defense, would spread through the city like a plague.

"Miquel, consider my side."

"Your side, your side. There's no other side, no other opinion, no other version but yours. As it always has been in saecula saeculorum." He stormed across the room, but before leaving, before slamming the door, he announced a curse I would not soon forget. "I'll see you next in eternity."

I didn't know then that his last words to me would be so prophetic. A week after this argument, Miquel left Barcelona for good and forever. I thought he would return, I thought I would have time to tell him what he deserved to know, but I underestimated his desire for stability, for peace, for a cast of people who offered him the moral support he needed to read, write, publish, think. In Madrid, his wife awaited, as did his editor and publisher, a circle of admirers willing to subsidize and promote whatever he wrote. He and I, we would remain separated by mountains and plains, by vineyards, orchards, and countless fields of wheat, barley, and oats. Something else, too, something unbridgeable: my cowardice.

Chapter 16

JUNE 1617, BARCELONA

What Might Have Been, What Could Be

We were doubly blessed in October of year past when Elisabet was delivered of two infants, a girl and a boy, scrawny in size but vigorous in lung power. They're pink and plump now, but no less loud. When they bawl, often in synchronized shrieks, they sound, to me at least, like birdsong in the morning, sweet even when cacophonous. I think of these babes as the gift owed for so much loss and despair.

"*Mare* Dolça, will you help with Dorotea?" Elisabet calls out from her bedchamber, flustered by last-minute preparations for the annual Corpus Christi celebration. "She's not cooperating."

In the nursery the flailing child fights all attempts to slip her fat, little arm through a sleeve of soft lace. Says the nursemaid, "She's feisty, this one. As soon as I put in one arm, she manages to slip off the other one."

Dorotea stops her howling when she spots me, moving seamlessly from tears to smiles as only children can. I adore her. Though as bald as her twin brother, she possesses the most intriguing eyes, almond-shaped like Miquel's, neither brown nor green but the color of a leaf before it turns. She is the first in the family with this name: *Do-ro-te-a*. Jaume chose it though Elisabet had favored her deceased mother's. At first, I thought my son's selection unusual for he's always been so beholden to tradition, but on the morning of the child's baptism, he explained his reason—Dorotea is a character in the first part of the *Quixote*. The irony of this isn't lost on me, but it does leave me with an unsettling curiosity about my son's conflicted feelings.

I scoop up little Dorotea as soon as she's dressed and hold her close while the nursemaid ties the bonnet under her double chin. The child smells of drool and lavender water.

"Now my beautiful princess is ready!" I exclaim, with all the enthusiasm and gratitude only second chances offer. "She can join her sister and brothers, but only if she doesn't cry anymore. Can you do that for me?"

Dorotea headbutts me and I yelp in surprise. She gurgles her amusement at my reaction. Though I massage my forehead, a glance in the mirror reveals a lump the size of a unicorn horn. One more injury of love.

Later, we stroll the city streets accompanied by Pau—Joana and Gabriel's youngest son—and his family. Jaume has secured a roped-off area for the family, so we're close enough to enjoy the crowds without being subjected to the beggars, vagabonds, and pickpockets that turn out for these festivities. The procession of the Holy Sacrament is, as always, long and solemn. All the parishes are represented by the clergy, who file past us in simple tunics and ornate chasubles. As soon as the *gegants i capgrossos* with their giant papier-mâché heads appear, my two oldest grandchildren squeal with delight. Margarida claps and little Françesc runs in circles. At the tender age of three, he looks very much like my dear father. Broad-chested and thick-legged, with black curls and long lashes that will one day be the envy of every woman, the little fellow towers over his playmates and is not above using his size to impose his will.

Eventually, in the distance, from the direction of the Church of Santa María del Mar, I spy an enormous cross, and I know that behind it comes the high-backed silver chair of King Martin, where the Holy Host is enthroned. I remember another Corpus Christi, many, many years ago, when Miquel met his son for the first time at the cathedral's cloister fountain. Jaume was two years old then, more amused by the dancing egg atop the spray of water than the man who remained oblivious to their shared bloodline. Now I'm certain that was for the best. Secrets exist for a reason—this I've come to accept.

"Mother?" asks Jaume, tapping my arm. "You don't look well."

"I'm fine." I do not tell him that thinking of the past always leaves me addled, unbalanced.

"Are you sure? You're pale."

He worries about me, my dutiful son. I could never utter an ill word about Jaume in that regard. However, I sense a certain detachment in him. At times I'll catch him watching me fixedly as if he were trying to understand the incomprehensible, as if he were reminding himself that I'm not to be trusted. When this happens, I nod and smile sweetly. None of this changes how much I love him. Nothing can.

As it turns out, his concern over my health provides an excuse for me to miss the festivities that follow the procession. When the crowd finally disperses, I decline Pau's invitation and happily accompany the children and their nursemaids back to Jaume's house—actually, it is Elisabet's, for she inherited it from her parents. Then once everyone has surrendered to naps, I continue to my own residence, eager to take advantage of the afternoon light.

I take a circuitous route, one that will lead me by the building on Sota Muralla where Miquel made his temporary home in those final years we had together. I remember the pleasures we found all around us—the clamor of the horns announcing a joust, the red roses for La Diada de Sant Jordi, the onion-and-tomato aroma of our *sofregit*—and the ones we took from each other. No longer do I dwell on Miquel's frustrations and churlishness. Rather, I imagine the effervescence of our early days, the hope and sensuality, the sense of possibilities. Wherever he is—and I believe him in heaven, sitting at a fine walnut escritoire with an inkpot that never runs dry—I want to believe that money is no longer a worry. I want to believe he is content.

At home, in the solitude of my studio, dressed in the old painting smock that is too snug around the waist, I settle on the stool strategically placed in front of my easel. I'd like to sketch the underdrawing of bandits hanging from a cork oak but hesitate to do so. These days I'm very careful of what I paint because Margarida has shown an aptitude and interest in art, much as I once did, and I don't want to frighten her away with my personal demons. I'd rather see her tracing joyful childish fantasies with her mother's quill. Now that I've experienced the life of the common man with all its deprivations and afflictions, I recognize the ignorance, and some might say the arrogance, with which I once approached my subject matter. Truly, there is nothing exotic or romantic about an existence of perpetual want. Not that I've changed my artistic choices, only that I proceed with humility and caution.

As I study the blank linen before me, I consider potential scenes for my work. The Martorell laborers in their short trousers and *faixa*. El Musulmán with his *barretina*. The muleteers astride their beasts. And Aldonça—yes, yes, Aldonça, arms akimbo, gaze steady, mouth pursed. I can't help but think back to the journey that brought me so much heartache and loss. I now know that Núria fled to the New World before any charges could be drawn, but I still wonder about Constanza and Catalina, what life has been like for them in the aftermath of Miquel's fame. I also remember and have several times considered asking after Xirau and his band. Surely Jaume has continued his business relationship with them, but I don't know how my son will react to my questions so I keep my counsel.

I remain in this meditative mood until Ermessenda announces that Jaume has come to look in on me. As I've mentioned, he worries.

"So, you weren't tired," he says in greeting. "You just wanted to be alone."

"Maybe."

"Gabriel said he was sorry he missed you."

"I can't say I missed him."

Jaume chuckles. He's well aware that my relationship with my brother-in-law is merely cordial. Yet Gabriel has mentored my son for these many years, and Jaume has named his younger boy child, the twin, after his uncle, proof that affinity can defy logic—just as love can defy class and rank.

"Should I tell Ermessenda to ready an early dinner, Mother?"

"No, not yet."

"But you're sitting in the shadows, alone. Why don't you light the lantern?"

"I like it this way. It gives me space and time to think."

"If that's what you want."

Nothing more needs to be said.

Tomorrow a rising sun will gift us the miracle of another beginning, and with it the usual flurry of social duties. There will be mandated church attendance, the joy of my grandchildren at play, the entertainment of a parade or festival: repetition and refrain. But also, the not small enjoyment of my studio, my painting. I once was careless in the harvest of my art. My passion for it was erratic, my persistence deficient, and that vacillation robbed me of both vision and mission. Miquel was correct about that. Our commitment to our individual arts was as dissimilar as silk and sackcloth—where he persisted, I fiddled; where he battled, I dabbled. No more. Now, without a secret to burden me, without the ruse of unlimited time, I am managing, slowly but steadily, to steal light from shadow and structure from imagination. Even in my sleep, I feel the contours of the brush in my grip, be it miniver tail or hog's bristle.

"Do you mind if I sit with you for a while, Mother? I need some quiet too."

I peer into Jaume's inscrutable face and then back at the canvas, which awaits what only I can give it, and wherever my gaze alights, my eyes find clarity and color.

Acknowledgments

This book wouldn't have been possible without the generous support of the CINTAS Foundation, whose creative writing fellowship gave me the time and financial freedom to finish a project that has taken me, in many ways, half a century to write. Special thanks to the foundation's Laurie Escobar and Cristina Nosti for their enthusiasm.

Thank you to my writing tribe, led by the incomparable Diana Abu-Jaber. Early drafts of *Dulcinea* were much improved by the suggestions of Diana, Andrea Gollin, Jake Cline, Jeff Slone, Aaron Curtis, Scott Eason, Dave Hayes, and Lauren Doyle Owens. Another shout out to Ileana Oroza and Margaria Fichtner for championing my work over these many years. Also, a hat tip of endless appreciation to friends who held my hand and heart through the darkest of days. You know who you are.

Thank you to Andromeda Romano-Lax, whose advice and critical eye were invaluable in crafting the plot and characters. (Maybe one day we'll cross the continent and meet in person.) A hearty thanks, too, to my agents, Sarah Yake and Frances Collin, who believed as strongly as I did in this sixteenth-century woman who existed only in my imagination.

A nod of gratitude to the Blackstone crew: editors Daniel Ehrenhaft, who understood Dolça from the very beginning Toni Kirkpatrick, who polished the prose to a glorious shine, and Caitlin Vander Meulen, who made sure I had my commas right; cover designer Sarah Riedlinger; and publicist Isabella Nugent.

And last but certainly not least, thank you to David Freundlich, my husband and first reader, who made sure I subsisted on more than Cheetos and chocolate and who insisted I occasionally venture away from my computer screen to impersonate a breathing, living human.

Couldn't have done this without all of you.

Author's Note

The idea to write about Dulcinea first came to me in Mrs. Olmos's Spanish IV, when my classmates and I were muddling through *El ingenioso hidalgo don Quixote de la Mancha* in its original language. I was a tenth grader at the American Cooperative School in La Paz, Bolivia, a gawky bookworm who dreamed of authoring something, *anything*, even though at the time I showed more aptitude for mathematics than for writing. (That might be why it took me half a century to pen this story!)

Dolça Llull Prat, like Dulcinea before her, is a fictional woman, created by a writer's imagination, and there is no historical record that Miguel de Cervantes ever had a lover in Barcelona. However, he did live there for a time, and this city is the only one he praises in his plays and novels. In 2017, that tidbit was enough to send me down the rabbit hole of possibilities, particularly since Catalonia is my ancestral home, where my mother was born and also where most of my father's relatives still live.

I was fortunate to have access to several books, theses, and assorted documents about Cervantes, early modern Barcelona, and Golden Age Spain. But like all novelists, I made ample use of literary license to flesh out what I didn't know about these subjects, while also trying to stay true to the timeline of Cervantes's life.

Though the COVID-19 pandemic and the corresponding lock-downs limited my research, technology raced to the rescue. On the web I found a trove of information, including a map of old Barcelona and another of sixteenth-century roads through the peninsula. *Repertorio de caminos* by Alonso de Meneses and *Repertorio de todos los caminos de España* by Pero Juan Villuga were especially helpful in guiding the route Xirau the muleteer would have taken from Barcelona to Madrid. In addition, *A Handbook for Travellers in Spain* by Richard Ford, although published in the mid-1800s, provided useful descriptions of the countryside. The discovery of Barcelona resident Jeroni Pujades's diary proved a gold mine of quotidian details, as did a website that included "meteorological happenings" in the first three decades of the seventeenth century. When my rudimentary Catalan wasn't enough to understand longer texts, Google Translate was helpful—sometimes hilariously so.

Once finished with the research and the writing, I found myself daydreaming about a historical period that was fraught with contradictions and conflicts. So many parallels exist between then and now, between a society beholden to the politics of religion and a society divided by the religion of politics. Though we live four hundred years later, our superstitions and enmities don't seem all that different.

If you are interested in old Spain and Barcelona or in the man who wrote what many consider the first modern novel, here is a list of reference material I found particularly helpful:

On Cervantes:
  La Barcelona de Cervantes by Luis G. Manegat
  Cervantes en Barcelona by Rafa Burgos
  Cervantes en Barcelona by Martín de Riquer
  Cervantes, el "Quijote" y Barcelona by Carme Riera and
      Guillermo Serés
  Miguel de Cervantes by Harold Bloom
  Cervantes: A Biography by William Byron
  Cervantes by Jean Canavaggio

On Barcelona and Spain:

> *Un siglo decisivo: Barcelona y Cataluña, 1550–1640* by Albert García Espuche
>
> *For the Common Good: Popular Politics in Barcelona, 1580–1640* by Luis R. Corteguera
>
> *La ciutat del Born: Economia i vida quotidiana a Barcelona (segles XIV a XVIII)* by Albert García Espuche
>
> *Honored Citizens of Barcelona: Patrician Culture and Class Relations, 1490–1714* by James S. Amelang
>
> *Historia social de España, 1400–1600* by Teofilo F. Ruiz
>
> *The Mediterranean and the Mediterranean World in the Age of Philip II* by Fernand Braudel
>
> *Spain and the World: 1500–1700* by J. H. Elliott
>
> *Daily Life in Spain in the Golden Age* by Marcelin Defourneaux
>
> *Cultura y costumbres del pueblo español de los siglos XVI y XVII* by Ludwig Pfandl
>
> *Anales de Cataluña Y epílogo breve de los progresos, y famosos hechos de la nacion Catalana . . . desde la primera poblacion de España . . . hasta el presente de 1709* by Narciso Feliu de la Peña y Farell
>
> *A Drizzle of Honey: The Lives and Recipes of Spain's Secret Jews* by David M. Gitlitz and Linda Kay Davidson